The Witch, The Seed &
The Scalpel

Scott O'Neill

M^cNIDDER |&
GRACE

Published by McNidder & Grace
Jedburgh
Scotland
United Kingdom
www.mcnidderandgrace.com

Original paperback first published 2025
© Scott O'Neill

A catalogue record for this work is available from the British Library.

ISBN   9780857162915
eISBN 9780857162922

Cover design: Tabitha Palmer, Wales
Designer: JS Typesetting Ltd, Porthcawl, Wales
Printed and bound in the United Kingdom by Short Run Press, Exeter

For Net

CHAPTER ONE

Waiting for Lachlan

The winter sky scything in from the Firth of Forth fairly thrummed with the pigeon-chested sails of bobbing schooners, skiffs and whalers. The snap and flap of their cloth seemed to scold their steam-powered cousins for their brazen modernity. Everywhere squealing gulls, hoping to snatch a glittering morsel from the deck of a herring boat, keened and swooped through air thick with the heady stench of whale oil and salted fish. There were so many vessels packed inside the harbour, with countless others riding the waves in the great river beyond, that I fancied I could walk across their serried decks all the way from the docks at Leith to the Kingdom of Fife.

The dockers, apparently impervious to the remorseless chill, cheerfully set about loading and unloading their cargos with dextrous speed and precision. The whaling ships carried a different breed of men altogether. Sporting complexions like scuffed boots etched and creased by the fierce Arctic blasts, and with manners blunted by months patrolling the frozen oceans far from the reach of a chastising wife or mother, they cursed and spat freely as they landed their haul. The rumbling thunder of blubber barrels rolling for the boilyard stuttered as many a lascivious eye paused to admire my mother as we made our way across the wharf to greet the latest arrival.

One grizzled specimen, teeth clenched hard around a clay

pipe, tipped his peak and examined the lines of Mother's coat from the hem all the way up to her tightly fastened collar. Head held proudly aloft my mother strode forth wholly undaunted by the attention, whilst I marched at her side, affecting the air of the invincible protector, hoping a straight back and stern expression would prove sufficient disguise for the cosseted student cowering within. Truth be known I could not have chosen a more ill-fitting costume, for I had never successfully engaged in physical combat with any individual in my life and knew with absolute certainty that if I took to the ring with any one of those brine-soaked dogs, I would be fortunate to escape with a single bone left intact.

But such worries were misplaced. Most of the men who plied the docks knew Mother as the sister of Thomas 'Tam' Keane, chief harpooner of the *Majestic North*. A man singularly suited to tackling monsters of the deep. He was a full head taller than myself and twice as broad, and it would take a fool indeed to test his usually jovial manner. Prior to visiting the docks, we had dined with Uncle Tam at the Ferryman's Inn on Sandport Street. Recently returned from a successful hunt in the seas around Svalbard, he was in fine, mischievous fettle.

'How old are you now, Joseph?' he asked, stroking his leathery fingers through a beard as black as Whitby Jet.

'Nineteen,' I replied, knowing exactly where my uncle intended to take the conversation, as did Mother. She smiled tolerantly before returning to the newspaper resting on her lap, tapping its pages in an agitated manner; an indication of her excitement at the imminent arrival of her husband whom we had not seen for ten long months.

'Nineteen, eh? Time enough to learn the trade yet. Yer skinny arms will do fine for scalin' the riggin'. I can see you reachin' the nest in half a blink. And you've a keen eye for detail. An essential quality when pickin' over a vast expanse of ocean for a tell-tale flick of a fluke or a blast from a spout. You'd be a fine addition to any crew. So what do you say nephew, eh? You and me on the high seas together. We'd be unstoppable!'

'Sorry, Uncle Tam. My mind is set.'

'Come on, man. Will ye no' try it for size?' He slapped me heartily on the shoulder and gripped hard, his hand as broad as a shovel, scarred and tarnished with a lifetime of hard toil. *'There she bloooows!'* he suddenly bellowed, drawing a few quizzical looks and smiles from our fellow patrons. 'Your turn, Joseph, let's hear ye roar!'

'Here's an idea. What say you leave those poor whales be and let me teach you all about the wonders of botany? You and I in the open fields together. We'd be unstoppable!'

Tam transferred his mighty paw from my shoulder to his ale. Wiping the froth from his whiskers, he made his disappointment known with an exaggerated sigh and a slow shake of his head.

'Pluckin' a dandelion from the dirt is no match for pluckin' forty tons of angry leviathan from the sea. Fair makes a man's pulse rattle like a lion in a cage. Excitement, boy! A life on the ocean! I'll teach ye all the tricks of the trade. With me as yer mentor ye'd become the best harpooner in the northern seas. Beg yer pardon, ye'd become the second best harpooner in the northern seas. It's all in the timin'. That's the secret. Tell him sister!'

Tam directed his beery gaze to Mother, still distractedly tapping the columns of *The Caledonian Mercury* with a nervous forefinger.

'Did ye no' hear me, Bil'ty? Tell yer boy to leave the weed-pickin' to his father. Tell him it's time to swap the dullest of occupations for the highest of adventures!'

Mother blinked from far to near. 'What's this you say? Oh, behave yourself, Tam. Is it not enough to have entrusted my brother and husband to the sea's mercy that I should also hand my only son into its fickle care?'

'The sea is no more dangerous than solid ground. And there's the proof,' said Tam, stretching across the table to prod the most prominent headline on Mother's newspaper:

'MURDER AT ADVOCATE'S CLOSE.'

Mother promptly folded the newspaper into her coat. 'Joseph and I have loitered long enough. We must away and collect the wanderer. Give the girls a hug from me, will you, Tam?'

'Aye, and be sure to give that useless big weed-picker a kiss from me, eh sister?' grinned Tam.

*

We continued along the quayside. The faraway quality she first displayed in the Ferryman's Inn continued to dampen Mother's usual effervescence. I suspected her sullen mood to be a lingering symptom of her displeasure at Tam's repeated attempts to lure me to a life on the ocean. Where my uncle saw waves, my mother saw only rocks.

I shared my mother's natural distrust of the sea. Much as I daydreamed of one day accompanying Father to the far-flung regions of the Earth, I knew my delicate constitution would render me little more than ballast to any vessel unfortunate enough to count me amongst its passengers. I can still vividly recall my first voyage across the Forth to North Queensferry, the entire duration of which I spent contemplating the contents of my stomach from the side of the boat as they floated away on the heaving surface and into the beaks of the grateful gulls.

And even on those summer outings to the beach at Portobello, I would never stray more than ankle deep into the surf, so fearful was I of falling foul of an undertow or of feeling the stings and bites of the creatures bristling in its grey depths. The sea commanded my respect, and I conveyed my respect by steadfastly avoiding it.

My feet were never more at home than when planted in

soft fertile soil, helping the resident shrubs and flowers of our garden to take root and grow. Phytology had always held a particular fascination for me, due in no small part to my father's infectious passion and encyclopaedic knowledge of the subject. I was in my second year at Edinburgh University studying Botany under the tutelage of Professor Gilchrist, a teacher who was singularly uninspiring and unimaginative, relying as he did on a rather too rigid adherence to a staid syllabus of academic texts predating the Napoleonic Wars.

In spite of Gilchrist's mission to remove every last atom of joy from our minds, my enthusiasm remained undimmed, as did my ambition to dedicate my entire career into the eradication of disease and blight in crops. Far too many of our farmers and crofters existed in that awful realm between starvation and mere survival, always one inclement season away from ruin. Our nation depended upon their toil and sacrifice yet showed precious little in the way of gratitude for their endeavours. I dreamed of discovering new techniques to protect their harvests from the ravages of the unpredictable Scottish climate and the at times cruel topography and had begun work on a treatise advocating the importance of cross-pollination and the benefits to be derived from taking the finest qualities of the various wheat crops and creating new strains capable not simply of surviving but *thriving* in hitherto unforgiving conditions. I wanted to strengthen their grains, increase their yields and thus bolster the farmers' income and independence. Independence from landowners who saw fit to forcibly evict their human tenants and replace them with sheep. My mother saw this systematic destruction of an ancient culture and heritage as our nation's shame, one which future generations would look back upon with bewilderment and rage. My father, to Mother's irritation, summarily dismissed every report of cruel treatment and enforced emigration as Chartist propaganda, arguing that it was a matter of cold, hard economics that drove these Highland families to the colonies in search of a better future and not the selfish whims of a greedy Clan leader or the toe of a soldier's boot.

Mother fixed her gaze on a dark shape picking its way through the Firth. A plume of smoke trailed from the steam packet's funnel, leaving a smudge of black against the blanket of white cloud. Soon the SS *Jupiter* had berthed and for the first time in almost a year, my father wrapped his arms around his wife.

'My God, you are a sight for weary eyes! But you needn't have waited in this foul weather for me. You both look positively frozen,' he beamed, widening his embrace to include his son.

'How was the expedition, Father?' I asked, my smile every bit as broad as his.

'It was everything I could have wished for and much more besides. Come now, let's get you both home, where I shall gather you round the fire and tell you all about it.'

He then turned and beckoned to one of the men busily securing the ship's ropes. Mr Maybury, my father's loyal assistant, was a man handsomely weathered beyond his years with an impassive blue stare that hinted towards a sinister past. He leaned down and listened attentively as Father imparted concise orders with regard to the transportation of the ship's precious cargo of rare Manchurian ferns and Mongolian orchids. These precious, delicate specimens were due to provide the main source of wonder for volume eight of *Botanica Fantastica*.

A volume that has yet to see the light of day.

CHAPTER TWO

Braid House

Amongst an undulating expanse of verdant glen and ancient woodland in the lee of Blackford Hill several miles to the south and west of Edinburgh's blackened streets, lay Braid House; a castellated jumble of architectural styles, each reflecting the passing tastes and whims of its owners stretching back many generations.

The Ware family acquired the estate when Lachlan's great-grandfather John Ware purchased it from the last surviving member of the Braid family line almost a full century before I was born. Elizabeth Braid, an elderly and by all accounts eccentric spinster, had allowed her property to fall into a serious state of disrepair. The attic and the empty rooms of the upper floor frequently echoed to the sound of rain dripping through a roof pocked with holes. The tumbledown outhouses and crumbling border walls had come to represent the state of her own disintegrating faculties. Too infirm to climb the stairs, Elizabeth confined herself to the ground floor, where she whiled away her existence sitting by the drawing room window, staring fearfully across a lawn overcome by weeds and moles to the darkly brooding woods beyond.

A strange and terrifying conviction had taken hold of her deteriorating mind. Elizabeth had come to believe that the woods were shielding something ungodly. An unseeable presence of indescribable malevolence forever watching her from its shadows. It became a common sight for the villagers of nearby Liberton to see the old woman pounding on the doors of the kirk, begging the minister to silence the distant screams and the murmuring phantoms tormenting her from sunset to sunrise from deep within the trees. But Elizabeth's entreaties received nothing but hostility and were roundly dismissed as the ramblings of a lonely old madwoman.

And then the little bodies began to appear.

One morning in the winter of 1725, awaking from a fitful sleep, Elizabeth rose to part the bedroom curtains, whereupon she saw a dead hare laid upon the lawn. The animal's throat had been cut and its pelt carefully removed and spread over the ground at its side. Terrified, she dashed from room to room, shuttering every window and bolting every door. The following morning, she opened the curtains to find the hare replaced by a fox, killed in the very same manner, its throat cut and its flayed skin neatly arranged upon the frozen ground.

For several days this grisly routine continued, each new dawn bringing a different victim to her window; an otter, a rabbit, a swan, a badger, a stoat, a jackdaw, their throats cut and all feathers or fur removed.

Finally, one crisp February morn, she encountered the most heartbreaking little death of all. Her own pet Highland terrier Henry, whom she loved above all other things in the world, lay skinned upon the unkempt lawn. Elizabeth rushed outside and fell to her knees in grief at the side of her beloved companion. Through a mist of tears, she turned her eyes to the woods and there came the sight that tore away the last shred of her sanity and endurance.

A woman in a bedraggled, soot-stained dress was standing amongst the trees. Her face lost to the gloom, she raised a hand and pointed to Elizabeth, releasing an evil cackle so loud it sent the crows scattering from the treetops. The awful, unearthly mirth shivered Elizabeth's blood to ice, and without once daring to look over her shoulder, she fled from the house and did not stop until she arrived at the door of her solicitor, bearing instructions to sell her ancestral home without delay. She accepted John Ware's offer immediately (a relative pittance even for a property in such sorry condition) and signed the contract in his presence with a warning that he stay away from the woods and avoid the view from the bedroom window.

Thankfully, neither the old woman's forebodings nor the serious state of disrepair into which Braid House had fallen, discouraged my great-great-grandfather who, seeing only its potential, invested a not insignificant sum in restoring the house to its former glory.

Since that time, each generation of Wares has added their own unique architectural flourishes, some more aesthetically pleasing than others. It was Lachlan's father Malcolm who re-established, then expanded the gardens with the addition of the fernery and arboretum.

The foremost dendrologist of his age and author of many respected monographs upon the medicinal and toxicological properties of arboreal fungi, Malcolm spent the majority of his working life as Regius Keeper of the Royal Botanic Garden and lectured regularly at Edinburgh University. But this most brilliant of careers was dashed against the rocks the day fate intervened to deliver a blow both cruel and twisted in its irony.

It was a warm, airless, late summer afternoon when Malcolm Ware accepted his son's invitation to spend a few pleasant hours in that section of the arboretum set aside for the cultivation and encouragement of a perfect rogue's gallery of fungi. Malcolm was quite content to sit himself upon a stump, light his pipe and watch with mild amusement as the young man, enthralled by the fleshy polypores bulging from the fallen branches and rotting trunks, flitted from tree to tree, sketching and recording the latest arrivals.

Malcolm's peace did not last beyond a few languid puffs before his son came hurrying across, holding a large round object in his excited hands. In his eagerness to share his discovery, Lachlan tripped over an exposed root. The leathery sphere flew out of his hands and landed in his father's lap, where it burst open with a dull pop. Malcolm understood the full gravity of his situation at once, but the realisation came too late. His last frantic act as the deadly spores invaded his lungs was to beg Lachlan to keep his distance, but his distraught son foolishly paid no heed and carried his father as far from the lethal Clyne's puffball as he could before he too succumbed to its poisonous dust.

When Lachlan awoke some hours later, the setting sun had made a nest in the trees and a latticework of cool shadow had spread over the manicured lawn of Braid House, where he shared the same pillow of grass as his dead father.

*

The blighted history of the Braid Estate was littered with such tales of violence, death and the supernatural, but there was one particular story, even more extraordinary than the sorry narratives of Elizabeth Braid and Malcolm Ware, that Father took a particularly fiendish delight in presenting to my young, impressionable ears.

And once again it began in the woods.

I was eight years old when I first accompanied my father on his annual pilgrimage to harvest the fruit of one very peculiar tree.

'Elizabeth Braid sounds like a very silly old woman. I can see these woods from my bedroom window and I have never seen or heard anything. There are no such things as ghosts,' I said, folding my arms across my chest in a display of petulant certitude.

Father sat himself down on a rock to watch the fast-flowing

burn wend its way through the dank autumnal woods, twisting in and out of view before eventually it was lost for good amongst the banks of hazel and gorse. The trek had left him short of breath, a chronic symptom of the damage inflicted by the spores inhaled on that tragic, warm and airless summer's afternoon twenty years earlier.

'Except I shall see in his hands the print of the nails, and put my finger into the print of the nails, and thrust my hand into his side, I will not believe,' quoted Father, now fully recovered. 'Perhaps we should have named you Thomas!'

We set off again, Father leading the way to a crumbling section of the burn's bank where a willow stooped to touch the water. I clung on for dear life as Father scooped me up, gripped the rope hanging from the tree's lowest bough and swung us across the stream. Safely ensconced on the other side, we proceeded along a narrow path flanked by ever thickening undergrowth.

'Thomas is the most unfairly maligned of all the saints,' continued Father. 'To have doubts is a sign of a balanced mind. A mind not to be swayed by empty theories and cheap supposition. We are men of science, you and I. We require evidence. Our quest is and must always be, to discover tangible, irrefutable evidence! Evidence is the bedrock, the foundation upon which all science must be built. Evidence provides validity, and validity provides respect. And when you have respect, people listen. And as respected men of science, we must never close our eyes to possibility. Ours is a world of endless wonder and hidden truths and we are duty-bound to continue searching for these truths until we have exhausted every means at our disposal. Then, and only then, can we dare to form our conclusions. Perhaps you are right. Perhaps Elizabeth Braid was a silly old woman. Perhaps there are no such things as ghosts. Or perhaps you have allowed instinct to rule over reason. You would not be the first to do so, believe me.'

'I have not!' I spluttered indignantly. I had hardly understood a single syllable of what my father had said, yet somehow I felt I had been gravely insulted.

'Ah! Here we are!' said Father. The path had come to an abrupt end at the lip of a broad depression. He spread his arms to encompass the view below. 'It is a magnificent specimen, is it not?'

Rising from the centre of the hollow there stood an ancient and solitary horse chestnut tree. The tree looked like no other of its kind in the woods. Its gnarled and twisted limbs, thrown with a flourish of grotesque eccentricity, criss-crossed the sky in all manner of unlikely directions. Deep clefts and scars ravaged the trunk whilst great bumps and lesions pocked the bark like some horrible affliction of the skin. With the crooked tree's brittle brown leaves crunching under our feet, we descended the steeply sloping sides and began collecting the nuts from the ground.

I quickly grew to regret my haste in agreeing to assist my father with so mundane and pointless a task. I had a million other infinitely more important things to attend to. My collection of mollusc shells were not going to clean, catalogue and sketch themselves.

'Why are we doing this?' I asked.

'We are looking for evidence,' he said. 'I shall take these samples home and dissect them. It is just possible that one of them may hold the key.'

'The key to what?'

Father stared up into the ancient tree's canopy, his gaze tracing the erratic reach of its branches against a leaden sky. 'Elizabeth Braid was not alone in her belief that these woods are filled with dark secrets. And there are some who say this chestnut tree holds the darkest secret of them all.'

'What secret? It looks like a boring old tree to me,' I said. This was a brazen lie, for I had never seen another tree so wildly contorted.

'A boring old tree? Well, I must say, I have never heard anyone describe the Witch Tree as boring before.'

'The Witch Tree?'

Father leaned against the grey, furrowed bark of the trunk and turned to me with an insolent smile.

'That's what people call it. Do you want to know why it is called the Witch Tree?'

Irked as I was by my father's condescension, I briefly considered feigning disinterest, but my curiosity, as he well knew, had been fatally hooked.

'Why?'

'Because its roots are nourished by a soil made fertile by the ashes and bones of a diseased and supernatural mind. This tree marks the very spot where, on the tenth day of December 1567, Margaret McKay was executed.'

I placed a hand against the tree. An unsettling, pricklish warmth gathered under my fingertips.

'Who was Margaret McKay? And why was she executed?' I asked, pulling my hand away.

'Margaret McKay was an evil woman. A wicked woman. The most powerful witch in Scotland, feared above all others for her ability to cast spells of the deadliest potency. She had the power to make men hurl themselves to their deaths from the cliffs of Salisbury Crags. But worst of all, she is said to have wandered the closes and tenements of old Edinburgh in the dead of night searching for an open window. And if ever she found one, the witch slipped inside as quietly as smoke to steal infants from their cots and carry them back to her hovel, where she dined on a stew of their flesh and drank their blood in order to preserve her youth. Happily, the people soon grew wise to the evil in their midst and even on the warmest of nights every last window in the city was securely locked and bolted. The Witch McKay, as you may well imagine, did not take kindly to having her supply of fresh blood taken away and so she wreaked a horrible revenge.'

'What did she do?' The question issued from the back of my throat in a dry, nervous rasp.

'She did what all witches do when their monstrous intentions are thwarted. She prayed. But she prayed not to our one true Lord God in Heaven, for her heart did not flow with the love and truth of Christian blood. No, her heart was a coal-black stone of hate and spite. So at midnight on All Hallows' Eve she climbed to the top of Calton Hill, sat herself upon the grass and lit a small fire made from the bones of her most recent victim. With eyes closed and the flames warming her cruel, hideous face, she pushed her hands into the dirt and prayed for her master to appear before her. When at last she stopped her incantations, she opened her eyes and with immense joy she saw the Devil himself standing before her. He smiled, ran a hand through the hair of his adoring disciple and asked why he had been summoned. The Witch McKay begged him to grant her the power to enter the dreams of all Edinburgh's children so that she might fill their sleep with nightmares of such terror and horror that they would die in their beds of fright.'

As Father said this, a little pile of rust-coloured leaves became entangled in a spiralling breeze and were scattered across the hollow.

'And did he?' I swallowed, anxiously. 'Did the Devil grant her the power?'

'Satan said not a word. He simply kissed the witch on the cheek and was gone. The very next night, from the Castle to the Tolbooth and all the way to the Palace of Holyrood, the air was filled with a terrible noise. A noise so awful it chilled every last soul in the city to their very core. Can you imagine it? The screams of all those infants echoing through the alleys and streets. Can you imagine the sheer terror of all those sleeping children? Their nightmares filled with visions of the Witch McKay, her eyes as red as fire, her teeth sharper than broken glass? Can you imagine them in their beds so terrified that their poor hearts simply burst with fear? That is no way for any Christian child to die. But die they did. In their scores. Eventually the screams faded and were replaced by the sobs of countless mothers and fathers mourning their dear departed children. It was undoubtedly, the bleakest night in all of Edinburgh's long and cruel history.'

My gullible young mind had no difficulty at all imagining in stark, unhurried detail all the macabre horrors Father described. I retreated from the twisted, malformed tree with a shiver.

'But the witch was caught, wasn't she? You said she was executed. That means she was caught, yes?'

'She was discovered hiding in a cave near the summit of Arthur's Seat by a group of boys not much older than you are now. Margaret McKay tried to scare the boys away, but they were a cocksure and insolent bunch and not easily frightened. They had no inkling as to who this strange hermit woman was, living in a grubby hole full of animal bones and foul-smelling potions. It was not until they came upon a horde of strange little boxes piled one atop the other at the back of the cave that they began to understand her true nature. The oldest boy opened one of the boxes and found inside a tiny doll, its eyes closed and little arms folded across its chest, looking for all the world like a tiny body at rest inside a coffin. It was then they realised they were in the presence of a witch and the miniature coffins were in fact the tools of her devilish trade; the very tools used to cast spells on those innocent children who went to bed with their heads full of pleasant dreams until the witch's curse turned them into the terrible nightmares from which they would never awake. But thanks to those foolhardy lads, Margaret McKay was apprehended before she was able to lay waste to another soul.'

Father reached down to gather a handful of the rich, mouldering earth. He brought the little heap close to his keen eyes, studying it minutely.

'It was here that the witch was hanged, her body burned to ash and the ashes buried where no one should ever find them.'

'Good. I'm glad. It was no more than she deserved,' I said, heartily relieved to hear the story had a happy ending.

'And yet, the old legend persists…' he mused in a worrying undertone as he allowed the soil to crumble through his fingers.

'Legend? What legend?'

Father brushed the last granules of dirt from his hands. 'Perhaps I have said too much already. Your mother will have my hide if she learns I've been scaring you with these things.'

I tugged insistently at my father's cuff as he turned to stride for home. 'I'm not scared. And I promise I won't tell mother.'

'Very well,' he sighed, then patting a slab of bulging root, he encouraged me to sit with him beneath the Witch Tree. 'Have you ever heard the legend concerning the last chestnut.'

'No. Never. Tell me.'

'Up there. Do you see it?' said Father, pointing to the top of the Witch Tree.

Try as I might, I could see nothing out of the ordinary amongst the curling brown fronds and the healthy crop of chestnuts hanging from its branches. I shrugged in defeat.

'There, just beneath that jay. See it? The big one?'

And there it was. The highest in the tree. A monster of a chestnut. As large as the bird perched immediately above.

'I see it!'

'You'll find it growing there every year without fail on that very same branch. Despite being substantially larger than all the others, it is always the last to fall. There is a legend that says this strange chestnut is imbued with a dark magic.'

'What kind of dark magic?'

'Witchcraft,' said Father. 'It is said that should any person catch the falling chestnut before it touches the ground, the ghost of Margaret McKay will appear and bestow the catcher with abnormal strength and longevity and grant their every wish and desire.'

'Like money and gold. Or endless cake?' I said, excitedly.

'All the cake you could ever eat!' he laughed.

I stared unblinkingly at the tempting bauble, willing it to fall.

'Have you ever tried to catch it?'

Father lowered his rueful gaze and idly swept a boot back and forth, brushing aside the carpet of leaves and twigs.

'Oh, I have spent many a day sitting under this tree waiting for it to drop,' he said. 'As have many others over the centuries. Alas, no one has ever managed to catch it.'

'Why don't we climb up and pick it from the branch?'

My suggestion, which I thought a perfectly reasonable one, was received with a sour twist of Father's lips.

'Ah! Firstly, the legend insists the chestnut must fall of its own accord and not be plucked by an unworthy hand. Secondly, it is far too dangerous. To fall from that height is to fall to your death. I fancy the chestnut is like Excalibur waiting to deliver itself into the hands of one possessed of true virtue. And as your mother will readily attest, I am no King Arthur,' he smiled. 'Speaking of your mother, it is time we returned home before we risk a fate far graver than any witch's curse.'

*

Eternal youth, untold riches and infinite cake. All potentially mine. Thus the seed had been sown and the damage done. The legend of the Witch Tree had stoked the fires of my boyish imagination, and so began an annual battle of wills between myself and that last, stubborn chestnut.

For several weeks each year I whiled away every spare hour

I had beneath the Witch Tree, watching its uppermost branches bend and dip, hoping the great seed would simply fall into my lap. Day after day I returned, but even as its fellows succumbed to the bludgeoning downpours and numbing squalls of late autumn the last chestnut remained, obstinate and unyielding, as though it were somehow exempt from Newton's Law.

My efforts invariably met with the same unhappy outcome experienced by my father in his younger days. With patience worn thin by the unremitting cold and my resolve broken by the lure of the comforts of home, the day inevitably arrived when I would abandon my vigil with a promise to redouble my efforts the following morning, only to find upon my return the bloated chestnut dehisced upon the ground.

These frustrating pilgrimages came to end as I entered my teenage years, whereupon my interest in the Witch Tree waned completely and I saw the legend for what it truly was: a fairy tale. One of many told by a mischievous father to his credulous young son.

To his credit, Father, for all his shortcomings as a storyteller, opened up an entirely different world of magic and wonder for me. A world of endless beauty far greater than anything an enchanted chestnut could possibly hope to offer. My father's boundless enthusiasm for all things botanical was his greatest gift to me. A gift he in turn had inherited from his own father.

I never met my grandfather. Malcolm Ware's unfortunate encounter with the Clyne's puffball occurred two years before I was born. And if another of Father's fanciful tales is to be believed, I should not have been born at all had my grandfather been spared. For his untimely death proved serendipitous in setting in motion a far happier chain of events.

The funeral of Malcolm Ware took place on the first of August 1820. The bright aspects and edifices of the New Town gleamed in the summer sunshine, the clouds having left the sky to hang heavy in the hearts of the mourners gathering on the steps of St Andrew's Church. Unbeknownst to the six men in black frock coats carefully easing the coffin from the hearse, a young Irishwoman was hurrying from a shop on Hanover Street with a freshly purchased supply of art materials under her arm. A resident of Leith, where she shared a home with her recently widowed mother, the young Irishwoman was in a careless rush to return in time to bid farewell to her brother before he set sail for the whaling grounds of the North Atlantic. Dashing into George Street, the low sun blazed directly into her eyes, forcing her gaze downwards to the pavement. Determined not to be late, she quickened her pace and pressed on.

Lachlan Ware and his fellow pall-bearers, having shouldered the burden of Malcolm's coffin, had advanced but one step towards the church doors when they absorbed the shock of an impact. Struggling to adjust his balance under the swaying load, Lachlan looked for the source of the blow and saw a young woman in a dress of forget-me-not blue, slumped on the pavement nursing her brow with one hand whilst the other reached to gather the brushes and pencils spilled at her side. The cortège continued inside minus my father, who stepped aside to attend to this poor, unfortunate... and strikingly beautiful woman.

He guided the hapless creature to the church steps and with the corner of his handkerchief, gently dabbed at a small cut on her forehead.

'Portraits or landscapes?' he asked, picking up a stray paintbrush.

'Oh,' she said, still somewhat dazed. 'Neither. I specialise in botanical illustrations.'

And with this perfectly innocuous reply, Miss Capability Keane had ensnared the heart of Mr Lachlan Ware as surely as the flame beguiles the moth.

Seven months after she had so fortuitously banged her head against Malcolm Ware's coffin, Miss Keane returned to the very same church to accept Lachlan's hand in marriage. The very same church where, fifteen months later, Mr and Mrs Ware christened their newborn baby: Joseph John Malcolm Ware.

My parents' partnership was driven not only by their mutual affection but also by a symbiotic creative flair. Together they published several extremely successful volumes on the world's rarest and most exotic flora, all beautifully illustrated by my mother's delicate brushstrokes. Widely regarded as the finest publication of its kind, *Botanica Fantastica* enjoyed a success that made my parents one of Edinburgh society's most celebrated couples. Not that they cared for such acclaim. Furthering the understanding of their chosen branch of science was all that mattered to them. Aside from myself, of course.

An only child but never a lonely child, they nurtured in me, as Mother has often described:

'A very happy little seedling.'

CHAPTER THREE

Toor root

The grounds of Braid House buzzed with activity. Three carts had arrived from Leith docks fully laden with the *SS Jupiter's* haul of treasures. The eleven-month long expedition had resulted in the collection of no less than three-hundred and twenty-seven species of the rarest ferns and sixty-three precious orchids. Cuttings, seedlings and mature growths harvested from across the vast territories of Central and Southeast Asia. Father welcomed each meticulously packed specimen in triumph and proceeded to regale us with the extraordinary tales of adventure and derring-do behind every hard-won procurement.

'Oh! this is the Glory Fern from the Himalayan foothills at Kathmandu... Ah! and here we have the Wreath Fern found only on the highest tidelines of the Irrawaddy Delta. Oh! but you must look at this,' he exclaimed with a feverish excitement. 'The most exquisite prize of all. From the wild plains of the Yunnan province of China with its perpetually feuding warlords where our entire company was but a whisker away from falling under the bloodthirsty swords of the Hui. Ah! but was it not worth the risk to secure this Emperor of the Filicopsida – the Equisetum Nocturna? Night Horsetail. This beautiful fern grows exclusively on the westernmost shores of Lake Lugu, where it pursues a very singular life cycle. Its silken fronds are uniquely bashful and will only unfurl to release their precious spores in the light of a full moon. The indigenous Moso people dissolve these seeds in goat's milk and drink the resulting solution before going to bed. They believe it fills their sleep with dreams of the most enlightened and divine insight.'

Ably assisted by the ever-present Mr Maybury, Father orchestrated the delicate transfer of his precious new guests into a purpose-built dome of glass and whitewashed iron. Inside, an ingenious system of irrigation of Father's own design spilled water down a stepped trough to feed little pools and streams, which in turn syphoned carefully measured flows to each individual plant. The fernery's gleaming cupola trapped the sun's rays, maintaining the perfect conditions of temperature and humidity the finicky residents demanded.

With the ferns happily settled in their new home, Mother, Father, Mr Maybury and I retired to the dining room, where we raised a glass of wine in celebration.

'You are most welcome to stay for supper. We are having roast lamb and vegetables,' said Mother.

'It is a kind and tempting offer, Mrs Ware, but I have a few errands to attend to in town. I shall see you all very soon, I trust. Good night to you all.'

Mr Maybury tipped his cap and left so swiftly I suspected he viewed my mother's offer as more of a threat than a treat. And, if truth be told, there was some merit in his assessment. My mother's cooking was not for the faint of heart.

Father wiped his lips and draped the napkin over an empty plate. A gesture of victory if ever I saw one.

'Delicious! You have surpassed yourself my angel,' he said, jaws still arduously engaged in a war of attrition with his last forkful of meat. 'You have no idea how much I have missed the simple pleasure of a home-cooked meal.'

Mother fixed her husband with a wry glint. 'And you have no idea how much I have missed the simple pleasure of your patronising if well-intentioned lies.' She kissed his brow and began to clear the table.

'Can we not afford to hire a maid to help with the cooking and the housework?' I suggested after successfully chiselling my way through the fortified skin of a roast potato. 'Especially the cooking?'

Father threw me a look which managed to convey both sympathy and amusement, qualities which were noticeably absent in Mother's expression.

'Why should I needlessly press some poor stranger into servitude? What, after all, is the purpose of having children if not to provide oneself with free labour?' She handed me a collection of soiled dishes and indicated a path to the scullery door. 'Now go and make yourself useful.'

*

Professor Gilchrist struck me as man for whom the colour grey had been invented. The senior tutor of Botanical Studies at Edinburgh University despised *Botanica Fantastica* with a passion. From our very first introduction it was evident that the son of Lachlan and Bility Ware was but a stray weed in his otherwise carefully cultivated lecture theatre. With each exponentially lauded publication (from Vol. I: – *The Wildflowers of Scotland* to Vol. VII: – *The Fruits & Berries of Australasia*) my parents' continued success merely served to inflame his envy. Gilchrist himself had written several pamphlets and monographs on Scottish flora, all as dry as the dust they collected on the shelves of the University's library, whereas the bindings of the neighbouring copies of *Botanica Fantastica* had become creased and frayed through overuse.

'Mr Ware? I understand your father has recently returned from his latest global meanderings. Is that correct?' said Professor Gilchrist. His voice, clipped with accusation, targeted me from the moment I entered the classroom.

'Yes, sir.'

I hurried to my desk, hoping the conversation was over, but the professor was not to be denied his morning's entertainment.

'And what delights has he pilfered this time? Anything of interest?' he asked, raising his scornful brows.

'Ferns, sir.'

'Ferns, you say?'

'Yes, sir. Ferns. And orchids from across Southeast Asia,' I said.

'Hmm.' He stroked his thin white beard which gave him the look of an undernourished billy goat. 'Interesting. I myself have written extensively on the subject of ferns. Have you read my monograph on the development of the rhizome structures in the Polypodiales?'

'Yes, sir. I found it most useful and instructive.'

Professor Gilchrist rose languidly from his chair. Hands clasped across his chest, he positioned himself in front of my desk, nostrils flaring as a contemptuous leer slid down the length of his upward tilted nose. He held this position until he had secured the undivided attention of every student in the room.

'Useful *and* instructive,' he mused. 'I feel blessed that my work has proved to be of some small value to you. For my humble scribblings to have found favour with a member of the esteemed Ware family is indeed an honour. One which I shall forever regard as being amongst my finest achievements. Our roles ought to be reversed, would you not agree? I should be the student and you the Professor?' Emboldened by the snorts of mirth his mockery had elicited, he leaned a tad closer. 'Tell me, Professor Ware, as one of the foremost pteridologists of our age, where do you stand on the ongoing debate with regard to the taxonomy of the Marattiaceae and the leptosporangiate? Should they not be regarded as a subclass of the Lycopodiophyta?'

As my stupefied mouth widened, the Professor's stare narrowed further.

'Why, sir! You appear to have no opinion on the matter? That is disappointing. You, sir, as the world's foremost authority on the botanical sciences, ought to have exposed me as a charlatan for posing a question that, in and of itself, is complete nonsense. However, it seems the reverse is true and that it is I who has exposed a charlatan.'

He turned to the student seated to my right; a tall, powerfully constructed fellow with a shiny complexion and dark hair curling greasily at his hunched shoulders.

'Mr Tulland? Have you read any of the revered volumes of the *Botanica Fantastica*?'

Robert Tulland's sneer twitched. 'No, sir.'

'Then you must rectify that oversight at once. For I promise you will find them both *useful* and *instructive*,' said Professor Gilchrist, returning to his desk, where he applied his pen to a scrap of paper and scribbled a note.

'But sir, I've heard some say they are boring to look at and dull to read,' yawned Tulland.

The professor nodded sagely. 'I too have heard similar criticisms from many a quarter.'

Though he tried to disguise the action behind a stack of books teetering at the corner of his desk, I watched Professor Gilchrist take a shilling from his pocket and wrap it carefully inside the note. The little package gripped in a closed fist, he set off on a meandering tour of the room.

'Be warned, Mr Ware. Success can be a capricious mistress. So, heed my advice and enjoy the privileges she brings while you can. And please, spare a thought for us mere mortals who sadly, have not been blessed with your advantages and have had to grasp what modest achievements we have made through our own hard work and sweat. Take, for example, our friend Mr Tulland here. His father, a man of considerable skill, has had to work like the devil in order to fund his son's education.'

Tulland turned his blushes to the rain lashing at the windows and failed to notice the little package enter his pocket.

'A man, unlike your own father,' continued Professor Gilchrist with a haughty sniff, 'who understands the true value and satisfaction that only a day's honest toil provides, would you not agree, Mr Ware? Therefore, why should the son of a cabinetmaker be any less worthy of respect than the son of a man who idly saunters off around the world, digging up pretty flowers and ferns?'

Accepting my continued silence as a sign of capitulation, Professor Gilchrist returned to his desk where, chest puffed with pride at his small victory, he invited us to consider the relative methods of conjugation employed by freshwater and saltwater algae.

*

The sky had grown dark by the time Professor Gilchrist's lecture, delivered in his usual dreary monotone, had reached its conclusion. My mind befuddled with the intricacies of algal reproduction, I left the university and set off on the long walk for home. But as I exited Potter Row for Buccleuch Street, I felt a sharp tug on the strap of my satchel.

'I hear your mother spends her nights at the docks selling herself to the lowest bidder.'

I was by no means a weakling and quite reasonably regarded myself as being above the average in both height and athleticism and yet, in the presence of Robert Tulland, my physical inadequacies were thrown into stark, humiliating relief. We were standing face to face, his chin hovering some distance above my nose whilst his thickset frame carried twice the weight of my own and contained enough aggression to arm an entire field of battle. Grabbing great fistfuls of my collar, he picked me up and threw me bodily against the wall of a grimy coal yard.

A fist drilled hard into my stomach. A second blow to the temple knocked my head hard against the bricks. The third fired a bolt of pain from my neck to my toes. My innards lurched and spasmed. I tasted blood on my tongue. Tulland thrust me against a heap of loose coals.

'I think I shall pay her a visit tonight. After all, I do have a shilling in my pocket. Far more than I need. Every fellow knows your mother is a ha'penny whore,' he sneered.

He pushed a knee against my chest. The lumpy black slope crumbled and shifted under my spine.

'Twice the value of yours then!' I gasped, launching a handful of soot and grit into his eyes.

Half blinded, Tulland growled furiously and flung himself into another attack. His momentum sent us tumbling in a tangle of thrashing limbs and flailing knuckles. For every blow I landed, Tulland struck two or three in return. Eventually I slumped to the ground in a spent bundle of exhaustion and pain. Face crimped like an angry accordion, Tulland sealed his victory by forcing a lump of coal into my mouth. Happy I had learned my lesson, he pulled himself upright and staggered off into the street rubbing his smarting eyes.

I spat out the coal, rolled gingerly on to my throbbing side and lay there until I gathered strength enough to take to my feet. Dusting myself down I noticed a small fleck of white lying on the filthy cobbles. A scrap of paper. Composed in Professor Gilchrist's unmistakable script, the note contained only two words:

Hurt Ware…

*

I entered Braid House treading as lightly as my aching feet would allow in the hope of reaching the sanctuary of my bedroom without detection. Blackened eyes obscured under the peak of my cap and with the torn stitching of my fatally wounded coat pocket shielded behind the satchel, I advanced through the hall more in keeping with an intruder intent on misadventure than a resident. I successfully bypassed the drawing room, where Mother sat at her easel humming sweetly to herself. She dabbed her brush in the palette, then deftly added a stroke of detail to a beautiful painting of the Wreath Fern.

I limped quietly towards the staircase, whereupon I glanced inside the half-open door of the study. My father was at his desk, surrounded by a lush spray of greenery. He held a handglass to the nearest fern, studying every intricate facet of its structure. Observations completed, he dipped his pen in the ink and recorded his findings in the closing pages of a notebook.

'Ah! Joseph! Come, join me,' cried Father on hearing the telltale creak of the stairs. 'I want to show you this marvellous *Platycerium*! Come. And please, close the door, lest my enthusiasm disturb your mother.'

Preparing myself for the inevitable inquisition to come, I abandoned my ascent and acceded to Father's beckoning hand.

'You really must take a close look at the extraordinary sporophylls on this fern. I have never seen anything... Hello? What's this?' A sudden cloud of concern dampened Father's ebullience. He dropped the handglass and rose from his seat to lift the cap from my head. 'Who did this to you?'

'It's nothing. A result of my own clumsiness.'

He took my head in his hands and inspected the damage closely.

'And that is the very lie we will tell your mother when she sees this mess. Look at your hands!' he said, grimacing at the sight of my burst knuckles. 'And your clothes! Dear God. Sit.'

Father gestured to the old threadbare couch hogging the

glow of the fireplace, where Mother and I would often catch him snoozing after a full day of research and cataloguing, an open book on his chest and dozens more scattered on the hearthside rugs.

By day the study was a big, bright, south-facing room affording excellent views across the rear garden to the woods beyond. By night, as now, the space appeared to diminish amongst the grasping silhouettes of the abundant plant specimens perched on sills, side tables and mantelpieces. On shelves bowed like toothy smiles under the mountainous weight of hundreds, perhaps thousands of haphazardly stacked books, a small army of precariously balanced lamps cast their soft yellowy pools of trembling light over walls decorated with maps and botanical illustrations so numerous as to almost completely obliterate the underlying wallpaper.

I dropped my satchel of textbooks and slumped my bag of bruised bones on the couch. Through the broad windows overlooking the rear lawn, I saw sparks and flames rising into the darkness from a brazier near the treeline. Mr Maybury, his face a flickering mask in the firelight, tipped an armful of garden debris into the blaze. Brushing his hands together, he looked towards the house with a singular grimness of expression which I found deeply unnerving.

'Here, drink this. I've added a little something to ease the pain,' said Father, handing me a glass of water. He dabbed a corner of his handkerchief into a small jar of liniment and applied the salve to my impressive assortment of scrapes and scratches. 'You look like you've fallen under all the horses on Princes Street. Tell me how you came to be in such a state. The truth now.'

I drank thirstily, pleased finally to rid the oily film of coal and blood from my mouth. I briefly considered the merits of telling another falsehood, but as the soreness eased I became infused with a pleasing warmth at odds with the coolness of the water and saw no harm in relaying everything exactly as it had occurred.

At the conclusion of my tale, Father pursed his lips and pondered for a moment.

'The lad's a coward. Much like his father. You may have lost this particular battle, but should hostilities resume, which I fear they most certainly will, I am confident that with a little preparation, you will win the war.'

'But how? Tulland is twice my size!'

Father opened his arms with a theatrical flourish.

'*So David prevailed over the Philistine with a sling and with a stone, and smote the Philistine, and slew him; but there was no sword in the hand of David.* Samuel, chapter seventeen, verse fifty. What you lack in firepower, Joseph, can be compensated by the application of a little knowledge. Allow me one moment and I will furnish you with a slingshot guaranteed to bring down this Goliath.'

Taking up a lamp, Father crossed the room to consult the huge apothecary chest which occupied the entire wall behind his desk. A gallery of hundreds of little drawers stretching from the floor to the ceiling and from corner to corner, each one painstakingly labelled with the strangely exotic Latin binomial and the equally intriguing common name of its contents. The highest examples were serviced by a sliding ladder fixed to a rail which ran the whole length of the collection.

'Let me think, let me think,' said Father, his fingers fluttering back and forth across the lacquered cherry wood and brass handles. 'St Matthew's Wort? Two grains of this, and the lad will lose all his teeth within twelve hours. No. Noxious as he is, it would be extreme revenge indeed to leave the lad without a smile.' He opened another drawer and frowned in contemplation. 'Philasia root. It's a possibility. He'll be scratching his knees for days. No, not nearly interesting enough... Ah!'

Descrying a promising label on one of the topmost drawers close to the study door, he hurriedly slid the ladder along the rail, brought its castors to a rumbling halt at the desired section, then with a devilish smile he climbed up, pulled the handle and removed a small jar of greyish powder.

'Perfect! Toor root! The name is a little joke of mine. Dried and crushed. Unique to the Tupinambas region of the Amazon Delta. A strange tuber similar to the humble potato but when ground together with a half scruple of red nutmeg... Wonders occur! The results are astonishing if relatively short lived, lasting no more than an hour or so. I can personally attest to its efficacy. The tribal elder of the Eru Indians introduced me to this astonishing concoction during our South American expedition of '37. Intuquo was his name. A man of rare mischief. He insisted that only by ingesting a morsel for myself could I prove our party's intentions were honourable and thereby win the trust and co-operation of his people. This much we managed to decipher through a mixture of enthusiastic gesticulation and what little Erunese dialect our guide possessed. And so I agreed. What else could I do? No more than a pinch sprinkled on a piece of fruit, mind, but by God! My ears have never rung with such laughter! The whole village laughed till they cried with the pain of it. I had no idea I was doing anything out of the ordinary until Maybury described my antics shortly afterwards. But his description was so ludicrously outlandish I refused to believe a single word. Maybury generously volunteered to take a pinch himself in order that I might witness the effects first-hand. I promise you, Joseph, I do not recall ever having laughed so much in my life. As a reward for providing his people with such sport, Intuquo granted us unfettered access to his domain. A humorous bunch of practical jokers, the Eru. Unquestionably the loveliest people I have yet encountered.'

Father descended the ladder and carried the precious vessel to his desk where, eyes wrinkled and brow furrowed in utmost concentration, he uncorked the glass and employed a set of delicately calibrated weighing scales to measure out a tiny amount of the mysterious Amazonian potato powder.

'But what are the effects? What does it do?' I asked.

A wicked twinkle appeared in Father's eyes.

'Would it not be more fun to see the magic unfold for yourself?'

*

The inevitable confrontation happened sooner than anticipated. I had mistakenly imagined Tulland would perhaps bide his time and wait for the lunch recess bell or, as seemed more likely, wait for the conclusion of Professor Gilchrist's afternoon lecture – *Epiphytes: In Relation to Their Hosts and Habitats* – and, in a repeat of our previous tussle, pounce from the shadows as I walked home.

I was still pondering these various scenarios on my way to morning tutorial and had set but one foot inside the university gates when Tulland and two of his equally sour-faced associates surrounded me. I recognised the wiry straw-haired lad on Tulland's left from the library, where he could often be seen with his nose buried in the *Complete Works of Shakespeare*. Bartholomew had designs on becoming an actor and thought the best way to achieve this goal was to learn the entire output of the great bard by rote. The other lout standing to Tulland's right was unfamiliar to me. Roughly the same physical stature as his leader, he had an alarming scar, pink and raised, which traced the contour of his hairline for several inches.

'Good morning, class,' said Tulland. His eyes and nose still bore the painful legacy of the coal yard. 'Today we are going to be studying anatomy.' He opened his coat just wide enough to reveal the knife concealed inside.

After a final glance to ensure there was no one of any authority in view, Tulland signalled a brief nod to his accomplices and I was dragged swiftly between the foyer's imposing columns of Craigleith stone and wedged into an alcove beneath the broad steps which curved upwards to the courtyard terrace. Bartholomew retreated a few paces to keep watch on the increasing flow of students, enabling Tulland and his scarred companion to carry out their business unhindered.

'I like your bag,' said Tulland, taking the satchel from my shoulder. 'I think I'll keep it. The perfect place to store your teeth when I knock them out. Where did you get it?'

'It's from China. A gift from my father,' I said, glancing nervously at Tulland's coat.

He unbuckled the satchel and peered inside. Nostrils snorting in derision, he removed a book, *Botanica Fantastica: Volume I – The Wildflowers of Scotland*. My personal favourite due largely to Mother's stunningly delicate illustrations of a whole host of blooms, from the cranesbills, sea thrifts and campions of the coast to the spotted orchids, ribworts and bugle flowers of the moors.

Tulland handed the bag to his lackey. Holding the book in front of my face, he gleefully tore away the pages in several great clumps before dropping the mutilated remnants to his feet, where he added a final note of criticism by crushing the whole sorry mess under his heel.

His taciturn friend issued a jubilant grunt. The bag had offered up a new treasure: my lunch. He pocketed the apple and unwrapped a neatly folded parcel of cloth, revealing the mutton pie Father had placed inside. Tulland seized the pie for himself.

'Smells good,' he said, sniffing the pastry. Then, lowering his greasy head close to mine, he crammed the entire pie into his mouth. Crumbs tumbling from his lips, Tulland looked closely at the satchel and said something incomprehensible behind the enormous lump of mushed meat and pastry stuffed inside his cavernous mouth. Acknowledging the look of puzzlement on my face, he forced the whole glutinous mass down his throat in one mighty gulp.

'What are these marks on my bag?' he asked.

'It's Chinese.'

'What does it say?'

According to my father the swirls of exotic calligraphy embossed between the satchel's buckles simply stated: *Guangzhou Leather Company.*

'It's a warning. Beware of poisoned pies.'

Quite what possessed my insolent mouth to replace the truth with a retort guaranteed to test his patience to the extreme, I do not know.

Tulland's glare dissolved into a prolonged and silent distillation of hatred.

'Lift up your shirt,' he said, having at last determined which part of me to damage first.

I cleared my arid throat.

'No.'

'Lift up your shirt!'

He raised the knife. The blade's patina of spotted rust spoke of a long and violent history. And though it measured no more than four inches it was quite long enough to puncture everything of importance, including every last speck of bravado. My trembling hands made heavy work of Tulland's instruction.

'Higher!'

The flat of the blade pressed coldly against my exposed stomach. Tulland drew his face so close I could smell the seasoned meat in each warm billow of his breath.

'Bartholomew is sensitive to the sight of blood. If he sees a single drop, he collapses like an old granny. That's why he volunteered for lookout duty.' Tulland edged the tip of the knife into my belly button. 'Myself and Andrew, we enjoy blood. We like to visit the slaughterhouse and watch them strip the hides from the cows and the pigs.' Tulland leered closer still. 'Their skins come off so quick! One good cut and it all peels away like a glove. But first they have to remove the guts. That's the best bit. I wonder if your skin will come off so easily. Shall we find out?'

Rigid with fear, I closed my eyes and waited to feel the cut of the knife and to hear the first soft splash of blood hit the ground. But the cut and the splash never arrived. Their absence was filled by a most alarming and protracted gurgling noise. When at length I dared to look, I saw Tulland drop the blade and grasp his rumbling stomach.

'What have you done to me?' he rasped, fury and fear battling for supremacy on his wan, perspiring face.

'Beware of poisoned pies,' I said with a smile.

'Hold him!'

Watching Tulland fold his broad knuckles into a set of battering rams, I struggled in vain to free myself from Andrew's iron grip.

And then, at the precise moment he attempted to launch the first punch towards my face, the powder's extraordinary effect seized control. Having braced myself for the arrival of a bone-shattering impact, I stared in astonishment as Tulland's fist suddenly halted in mid-air, where it tremored momentarily before hurling itself with equal ferocity back from whence it came.

His belly continuing to gripe and whine, Tulland's face ignited in alarm as his fist stubbornly refused to pursue a forward, nose-crunching trajectory, preferring instead to bash harmlessly at the air behind his head.

Andrew released me with a bemused grunt and sidled beside an equally perplexed Bartholomew as their leader repeatedly jerked his fist backwards over his shoulder, the sinews and tendons of Tulland's neck bulging and quivering under intense strain as he battled with some immense and unseen force. He tried repeatedly to face his allies and plead for their assistance, but rather than turn to the left as desired, his head spun sharply to the right, whereupon he saw me gathering my possessions and return them to my bag.

A flash of rage purpled his cheeks and he started towards me with malevolent purpose, but again the invisible foe took possession of his limbs. His knees trembled and locked to a momentary standstill before, slowly at first but then with increasing momentum, they began to propel him backwards.

Tulland's eyes gleamed with a wild mania, but no matter how hard he wrestled to steer himself forwards, he succeeded only in achieving full speed astern. Truly, it was a sight to behold. The students now pouring inside the quadrangle stared with mouths agape, pointing and laughing as he lumbered in reverse with chaotic celerity up the steps and through the cloisters like a demented escapee from the Morningside Lunatic Asylum. Faster and faster he went, his wildly flitting eyes trying to evade obstacles and walls whilst his feet motored backwards, toe to heel, toe to heel, weaving him madly between the pillars and into the courtyard. Tulland had become a hapless marionette dragged hither and thither, in direct contradiction to where his brain desired him to go, by a merciless and sadistic puppeteer.

Humiliated by the peals of laughter echoing from every quarter, he gathered speed and began to yell at his detractors in what I imagined was a foreign tongue until I realised his speech, like everything else, was flowing in the wrong direction.

'On going what's! Me to happening what's! Help! Help! HELP!!'

The rising volume of consternation drew forth several stern-faced professors into the courtyard, all of whom stepped aside when the Principal himself marched into the centre of the maelstrom, the tails of his long black coat billowing in his wake. Mortified, Tulland tried to run and hide from Sir David Henderson's wrath, but the contrary influence of the Toor root saw him sprint towards the Principal at such speed he tripped on a broken kerbstone and landed in a heap at the polished buckles of the great man's shoes. Sir David calmly folded his arms across his chest and leaned over the luckless Tulland like some monstrous raven poised to peck an irritating bug.

'What *are* you doing, boy? Stop behaving like an imbecile. Do you not have a lecture to attend?' Delivered in Sir David's customary soft and measured tone, the admonishment contained far more authority and instilled far more fear than the vocal histrionics employed by many of the other professors when registering their displeasure.

'Sir yes. Sir sorry I'm.'

Tulland attempted to haul himself upright but succeeded only in pressing himself harder against the flagstones until he resembled a deranged seal squirming helplessly on the rocks. His antics inspired a fresh paroxysm of merriment from the assembled masses, which now appeared to comprise the entire population of the University.

'Get up now before I lose my patience.'

'Sir can't I!' Tulland yelped. 'Me not it's! Fault Ware's Joseph it's! Me poisoned he!'

Sir David, who was not one to suffer fools, especially those incapable of sustaining forward momentum, gripped Tulland by the ear and heaved him to his feet.

'My patience has expired. Report to my office at once.'

'Sir yes. Sir away right.'

At which Tulland proceeded to march backwards across the courtyard, through the gates and disappeared on to South Bridge Street, all the while staring at Sir David with an exasperated expression of apology on his face, the audience cheering and applauding enthusiastically as he went. Andrew and Bartholomew quickly scarpered after their leader.

The Tulland Episode firmly established itself as the main topic of conversation in both staff and student circles for the remainder of the day. In the library, rumours abounded in hushed whispers that, half an hour or so after his brazen insubordination, Tulland aided by Bartholomew and Andrew, returned to the Principal's office to beg for leniency. Sir David sentenced Tulland to perform a recital of 'To A Mountain Daisy' in front of the most senior members of staff, this being his favourite form of punishment. Alas, the Toor root had not yet fully relinquished its hold on poor Tulland who received six lashings from Sir David's tawse for mangling the beauty of Robert Burns' words with his incoherent, mumbling nonsense:

> *Flow'r tipped-crimson, modest, wee,*
> *Hour evil an in me met thou's,*
> *Stoure the amang crush maun I for,*
> *Stem slender thy,*
> *Pow'r my past is now thee spare to,*
> *Gem bonnie thou.*

Toor root…
What was it Father had said?
'The name is a little joke of mine…'

CHAPTER FOUR

Tulland & Son

Cold, perpetually damp and always foreboding, this was Edinburgh dressed in all her December finery. The North Sea winds having shaken aside the last vestiges of autumn's russet embrace now carried gowns of winter grey. The haars and mists wreathed through the wynds and closes of the Old Town, their dun veils trapping the stench rising from the gutters' stagnant stew of butcher shop blood and pails of tenement slurry thrown from the windows of the unseen hovels above. A fine cocktail indeed for the rats and the mice.

And everywhere, hands and caps outstretched, the decrepit and the broken squabbled with each other as they laid claim to the most profitable corners of the High Street and Canongate before returning home to tally up the day's meagre takings of coins, raindrops and spittle. Elsewhere, figures lurked in dram shop doorways, eyes peering from under frayed brims with sly, silent menace at all that passed before them, seeking the unwary and an easy pocket.

Leaving the labyrinthine thoroughfares and passageways of the Old Town, the fog tumbled down The Mound towards Princes Street, that great dividing line where the two faces of the city pressed nose to nose. Busy shapes bustled and harried with heads bowed to the elements and shoulders slouched under the seasonal burden of heavy coats, hats and scarves.

Their breaths punctuated the frostbitten air with little grey wafts gradually fading into an ashen sky scented with roasted nuts and warm fudge. These pleasing aromas billowing from the street pedlars' barrows were a welcome distraction from the ever-present background odour drifting from the mess left on the streets by the working horses.

The broad boulevards and squares of the New Town glistened with a sheen of fresh lacquer as the mist permeated its grandeur, dampening the spirits of the lamplighters who complained of having to set about their work earlier and earlier with each passing evening. And looking down upon the appallingly bleak poetry of its domain, from every crawling shadow of the Old and respectable glow of the New, the Castle sat isolated atop its tower of basalt.

As had become her custom for many years, my mother set off from Braid House with her sketching-bag and a small folding seat every second Friday, immediately after breakfast, come hail or shine, to while away several meditative hours in the cemetery of Greyfriars Kirk. Here she would sit upon her little stool, tip the pencils and charcoals from her bag and use them to capture the garden of the dead in a monochrome outline with perhaps just a single stroke of green or yellow to signify the presence of a bloom or a fresh shoot amongst the decay.

This fortnightly pilgrimage invariably concluded with Mother paying her respects to the memory of Mr George Buchanan by tucking a modest flower behind a loose stone at the base of the philosopher's memorial. The pressed and dried petals of a blue cornflower represented her most common offering, but occasionally she preferred the brilliant yellow of a buttercup. As a young boy I regularly accompanied my mother on these visits to Greyfriars, but it was quite some time before I eventually witnessed this odd little flower ceremony, and when I did, she appeared uncharacteristically perturbed, leaving the distinct impression that I was not meant to have noticed her sleight of hand. She knelt to match the height of her inquisitive wee boy and gripped me by the shoulders.

'You must never tell your father about my small tributes to Mr Buchanan. He will think me foolish. Let this be our secret. Promise me you will keep it forever.'

I made my most solemn promise and asked why Mr Buchanan deserved her flowers.

'Because he has an honest face, just like you,' she smiled.

I peered up at the coldly pious eyes and verdigris-stained complexion of the bust staring out from the centre of the memorial and questioned the efficacy of Mother's eyesight.

My mother's inexhaustible enthusiasm for the place and the stories she'd weave whilst working on her art opened up an entirely new and wondrously macabre world to me. She seemed to know the history of every soul buried within the kirkyard walls whose ghosts convened nightly to discuss the woes and triumphs of their mortal existence, their spectral gossip exposing the innermost secrets of Edinburgh's turbulent past. She explained the symbolism behind the memento mori everywhere carved into stone; the gargoyles, the death heads, the scythes, the snakes, the weeping angels and the grinning skeletons carrying books in the weathered bones of their fingers.

Some of the graves were protected by cages of iron, grim reminders of those nights when, in the light of a dimmed lantern, the resurrection men crept between the slabs to ply their unwholesome trade. There were many, including Mother, who remained far from convinced that these grisly embellishments were no longer required.

In recent months these visits to Greyfriars, hitherto undertaken purely for recreation, had taken on a scientific purpose for Mother. She and Father were planning a future volume of *Botanica Fantastica* dedicated to lichens and mosses, which they hoped would represent the most exhaustive survey of these hardy growths ever committed to print. To this end she had selected three distinct headstones for her study – one of sandstone, one of granite and one of marble – with a view to discovering the effect different surfaces had, if any, upon the growth rate of the lichens.

The minister of the Kirk, initially somewhat bemused, had become inured to the sight of this eccentric woman, the front of her dress muddied and stained by repeatedly crouching on all fours with a magnifying glass and measuring rule for an intimate examination of her chosen stones. Her initial findings revealed that the plants appeared to favour the porous sandstone, covering this surface at a faster rate than the smooth impenetrable marble. However, fast by lichen standards remained infinitesimally slow in comparison to the weeds and grasses sprouting from the fertile soil from which the stones themselves seemed to rise, benefitting as they did from the plentiful nutrition stored below.

It had been some considerable time since I last accompanied Mother to Greyfriars, so it came as a pleasant surprise when, two days after the Toor root incident, she invited me to join her. I had no lectures scheduled on that particular Friday and accepted the invitation gladly, but my enthusiasm for the trip was soon tempered by Mother's sombre demeanour. The joy and smiles I remembered from previous outings had been replaced by a despondency I had seldom seen her exhibit.

Not a word had passed her lips since we departed Braid House for the cemetery. Not a word since she learned that the body recently discovered on the steps of Advocate's Close had now been identified. It belonged to a young solicitor by the name of Francis Baxter.

'*The victim's body displayed evidence of a most horrific and frenzied attack. He had been stabbed repeatedly about the chest, abdomen and arms, his throat was cut and his face further mutilated by a strange mark scored into the flesh of his brow...* Well, well, these are dark times indeed,' Father concluded, folding his breakfast newspaper. 'However, the legal profession is by no means underpopulated and the world will not suffer from having one less lawyer to feed.'

'There is no need to take such delight in this poor man's demise!' replied Mother, visibly upset by her husband's callous remark. Father's contrition was immediate.

'Forgive me, my dear. It was a poor jest. I take no pleasure in this tragedy. It is merely the irony that causes me to smile. I have spent my entire life travelling through some of the most violent places on earth. Jungles rife with cannibals. Deserts ruled by murderous barbarians. But none of these it seems, are more savage than my own home.'

My disconsolate mother, having completed her measurements and sketches detailing the latest advance of the lichen across the three headstones of her ongoing study, produced a single dried rose petal from her purse and placed the little splash of red delicately behind the loose stone at the foot of Mr Buchanan's memorial.

'Poor, poor man,' she muttered, carefully packing her implements and drawings inside her sketching bag. 'Awful. Truly awful.'

We exited Greyfriars for Candlemaker Row. I walked closely by her side, wracking my brain for something humorous to say to disperse the cloud of gloom gathering about her head, when I noticed a figure, face obscured under the upturned collars of a coarse woollen coat, lurking in a doorway across the street, surveying our every step. The man's hard blue eyes retreated smartly into the shadows when I caught his stare. I had half a mind to cross the road and confront the fellow, but Mother, continuing to mutter ruefully to herself, marched on at such a rate that it was all I could do to keep pace with her as we descended towards the Grassmarket.

The square, as ever, was abuzz with the gossip and holler of its resident victuallers all fighting to be heard above the clatter of hooves and cartwheels, the whole swirling cacophony enriched by a chill air pungent with cheap tobacco, wet straw and warm manure. To the relief of our battered senses, we left the clamour of the Grassmarket behind and turned smartly at the corner of Grindlay Street, where Mother drew to a sudden halt. Through gritted teeth she inhaled a long slow breath and locked it away for a moment to cool the turmoil simmering inside her chest.

'Cowards,' she said in a whisper scarcely audible over the icy squall blustering at my ears. Then, straightening her posture to present her full height, Mother wiped the dampness from her eyes and with head proudly raised, she marched steadfastly onwards until she arrived at the generously proportioned windows of Tulland & Son.

A little notice perched within the shop proudly proclaimed: *All items created by master craftsman Hugh Tulland, former apprentice of Mr Brodie.*

Mother cupped her hands to the glass and peered inside to admire an exhibition of the cabinetmaker's finest wardrobes, bureaus and dressers; beautiful pieces of oak, walnut and satinwood all expertly turned and inlaid. Yet it was the most unassuming piece on display that caught my mother's eye. She tapped the window.

'What do you think, Joseph? Quite beautiful, is it not?'

Aside from being at least as tall as myself and sporting a few unusual appendages, the object appeared, to my untrained eye, no more or less remarkable than any other artist's easel.

'I must have it,' she declared, pushing through the door.

I hesitated on the threshold, pondering whether or not to wait outside, as I had no desire to endure another encounter with a Tulland, father or son. I had met with Mr Hugh Tulland only once before when, at Father's behest, he arrived at

Braid House to collect an antique dresser in urgent need of restoration. He was a man of tawdry appearance with sleekit, scheming eyes. My father nevertheless held his skills in the very highest regard: 'Simply the finest in the country. No one else will do.'

I suspected my father's loyalty, like so many of the cabinetmaker's clients, reflected a morbid fascination with his association to the infamous Deacon Brodie (a spurious claim, as Hugh Tulland could not have been more than a tot when Brodie was hanged) than to any real appreciation of the man's talent. And to my mind, the elder Tulland's willingness to exploit a dubious connection to a long deceased housebreaker merely served to indicate his own questionable morality.

With these reservations preying on my mind, I entered the shop and followed the little chime of the doorbell into a long and broad room, its dimensions heavy with the scents of polished veneer and sawdust. Slow to dispense with the hard daylight of the street, my gaze required a little time to adapt to the dim cave of the shop's interior. Gradually, shapes in turn bulky and delicate, many gilded with fine marquetry, sparkled forth from the sparse candlelight. Everywhere, pressed against the wainscots and tucked into alcoves, stood further examples of the cabinetmaker's artistry; tables and desks, cabinets and exquisitely designed armchairs. And in all the spaces in between came a plethora of smaller items; chessboards, coat stands and walking sticks. Above the counter there hung a most peculiar crucifix fashioned from two gnarled lengths of bone grown yellow with age and pitted with disease. A cold, morbid thrill ran through my skin when I realised the bones upon which Jesus stared down in his anguish were quite possibly human and that the crown of thorns secured to his bloodied brow were, in fact, a crown of broken teeth.

From an unseen room somewhere to the rear of the premises came the rhythmic sound of a carpenter's plane at work. Mother tapped the bell on the counter. The plane continued unabated. She tapped the bell again. The slicing ceased. A brief interlude of silence was quickly filled by the dulled rush of a cart passing by on the street.

A candle appeared from the carpenter's workshop. Its meagre flame too weak to expose its carrier, it floated towards us through the gloom as though propelled under its own volition like some magical firefly. The illusion soon evaporated when the proprietor advanced a little further.

'Ah! My dear Mrs Ware. And you, Joseph. Welcome. Have you been waiting long? Apologies. My hearing is not what it once was,' said Hugh Tulland, loudly.

Sporting a broad smile punctuated by a scab crusting at his lower lip, he slowly raised his candle to guide his licentious gaze along the folds and contours of my mother's dress.

'And may I say,' he added when at last he arrived at her own, unwavering stare, 'that you are a positive beacon of sunshine on this dreich and chillsome day. What may I do for you?'

'The easel you have on display. I would like to purchase it.'

'Ah! Certainly. One moment.'

With hands as coarse as his manner, he set his light upon the counter, brushed the sawdust from his apron and hurried to the window.

'As you can see, it is both sturdy and practical,' he boasted, planting the easel before us and proudly running his fingers along each expertly crafted component. 'It is of my own design and features a few unique additions such as this caddy to hold the artist's brushes. And here we have an adjustable tray, which may be filled with water for cleaning those same brushes or, indeed, for mixing colours. The whole piece is made of cherry wood which, I confess, I have never worked with before, but I cannot help myself when it comes to trying new and unusual materials. How else are discoveries made? It proved most accommodating to the chisel and the plane and I believe it will provide added durability, particularly for the landscape artist who regularly ventures to the great outdoors to undertake their work. And as I see by the mud staining the hem of your skirt and the toes of your shoes, the great outdoors provides much inspiration for your own art. In addition, as a gesture of gratitude to a most highly valued customer, you will also receive a complimentary palette.'

Mother removed a solitary coin from her purse.

'I believe this should be enough?'

Hugh Tulland's smile faltered at the paltry sum.

'You are in fine humour today, I see, Mrs Ware.'

'You think it too much, Mr Tulland?' said Mother, making it quite plain that she was not in a jesting mood.

The cabinetmaker's jaws tensed and flexed as he ground his teeth, biting down on his growing rage.

'That will be quite sufficient,' he muttered.

'I would like it delivered to Braid House before the end of the day.'

Mother's request was met with a dark glower.

'Certainly, Mrs Ware.' He turned to the staircase curving up into the darkness behind the counter. 'Robert!'

'Coming!' cried a voice from the floor above. Footsteps hurried down and there appeared Robert Tulland, eying me with wary surprise. Not so much as a syllable had passed between us since the escapade involving the Reverse Root. Robert's father placed a hand on the back of his neck and coaxed him closer to me, close enough to notice the mottle of fresh bruises colouring his temples.

'Robert! Look who's here! This is a happy coincidence. I believe you owe young Mr Ware an apology.' Mr Tulland tightened the grip on his son's neck. 'Don't be coy, son, say it. Say it now.'

'Sorry.'

'That's sorry *Mr Ware* to you, boy. Try again,' the father growled.

Robert now cut a very different figure from the fearful thug who had threatened to flay me alive. I had spent the intervening days longing to see my tormentor receive his much-deserved comeuppance, so I was greatly surprised when, instead of relishing the flush of humiliation warming his face and the moisture welling in his downcast gaze, I felt a pang of sympathy for him. The change was every bit as striking as that which had overtaken Professor Gilchrist. Gone were the contempt and disdain with which he habitually greeted me upon entering his lecture theatre the previous morning, and in their stead I received a fulsome handshake and a succession of supplicatory enquiries as to my health, happiness and comfort. Evidently, I had somewhat underestimated my parents' influence within the University.

'Sorry, Mr Ware.'

Hugh Tulland released his hold on Robert's neck.

'There! Now we can all put this sorry business behind us. Be assured, Mrs Ware, the boy has been spoken to in the sternest possible terms and is well aware that I do not expect him to squander the education I have sacrificed my every last ha'penny in providing, by involving himself in needless squabbles and tiffs. However minor they may be. It will not happen again.'

Mother placed the coin on the counter.

'I hope not, Mr Tulland.'

Hugh Tulland's mouth twitched as he collected the six-pence. He passed the easel to his glum-faced son. 'Take extra care when you load the cart, Robert. You could not be delivering to a more distinguished home. Truly, we are blessed and humbled. To have no less than Mrs Bility Ware, the artist behind the wonderful *Botanica Fantastica*, purchasing our wares is indeed patronage of the highest order,' he scoffed.

Once Robert had taken his load through to the rear of the shop, his father took a small step towards Mother.

'I trust this settles our account?'

'Your son will join us for supper after he makes the delivery. My husband was most insistent on that point.' Mother, sensing my consternation at this deeply unwelcome plan, raised a hand to silence my dismay.

'And then the account will be settled?' Hugh Tulland persisted, advancing another inch.

'And then the account will be settled,' confirmed Mother.

They stared at each other, my mother parrying his enmity with a calm assuredness. The cabinetmaker sniffed, then retreated behind the counter, where he deposited the coin into a small metal box.

'Very good,' he said, slapping the lid on his derisory takings. 'May I humbly offer a small piece of advice with regard to your new purchase, Mrs Ware?'

'By all means, Mr Tulland.'

'You are a singularly gifted artist, Mrs Ware. But like all artists your eye is naturally drawn to the beauty and wonder of our world yet slow to recognise its dangers. You do not see the ugliness and violence that resides all around us. Even in the bonniest of places. Take the poor soul found slain not a stone's throw from where we now stand. A young man not much older than our own sons, slaughtered like a mangy lamb. So I beg you, Mrs Ware, imagine how much more vulnerable is the woman out on her own, innocently painting the butter-cups and daisies whilst the nettles and thorns rise up behind her?'

'I have no difficulty in recognising where the danger lies, Mr Tulland,' said Mother.

'I am very glad to hear it.' The smile had returned to Hugh Tulland's sluglike lips.

'Then we shall bid you good day.'

'One more request, please,' said the cabinetmaker hurrying to block our advance towards the door. 'You have some fascinating trees in your arboretum.'

'I beg your pardon?'

'At Braid House? I am told your husband's collection of exotic trees is a sight to behold. May I be so bold as to ask that, should the winter storms dislodge the branches from say, a Chilean pine or a baobab, you will allow me to purchase them from you?' Hugh Tulland lifted a chisel from his apron and ran the tip of a finger along its edge. 'As I have said, new materials fascinate me and I would love to experiment with some of the rarer species to see how they compare with the tried and the trusted. How else can one further one's artistry and craft? Rare trees! Rare woods! These are what my blades desire above all.'

'If we suffer the same winter this year as we endured last, you may have more material than you can handle,' said Mother.

Hugh Tulland blinked slowly. 'The more, the merrier, Mrs Ware. I cannot wait to carve my chisel into something new.'

'A novel experience is often a disappointing one. Good day, Mr Tulland.'

'Good day, Mrs Ware. And to you, young Joseph.'

The shop door closing at our backs, I turned angrily to Mother.

'Have you any idea how humiliating that was? I have 206 bones in my body and you have just ensured that Tulland is going to break every last one!'

Mother ignored my outburst and trekked on in silence. We arrived at The Mound, where we paused to look down upon the spread of Princes Street Gardens.

A small crowd had gathered at the bandstand, where an accordion player worked a merry tune complimented by squawks of spinning laughter from the children riding the nearby roundabout. The joyful vista soon dispelled my anger.

I turned to Mother, ready to issue an apology when suddenly she clasped my hands so tightly I heard a knuckle crack. The sorrow in her eyes had been replaced by another quality I had rarely encountered in them before.

Fear.

'Listen to me!' she pleaded. 'The shadows are closing in on us all. Never drop your guard. Not for one instant. And above all, trust no one. Do you hear? No one!' This last she uttered in a terse whisper after a drunkard appeared at the railings a few paces from where we stood. The man peered down to the gardens and began to tap his toes and hum cheerfully along to the accordion.

Mother's usual composure returned as swiftly as her momentary alarm had appeared. She placed a finger to my mouth to stifle the questions gathering there, then stepped to the kerb to hail a cab. Those same questions continued to rattle inside my mind, echoing the clatter of the wheels upon the road as we journeyed homeward without exchanging a word.

Chapter Five

Fistulina hepatica

Robert Tulland steered his pony and cart through the gates just as the sun's insipid radiance stymied by layers of gauzy cloud, began to slide behind the Braid Hills. Mother hurried from the house to greet him. She pushed a shilling into his hand and threw aside the jute blanket covering her easel – complete, as promised, with complimentary palette – then strode towards the glasshouse, where Mr Maybury, Father and I were busy watering and labelling the newly installed ferns.

'Mr Maybury, would you be so kind as to fetch some hay for Robert's pony while I assist the young man in unloading the cart?'

'Certainly.'

As Mother and Mr Maybury set off to perform their respective tasks, Father leaned to my ear and said in a conspiratorial whisper, 'So this is the fellow who experienced the Toor root?'

'It is.'

'I wish I had been there. It must have been something to behold. Have you had any further trouble from the lad?'

'None.'

'Excellent! Then let us not keep your friend waiting a moment longer.'

'He is not my friend,' I said, addressing my father's back

as he unhooked three lanterns from the fernery's iron ribs, set them aglow with a lucifer and strode out of the glasshouse.

'Pleasure to meet you, Mr Tulland!'

Unused to exchanging pleasantries, Robert hesitated for an awkward moment before removing his cap and shaking Father's outstretched hand.

'Pleasure to meet you, Mr Ware, sir,' he murmured.

'Your father is an exceptional craftsman. He has supremely gifted hands. My cumbersome old paws have difficulty enough in folding a sheet of paper,' laughed Father. 'But happily, Joseph tells me you have no such difficulties and that God has seen fit to bless you with your father's dexterity when it comes to handling a blade.'

Robert threw me a glance, then stared sheepishly at the cap squirming tightly in his grip.

'Relax, Mr Tulland,' said Father, squeezing the cabinet-maker's son's shoulder. 'You are amongst friends. Here, take this.'

The bemused visitor accepted a lantern.

'You will of course stay for dinner, but first we must visit the woods. After all, dinner will not harvest itself.'

'But I must help the lady carry her easel,' Robert protested meekly.

'Don't you worry about that. I shall manage,' said Mother.

'Come!' said Father, handing me a lantern. 'We must hurry. The light is fading and the woods are difficult to navigate at the best of times.'

We followed him into the dense shadows, where a narrow path laid thick with damp leaves of gold, rust and bronze led us deeper into the last gatherings of twilight. We delved and weaved erratically through the trees to meet the brackish flow of the Braid Burn snaking its way north-westward to marry itself with the Water of Leith. The burn, too broad to leap and too deep to wade, kept us pinned to the bank for another hundred yards, its bends and loops guiding us to the familiar old willow straddling the water's edge. Hanging the lantern around his arm, Father reached up to seize the rope dangling invitingly from the tree and swung himself across. Robert and I followed suit and on we pressed through a tangled thicket of broom, both of us struggling to match the older man's brisk pace.

'Where is he taking us?' asked Tulland breathlessly.

'To the Witch Tree.'

'The what tree?'

'You'll see soon enough,' said I, watching Father's light disappear into the hollow.

Robert Tulland planted himself in front of me and stretched his spine to meet his full, menacing extent.

'I hope you're not planning to make a fool of me again, Ware.'

I defiantly arched my own back but even after attaining full height I could do no better than stand nose to throat with my nemesis.

'Why would I waste my time when you're so adept at making a fool of yourself?' I said, refusing to yield an inch of ground and presenting what I hoped was the most intimidating stare I had ever produced.

He responded by raising his lantern, its flickering glow exposing every last pockmarked measure of contempt upon his face.

'You have no idea how lucky you are, do you? With your perfect home. Your perfect parents. Your perfect future all ready and waiting. I look at you and all I want to do is break your perfect teeth.'

'Then why not indulge yourself?'

He lowered his lamp and I readied myself for the blow my foolhardy bravado richly deserved, but it never arrived.

'Why do you think I'm here?' he scowled.

'Because you've been paid. Why else?'

'Paid?' he said scornfully. 'Far from it. I am being punished!'

'Punished? Why?'

Robert tugged the collar from his neck to reveal the palette of yellows, blues and purples staining his skin.

'Because the son of Hugh Tulland cannot lay so much as a finger on the son of Lachlan Ware without there being serious consequences.'

'But you apologised and I accepted your apology, so why can't that be the end of the matter?'

Robert's malice suddenly melted away with a sorrowful sigh. Shoulders slumped and head drooped, the once impenetrable mountain now looked eminently scalable.

'Because my father says a man who is forced to apologise is no man at all. He says I am living proof of God's ability to make mistakes.'

'Then forgive me for saying so, but your father is a first-rate idiot.'

'But he is an idiot who knows the truth. I *am* God's mistake. I arrived into this world a murderer. That is who I am. And that is who I always will be.'

'You are many things, Robert, but you are not a murderer,' I said, not wholly convinced by my own words. 'I mean to say, that business with the knife? You had no real intention of stabbing me. Did you?'

'Why not? There is no denying it. Killing things is all I'm good for. This is what my father will doubtless remind me of tonight when I pull him from the Grassmarket gutter, load him on to the back of the cart and throw his drunken carcass into his bed.'

I stood dumbstruck as he turned to trudge onwards through the undergrowth, and for the second time in a single day, despite my very best efforts to quash this most alien of emotions, I felt sorry for Robert Tulland.

I hurried after him and caught up just as he finished wiping a cuff across his eyes.

'Do you think it would be possible to put our differences aside? I understand friendship may be beyond us, but perhaps we could at least agree on a truce? An end to hostilities if nothing else?'

Robert eyed me at length. 'I can agree to that. As long as you promise not to blow that magic powder in my face again.'

'You have my word.'

A cursory meeting of hands, and the uneasy agreement was sealed.

The ancient chestnut tree creaked and shivered against the rising wind, its branches dipping into the wide bowl of the hollow to savour the sweet necrotic scent of decaying leaves. We found Father resting upon one of the exposed roots, allowing his spore-damaged lungs a moment to recuperate from the exertion of the journey.

A small thud deadened by damp moss hit the ground at Robert's feet. A chestnut, its spiky casing slit like an open eye. He picked it up and removed the nut. A good size. He stepped back and peered high into the tree.

'Look at that huge one up there!'

The sky had adopted the colour of wet stone, but I had no difficulty in distinguishing the specimen that so excited Robert. Its jagged silhouette drooped from the end of the highest branch. There were perhaps less than a dozen chestnuts remaining on the tree, but the others were mere berries compared to this swollen oddity.

'I must get it,' said Robert, more enthused than I had ever seen him. Placing his lantern on the ground, he located a hefty stick and threw it into the canopy but missed his target by several feet. A second attempt succeeded only in showering us with broken foliage and twigs. He raised his stick for a third time, but Father took it from his grasp and casually tossed it aside.

'This fine old tree deserves your respect. Not your vandalism. You would do well not to provoke its ire.'

Robert was not at all pleased at having his fun curtailed. 'Provoke it? It's only a tree.'

'*Only* a tree, you say?' said Father, astonished. 'I take it you have not heard the legend of the Witch Tree?'

'No, I have not.' The flash of anger aimed in my direction suggested our nascent truce was in imminent danger of collapse. 'And I will not be made a fool of again. I have no interest in your witches and legends.'

Father rose from his seat and laid a friendly hand on Robert's arm. 'Quite right. You did not come all this way to listen to some old fairy tale. You came here for supper. And look here! We have found our main course!'

He crouched excitedly into a cleft at the base of the wizened tree's distended trunk. Lowering his lantern into the cavity, he revealed an ugly, spongy protrusion, its surface moist with glistening beads of red sap. The whole unsavoury swelling resembled a freshly picked scab as big as a man's head.

'*Fistulina hepatica*!' Father proclaimed triumphantly. 'The ox tongue fungus. More commonly found on oak. And only ever in springtime. So how can it be that we find it here, ripe and ready on the tenth day of December? How can it be that every year without fail, on the anniversary of the Witch McKay's execution you will find it growing on this spot and yet, come tomorrow, not a trace of it will remain? But, alas,' he added, glancing at me with a waggish smile, 'these questions are immaterial to those with no interest in witches and legends.'

Robert's face was scrunched in distaste.

'Looks disgusting.'

'Ah! You are making the cardinal sin of allowing yourself

to be deceived by appearances. It is no rose, I grant you, but it possesses a flavour every bit as succulent and tender as the finest cut of meat. Come now, Robert, don't look so perturbed. You don't believe me? Then let me prove it to you.' Father rested his lantern on the damp earth and unfolded his Barlow knife. We watched the blade glint as he cut deep into the fungus. Blood red juice dripped from the incision and when lifted free from the bark, the growth looked for all the world like a lump of raw beef.

'I dare say your pony by now has been well watered and fed. I suggest it only fair we offer you the same treatment. So let's go. Fine dining awaits!'

Staring sourly at the thing dripping from his fingers, Robert trudged out of the hollow behind my father. As I made to follow them, something tumbled softly to the ground at my back. I turned to search the highest branches of the Witch Tree.

The obese chestnut was still there, bobbing and swaying in the breeze.

My heart began to beat a little faster.

It's only a tree...

*

Glad to have swapped the gelid night air for the homely warmth of the hearth and the welcoming radiance of the abundant candles and lamps, we took our places around the dining room table. Robert Tulland sat rigidly in his chair, his eyes flicking nervously around the walls, taking in the higgledy arrangement of Mother's paintings, sketches and lithographs. This joyful exhibition of the wonders of the plant world extended to the dining table itself where we conversed across a miniature garden resplendent with wildflowers, pine cones, vines and holly.

'Help yourself to whatever takes your fancy,' said Mother, adding a salver of green beans to a landscape of boiled potatoes, carrots and cabbage.

'Thank you,' replied Robert, timidly.

'You are most welcome.'

'You must try a piece of the *Fistulina hepatica*,' said Father, ladling a portion of the braised fungus onto our guest's plate.

Robert looked sceptically at the deep maroon slices, all shiny with melted butter. He lifted his knife and fork and cut hesitantly into the mushroom's flesh.

Father followed the morsel as it journeyed from plate to mouth with increasing excitement. Mother and I shared a knowing glance. The trap had been sprung. We had borne witness to this experiment for many a year and had even ourselves been used as subjects, hence the mushroom was no longer shared to our plates. My father had long convinced himself that this rare fungus must contain some residual trace of the witch's power. For why else would it flourish on a spot so blighted by her corruption and then only on the anniversary of her wretched demise? What form this power took he knew not but surmised that it must surely manifest itself when eaten. And so, on those occasions when he was not away from home on the day of the ox tongue's ripening, it had become a custom of Father's to invite an unwitting guest to dinner where, amidst the pleasant chatter and smiles, a sample of the 'uniquely flavoursome' mushroom, would inevitably, find its way to their plate.

I was an unsuspecting five-year-old when Father fed me my first piece of *Fistulina hepatica*. I ate it without fuss and though I remember its flavour being distinctly earthy, it was not unpleasant and I suffered no ill effect. No effect, that is, except for the dream. The same lucid dream I have experienced sporadically throughout my life. A dream so vivid in its every detail that when I awoke from its grip, it always came as a great surprise that I had been sleeping at all.

The dream always began with me climbing into a rowing

boat on the shore of a loch. I had a companion. A young woman, her back towards me as I took the oars and steered our boat across the unfathomably deep black water. We were escaping some awful danger and repeatedly glanced back over our shoulders towards the thick veil of mist and rain obscuring the hills and woods. And as I rowed she would sing 'Sweet Tibbie Dunbar' in a voice as beautiful as I suspected her face to be, but I was never permitted to glimpse that beauty, shielded as it was by an abundance of curls. A small islet bursting with trees rose from the centre of the loch. I pulled the boat ashore and the young woman took my blistered hand and led me to a clearing at the heart of the islet, where we looked up to admire a perfect circle of clear blue sky framed within a ring of treetops.

'You're safe now.'

Her words, so softly delivered, stirred a whirlpool of emotions. Of joy and sorrow. But, as she turned her face to mine and lifted her hands to part her hair, there the dream would end and I awoke with a jolt every time.

I never shared this mysterious side effect of the *Fistulina hepatica* with Father. The dream was to remain my secret and mine alone.

Disappointingly for my father, Mother also reported nothing of note after sampling the mushroom other than a single bite had proved sufficient to sate her appetite for several days. The most recent experiment, however, did succeed in producing a set of far more intriguing results when Uncle Tam and his daughters Molly, Grace and Bethany unknowingly partook in Father's study.

One mouthful, and Tam lost all control of his senses. He leapt upon the dining table and entertained us all to a drunken cabaret of singing and dancing interspersed with a string of lurid jokes. All this without a drop of whisky having passed his lips. The performance lasted a full hour before Tam returned to his chair and abruptly fell into a deep, snoring slumber.

Little Grace collapsed into a fit of giggles, which continued long into the night no matter how hard she willed herself to stop. Whether this was due to her father's antics or the buttered fungus, it was impossible to determine. Baby Bethany wisely wrinkled her nose at the spoonful of mushroom paste and refused to eat it whereas Molly, the eldest of the girls, obligingly devoured her share with no obvious distress. But a short while after dinner a peculiar crescent-shaped irritation appeared on the back of her hand. The rash began to spread at a most disconcerting rate. Father managed to put an end to its itching progress with a salve of ground buttercup stamens and milk. I remember my father himself braved the mushroom on three separate occasions, succumbing each time to a prolonged and violent bout of sneezing that continued unabated till the first chime of midnight finally released his inflamed nose from its torment.

Interesting as these varied outcomes doubtless were, the evidence remained frustratingly inconclusive for my father. Were these strange symptoms the result of witchcraft or did they merely show that the *Fistulina hepatica* was not entirely suitable for human consumption?

'This is the best thing I have ever tasted! I must have some more.'

We sat and watched in quiet amazement as Robert Tulland launched into a second helping, chewing and swallowing with the rapacity of a starving dog.

With the last forkful greedily dispatched, he raised the plate to his mouth and sucked the residual oily brown pool noisily through his teeth. Satisfied he had obliterated every last trace of the mushroom, he wiped his lips on a cuff, sat back in his chair, patted his stomach and belched.

'What are you all staring at?' he demanded, haughtily. 'Have you never seen someone eat before? Stop staring at me!'

He directed his escalating rage first to Father: 'STOP!' And then to Mother: 'STOP!'

At first I assumed it was the ferocity of his anger that left my parents stunned and motionless, but when they remained suspended in a statuesque, unblinking stupor even when Robert smashed his plate against the table in a fit of brutish temper, sending broken pieces scattering in every direction, it became apparent that some other force was at play within them.

'You know, don't you?' he said, still holding one fragment of the plate between his fingers. He placed it carefully upon the table. The rage had gone. And in its stead, I glimpsed an aching sadness.

'Know what?'

'You know I murdered my mother.'

'You did what?' I gasped, astonished by this extraordinary confession. 'When?'

'As soon as I was born.'

'She died at childbirth? But that's not murder. You cannot possibly be held responsible.'

'My mother is dead. I killed her. God recognised the evil in me and took mother straight to heaven rather than condemn her to a lifetime of humiliation of having me for a son.'

Robert, no longer able to suppress the torrent of guilt he had kept dammed from his heart for all the years of his existence, pounded both fists on the table and raised his guilt-soaked eyes to the ceiling.

'I am God's mistake!' he screamed. The primal violence of his cry had torn his voice to shreds and he began to choke and rasp.

He threw back his neck, stretching it so tightly his Adam's apple threatened to tear through its thin pale covering. Then, to my horror, there came a pronounced crack as his jaws separated themselves from one another and his mouth gradually widened beyond all natural limits. Above this mute, cavernous gape, Robert's eyes bulged and rolled to a blank white stare in their sockets. And with blood seeping from his straining lips, a horrible gargling sound crawled up from the depths of his throat to escape between his teeth in a fierce whisper that chilled me to the core.

'*The tree is dying.*'

The voice did not belong to Robert Tulland.

I sat petrified as a slimy mass beaded with crimson sap retched and frothed like an enormous swollen tongue from his mouth. I looked to my parents, but they were as marble. Unseeing and unmoving. The mass grew larger still, so large it obscured his head. Soon the sheer weight of the thing proved too much to be held in his mouth and it fell with a hefty thump upon the table. All I could do was stare at the repulsive *Fistulina hepatica* resting there, reconstituted exactly as it had been when Father had cut it from the tree. Red, raw and fleshy. A sudden instinct led me to spring from my chair, snatch the fungus and throw it into the fire. A short, sharp scream of anguish from Tulland's slack mouth pierced the room. Several candles guttered and died, casting ribbons of smoke to the ceiling. The awful sound vanished as the fungus shrivelled and bubbled in the engulfing flames.

'Thank you very much, Mrs Ware. That was the best meal I've ever had,' said Robert.

I turned from the fire where the last crackling remnants of the fungus melted away to see our guest wipe his now perfectly normal mouth and set his knife and fork down on the empty, undamaged plate before him.

'You are most welcome.'

My parents had returned to full wakefulness and exhibited no ill effects from the strange paralysis that had held them captive, nor did they betray even the slightest indication that anything untoward had taken place.

'Glad you enjoyed it, Robert,' said Father, failing to mask

his disappointment at the mushroom's apparent failure to produce a meaningful result.

By the time Robert trundled away from Braid House, I had developed serious doubts as to the veracity of the uncanny display I had earlier witnessed. After all, how could such a thing be? The whole episode railed against nature herself. There had to be a simple explanation. A stray splash of uncooked mushroom sap on my food may well have produced those unpalatable hallucinations.

A sound theory.

But that night, as I laid upon my pillow, my mind quickly became entangled in a swirling skein of paranoia and doubt.

And whispering through it all, came the haunting words which emanated from Robert Tulland's borrowed tongue:

'The tree is dying...'

CHAPTER SIX

The Chestnut

'The tree is dying...'

What if this simple statement were true and this was to be the tree's final winter? A final opportunity to catch the chestnut and walk away holding an oversized but otherwise unremarkable seed, or a final opportunity to catch the chestnut and walk away holding the key to a host of magical powers? Either way it was an opportunity I dared not squander.

And so I returned to Braid Woods at first light, determined to resolve the mystery once and for all.

The overnight winds had stripped the Witch Tree of all but the most stubborn of its leaves and spared a grand total of seven chestnuts – including, I was relieved to note, the great jagged ball itself.

I examined the scar left by Father's blade where the *Fistulina hepatica* had been harvested. A layer of sap had exuded over the wound, now hardened and healed. It had been my intention to remain under the tree until nightfall, but in my haste I had foolishly neglected my gloves and scarf, nor had I brought so much as an apple to bite from, and within a few short hours the twin onslaught of cold and hunger forced me into a chastening retreat.

The next day, having properly furnished myself with

sufficient clothing and provisions, I endured an entire day at the base of the tree and witnessed two chestnuts fall to the ground.

Now, only five remained.

On the Monday an incessant downpour made the trek even more arduous than usual and I slipped several times before resuming my regular seat beneath the tree. Damp and covered in mud, I cursed the blasted chestnut for its obstinacy and my own foolishness in allowing fantasy to overcome reason.

Four chestnuts remained...

A day later and I had attached a large sheet to the tree. The corners tied between two large boughs situated close to the ground, I spread the net beneath my quarry's projected descent and resumed my vigil, satisfied that I had installed the perfect solution to the ever-present problem of the chestnut falling when I was not in attendance.

Three remained...

Wednesday. An ill-tempered north-easterly had torn the sheet from its tethers and blown it clear out of the hollow and into the canopy of a silver birch, where it hung like a slack smile mocking me for my impudence.

Two...

Conditions on the Thursday were dry and settled as I took my place ready for a long day's wait. I opened my satchel and unwrapped a mutton bridie. My teeth closing in on the pastry, I happened to glance upwards on hearing the branches sway against a sudden gust. The two surviving chestnuts bobbed furiously at the end of their gallows and then, with a little snapping sound, the smaller one broke free and tumbled earthwards.

I sprang to my feet, watching it hit first one branch and then collide wildly with another as I dashed to intercept its fall. It closed to within a mere yard of my cupped hands when it struck one of the trunk's many great bulbous outgrowths and looped over my head. I spun round and threw myself after it, but the chestnut landed in the soft carpet of leaves an inch away from my outstretched fingers.

One...

Head propped on my satchel and heart hammering at my chest, I laid on the ground, eyes fixed on the object now hanging perfectly still, and concentrated all my efforts into plotting the likely course of last chestnut's descent. I factored in every obstacle with the potential to influence its journey and made the necessary adjustments till, confident my calculations signified there would be no repeat of the scramble to reach its predecessor, I felt my hands tingle in anticipation of the catch.

The next thing I knew, snowflakes were settling on my eyelashes. I sleepily blinked them clear and watched the soft silent flurry descend through the branches where the chestnut hung in prickly silhouette against the gloaming. The hollow had wrapped itself in a glimmering gown of frost, the chill touch of its hem gnawed at my hands and toes. I sat up, rubbing my fingers, determined to wait a little while longer, but the lure of a glowing hearth and a hot warming meal soon persuaded me to abandon my post with a promise to return at the earliest opportunity.

*

'So when do you next weigh anchor, Lachlan?'

'January the sixth.'

'The Epiphany? Perfect! God is sure to watch over ye. And where are ye goin' to pick yer weeds this time?' railed Tam, good-naturedly.

'The Comoro Islands. They have some very fine weeds indeed. And yourself, Tam? When is the Majestic North heading back to sea?'

'Monday next. Repairs permittin'. The old girl broke her 'sprit this last hunt but I hear the replacement is near done.

Need to land those bowheads before the Dutch steal 'em. A short trip. Be back by Easter, God willin'. Grace, will ye no' eat yer greens?'

'Yes, daddy.'

Grace pushed a bean into her puckered mouth and proceeded to chew the unpleasant article. She swallowed, then opened her mouth wide to let her father inspect the empty chasm.

'All gone, see?' she beamed.

'Aye, yer a brave lass,' smiled Tam.

The dining room fairly clinked and thrummed as cutlery cut and jabbed, and feet too young to reach the floor tapped impatiently at chair legs. I had completely forgotten Uncle Tam and his three daughters had been invited to dine with us at Braid House, thereby scuppering my hopes of an immediate return to the Witch Tree. Good manners forbade any notable absence and ensured there would be no escape from my customary duty to entertain and amuse my cousins throughout their stay.

In Bethany's case this was a simple enough task. She was a but a bairn, having only recently celebrated her second full year on earth; a year dedicated, as she had the first, to perfecting the twin arts of sleeping and eating. Propped on Mother's lap, she happily treated us all to a masterful display of the latter by gulping down two glasses of warm milk.

Grace, however, was an altogether more taxing proposition. Her eight-year-old mind was the most inquisitive in all Edinburgh, possessing as it did, an innate desire to know the where, the why and the how of everything – a trait that quickly became exhausting after less than a few minutes in her company. But thankfully there was a sure-fire trick to keeping her amused: reading. Place a thick illustrated encyclopaedia in her hands, and Grace would disappear inside its pages for hours, raising her eyes from the text only in order to find out the meaning of a certain word she had never before encountered.

There was a tiresome period when Grace could not negotiate a simple paragraph without demanding I provide her with a definition for this word or that. A problem soon resolved with the discovery of another trick: I placed a dictionary by her side and encouraged her to discover the meanings for herself, a task Grace pursued with gusto. Her eyes burned with intelligence and a maturity way beyond her meagre years. She had all the attributes in place to achieve great things, but I acknowledged with a certain sorrow, that her future ambitions were set to encounter resistance at every turn by a world unsympathetic to her sex. This said, I had every confidence that Grace would grow into a woman capable of breaking down such walls, and with Bility Ware as her aunt, she possessed a formidable ally.

'Checkmate,' said Molly leaning back; the eddies of lustrous red hair pooling at her shoulders absorbed the radiance of the flames dancing in the hearth behind her.

The eldest of Tam's brood, Molly had always taken a singular delight in beating me at chess. Also draughts, back-gammon and cards. She was a natural game player. A wily tactician. She was fiercely independent and earned a few extra bawbees at the dock mending gloves, scarves and boots for the thrifty-minded sailors. Molly had also uncovered a ready market for her father's scrimshaws. The bankers and insurance brokers of the New Town had seemingly no end of a need to adorn their desks and mantelshelves with engraved whale teeth and baleen.

'But how?' I protested. The game had been in progress not five minutes since we'd cleared our plates to make room for the board. A pitiful performance, even by my admittedly modest standards.

'You are too predictable, Jojo. Stop looking to bring your rooks into play so early. It leaves your queen exposed to my knights,' she explained, folding her arms and exuding that calm, unhurried confidence that I so envied. Nothing fazed

Molly. She shielded herself from the cruellest of life's blows with an unshakeable fortitude and an iron will to survive. But those shields had been left battle-scarred and weakened by repeated attacks.

Because life had been particularly cruel to Molly.

As it had to all the girls.

To Tam.

To us all…

*

Aunt Kathryn had lit up all our lives with her boundless energy and enthusiasm. She carried joy and cheer into every room she entered. She and Tam were the perfect match. Where he wielded a harpoon and rope, Kathryn wielded a needle and thread.

'The finest seamstress in Scotland!' Tam proudly boasted to all he met.

Their union appeared to me, to be the most unbreakable of bonds, enduring many hardships including near financial ruin and the heartbreaking loss of two infants. The first, a son, entered the world stillborn. The second, cousin Annie, survived three precious weeks before a fever snatched her away.

Then, seven months after Bethany's birth, the spiteful hand of fate did finally break the bond between Kathryn and Tam in the most mysterious of circumstances.

Kathryn disappeared at the end of the warmest summer's day Molly had ever known. The *Majestic North* had set sail for the fertile fishing grounds of the Barents Sea that very afternoon. Kathryn and the girls accompanied Tam to the docks and bade him farewell as they always did, with hurried kisses and tight embraces offered in exchange for promises of a safe return. From the deck of the departing ship, Tam watched his wife wave tearfully from the harbour till she was no more than a speck on the ever-distant shoreline, little realising that this was to be his final memory of her.

Upon returning to their Coatfield Lane home, Molly and Kathryn applied their needles and threads to a new, long promised dress for Grace's favourite doll. The tragic loss of Annie had left an immovable splinter at the centre of Kathryn's heart and so, naturally, her attentions were frequently diverted from her sewing by the sound of Bethany's obvious distress. The baby, who had for some days been incubating a fever, loudly voiced her woes, leaving Kathryn no choice but to set down her needle and soothe the infant's discomfort with a breast and a soft lullaby.

The potency of Kathryn's cradle songs must have lured Molly on to the rocks of her own sleep for at the approach of midnight, she woke with a start to a pounding at the door. Rising from her chair, she opened the door to find her mother standing on the other side in a state of extreme agitation.

'Ma? What's the matter? Look at you, you're trembling.'

Peering fitfully up and down the pitch-dark lane, Kathryn handed Molly a basket containing a small bowl filled with a thick green paste. Fragments of thistles, buttercups and grass clung to the sides of the bowl.

'Take this!' she urged in a terse, fraught whisper. 'It's a balm for your sister. Rub it on her chest. Hurry!'

'Aren't you coming inside?' said Molly, bemused.

'No. I must go to church. I must light a candle for your father's safe return and another for Bethany's quick recovery. Please, you mustn't worry yourself. I will not be long.'

'But Ma, it's not safe to be out at this hour. Let me come with you,' offered Molly, reaching to collect her shawl.

'No! Stay and look after the girls. Make sure to rub the balm into Bethany's chest and brow. Do it now.' Then with eyes glistening wetly, Kathryn took Molly's head in her hands and laid a kiss on each cheek. 'I will be back soon, my darling. I promise,' she said before turning heel and hurrying into the darkness.

Molly waited and waited, but with each passing hour the sickening feeling that something truly awful had happened spread like a poisonous vine to engulf her heart and drain it of all hope.

She left the house at dawn, carrying Bethany in her arms and with a frightened and confused Grace clutching at her skirt, struggling to keep pace as she scoured the surrounding confusion of streets and alleyways. They visited the Chapel of St Mary's, where Father Slaven confirmed he had seen neither hide nor hair of Kathryn and that no new candles had been lit in the transept where the statue of St Mary gazed down upon the devoted. The priest escorted the distressed sisters to the home of a local constable, who promptly organised a search for the missing woman. But not a trace did they find. Indeed, aside from a single report of two undesirables seen loitering suspiciously about the corner of Tolbooth Wynd and Riddells Close on the night of her disappearance, no evidence of any kind was ever uncovered.

Kathryn Keane had simply vanished from the face of the earth.

Every day thereafter, under the care of our grandmother, Nana Keane, who had moved in with the girls immediately upon hearing of their plight, Molly prayed for her mother's safe return. The days became weeks and the unanswered prayers were piled high about the house when Tam, unaware during all his time at sea of the tragedy that had befallen his family, arrived home to receive the miserable news. The shock very nearly destroyed him.

He refused to accept the truth of it and spent his every waking every hour knocking on all the doors of Leith and Edinburgh, determined to find some hint as to the whereabouts of his wife. His desperate quest expanded outwards from the city until he'd climbed every hill, explored every wood, investigated every loch, riverbank and inlet in Lothian. Each successive failure chipped another piece from his shattered soul. Eventually, the threat of penury forced him to abandon his futile search and return to the sea, leaving the girls once more under Nana's safekeeping.

During all this time there did appear one beam of sunshine to break the unending gloom, and it came with Bethany's return to the full rosy pink glow of rude health.

Kathryn's balm had broken the baby's fever with the first application.

*

'Here. This is for you, Joseph.'

Tam tossed something across the dining table. It was an enormous tooth, as thick as my wrist and as long as my hand. My uncle had skilfully etched a fine depiction of a ship sailing on a storm-tossed sea into the ivory.

'Dug that out of what was left of our boat. Imagine it sinkin' into yer skull. It would make yer head burst open like a ripe fruit, no question. Now imagine a mouth bigger than this room with forty or more of those spikes ready to bite down and swallow ye whole. That's how we lost one of our men on that last trip. I watched it happen.'

Pleased to have captured everyone's rapt attention, he dabbed another pinch of tobacco into his pipe, lit the bowl and expelled a cloud towards the ceiling rose.

'Biggest bull I've ever seen, it was. We hunted that monster for two days and two nights. And for two days and two nights it swam beyond our reach till finally, on the third morning, we pulled close enough for the *Majestic North* to drop her boats. Mine was first to hit the water. I took my position at the prow and shouted to wee Jack Sperrit, our steersman, to keep our course true while the oarsmen heaved us over crests higher than the highest chimneys ye have here at Braid House. Risin' and plungin', risin' and plungin', like a cork in a drunkard's tankard we went. Closer and closer we chased till we saw the fear in its eye. Three times I pierced the beast's hide! If this had been any other whale we should have sat back and cheered the chimney catchin' fire. But no! Not with this devil! When he blew, it was not blood we saw comin' from his spout, it was the white steam of his rage. Then he gathered that rage within him and dived. And he dived deep.

'We steeled ourselves for the mad ride to come and watched the rope fly from the line-tub so fast it started to draw smoke from the gunwale. A hundred feet. Two hundred feet. Three hundred! And still he sounded! I was ready to cut the rope lest the monster drag us down with him into the seethin' abyss. Then the line fell slack. I readied another harpoon and peered over the sides, searchin' the rollin' blackness. The birds began to circle above us. A bad sign. "Abandon ship lads!" I hollered. But too late. With an almighty crash the leviathan's head exploded from the deep and smashed our puny wee boat as if it were nothin' but a child's toy, scatterin' the men to the waves and I with them. Let me admit freely to ye, as I treaded a sea cold enough to numb the very fires of hell, that I was terrified. Terrified beyond all measure.'

Tam leaned forward and puffed another blue fog into the air.

'It was all I could do to stay afloat. I twisted and turned in that boilin' black ocean to see my crewmates bobbin' like tops, wavin' and splutterin' their terrified appeals towards the *Majestic North* which was comin' to our aid, but it still seemed so hopelessly distant. I saw nothin' of the great beast himself but knew the wily old devil was close at hand. Then, a few short yards beyond the reach of my flailin' arms, I saw a figure rise with the swell. It was wee Jack Sperrit, clingin' for dear life to a broken oar. I tried to swim for him, but at that moment a great cave of a mouth breached the surface! Wider and wider it grew till it threatened to devour the very sky! Water rained down from those enormous lips in great fizzin' downpours. Its shadow yawned over the sea, coverin' Jack in its great, dark cloak. Then those mighty jaws slammed over my friend and swallowed him whole! The blade of his oar sprang from the whale's mouth and knocked me near senseless.'

Tam lifted the black curls from his forehead to reveal an impressive scar. The wound, a thumb in length, appeared recently healed, lending credence to my uncle's extraordinary story.

'The sea splashed the blood from my eyes and I watched the monster wave a cold goodbye with one last flick of his massive tail before he slipped into the depths, taking Jack Sperrit to his dark and watery end. The rest of us were hauled aboard the *Majestic North*, where we collapsed on deck, offerin' our shiverin' gratitude for God's salvation and prayed for poor Jack's soul.'

'What happened next, Daddy? Did you see the whale again?' asked Grace, her eyes like saucers.

'Aye, we did, Sweet Pea,' said Tam, lubricating his throat with a swig of whisky. 'As soon as we regained our strength, we vowed to avenge wee Jack. We scoured those frozen seas for nigh on a week till we heard Francis cry from the mizzen head: "There, there, there she blows!" We had found him! Our sworn enemy! The *Majestic North* lowered her boats and off we chased. We were on him in a heartbeat for the beast was sorely tired. My lances, still piercin' his thick black hide, had performed their duty. I drew eye to eye with him. I swear I saw terror in that wretched stare. He knew his fate was sealed and I had no wish to disappoint him, so I cursed him loudly for darin' to eat our friend Jack and drove my harpoon clean through till his eyes rolled and his spout hole showered us all in hot blood.

'We towed our prize back to the ship and once it was safely secured, the flensers set to work with their cuttin' spades and pikes, peelin' strip after strip of precious blubber from the mighty carcass but when they exposed the creature's belly – a belly as big as this house! – they suddenly dropped their tools in shock.'

'Why?' gasped Grace.

Tam leaned forward and in a dramatic whisper, said, 'Because there was something wriggling inside.'

Grace clung fearfully to Molly.

'Did you cut the belly open?' she asked breathlessly.

I admit my own heart did beat a little faster as we all waited for Tam to finish drawing on his pipe.

'We did indeed, my wee lamb. And what did we find among that great stinkin' flood of belly juices and slimy squid tentacles slippin' and twistin' over the deck? Why, it was none other than wee Jack Sperrit!'

'Was he dead? Was he dead?' Grace chirped impatiently.

'Well, when we crowded round that motionless body, his skin and clothes bleached white by the whale's belly acid, we thought Jack had surely breathed his last. But when Captain Harris prodded him with the toe of his boot, wee Jack's eyes sprung open and he started howlin' and splutterin' like a newborn. We quickly fetched soup and blankets, got him nice and warm. He seemed fine 'cept he couldn't remember a thing about being swallowed. Said last he recalled was slidin' like Jonah down the whale's throat, graspin' at the sides which quivered under his fingers. But after that? Nothin'. Nothin' but darkness.'

Grace climbed aboard her father's lap.

'Are you going to cut my belly open, Daddy?'

'I think not. We already know what's inside your belly, don't we?'

'What's in my belly?'

'Green beans!'

Tam tickled Grace, sending her sliding to the floor in a useless heap of squirming laughter.

'I feel sorry for the whale,' declared Molly. 'Poor thing. Chased halfway across the ocean to be stabbed, cut, sliced and boiled. And for what? So we can have some oil for our lamps?'

Tam exchanged a tired look with Molly. He had discussed this subject with his eldest daughter on many an occasion.

'You need not waste yer sympathy on the whale. God has given them their purpose which is to provide for Man. And I believe it is a fair fight. I have seen many a good man killed so that you may have oil for yer lamp.'

'And that is my point! I for one have no desire to see any more good men killed. I wish you would leave the whales be.'

'Would you rather I travelled the world pickin' daisies like your uncle Lachlan? Is that how you'd like me to live? Would you see me die of boredom, young lady?'

'She only wants you to be safe, Tam,' said Mother. 'We all do.'

Tam looked about the room with a melancholy air.

'Aye well, you may get yer wish sooner than ye think. There's rumours at the docks. They say the whale fishery in Leith will soon be at an end. Seems yer wise to stick to the weeds, Joseph. There's money to be had in their picking for sure. But where's the thrill?' he railed, slamming a fist against the table and startling Bethany from her milk-induced slumber. 'What is life without a little danger? Without a little risk?'

'The life of a botanist is not a life without risk, Tam,' said Father, gravely. 'It would appear that you have never encountered the Giant Carnivorous Pasque-flower of the Mongolian Flatlands. A flower as tall as an oak tree with petals the size of barn doors which droop to the ground where they await an unwary foot.'

'Petals like barn doors? Ha!' scoffed Tam, returning Grace to his lap.

'It's true. The petals are the colour of purest gold. They sparkle and gleam, luring you closer and closer to admire their beauty like the sirens of ancient Greece, until... Boom!' Father clapped his hands sharply, raising a frown from Mother who now had to soothe the bairn back to sleep for a second time. 'The flower snaps around you, lifts you up and drops you inside a great bowl at its stem. This is where the Giant Carnivorous Pasque-flower of the Mongolian Flatlands slowly dissolves you into a paste from which it derives its sustenance. Eventually nothing will remain but your hat and your pipe.'

Tam released a hard glare and steady plume of smoke towards his brother-in-law.

'The Giant Carnivorous Pasque-flower of the Mongolian Flatlands,' he growled. 'You have excelled yourself, Lachlan.'

The two men glowered at each other for a few charged seconds before both collapsed into uproarious laughter.

'To weeds in all their man-eating glory!' said Father, raising his glass.

'To weeds!' cried Tam.

*

The weather had taken an unfavourable turn, and with the snow now lying in a thick carpet over the lawn, it was decided that Tam and his daughters should spend the night at Braid House. The fires and lamps were lit in the guest rooms and as the clock chimed midnight I sat alone in the drawing room, listening to a steady stream of deep volcanic rumblings reverberate down through the ceiling. But it was not my uncle's cataclysmic snoring that kept me awake. It was the thought of the chestnut dangling from its flimsy firmament deep in the woods where even the weight of a single snowflake might prove a burden too far and send it hurtling earthwards. I imagined it lying in the snow, its secrets forever lost. Having invested so much time and energy waiting under its shadow, the prospect of being absent from the moment of its fall vexed me to the point of distraction.

The clock ticking in the corner reminded me that with every passing second, the bleak prospect of my imaginings moved closer to becoming a reality.

Something fell from my lap as I stretched to place a log on the fire. I picked up the whale tooth and, cradling its cold heaviness in my palm, tried to envisage the unimaginable depths it must have reached inside the mouth of its gigantic host. The coldest, darkest realm of the unknown where great tentacled monsters haunted the blackness. I rose to the window and stared into the night.

'What can you see?'

I turned with a start to face a ghostly figure in a white nightgown pressing the drawing room door to a close behind her.

'Why are you still awake? Is something wrong?' I asked, trying to conceal my fright.

'I can't sleep. Unlike Pa,' Molly smiled and cocked an ear to the room above. 'I swear if the Apocalypse were to happen right now, he'd snore through the whole thing.'

She poured herself a glass of water from the jug perched on the little rosewood table and joined me by the fireside.

'Why can't you sleep?'

Molly remained silent for a while, her thoughts lost in the shifting glow of the flames. Then I saw a tear roll down her heartbroken face.

'Molly? What's wrong?'

'I miss her so much,' she said, softly.

'Aunt Kathryn?'

'It's been one year, six months and three days.' Molly lifted her gaze. The fire had thrown a spark of anger in her eyes. 'How could she do such a thing? How could she abandon us like that?'

'Aunt Kathryn would never abandon you. Not deliberately. Something must have happened. Something beyond her control,' I said.

Molly wiped her eyes and stared silently back into the coals. Her sadness was unbearable.

'I was thinking of going for a walk. Would you like to come?'

She turned to me, intrigued.

'A walk? At this hour? Where?'

'The woods.'

'The woods!'

'Why not? It'll be fun. Would you like to come?'

Molly flashed a smile.

'Wait here while I go and get dressed.'

*

We set off across the lawn, deep crisp footprints sinking in the white blanket, and pushed onwards for the great silent ranks of the trees, where we finally dared to uncover our lanterns.

'Where are we going?' whispered Molly. Her breath twisted and rolled like an impatient phantasm in the frosty lamplight.

'To the Witch Tree. Let's hope we're not too late.'

'Too late? Too late for what?'

Molly listened carefully as I shared everything I knew regarding the peculiar history of the Witch Tree and the legend of the last chestnut.

'You don't really believe that stupid old nonsense, do you?'

'I know it sounds foolish, but there is something about these old woods. Something strange. If there is even the merest possibility that there is some truth in these old stories, are we not obliged to investigate? I for one need to find out one way or the other. I need to catch that chestnut. But if you're too frightened to carry on, you can always return to your safe, warm bed. I'll understand.'

Molly landed a scornful punch to my arm.

'Lead the way.'

We stumbled deeper into the woods. The light from our lamps did not penetrate but an arm's length into the darkness. The silence closed in from all sides, broken only by the cautious advance of our feet. The crack of a twig under my heel triggered the startled flapping of wings in the branches close by. I looked up but could find no movement amongst the dense network of ink-black blood vessels printed against the night.

Molly stopped abruptly.

'Did you hear that?' she asked, a look of intense concentration on her face.

We had arrived at the rope swing. I listened closely but heard nothing other than the rapid flow of the burn passing under the drooping willow.

'No. What was it?'

'I thought I heard footsteps.'

I joined Molly in casting my light in a wide arc. The surrounding shadows remained silent and still.

'There!' she whispered fearfully. 'It's coming closer.'

'Where?'

I spun my lantern in ever more frantic circles. And then came a familiar sound. A soft, snorting laughter. The light settled on my cousin's huge mischievous grin.

'I am so sorry, I couldn't resist. Your face was such a picture! Admit it, you were terrified,' she said, poking a finger into my chest.

'You scared me half to death, Molly. Would you still be smiling if I were lying dead on the ground?' I said, irritated both by her evident amusement and by my own gullibility.

'Oh, Jojo, forgive me. There's no harm done. And a wee bit of fear is good for the heart. It keeps us alert and ready to fight the good fight. That's what Pa says.'

Her use of 'Jojo' had always rankled. We were no higher than the crown of a summer thistle when she first addressed me by that name, and I had never been able to determine whether it was intended as a term of endearment or jest.

Molly gripped the rope and pushed herself effortlessly across the burn. As I waited for the rope to return, I held my lamp aloft for one last glance into the darkness behind us. I could not shift the sense that something lurked there still. Something indefinable.

We pressed on through the undergrowth, hugging the narrow deer trail with our lamps swung low to avoid the hazardous array of roots and stones which jutted from the ground with alarming frequency. The notion that something or someone was watching our every move continued to linger and I began to sense the same growing unease in Molly. We attempted to mask our disquiet by engaging in a discussion on the relative merits of Father's and Tam's far-fetched tales and our own plans for the future. I listened attentively while Molly laid out her grand ambition to travel to London, where she planned to open a small shop selling medicinal balms derived from plant oils and extracts recommended by my father.

Arriving at the hollow, I held out a hand, hoping to guide Molly down the precarious slope, but before our fingers met she lost her footing on the crust of ice and slipped helplessly all the way down.

'That was fun!' she laughed, gathering her stricken lamp before the guttering flame died. 'I'm going to do it again.'

'Wait! Did you hear that?'

'We have already played that game, Jojo. I am not so easily fooled as you.'

I slid down the slope to join my cousin.

'I'm being serious. Listen!'

We waited in breathless silence. Then through the smothering darkness came a soft rustling sound.

'I hear it!' said Molly. 'Where is it coming from?'

I edged towards the Witch Tree, its eccentric branches

expanding, then fading in the sweep of my light as I carefully hunted for the source of the movement. Soon, a few spots of red appeared on the sparkling frost.

'Here!'

Molly hurried by my side.

'Oh my God! The poor thing.'

A pine marten lay at our feet. A mortal, ragged gash exposed the hapless creature's spine, rendering its hind legs useless while the front pair scrabbled frantically in the snow. It bared its teeth and squealed in a futile gesture of defiance at our unwelcome examination, but there was no hiding the terror in its little eyes and gasping chest.

'What do you suppose happened to it?'

I knelt down and collected the animal in my gloved hands.

'Perhaps it was attacked by a fox. Or an owl,' I suggested.

The pine marten stretched its claws in front of its nose and went quite still.

'Is it dead?'

'Yes,' I confirmed, sadly.

'Then let's bury it,' said Molly.

The soil beneath the layer of frozen snow remained soft and yielded easily to her boot heel. Soon she had scraped a hole large enough to accommodate the dead pine marten. The burial complete, we turned our focus to the Witch Tree. Molly skirted the bulging trunk and frowned up into the tangle of branches.

'This is impossible,' she shrugged.

I shared her frustration. No matter how hard I tried, I could not distinguish any detail in the upper reaches of the tree. The thick, snow-bearing clouds denied any possible assistance from the moon or stars. A return at first light seemed to me to be the most pragmatic course of action, but Molly had other ideas.

'Molly! Don't be foolish! Come back down!'

'We need to take a closer look. We can't see a thing from

down there.'

She hoisted herself higher into the tree and proceeded upwards with astonishing dexterity and speed.

'Please come down! You'll injure yourself,' I yelled in vain towards the diminishing bauble of yellow light cast from her lamp.

'I can see it!' she cried. 'One more branch and I'll be able to reach it.'

The glow changed direction and began to inch outwards from the main body of the tree.

'Be careful!'

My entreaty was met with a terrible reply. A fierce crack split the darkness like a rifle shot. I stepped smartly back from the ensuing deluge of twigs and splintered wood, narrowly avoiding a hefty branch which crashed to the ground in an explosion of frost and dirt. Molly's lamp landed at my feet, the impact spattering the glass with wax. Heart shrivelling with dread, I searched hurriedly under the tree.

'Molly!'

'Coming!'

To my immense relief her voice rang out strong and true from the limbs immediately above. I hoisted my lamp and watched her lower herself from the bottom-most bough.

'That was exciting!' she said, touching terra firma with a big gleaming smile on her face. 'Though, I think I may have torn my coat.'

I stepped in for a closer look. Her coat had indeed suffered a tear at the waist and there was a small scratch on her chin, but otherwise she appeared remarkably unscathed.

'What happened? Are you hurt?'

'No. I didn't fall far,' explained Molly, twisting to inspect the damage to her coat. 'I almost had it, Jojo! I was so close. It was an inch from my fingers when the branch broke! Did you find it? Is it on the ground?'

'You could have killed yourself, Molly.'

'Oh, ye of little faith,' she beamed. 'Come on. Let's see if we can find it.'

Molly borrowed the flame from my lamp to replenish the light in her own and together, our backs hunched to the ground, we encircled the tree, carefully examining the scatter of recently fallen debris.

It did not take long to find our prize.

The broken branch lay on the ground like some monstrous upturned wishbone. And there, dangling from a fibrous thread of torn stem, hung the bloated chestnut.

'It's bigger than my fist!' said Molly, astounded. 'What if it really does have magical powers! What if it can grant wishes like Aladdin and his lamp!'

'We will never know,' I said, staring morosely at the object of so many fruitless hours and days of interminable waiting, convinced that our mission had been one of abject failure. 'To release its magic, it must be caught before it touches the ground, remember?'

'But it hasn't touched the ground.'

Molly's simple statement produced a minor magical effect all of its own. I had become so blinkered in my despondency that I had overlooked the plain truth of the matter. The branch had most certainly touched the ground. But its cargo had not! A distance of half a yard yet lay between the chestnut and the snow-covered earth.

'Shall you catch it or shall I? We must catch it, mind. Not pluck it,' I said with nervous glee.

'This is your adventure, Jojo. You should be the one to catch it. Now get ready. I reckon one good tap will knock it free.'

I cupped a hand underneath.

'Ready?'

'Ready.'

'One... Two... Three!'

Molly struck the broken limb. The spiny green orb dropped into the palm of my glove. We both watched and waited expectantly as I rotated the freakishly large capsule slowly in my grasp. There was not a blemish to be seen anywhere upon its impressive circumference. Nor did its emerald surface offer any hint of a crack or split which would aid access to the nut within.

'Feel anything?' asked Molly.

'Nothing.'

'Try making a wish.'

'A wish?'

'Why not? It has to be worth a try. Go on, make a wish,' Molly insisted.

'What should I wish for?'

'I don't know. Whatever you like.'

'I've always wanted a telescope.'

'Is that it?' said Molly, singularly unimpressed. 'Is that the limit of your imagination? Why not ask for something truly impressive? Like the power to turn water into wine? Or sand into gold?'

'Or raindrops into diamonds?'

'Perfect!'

'No. I've thought of something else.'

I closed my eyes for a few moments.

'What did you wish for?'

'Ah! The genie says it must remain secret, or it will never come true.'

Molly prodded a finger to my chest.

'Tell me what you wished for or I'll –'

She suddenly abandoned her threat and snatched up her lantern.

'What is it?' I whispered fearfully.

Molly gestured for my silence and encouraged me to listen.

I did not have to wait long before I detected a frantic scrabbling sound emanating from the ground close by.

Our lights soon hit upon the source. A flurry of snow and earth rose up from the little grave we had dug. Hearts racing wildly, we stared in disbelief as the pine marten extricated itself from its crude burial chamber. A remarkable transformation had overtaken this diminutive Lazarus. The gaping wound on its back had now healed, hiding its previously exposed backbone. Its hind legs too, were now in perfect working order. The most remarkable change of all, however, was in its fur. When we had consigned the creature to the ground, its coat had been predominately brown in colour with a golden neck and chest but now it was of the purest white. The pine marten sniffed the air, shivered the dirt from its pelt, stretched itself to its fullest extent and then, throwing a contemptuous glance at the bothersome lights hovering above, it scampered across the hollow and was soon lost to the crowded blackness of the woods.

'I would like to go now,' breathed Molly, her countenance as pale as the ubiquitous frost.

We hurried from the hollow and clambered up the treacherous slope. Arriving at the summit, I could not resist one last look and there, caught in a splinter of moonlight escaping through the fragmenting clouds, I saw a pillar of mist slowly gather beneath the Witch Tree. The nebulous wisps spun and rose and, to my fretful imagination, began to adopt an almost human-like form when, much to the relief of my shattered nerves, the spectral mist succumbed to a brisk breeze and was gone in a blink.

*

The grandfather clock stationed on the landing beyond my bedroom door chimed thrice. Molly and I were seated on the hearthrug, the fire warming our bare feet and drying the damp footwear hanging from the mantel.

'I shall never set foot in those woods again,' said Molly, watching as I stoked the grate. The flames responded and clawed their way out through the fresh heap of coals. The image of the pine marten resurrecting itself continued to play over and over in my mind's eye.

'I don't understand,' I said. 'I thought it was surely dead.'

'Apparently not.'

'But you saw the wounds! It's spine. The blood. You saw its hind legs. They were useless! It couldn't walk! I cannot understand how it did what it did.'

Molly shrugged. 'The injuries looked worse than they actually were. What other explanation can there be?'

'Then how do you explain the white fur?'

'It was covered in snow.'

'No. Not to that extent.'

'I am not going back in those woods. Let that be the end of it,' said Molly, a flash of anger in her eyes.

I took the chestnut from my pocket and balanced it in the palm of my hand. Holding it for the first time without the protection of gloves, I felt its needle-sharp spikes probe and jag at my skin.

'What do you think would happen if we threw it on the fire?' asked Molly.

'Nothing good. It might release a curse and turn our hair as white as the pine marten's.'

'It was covered in snow!' Molly sighed, exasperated.

'Perhaps we should plant it,' I suggested.

Molly wrinkled her nose, unimpressed. 'And then?'

'We let it take root and wait for something magical to happen.'

'And how long will that take? Ten, twenty, a hundred years?'

'My father would say a seed taking root is magical in itself,'

I smiled.

'Hmmph! After all we've been through, I think I have every right to expect something far more impressive.'

'Then let's open it.' I dug my fingernails into the shell, but no matter how hard I tried, it proved impossible to prise apart. Molly reached for the brooch pinned to her chest.

'Try this.'

I had always regarded the simple wooden cross to be a rather dull adornment. A modest token of her faith. But when she gave the hilt of the brooch a little tug between her forefinger and thumb, its true nature was revealed.

'Pa made it for me. He says a Leith woman must always have the capacity to defend herself readily to hand,' she explained, unsheathing a small, lethal looking blade of polished silver two inches in length from the vertical spar. She handed me the miniature sword.

'Remind me never to upset you,' I said, admiring Tam's handiwork. I brought the secret weapon to the chestnut and pushed the tip through the burr.

An anguished howl rose up from one of the guest bedrooms. The wailing increased in intensity until, with an irritated shake of her head, Molly reclaimed the little dagger, collected her boots and headed for the door.

'It's Bethany. She's having a bad dream. I better tend to her. Let me know if anything magical happens.'

'I will.'

I listened to her footsteps hurry across the landing to enter the room she was sharing with her sisters. Another door opened. I heard my parents exchange whispers of concern as they made their way to investigate the hubbub. Eventually wee Bethany's sobs faded to nothing and the house fell into silence once more. A silence disturbed only by the muted rumblings of Tam's snores, my uncle having somehow slept through the entire commotion.

It was then that the centre of my palm began to itch under the chestnut. A minor irritation at first, but the tingle of perspiring warmth quickly expanded outwards utilising the network of lines and folds to spread an uncomfortable, inflamed rash over the entire hand. My fingers closed involuntarily around the shell, locking it inside a rigid, impregnable cage. The vice tightened in slow painful increments. The chestnut's spikes punctured my skin and blood oozed in trickling rivulets down my wrist. My knuckles stretched and blanched so tightly I feared the skin would split to the bone. More and more spines lanced the flesh of my fingers, thumb and palm. A fissure appeared on the surface of the green husk. The slit widened to unveil the single glossy brown nut within. It was the size of a billiard ball!

A pale radicle suddenly erupted from the nut. Reaching out like a hungry white worm, it twisted and spiralled, tasting the air. Then, evidently attracted by the flow of warm blood, it squirmed its way towards the spine embedded at my wrist. My head swam in panic as I watched the shoot ease the spine aside and plunge itself into the bleeding hole. I sensed the shoot burrow its way deeper into my arm, sensed it writhing under the surface of my skin, travelling towards the elbow.

The paralysis afflicting my hand advanced rapidly to consume my whole body and soon there was nothing to be done but watch.

Watch as the chestnut nestling in my bloodied hand began to shrink in size.

Watch as the seed followed the wormlike shoot and melted into the wound at my wrist till finally nothing remained but the shrivelled empty husk.

Gradually, my fingers relaxed, unfurling like the petals of a flower, revealing a hand dotted everywhere with a host of red punctures. Yet while the external shackles slipped away, the invasion within continued its relentless advance. I sat there by the fire, its warmth hopelessly inadequate in the face of the gelid terror stoked by the nauseating sensation of fresh offshoots striking out into new territories; a vanguard of rootlets and tendrils sprouting and sliding their way between bones, tendons and organs. Shivering with fear and exhaustion, I staggered to the bed and buried myself under the cold, black folds of the counterpane.

Is this your doing, Margaret McKay?
Did you grant my wish?
The wish I knew to be impossible?
For how can a dead creature return to life?
Is this your doing, Margaret McKay?

I received no response and passed into the void of colourless dreams.

CHAPTER SEVEN

The Whale Tooth

My eyelids flickered stickily to a sharp *rat-a-tat* at the door.

Mother poked her head into the bedroom.

'Good morning, sleepyhead. Tam and the girls will be going home soon. Come and join us at the breakfast table.'

'I'll be down soon,' I yawned.

A sudden frown replaced Mother's smile. 'You look pale. Are you unwell?'

'I'm tired, that's all.'

She sat herself on the edge of the bed and placed a hand to my brow.

'You feel so cold! It's this draughty old room of yours. We really must do something about that rickety window, I can feel the air coming in from here.' She rose to inspect the object of her disdain, pushing at its edges, testing the frame. 'Listen to it rattle. But first thing's first, young man, the dining room is warm, your place is set, so get yourself dressed and come and eat... Oh! What is this?' Mother gathered the empty chestnut shell from the hearthrug. All trace of vibrant green had been replaced by a dull uniform brown and the once potent spines now drooped listlessly. 'The nut inside must have been a giant! Do you have it?'

'I threw it on the fire,' I said, hoping the lie would put an end to her interest.

'Pity,' said Mother, ruefully. 'Even so, this will be an interesting thing to sketch. May I borrow it?'

'Keep it. I have no use for it.'

Pleased with her find, Mother departed and the door closed.

I threw back my blankets and rose wearily to the washstand, still fully dressed in the mud stains and scrapes from the previous night's foray into the woods. I studied my ravaged hand. Streaks of crusted blood had created a network of dried riverbeds flowing from the many deep pits puncturing the flesh from fingertips to wrist.

There is nothing like the sober light of a winter morn to stimulate that logical portion of the brain responsible for separating the ridiculous from the banal. I emptied the jug into the basin, and it was in this cleansing swirl of light and water that the flecks of russet dissolved, taking with them the ridiculous dream of the parasitical chestnut burying its way into my flesh. In all likelihood the chestnut's spines pierced my hand when I tripped and fell as we fled the woods in our fevered haste of fear and paranoia. Several times we strayed from the path, stumbling in unfamiliar darkness, through gorse and thicket before finally locating the rope swing and crossing the burn.

In a shameful display of weakness, I had allowed myself to be seduced by the romantic absurdities of witchcraft and magic. I had lost all sense of perspective and abandoned the fundamental scientific principles of fact-based reasoning and analysis. Driven to the brink of mania by endless hours spent waiting under an old tree in freezing conditions, my exhausted imagination had chosen to reveal things that had no basis in reality.

Take the pine marten. The creature's *recovery* was categorically not the result of a wish fulfilled! I had pronounced it dead. A pronouncement based on the evidence of a feeble lamplight. What nonsense! It is not uncommon for an injured animal, when at the mercy of a predator, to feign death, then sally forth and make good their escape when the opportunity arises.

And the pillar of mist? Is it so unusual to see mist rising from a hollow?

But to have recruited Molly into my circus of shame! This was the most unforgivable act of all.

Hands cleaned and dried, I moved to the window. The stark winter sunlight refracted harshly from the snow-smothered lawn. Deprived of night's black veil, the woods beyond had lost all their mystery. The only truly miraculous thing to have occurred during the night came with Molly's remarkable escape from serious injury. I shuddered at what might have followed had her natural dexterity failed and she had crashed to the ground to land with her limbs every bit as crooked and splintered as the treasonous branch that snapped beneath her. What possible explanation of mine would have satisfied Tam and my parents? I very much doubted her distraught father, uncle or aunt would find any degree of solace in learning she had sacrificed herself in pursuit of a chestnut with supposedly magical powers.

As I stood there thanking God for bestowing my cousin with the poise and balance of a cat, Mother appeared below. Throwing a shawl around her shoulders, she hurried over the lawn towards the fernery, where Mr Maybury was perched on a ladder, clearing snow from its glass roof. After a brief verbal exchange my mother appeared to hand something to Mr Maybury who, after a brief examination of the object, responded with a nod, tucked it safely inside a pocket and resumed his work. As I watched Mother return to the house, my right hand began to itch. I soothed the irritation as best I could with a splash of cold water and made my way downstairs.

'Well? What happened after I left? Anything magical?' asked Molly in a hushed tone even though there was little danger of our conversation being overheard. Between mouthfuls of bacon and boiled eggs, my father and Tam were embroiled in an argument regarding the merits or otherwise of the Chartists (Tam passionately espoused the merits, Father passionately decried them) while Grace and Mother amused a delighted Bethany with several raucous verses of 'I Saw Three Ships'.

'No. Nothing happened,' I replied, happy to note that our nocturnal excursion had passed unnoticed by the rest of the household.

'How disappointing,' Molly sighed. 'After all our efforts. Where is the chestnut now?'

'I threw it on the fire.'

'Oh, well. So much for turning raindrops into diamonds.'

Feeling suddenly ravenous, I reached for my knife and fork. Taking care to hide the puncture wounds dotted over my palm, I sliced into the meat on my plate.

A scream such as I had never before heard, skewered my brain with a violence so brutal I feared my skull would burst. The onslaught corrupted my vision with pulses of searing white making it impossible to fathom what lay directly in front of me. Fleeting images began to appear between the lightning strikes. Scenes of utter confusion and terror. A crowded pig pen. Trotters, frantic to escape, slipping and flailing in thick mud. Eyes bulging in terror. Snouts and mouths, pushing and shoving and biting. I was amongst them. Trapped. A squealing sow overwhelmed by an impending, mortal danger. Grasping hands reached down. Human hands. And I was dragged from my fellows. Legs tied. Hoisted and suspended. The ground beneath me span in a bewildering smear of wet muck. And the piercing visceral shriek continued, growing ever more hysterical in pitch. A song of dread. Of helplessness. Of a life aware of its imminent end. A man reached forth. The spinning stopped. He held a blade. Raised it to my throat. And the scream – *my scream!* – ceased. Blood rained against the stone floor in great spattering globs.

'Jojo? Whatever is the matter?'

The shock of the hand resting upon my arm tore the crimson pool from my sight. Another dazzling flash and I was returned to the breakfast table. Molly was close at my side, eyeing me with deep concern. And she was not alone. The entire room had fallen silent. The arguing and singing had ceased.

'Why are you all staring at me?'

'Because you were shaking like a terrified dog, Jojo. I've never seen you look so scared. We tried to talk to you, but you wouldn't answer. And look,' said Molly, gesturing to my hands.

My fingers were gripping so tightly at the knife and fork, the metal had started to bend. I withdrew the knife from the meat and pushed the plate beyond reach.

'He has a fever,' said Mother. 'And little wonder. His bedroom is freezing. That rotten window needs to be replaced as soon as possible.'

'I'll have Mr Maybury take care of it,' said Father. 'Meanwhile, I have several remedies suitable for all manner of fevers in my study. A measure of willow milk should do the trick.'

'Away with yer hubble-bubble potions, Lachlan!' railed Tam. 'Finish yer breakfast Joseph, then wash those eggs down with a warm toddy and ye'll be right as rain. I guarantee it.'

'There really is no cause for all this fuss,' I said, anxious to escape the unwelcome scrutiny. 'Some fresh air is all I need. So if you will excuse me, I think I shall take myself outside.'

'Would you like some company?' asked Molly.

'Thank you, but no. I shan't be long.'

'Make sure you wrap up warm,' said Mother.

'I will.'

I hastily turned heel on the gallery of worry staring in at me from all sides and made for the vestibule, where I donned my boots, coat and scarf. I tramped through the snow, tortured at every step by the screams of the condemned animals. The blood-drenched slaughter of the pig still vivid in my mind, I noticed Mr Maybury watching me from within the fernery. Hoping to mask my distress, I threw him a cheerful wave and he acknowledged in kind. I glanced back to the house to see my parents standing at the dining-room windows. Again I waved and smiled in an attempt to appease their obvious worry.

A few more yards and I reached the sanctuary of the woods where, removed from all prying eyes, my state of severe agitation began to ease.

I pushed onwards, guided only by the desire to put some distance between myself and the house, the confines of which had become intolerable under the pernicious if heartfelt concern of its occupants. And yet, caught in the thrall of some unfathomable instinct, I found myself following that same familiar path through the woods and soon arrived at the hollow.

In spite of its many eccentric twists and aberrations, the Witch Tree had always projected an air of defiance and strength. But now, with nary a leaf nor a chestnut left, it looked so frail and vulnerable under the glare of the bright morning sky. I gasped in shock when I saw the splintered limb high in the upper reaches which marked the truly dizzying extent of Molly's climb.

My palm started to itch.

I scratched at the warm tingling sensation, but this merely aggravated the irritation further. The inflammation blistered and peeled under my clawing fingernails and became so painful that in desperation, I dropped to my knees and thrust my hand into the snow.

Relief came swiftly. The blissful, numbing cold extinguished the fire. But as one torment eased another rose up to take its place. Hunger. My famished belly rumbled. I had not eaten since supper. But this was no ordinary hunger pang and I certainly had no appetite to return to the horror-laden plate of my aborted breakfast. The strange food I craved did not require a plate at all.

I buried my recuperating hand into the ground as far as the wrist. Immediately there came the taste of earth to my tongue. A mouth-watering tang of deep rich humus. I burrowed my fingers deeper still and while the heady flavours intensified, they carried with them a strange array of impressions and thoughts. I instinctively knew that I was being spoken to but in manner and in a language of untold antiquity far beyond my understanding. There was no doubt in my mind, however, that these ethereal messages were being conveyed directly from the Witch Tree itself.

I closed my eyes and pictured the filigree of its roots infiltrating far and wide beneath the hollow. I traced their progress, ploughing ever downwards until I arrived at the taproot; the starting point where hundreds of years before, the first radicle split hesitantly from its seed to embark on a mammoth journey which would ultimately result in this enormous pillar of life. There were bones at its tip. Lots of bones. The flesh long since absorbed by the soil from which the nascent tree gathered the nourishment necessary for its early growth.

Travelling between this network of rhizomes I detected hundreds if not thousands of tiny movements. The traffic of worms, nematodes and all manner of burrowing insects simply going about their business. A bustling of innumerable little lives all driven by the universal need to devour and reproduce. This communication with the subterranean world tickling at my fingertips rapidly expanded beyond the manifold creatures toiling beneath the immediate surrounds of the hollow to include the entire underground realms of Braid Woods, of

Liberton and Edinburgh and Leith, of Lothian, spreading onwards beneath all of Scotland, Great Britain, Northern Europe...

My mind swam with wonder as Mother Nature led me by the hand to reveal her innermost secrets. We journeyed across the land and into the oceans and under the seabeds to rise again and cross the continents, through forests, through bogs, across deserts, over mountains, whereupon she spread her magnificent wings and took flight. Through tingling fingers came the songs and chatter of the entire world, songs and tales of birth pains and deaths throes in all the keys of growth and decay but above all, *life*! Here was the most glorious symphony played out under intense sunshine, furious downpours and the star filled cosmos.

I saw it clearly for the very first time. The interconnectedness of everything. The *whole* planet – for that's how it was presented to me – as one unified entity. The sum of incalculable constituents, each intricately linked to the other. *Dependent* upon the other. The sheer majesty of Nature's work was a joy to behold. But there was pain in her experience. Her creation which had taken inestimable aeons to perfect was under threat. The delicate threads of existence were being picked apart by nefarious forces for whom beauty resided only in the colours of silver and gold. Utilising all their implements of plunder, they cut and hacked and scraped and tore at her treasures, unconcerned by the disfiguring scars they left. She showed me the wounds, each revelation more harrowing than the last.

I could endure no more and pulled my hand from the dirt. Astonishingly, the sores had all but vanished from the palm. Only a few of the deeper puncture marks remained visible. My stomach gurgled impatiently. Without a moment's compunction I greedily licked the abundant coating of soil from my fingers. Then, with a quick glance to confirm that I was indeed alone, I scooped a fistful of earth into my mouth and swallowed it down. Another helping followed. And then another.

After the fourth mouthful, the tears began to flow. I stared at my blackened fingernails. What in the name of Almighty God was happening to me? I picked myself up and looked to the heavens for an answer. Though its warmth was feeble, the benign radiance of the winter sun had strength enough to lift my spirits and soothe my fears. I departed the hollow with a renewed vitality. A fresh vibrancy now infused all the colours and hues of the woods, from the silver lichens and the emerald mosses to the iridescent plumage of a passing jay. The effect of this startling rejuvenation extended to enhance the sounds of nature's own orchestra. Everything from the faint whirr of a sycamore seed spinning for the ground, to the scrabbling beetle feasting on the torn carcass of a rabbit hidden in the scrub, to the tiny chime of a snowflake striking the surface of a stone. I fancied that if I listened hard enough I might even hear the whisper of the clouds as they scurried across the sky.

*

'I trust the fresh air had the desired effect, eh Joseph?' said Tam, pipe clamped between his teeth.

'I can honestly say I have never felt better.'

Mr Maybury waiting patiently at the reins, Tam boarded the carriage and shuffled himself in beside Grace, taking care not to jostle Bethany bundled fast asleep on Molly's lap. Molly scrutinised my every gesture and utterance with narrow-eyed suspicion but said nothing.

'Excellent! Now remember, lad. Botany is, unquestionably, the dullest pursuit in all humanity. And the day ye come to yer senses and realise this, let me know and I'll make good on my promise to turn you into the second-best harpooner in the Northern seas,' winked Tam.

'Thank you, Uncle. But I fear I may never come to my senses.'

'Away with you, Tam, before I stick a harpoon in your own blubber,' Mother warned with a smile.

'Forgive me, sister, I shall say no more on the matter,' he grinned. 'Goodbye all!'

Mr Maybury flicked the reins and the carriage pulled away to a chorus of cheerful farewells. Mother ran tearfully into the house as soon as the sweep of the driveway had curved the departing Keane family from view. I started after her, hoping to offer some words of comfort, but was halted by my father's discouraging hand.

'No. Leave your mother be. It still grieves her to see Kathryn missing from their number. Give her time. She will return to her usual self in due course. Meanwhile, walk with me, Joseph.'

I accompanied him to the pleasing light and comparative warmth of the fernery. Father cast a satisfied eye over his collection. The acquisitions from the China expedition, now fully settled in their new home, exhibited their satisfaction in a beautifully delicate explosion of green.

'This one is called the Eternal Fern,' he explained, crouching on his haunches to admire an umbrella-like specimen situated close to the central fountain. 'They are impervious to extremes of both heat and cold. Fire and frost have no effect. Some individuals are believed to be even older than The Great Wall itself. I am reliably informed that this one is over three hundred years old. A relative youngster by comparison.'

He brought himself upright and turned to me.

'Are you quite sure you are well, Joseph? Your demeanour would suggest otherwise.'

'I feel much better now, thank you.'

'Rarely have I seen a man who claims to be in such fine fettle look so vexed.'

Father snatched my hand and angled the palm upwards for the benefit of the hard white daylight.

'What are these marks?' he asked, closely inspecting the now sparse array of puncture wounds.

'Nothing.'

He lifted his eyes to mine. They saw straight through the lie and suddenly blazed with wonder.

'You caught it, didn't you? You caught the chestnut!'

'Yes.'

'How? When?' he gasped.

I furnished Father with a heavily abridged version of events. Omitting Molly's involvement, I told of my visit to the Witch Tree in the dead of night and how, after many preceding visits waiting in vain for the nut to fall, my patience and doggedness had finally received its reward.

'Where is it now. Let me see it.'

'I threw it on the fire.'

Father, who throughout my narrative had been paying minute attention to the entry wound at my wrist, stretching and studying the surrounding skin, released my hand and looked at me aghast.

'You threw it on the fire? But why?'

'Because nothing happened. Nothing magical. Nothing unusual. Nothing of any note whatsoever. It was a perfectly harmless chestnut.'

He considered this for the duration of a sigh.

'Perfectly harmless? That is not how I would describe the events we witnessed at the breakfast table.'

'That had nothing to do with the chestnut,' I protested. 'It was a momentary dizzy spell. I suspect I caught a chill from being out in the woods all night.'

Father retreated to cast his disappointment through the glasshouse towards the bank of trees beyond.

'Tell me, aside from this dizzy spell, have you experienced

any other symptoms since you caught the chestnut. Any visions? Nausea?'

'No.'

'I see,' said Father, with a nod. 'There will be no more nocturnal wanderings. Is that understood?'

'You have my word.'

'Then let this be the end of the matter.'

'It is already at an end,' I said.

'How so?'

'The Witch Tree is dying.'

'Ah, yes. You have noticed that too, hmm?'

'Is there nothing to be done? Surely you must know of some remedy?'

'If only that were so,' said Father, sorrowfully. 'Some outcomes are predetermined and no amount of interference, benevolent as the intent may be, can alter the course that nature has decided. The Witch Tree is dying. And that is as it should be. Its destiny has been fulfilled. But enough of this gloom!' He smiled and wrapped a sympathetic arm around my shoulder. 'Come. Let us retreat indoors, warm ourselves by the fire and raise a glass in celebration of a life well lived.'

*

Deprived of the bustle and energy supplied by Tam and his brood, the old house slipped back into peaceful quietude. We whiled away the remainder of the day in separate rooms; Father in his study transcribing the more pertinent notes from his China journals, Mother in the drawing room painting a spray of delicate fronds, whereas I retired early to my room and tried to lose myself in the texts of Hooker and the plates of Besler's *Florilegium* which, though undoubtedly beautiful, were not quite as wondrous as my mother's work for the *Botanica Fantastica* series. Under normal circumstances those excellent books would have secured my attentions with minimal effort, but the circumstances in which I now found myself were as far removed from any definition of normal as it was possible to conceive.

The printed pages I held in my hands disappeared and were replaced instead with woodcuts and lithographs of Molly's fearless climb, the falling branch and the chestnut driving under my skin, the horrible screams of the slaughtered pig and the dirt dripping from the tips of my fingers as they broke from a soil rich with secrets.

A whistling gust rattled the loose-fitting window and brought the flow of grotesque imagery to an end.

I had been sitting in the dark, staring vacantly at the same book, open at the same page, for hours. The room had grown deathly cold in the interim. I was so fatigued I could not bring myself to stoke the hearth back to life. I retreated to the bed and insulated myself from the debilitating draught inside a cocoon of blankets.

The sound of the squall buffeting the panes and harassing the creaking eaves became a soothing lullaby as I prepared to surrender to the forces of sleep. Turning on my side, I noticed the polished surface of an object reflecting the guttering light of a candle. I reached out to collect the whale tooth from the bedside table.

And touched Death itself.

A lightning bolt of the purest form of agony tore through my being. It flowed on and on, stabbing, slicing and flaying at my skin. A hundred invisible blades cut away my flesh to expose the bones for a hundred hammers to smash and splinter. From the crown of my scalp to the ends of my toes, the crippling spasms wrenched and scythed. I tried to drop the tooth, but my grip refused the command and tightened further. The wind howled down the chimney and burst from the flue in a great seething cloud of soot and ash. Not to be outdone, the rain thudded its fists against the window with increasing fury. The glass shattered, releasing a great frothing red torrent into the room. I tried to cry out, but the sea of blood gushed down my gullet to squeeze the last bubble of air from my lungs. Rising through the swirling confusion of ash, soot and blood, the bubble lifted me from the bed and propelled me into a terrifying whirlpool of darkness...

...I breached the surface of a vast ocean of black... The tooth had returned to its rightful position, fixed within the mouth of the great whale. Through his eyes I surveyed an endless rolling seascape of charcoal waves fringed with tumbling crests of white chalk. The whale dived gracefully into the depths, its purpose benign. Merely searching for food and calling for company. His mournful melody laced with hope. The magnificent animal's beautiful song garnered no response, but he continued to serenade the unfathomable darkness with verse after verse. He recalled a time, long ago it seemed now, when every refrain he sang received an invitation to join another in a joyful duet. But the ocean had become a lonely place. The distances he now had to travel to encounter another of his kind had become exhausting. His was a world of increasing silence, yet onwards he swam, defiantly filling the emptiness with his melancholy compositions.

The whale arced smoothly towards the rippling light above. He greeted the sky with a mighty blast from his blowhole and gorged himself on its sweet air. Enjoying the rise and fall of the swell, he rested a while on the surface, replenishing his cavernous lungs, gathering his strength. A cluster of strange creatures approached him, their spindly flippers dipping in and out of the water in an awkward, inefficient fashion. Above the splash and spray of the sea came their strange cries, urgent and persistent. Theirs was an ugly, dismal song.

Another creature, considerably larger than the ones drawing ever nearer, followed at a distance. There were no flippers protruding from this beast; instead it glided over the waves under a set of great white wings. He had seen one similar beast before many seasons ago, the day he heard his mate perform her beautiful aria for the last time.

I shared the whale's rising fear and panic. He prepared to make good his escape but had not yet taken enough air. The first spike pierced clean through skin, blubber and ribs. A hot spasm of agony rippled out from the barbs, biting close to the animal's noble heart. The whale convulsed and flexed his huge tail, ready to dive, when a second strike penetrated his body. A third punctured the flesh above his fin.

I sought refuge in the eternal darkness, but the blood choking my mouth and the tugging ropes soon sapped my strength and again I was forced to the surface. The little creatures swarmed around me. I thrashed at them in a confusion of distress and despair, trying to swat them free, but they held fast, riding in my wake till I could swim no more.

Exhausted, I could do nothing to stop the busy torment. The harrying, stabbing and hollering. Something cleaved my spine, putting an end to my feeble struggle, and left me floating helplessly in an expanding slick of crimson. Waves of my own blood lapped at my eyes as holes were gouged into my tail and more ropes attached. The spindly flippers set to work, hauling me towards the great mother beast.

Raised from the water and secured to her side, I watched in mute terror as her tiny offspring scurried everywhere. With gleeful voices and glinting appendages, they cut at my flesh in a frenzy of excoriating torture. But these lacerations were superficial compared to the soul-deep wounds of loss. The loss of my beloved ocean home with all its mystery and wonder. The loss of all those precious memories of the times we spent swimming the southern seas together, the warmth of the tropical sun upon our backs. The memory of our favourite song, loving and heartfelt, began to fade from my mind.

The tiny animals sliced away huge strips of skin and

blubber. They plundered my insides. One tiny animal leaned close to my clouded eye and loosed a hail of victory as he held aloft a trophy. And then I realised, as I succumbed to the soundless realm of the permanent dark, that I recognised this little creature proudly boasting a tooth hacked from my own mouth. I even knew his name.

Uncle Tam!

I sat bolt upright in bed and hurled the offending tooth across the room. The last echoes of the whale's anguish drifted away on a sea so full of blood the cresting waves rolled red. On the murderous ship, the laughing, singing whalers splashed in the blood pooling at their boots in a layer so thick the timbers reeked of its stench whilst the magnificent animal remained alive to every excruciating cut of their busy blades.

I wept in quaking, unrestrained despair at the awful senselessness of it all. I could not allow another fellow creature of God to experience such soul wrenching cruelty. Something had to be done. The beginnings of a plan were formed, the execution of which required the breaking of my earlier promise to my father.

I dressed quickly, pocketed a box of lucifers and made my way quietly downstairs. Two patches of soft yellow light illuminated the otherwise impenetrable darkness of the hallway. The first spilled out from the partially open door of Father's study. I stole a glance inside and saw my father, hunched at his desk, dip a pen into the inkwell, then work it furiously across a sheet of foolscap. Avoiding those particular floorboards I knew were waiting to betray my presence at the mere press of a toe, I crept towards the second spill of light escaping from the drawing room, where Mother had abandoned her easel for the piano.

The plaintive sweep of her playing accompanied me as I donned my winter things and closed the front door behind me.

CHAPTER EIGHT

The *Majestic North*

Pulling my collar tight against the cold night drizzle, I hurried through lanes of melting snow into Liberton, where I joined the Newington Road and pressed onwards for Edinburgh. The city's church bells were tolling midnight by the time I reached the North Bridge. Despite the rain and the lateness of the hour, a good number of people were still to be seen hastening along the pavements or loitering under the lamps. One woman in particular caught my attention. Hunched over the parapet, her threadbare skirt blotted damp at the hem where it skimmed the grey slush, she stretched her bony hands out towards the broken windows of the abandoned Orphan's Hospital, its ruins rising amidst a landscape of rubble and weeds from the square below. She sang a soft mournful tune to the building so frustratingly out of reach of her clutching fingers. The woman cut such a wretched, tormented figure, I felt compelled to stop and engage with her.

'Excuse my intrusion, madam, but I fear you are not adequately dressed for these conditions. You will freeze to death out here. You should go home. Please, allow me to hail you a cab.'

Seen at close quarters, her clothes were in a sorrier state of repair than I had first imagined. The shawl clinging wetly about her shoulders offered scant protection from the elements. And nor did the tired little bonnet perched on her head, its blue ribbon channelling water down the gullies and curls of her long, matted hair. The heel of her right boot had split from the sole. Untroubled by my intervention, the woman continued to sing her sweet lament to the empty black windows opposite.

'Madam?'

She fell silent, lowered her tremulous hands and turned slowly. I was greeted by a piteous sight. Though I surmised her to be no more than twenty-five years of age, a lifetime of hardship had creased and scored the youth from her emaciated face and stolen all trace of wonder from her eyes.

The woman gazed at me in silence for some length. Then to my astonishment, she rested a hand on my cheek and with an expression of the utmost pity said: 'I will pray for you, you poor, poor, broken thing.'

Without another word, the woman scuttled off in the direction of the Tron Chapel, where she dissolved into the darkness and was gone.

This baffling encounter added to a gnawing sense of unease as I made my way across Princes Street, fingers shielding the matches in my pocket from the dampness seeping through the seams of my coat.

At Leith Walk, I happened to glance over my shoulder and fancied I caught sight of someone shifting quickly between the shadows some yards behind. Fearing I was being followed, I slipped inside the doorway of a baker's shop and waited. As the minutes passed, the only discernible movement came from the street lamp opposite, where the mesh of fine rain trapped within its glow, swayed with all the restlessness of a swarm of silver midges above a summer-black lake. I watched this strangely captivating performance till the dancing rainflies dissipated, leaving the cone of light to shine upon an empty stage. I resolved to wait a short while longer but saw no further cause for suspicion.

Leith has its own distinctive aroma. A salty, industrial blend of flax dust, toasted malt, fired glass and the decaying fruits of the sea. This pungent blend of the art of the rope maker, the glassmaker, the distiller and the whaler reached its zenith along Great Junction Street. But, as I advanced towards the slumbering docks, it was the offensive stench of boiled blubber which grew in dominance, coating every breath in an acrid, waxy seasoning; the flavour so strong I was forced to wrap my scarf over my nose and mouth to mitigate its noxious assault.

The wharfs provided a wealth of recesses and crannies. Perfect places to hide oneself from wary eyes. Crouching behind a nest of barrels, I surveyed the creaking hulks fast asleep at their moorings, their riggings and masts thinly illuminated by the sparse dock lights and a feeble, liquid moonshine. The cloying odour of whale oil and smoked fish penetrated even the thick wool of the scarf. The stink of plunder and death. My palm itched against the surface of a barrel. The wood spoke of violence. Of axes cutting short an ancient life. A sensation of all-pervading sadness overwhelmed me as I hid there surrounded by hulls, crates and warehouses carrying the ghostly refrains of a thousand murdered creatures.

I will pray for you, you poor, poor, broken thing.

Slow footsteps studded the quayside timbers. A night-watchman approached, his cape and broad hat reflecting wetly in the throw from the lantern swinging idly in his hand. I squeezed deeper behind the barrels and studied him through a tiny sliver of a gap. So close did the watchman stand that I overheard every scratch of his fingers ploughing at a patch of yellow in the otherwise white field of his beard. He removed his clay pipe from a similarly discoloured set of teeth and proceeded to tap the bowl against a barrel before loading the pipe with a fresh pinch of shag; a task he performed whilst humming a familiar little shanty. It was one of Uncle Tam's favourites, invariably sung (or to be more accurate, *bellowed)* whenever he approached the maudlin end of a whisky bottle:

Make haste if ye please,
The ship is ready,
For the wild seas,
Where the wind blows steady,
In yer bonniest hat
And ribbons of blue,

The nightwatchman broke from the tune to present his pipe to the lantern's flame. Leaving a cloud of blue in his wake, he plodded on for the far end of the quay.

Yours is my heart
A beat strong and true
But the sea is my mistress,
And I must obey,
The song of the whale,
Till the end of my dying day,

I waited for the nightwatchman to enter the shelter of his hut and close the door on his song before scampering from my hiding place towards the nearest ship. A heavy sheet of sackcloth had been draped over her freshly lacquered bowsprit. The scatter of wood shavings at my feet provided further evidence of recent repair and prompted a knot to tighten inside my chest. I stepped to the very edge of the wharf, struck a lucifer against the massive hull and held the flame to the plaque bearing the vessel's name...

Majestic North.

I dropped the flame into the dark chasm separating myself from the hull and staggered back. Her slumbrous breath echoed in the soft creak of her masts, their black spikes piercing the night, and from the inky waters slopping languidly at her bows, came her heartbeat. I had not expected to discover Tam's ship quite so readily and to find her resting so peaceably and alone; it seemed particularly ignoble of me to countenance bringing harm upon her in this becalmed state and I confess my resolve buckled momentarily.

Majestic North...

It was a fitting name.

I boarded the ship and helped myself to a lamp hanging from a hook on the mizzenmast. The lamp lit, I made my way very carefully and very quietly below. The vessel was entirely deserted. The stillness reeked of blood and rancid oil, a reminder that whatever majesty she possessed was built on a foundation of shame.

Inside the fo'c'sle, I encountered a slew of empty bunks. The crew doubtless enjoying their precious shore leave with loved ones or collapsing into a stupor in one of Leith's plentiful hostelries where, in exchange for a shilling or two, Damocles will lay down his sword and for a few happy hours the fears and trepidations common to every whaler that the next hunt will be their last and that never again will they return to enjoy the warm embrace of home, are cast aside.

I discovered a little picture carved into the beam positioned directly above the top bunk adjacent to the bulkhead; the head of a woman in profile, her locks tumbling to encapsulate the name Tam had etched beneath:

Kathryn.

I reached up to touch the likeness of my aunt, but the instant my fingers came in to contact with the beam I received a fearsome, galvanic jolt of shivering horror. The timbers of the *Majestic North* were soaked in the anguish of countless trees slain in order to bring this ruthlessly efficient killing machine to life. They had borne witness to unimaginable cruelty. Their stories spoke of innumerable whales shackled to the side of the ship with chains and hooks while the men lowered themselves on ropes and platforms to gather their grisly harvest. The timbers recalled the slow thud of their dying hearts and the warm varnish of blood seeping into every knot and fibre of the wood. A storm of violence blazed through my mind; quick-fire flashes of men and their blades, cutting, slicing, hacking, chopping, sawing... Flesh and wood. Blood and grain. Death upon death upon death upon death upon death...

Every sacrifice incurred in the construction and operation of this murderous craft now seized the opportunity to use me as the unfortunate repository for all their histories of torment and woe. Yet somehow, amidst all this grief, I sensed life. Not one, but millions of tiny lives. Squirming, scratching and burrowing. The fleas, lice, maggots and rats; small but no less significant lives, busily exploiting the opportunities afforded by the *Majestic North*'s trade in huge deaths. The ship's bones ached with a desire to put an end to this perpetual cycle of ruin. It yearned for an angel of mercy to come and release it from the sea of its own desolation.

I formed a loose bale of pillow feathers and straw on the floor and opened the lamp. The flames reacted lazily at first but quickly gained enthusiasm. I gladly warmed my hands and watched the fire's ravenous progress in rapt fascination till the smoke filled every last corner and I was forced to scurry back to the dock and resume my position behind the barrels.

The *Majestic North*'s insides cracked and rumbled. A thick black plume spewed from her cramping stomach. The flames punched their way through her buckling waist and harried at the lower foremast. I felt the heat of the conflagration prickle my brow as I admired the fire's ruthless ascent, its agile fingers grasping at the ropes bridging the divide to the mainmast.

A shrill whistle cut through the air. Eyes shining with panic, the nightwatchman came running from his hut. He gave another blast and attempted to board the stricken ship but was beaten back by the belligerent fire. From all over the docks came the clang of alarm bells and soon the quayside was full of men sprinting from the darkness, some frantically tugging on their boots and pulling on their coats, while others ferried pails of sloshing water. The nightwatchman wiped his face and with a final defeated blast of his whistle he slumped on a capstan and refilled his pipe.

The men worked desperately, filling, passing and throwing the contents of their buckets. The blaze cackled in disdain, mocking their efforts as an exercise in futility. A thunderous snap sent the men scurrying to a safe distance, where they gathered to watch the mainmast, now a great pillar of flame, topple into the water. The great oak, suffering the ignominy of being felled for a second time, hissed in a swirling turmoil of smoke and steam. Then the *Majestic North* herself trembled and lurched, listing to a most alarming degree in a desperate bid to reclaim her lost limb. The men recognised the cause was lost and resigned themselves to stare in mordant silence as the ship descended further into the glittering harbour. Only when an order was hollered from the tallest of their number did the men, now eye-to-eye with the barnacles crusting at her upturned keel, spark back into action to dampen down the neighbouring ships from the embers swarming like fireflies in the updraught of the *Majestic North*'s funeral pyre.

'Hoy, you! Get back here!'

In the midst of the commotion I had crept from the safety of the barrels and started for the harbourside steps, thinking all attentions were safely diverted. But there was one face that was not fixed upon the endangered ships. The nightwatchman rose from his seat and jabbed his pipe in my direction.

'Stop him! It's arson! Stop him!'

Requiring no further encouragement, I bounded up the steps, hared across Commercial Place, recrossed the Water of Leith via the Upper Drawbridge and fled into the labyrinth of alleys that peel off from the Tolbooth Wynd. An eccentric jumble of erratic twists and blind corners, these narrow filthy setts with their rancid overflowing gutters splashing underfoot were a difficult enough proposition to navigate in daylight, but the fall of night rendered them virtually impassable. A handicap I hoped to use to my advantage, as it applied not only to myself but equally to the dozens of voices and boots hunting the adjacent thoroughfares.

The clamour prompted a few candles to appear in the windows of the overhanging, tumbledown houses. Another turn to the left and I would have arrived at Coatfield Lane. Thankfully, even in my fevered brain state, I possessed enough common decency to turn right. For to seek help at the door of Uncle Tam, the man whose livelihood I had just destroyed, would have been an act of the most scandalous hypocrisy. Here, the vennels were packed so tightly it was possible to tap the opposing windows of the inhabitants at the same time. The distended walls of one particularly cramped alley threatened to hold me fast, but my perseverance was rewarded when it conducted me unexpectedly to an open square dominated at one end by a large sullen building two storeys high.

Glad to steal a moment to catch my breath, I sat wearily on the kerb by the building's rear gate, but as I nursed my aching feet, the sound of baleful sobbing permeated the night. Scanning the regimented rows of windows at my back, I came across the shadow of a woman clutching at the bars of a room on the upper floor. She paid me no heed and continued to focus her mournful attentions in the direction of the docks, where the peal of alarm bells, dulled by distance, persisted. Lowering my gaze, I noticed a plaque fixed to the ironwork of the gate made legible by the solitary lamp fixed above.

The Female Asylum for Incurables.

I had passed this building once before with Mother and vividly recalled how she had railed against its very existence and expressed a particular loathing for its 'benefactor', Sir John Gladstone.

'Benefactor! Ha! *Tyrant* would be a more fitting title,' she raged. 'And this is no *asylum*. This is the desperate folly of a rich man trying to thread a camel through the eye of a needle. A salve on the fetid conscience of a slaver grown fat and rich on the chain and whip! May Heaven's gates remain forever closed to men like him.'

The woman at the window stopped her sobs and began to whistle, mimicking the alarms echoing across the rooftops. She looked and sounded for all the world like a sorrowful songbird, wings clipped and trapped in her cage. Falling suddenly silent, the woman lowered her haunted gaze.

'They're coming for you. Run!'

The spread of a lantern and the clatter of footsteps filled the passageway I had recently vacated. I took to my heels and ran for the dark tunnel of a close at the opposite corner of the square. Blindly I ran, turning corner after corner and escaped finally on to Easter Road, where I hurried onwards for the city, and before long my boots were struggling to find purchase on the slippery incline of Calton Hill.

Satisfied I had at last successfully outmanoeuvred my pursuers, I perched on the steps of the Folly and used this excellent vantage point to examine the sprawl of Leith laid out before me. The first bruising's of dawn now stained the skies over the Firth and the Kingdom of Fife in the deepest blues and purples. Beneath those hues, the irregular cobweb tangle of gold streetlights stretching to the docks, provided some measure of the distance I had travelled. Teams of horses pulling fire engines rumbled the length of Leith Walk towards the smoke still rising from the harbour.

My blistered feet baulked at the prospect of walking another yard, let alone the three miles southward, beyond the castle's charcoal silhouette and the gathering slates of grey cloud, to Braid House. I limped downhill, seeking a place to hide myself away from vengeful eyes and the raw northerly wind.

Calton cemetery provided all manner of accommodation for those seeking a place to rest. From the humblest tombstone to the most grandiose monument to decomposition any corpse could wish to inhabit. Yet finding a suitable spot in which to stow my own weary bones proved to be a source of some frustration. I attempted to force my way inside the great pillar box housing Mr Hume's mortal remains, but the gate served its purpose well and I consented to settle down on the narrow curve of earth separating the rear of the mausoleum's circumference from the cemetery wall. A dense knot of ivy provided a roof of sorts and the pillow of cool, damp soil soothed my fractious mind as I recalled the *Majestic North*'s final moments.

Soon the dreams encroached to douse the memory of the flames with a watery, faraway lullaby.

The song of the whale.

CHAPTER NINE

Growth

I awoke to the sound of a new song. A blackbird, perfectly untroubled by my yawning presence, jabbed its bright red beak into the earth directly in front of my nose. Claws anchored to the dirt, it pulled and pulled until the tug of war ended with a fat rope of a worm wriggling haplessly in its mouth. The victorious bird flew off, hunter and prey disappearing inside the umbrella of ivy above. I turned to the sun flickering between the trembling leaves and indulged myself in its faint warmth.

A small pleasure quickly stolen, for a sudden wave of nausea breached my throat with all the flavours of death. I attempted to stand upright but found myself shackled to the ground. Both arms were planted elbow deep in the bilious soil from whence I tasted every foul manner of putrefaction; from the sludge of blood and organs recently burst from bags of skin, to the dry mouldering bones of centuries past. The corrupted earth tingled with all the agents of decay; the maggots, the nematodes, the beetles and the fungi, all gorging themselves from the cemetery's munificent banquet table.

Every grave had a tale to tell. Some told of lives well led and well fed, others of trauma and extreme hardship, of disease and even murder. The most poignant stories, expressed in timid whispers amidst the hubbub, spoke of lives cut so tragically short as to merit but a footnote in this compendium of putrescence.

The coffins themselves had much to lament via the brutal sacrifice of the trees felled, then replanted to provide a home for the dead. A handful had been violated and their occupants removed. Raided by the resurrectionists. Proof, if proof were needed in this increasingly godless city, that nothing was sacred.

I tried to wrest my arms from the noisome ground, but they refused to yield. Back pressed against the curve of Mr Hume's mausoleum and my feet pushing the cemetery wall, I heaved with all my might. At last, as my arms threatened to tear clean from their sockets, my hands broke free, scattering lumps of dirt in all directions.

And when I first chanced to look down upon those filthy fingers, the sickness in my throat spread rapidly to engulf my heart.

Ten white growths as long as my forearms dangled hideously from my hands. The thin, gnarled tendrils had erupted from underneath each fingernail. I instinctively bit down on one of the roots and cried out in unimaginable agony as the deformity was torn from the quick. A clear, viscous liquid seeped from the wound. I put the finger to my mouth. It tasted sweet. I steeled myself, then set my teeth to work on the nine remaining obscenities.

In a state of near delirium, I balled my smarting, weeping hands into tight fists, pushed them inside the pockets of my greatcoat and left the cemetery. With head bowed to a quickening pace, I joined the bustle of Princes Street and proceeded for home in a daze of horror and confusion. The witch's curse had taken a most heinous turn. What, if anything, could be done to reverse it? Who, if anyone, could I turn to? Was it too late? And what was the purpose of Margaret McKay's spell? Mere spite? A final riposte against a world that had treated her so callously? If so, hers was an unjust and indiscriminate retribution. I had no hand in her suffering and therefore I did not deserve this cruel and unholy punishment.

At Braid House the sun had slipped behind the treetops, casting long shadows across the newly laid frost covering the lawn. Inside, I quickly threw off my coat and boots and hurried for the hallway, hoping to climb to my room unnoticed.

'Joseph! Where have you been?' said Mother, accosting me with wide-eyed concern before I managed to place a foot on the stairs. 'Is that dirt in your hair? And oh my! What have you done to your hands?' she exclaimed, first brushing the crumbs of cemetery soil from my hair before discovering the bite wounds at the tips of my fingers and thumbs. A varnish of hardened sap had formed over the injuries. 'Have you been in another fight? I thought you had made your peace with that Tulland boy? No matter. You're home now. Have you heard the awful news?'

'No. What news?'

'There has been a terrible fire. The *Majestic North* has sunk!'

She took my arm and led me to the drawing room. Uncle Tam was seated by the fire with his head in his hands, staring blankly at the flames, his usual good-humoured bluster swallowed up in a cloud of gloom.

'Daddy, please don't be so sad!' pleaded Grace, pulling repeatedly at his waist. Molly hauled her away.

'Leave him be, Grace. Help me look after Beth.'

'No! I want to look after Pa!'

'But who would do such a thing?' I asked.

'I have no idea,' shrugged Mother.

'I know precisely who is responsible,' offered Father with such stern-faced conviction that my guilty heart shrivelled to a halt.

He knew!

My father suspended his damning verdict momentarily to

decant a generous measure of whisky into two glasses, one of which he passed to Tam.

'Chartist louts hell-bent on bringing ruin to us all. They are behind this act of wanton vandalism. That man O'Connor and his ilk are a blight on civilised society.'

I sank into a chair, positively overcome with relief. Mistaking my reaction for one of shock, he filled another glass and passed it to me. I sipped delicately at the honeyed warmth while Tam drained his in a single gulp.

'Yer wrong. The Chartist cause is a just cause. And O'Connor is an honourable man,' he said in a low despondent tone.

'I assure you he is not,' Father insisted. 'He is a violent, mindless hothead of the lowest order whose sole aim is to incite the ignorant masses to take up arms and lay waste to our great nation. The man is a traitor and should be treated as such. The courts have been excessively lenient with him. He should be hanged. An example must be set.'

'Aye, let the noose silence all those who cry out for decency and fairness,' said Tam.

'Calm yourself, Thomas,' said Father, unmoved by the glower of disapproval he had provoked. 'It is only natural that you should seek to defend a fellow Irishman.'

'But why would the Chartists burn a whaling ship? Why destroy the livelihoods of the very men whose rights they claim to be fighting for?' asked Mother.

'I do not pretend to understand the logic behind their actions. Suffice to say our country is in the grip of a conspiracy designed to bring about chaos. The Chartists for their part, are merely pawns deployed by a far more formidable enemy.'

'And who do you believe is behind this conspiracy?' I ventured.

'The French, obviously. We humiliated them on the battlefield, so now they try to destroy us from within. They have gifted

Scott O'Neill

us a Trojan horse with a belly stuffed full of revolutionaries.'

'Nonsense!' Tam snatched the decanter from Father's hand and tipped the neck to his glass. 'The ship's owners sank her for the insurance.' He despatched another mouthful of whisky, wiped his mouth then added hotly, 'And what does it matter, the who or the why? The *Majestic North* now lies in the mud, I am without work and soon we'll be without a home. May whoever did this rot in hell.'

'Without a home?' I said, feeling the cold, slithery grip of shame.

'Mrs Jameson has heard of my misfortune and fears I will no longer be able to pay her rent. We have till week's end to pack our things and move out.'

'How absurd!' cried Mother. 'Ask her to reconsider. Let her know her fears are unfounded. We will cover any shortfall in your rent until you find new employment, won't we, Lachlan?'

'Of course.'

'Thank you, but her mind is set. The old hag has at last found her excuse to be rid of us. Ha! You know what she said? She said I ought to be grateful she ever opened her door to us in the first place – "There's precious few others round here would take in your sort", that's what she said.'

By 'your sort' I knew Mrs Jameson was referring to Catholics.

'But enough of this self-pity!' Tam bellowed, launching suddenly from his chair. 'I shall head to Kirkcaldy! The *Pole Star* is preparing to sail for Spitsbergen. The captain owes me a favour or two. He will gladly make room in his crew for the finest harpooner in the realm!'

'You will not stop killing whales?'

The question escaped my lips with unseemly haste and more than a hint of anger. My efforts had been in vain. The end of the *Majestic North* was not to be the end of the slaughter.

'Killin' whales is what I was built for. It is my God-given

122

purpose in life. And there is always great demand for a man of my undoubted skill.'

Molly threw out her hands in exasperation.

'Because so many of you fail to return! Can you not see? This is a sign. God wants you to stay ashore with us, Pa. Please stay, I beg you.'

Tam gently enfolded her delicate wrists in his meaty paws and stared into her glistening eyes.

'Don't you fret now, dear Molly. The sea and I have an agreement. As long as I pay her the respect she deserves, she'll not harm me.'

'You are a stubborn old fool,' sighed Molly, pulling free to brush aside a tear.

'Stubborn? Aye. A fool? Aye. But old? Surely not,' Tam smiled.

'While your father is away, the three of you will stay with us this time, and leave your Nana be. She's not been feeling too well lately.'

'Thank you, Aunt Bility, but we don't wish to be a burden.'

Grace, who perked up considerably at the prospect of an extended stay at Braid House, prodded an elbow into her older sister for recklessly endangering the offer.

'Don't listen to Molly. We would be no bother, Aunt Bility. We would earn our keep, do all the chores and everything.'

'Would that be acceptable to you, Lachlan? It would be a temporary arrangement, you have my word,' said Tam.

'It would be a pleasure. The girls will breathe some much-needed life into this dusty old house.'

Grace bounded from the settee to wrap Father in a big hug and an even bigger grin. 'Thank you, Uncle!' She dashed to offer the same appreciation to Mother, 'Thank you, Auntie!'

'You are very welcome.'

'What is this? My own daughter cannot wait to see the back of me!' laughed Tam.

'Don't go, Pa! Stay here with us.'

Tam engulfed Grace in his powerful arms and encouraged Molly to join the embrace.

'I'll return soon, I promise. And when I do, I will find us a new home. A much better home!'

The promise did nothing to lift the sadness in Molly's eyes. A sadness which further inflamed the guilt devouring my soul. The same guilt followed me to my room to plague my sleep with fitful visions and nightmares of the most violent nature.

CHAPTER TEN

The Dying Spell

Mother entered my room at dawn to find me in the grip of a fever. Ignoring my protestations, she insisted I remain in bed where, under the warm smothering of blankets, I listened to the crack of the reins as Mr Maybury carted everyone off for Coatfield Lane to collect the Keane family's belongings and onwards to South Queensferry, where they planned to see Uncle Tam safely on his way across the Forth.

I must admit, I was heartily relieved to have been excused the trip, as I would not have been able to meet Tam or Molly in the eye for fear they would instinctively recognise the man who had put a torch to their futures.

And all for nothing!

The sickness continuously announced itself in new and ever more inventive ways. The most immediate manifested itself in an excruciating burrowing sensation as though an army of worms were methodically tunnelling through every bone in my body, excavating the soft tubes of marrow and replacing them with rods of stone. My obscenely weighty bones refused all attempts to hoist them out of the bed. I soon tired of the battle and opted to remain horizontal. Indeed, the longer I lay there, the more appealing became the idea of surrendering myself completely to a permanent state of inertia.

Why move?

At all?

Ever?

To remain fixed and still, what could be better?

I summoned the minimum volition required to raise both hands in front of my face. I picked the crusting of hardened sap from the fingertips. Underneath I discovered the nails already reformed, but they were not the familiar clear and flexible structures of old. A set of ten rigid plates of a polished chestnut colour had taken their place. I buried the offensive articles under the counterpane and stared at the pendant hanging from the ceiling.

Something twitched inside the bowl. A moth, its wings beating a rhythm of circling distress against the frosted glass.

The insect climbed to the lip of its cage, where it waited, wings opening and closing as it pondered its next move. The moth fluttered down and settled on the corner of the pillow. It was unlike any species of Lepidoptera I had ever seen. The wings were separated into four stained-glass panes of twilight blue, set in frames of black with the shape of a brilliant white crescent moon at the centre of each. This was far too exotic a creature to be a Lothian native. It most probably arrived as a stowaway amongst the Chinese ferns. I reached out and very gently cajoled the moth aboard my hand. Its prodigious tongue unwound to probe the faint pits and scars left by the chestnut. Examinations concluded, it flew off towards the fireplace and disappeared up the flue. Inspired by the moth's decisive action, I dragged myself from the cocoon of my bed and dressed quickly. There had to be an answer, an antidote to the sickness hidden somewhere in the pages of Father's books.

Arriving downstairs, I had the strangest impression that the timbers of the old house were whispering to me. From every shadow came the same urgent demand:

Hurry!

As I entered Father's study, the sickness conjured a strange sensation within me. A small, distant feeling of desolation. Of something slowly falling into an abyss.

A pair of portraits claimed pride of place above the mantelshelf. A man and a woman. Hitherto, the knowledge that this diptych represented my mother and father was as obvious to me as my own name. However, standing there staring at their features, I had to consciously remind myself that these individuals were indeed my parents. Bility Ware and Lachlan Ware. My mother and father. Side by side. In separate frames. Together. Yet apart.

Disconnected.

The sickness had taken a blade to the cords of empathy that bound me to family, to home, to everything I had thought unbreakable and was now slowly cutting them apart.

Hurry! Hurry! ...

I turned to the vast bank of apothecary drawers. One of them simply had to contain the key to unlock and reverse the Witch McKay's nefarious spell. But which one? There were so many samples. So many powders, cuttings, roots, seeds, extracts, resins, bulbs, spores and pollens stored in the collection, it was impossible to know where to start. More research was required, but a quick glance at the hopelessly overburdened bookcases revealed the truly daunting nature of the task.

To make matters worse, there was no discernible order or logic to the way Father had chosen to catalogue his life's work. Thousands of handwritten notebooks – balanced precariously in piles so heavy they bowed the shelves upon which they sat into lopsided smiles – nestled alongside published texts boasting obscure and archaic titles on their split spines and bindings rubbed raw with study... *On The Nature of Hermaphrospores, The Anatomy of Moonwilt, Holbert's Guide to Woodland Anomalies, Lingua Arboribus...* These were a few of the more intriguing examples to catch my eye.

Then, as I continued to circle the haphazard library in increasing exasperation, my fingers inadvertently brushed a set of notebooks bound in burgundy calfskin and I was suddenly infused with an unnatural warmth. I instinctively gathered them up and transported *Plants & The Human Body: Vols I–IV* to Father's desk.

As I held the pages of Volume I, wave upon horribly familiar wave of vicarious sufferings fell upon the shores of my imagination. First came the young animal restrained and terrified at its moment of slaughter, whose own covering had been removed and transplanted to bind the book I now held. And as I leafed through a succession of chapters with headings such as *Hallucinogens, Toxins, Medicinal Benefits, Temporal Confusion, Transformative Effects*, the paper itself interrupted the calf in order to convey the pain and wastefulness employed in its own manufacture. This anguish flowed outwards to encompass first the floorboards under my feet, then upwards through the beams and supports which formed the very bones of Braid House. A skeleton of trees torn from ancient woodlands to be chopped, split, planed and varnished.

Within this wretched ossuary I detected the presence of life. Woodlice scurrying through gaps in the skirting. A family of mice nesting in the attic. A bristletail dining on a flake of skin. And the jasmines in their pots, the petals turned to embrace the squares of sunlight held in the misted windows.

Hurry!

The mantel clock chimed. They would be home soon. I had an hour, perhaps two. I skimmed the remaining volumes of *Plants & the Human Body* with decreasing optimism. Not a single recorded incident of a parasitical chestnut did they contain, let alone a potential cure.

I closed the fourth and final volume with a dull, petulant slap and was halfway towards slamming it down on top of its equally unhelpful companions when I noticed something protruding from the gap separating the pages from the spine. I carefully teased the tightly folded slip of paper from the hole and laid it flat upon the desk:

Archibald Finlayson Esq.
Bookseller & Linguist
90 West Bow
Edinburgh.

September 14th, 1828.

For the translation of the Witch McKay's dying spell from the original Gaelic into English – the sum of two shillings received from Mr Lachlan Ware of Braid House with much gratitude.

A charge of excitement shot through me as I read the florid, sweeping strokes of Finlayson's handwriting. A quick calculation confirmed that I was a mere six years of age when he had composed the receipt. The age Father first introduced me to the Witch Tree and the legend of the last chestnut. Fragments of all the conversations I'd had with my father regarding the tree returned to gather in my mind like leaves caught in a stiff October breeze, spinning and rising in a flurry of suspicion. Year after year, he had taken me to the resting place of the Witch McKay and encouraged – no, *dared* me to try and catch that last chestnut of the season. I always assumed his motivation to be the benign teasing of a father wishing to test his son's gullibility, but the note in my hand suggested a deeper purpose to his games and that he knew a great deal more about the legend than the scant details he had deigned to share with me.

A re-examination of the gap behind the spine of *Plants & The Human Body: Vol I* revealed nothing. However, Volumes II and III had secreted within them, two further documents.

Unable to retrieve them with my fingers, I quickly raided the cabinet containing the delicate instruments Father used for the dissection of seeds and capitula.

Using a pair of tweezers, I plucked the inclusions free and placed them on the desk beside the receipt. The first document comprised a single tatty sheet of quarto, much yellowed with age and splitting at the time-worn folds. Two verses written in what I recognised to be Gaelic (though I did not speak the language myself) occupied one side of the mould-speckled leaf. The lines were arranged in a messy, sloping fashion to the point of near illegibility. Save for a small crudely drawn and much faded symbol, the reverse was blank.

The second document also boasted two verses, this time in English and composed in the same assured hand as the receipt. The paper, when compared to its Gaelic counterpart, was evidently not of the same great age.

The verses ran thus:

Murderers of mine!
Heed this promise
From this dust I shall rise
And my dust become bone
And my bone become wood
From these branches will grow
The seed of my magic
And with Nature's justice
Thine actions I shall judge

For whomsoever will catch
My last autumn fruit
Before it enters the dirt
Shall taste my power
And with the blessing of the sun
The moon and earth

I curse to see as I see
A world of death
For you murderers of mine!

At the sound of hooves and wheels on the driveway, I returned the books to the chaotic shelves and dashed to my room. The discoveries safely tucked inside my pillow, I climbed into bed and listened to the animated voices of my parents and cousins entering the house. There was much huffing and puffing as everyone made their way up the stairs, hauling bags and trunks laden with belongings.

Grace's breathless enthusiasm filled the hallway beyond my door.

'Can I have this room? Please, may I have this room?... Thank you, Auntie Bility!'

The commotion travelled onwards. Doors opened. Doors closed. Muffled laughter and creaking floorboards. My weary eyes settled on the snow bustling at the panes and drifted off between the crystals towards the welcoming embrace of sleep.

*

'Hello, sleepyhead. I'm so pleased I haven't been given the room next to yours. You snore even worse than Pa.'

'What time is it?' I yawned, sitting up. The snow at the windows had been replaced by the solid black of night. A fire blazed in the grate and the room candles had been lit.

'A little after seven,' said Molly, seated by the hearth with a book upon her lap. 'Your mother did call on you to ask if you wanted to join us for supper but thought it best to let you sleep. There is still plenty of chicken broth left. Would you like me to fetch you some?'

'I'm not hungry. But thank you.'

My famished stomach grumbled at the lie, and the heady flavour of the soil I devoured at the hollow returned to taunt my salivating mouth.

'Do I really snore?'

'Like thunder,' she smiled. 'How are you feeling? Any better?'

'A little,' I said.

'Jojo, I know you're hiding something. I can tell.'

'I'm not hiding anything.'

Molly leaned forward in her chair.

'I don't believe you. You've been behaving very strangely ever since our trip to the Witch Tree. Don't think I've forgotten your funny turn that morning at breakfast. Something happened, didn't it? Something to do with the chestnut.'

The fire slipped and crackled. The rising smoke whispered memories from aeons past where outlines of huge and magnificent creatures wandered between forests of vast, towering trees. The moon moth reappeared from the flue and hid itself on the underside of the mantelpiece.

'Yes.'

'I knew it!' cried Molly. She perched excitedly on the edge of the bed. 'Tell me everything. Did something magical happen? You must tell me!'

And so I relented and told her all that had occurred since she left my room that fateful night to tend to her crying sister, excluding of course, my involvement in the fate of the *Majestic North*. She listened open-mouthed as I described how the chestnut had entered my flesh, its tendrils pushing, sliding and twisting between the bones and organs. I told of my return to the Witch Tree and how I'd devoured handfuls of dirt and pushed my fingers into the ground, where through dreams and visions, Nature herself shared all the beauty and wonder of her realms, allowing me to fly over the highest mountains and sink to the depths of the oceans, escorted everywhere by the joys and tribulations of her creatures.

Molly gasped when I recounted the tale of the pig in the

slaughterhouse. Her horror turned to disbelief at the description of the loathsome roots growing from my fingertips and the torture I endured in biting them off. My narrative, it seemed, had reached the limit of her credulity.

'Your stories are almost as far-fetched as Uncle Lachlan's,' she laughed.

Her amusement promptly vanished when I held out my hands and angled them towards the candlelight to give her a better view of the little pearlescent buds, perhaps no more than an inch in length, coiling from the ends of every finger.

'My God!' she cried. 'But how? How is it possible? Do they hurt?'

'I can cope with the pain. It's the death! This never-ending death. I sense it everywhere. In the very fabric of this house. I touch this bedpost and I feel every blow of the axe and hear every scream of the tree. I touch the leather of my boot and I feel the blade at the cow's throat. And I see the floor covered in its blood. I feel the tug of its skin as its flayed from its body. The ghosts are everywhere, Molly! I cannot escape them. They hound me even as I sleep! And all I want to do is sleep. Sleep until they all fall silent. But they never do. Do you understand? They never do!'

Visibly shocked by the violence of my fevered agitation, Molly headed for the door. I grasped her by the arm before she could turn the handle.

'Where are you going?'

'You've been poisoned, Jojo. Let me fetch Uncle Lachlan. He'll know what to do.'

'Please, Molly. You mustn't. This is not poison. This is witchcraft! Here, see for yourself.'

I removed the papers from the pillow and handed them to her. Molly consented to sit and read. When she finished, she raised her astonished eyes to mine.

'Where did you find these?'

'They were hidden in the spines of my father's notebooks. But do you not see? You are holding the Witch McKay's spell. The curse of the Witch Tree. It's all true!'

Molly turned suddenly very pale as she gazed nervously at the words in her hands.

'You should put them back, Jojo. As soon as you can.'

'Promise me you won't tell my parents anything about this.'

'Why?' she said, her voice as pained as her expression. 'They need to know what's happening to you.'

'And they shall. But not yet. There is someone else I must speak to first.'

CHAPTER ELEVEN

Mr Archibald Finlayson Esq.

All attempts to dissuade Molly from accompanying me on my quest had foundered against a wall of stubbornness; 'I'm going to help you, Jojo, whether you like it or not!' And so together we arrived at the apex of the West Bow's sweeping incline, where the bright red façade of Number Ninety cast a pink blush upon the snow. Above the shop's generous windows, printed in a crisp white script, came the confirmation we had been searching for:

Mr. Archibald Finlayson Esq. – Bookseller & Linguist.

After a brief overview of the books on display – a singularly dull collection of academic texts notable only for their great age and heft – we pushed our way inside.

A little bell tinkled over the door as we entered, but there was no one in attendance to greet us and we were left alone to browse a series of bookcases as orderly and meticulously maintained as those to be found in any academic library. The shop was divided into neatly arranged sections covering a variety of scholarly interests, including *Comparative Philology*, *Classical Languages* and *Antiquarian Texts*. The dryness of the subject matter effectively killed any desire to investigate further, but then, as if seeking to make a final outlandish attempt to maintain our interest, the bookcase labelled *Etymology & Linguistics* suddenly swept outwards and a man appeared.

'Ah! I apologise for my absence. I trust you have found something to your liking?'

His was a beaming, rotund face, clean shaven aside from a straggly caterpillar of a moustache. A blue felt hat, the brim spotted in several places with drips of tallow, sat atop an equally uncultivated thatch. As the lines crimping his forehead betrayed the advancement of years, so his sparkling eyes contained a youthful zest which, in addition to an infectiously enthusiastic demeanour, made him an instantly likeable fellow.

'Are you Mr Archibald Finlayson?' asked Molly.

The man bowed. 'I am indeed. And how may I be of service? Are you both collectors? You'll find my prices are most reasonable.'

'My name is Molly Keane. This is my cousin, Joseph Ware. We were hoping you may be able to provide us with some advice.'

'I shall certainly endeavour to meet your needs. What is the nature of your enquiry?'

'Do you remember these?' I asked, handing the bookseller both variations of the spell along with the receipt for his services.

Finlayson unfolded a pair of half-moon spectacles from his breast pocket, nestled them on his nose and concentrated on the papers.

'The Witch McKay's dying spell,' he muttered, a small frown furrowing his brow, 'Lachlan Ware...' He peered over his spectacles and regarded me closely. 'You are the son of Bility and Lachlan Ware? Authors of the *Botanica Fantastica* books?'

'I am.'

'Interesting,' he mused. 'The answer to your question is, yes. It was a long time ago, but I do remember performing this little commission on behalf of your father. The Celtic languages are a speciality of mine. And I am, it is not unreasonable to say, something of an authority on the life of Margaret McKay.'

'Do you believe she was a genuine witch with magical powers?'

'Why do you ask?'

I removed my gloves and held out my hands, fully expecting Finlayson to recoil in horror. Instead, I was hurriedly invited to take a seat while he scurried off in search of a magnifying glass. When he returned, he studied the shoots curling from my fingertips and the indentations on my palm in minute detail, treating each in turn like an intricate piece of jewellery. Finlayson next raised the glass to peer into my eyes, then into my ears before moving upwards to part my hair and examine the roots.

'Open wide,' he said, keen now to explore the interior of my mouth. I obliged and much to Molly's amusement he set about tapping my teeth and prodding my tongue. Satisfied he'd gleaned all he could, Finlayson stepped back and viewed me with an expression of sombre concern.

'You caught the chestnut, yes?'

'Yes.'

A man appeared at the shop window, his face obscured by the hat bowed to the books on display.

'Hmm, follow me,' said Finlayson.

Moving swiftly to discourage any potential interruption, Finlayson locked the door and then, picking up a candle, he ushered us through the secret opening behind the *Etymology & Linguistics* bookcase. Closing the singular doorway behind him, he led us down a set of narrow stone steps to a capacious basement dominated at its centre by a large elliptical table of polished walnut, on which rested a pipe, a generous supply of tobacco, two candlesticks and an inkstand. Our host swept through the room, stoking the grate and lighting a succession of sconces and candelabras festooned with stalactites of wax. The gloom lifted to reveal a wondrously chaotic Aladdin's cave of the macabre. Finlayson threw his arms as wide as his smile.

'Welcome to my little sanctuary from the humdrum world above. This is where I keep my *real* treasures. Please, take a moment to look around. There is much to see.'

There was indeed so much to see that the eye had trouble deciding where to begin. The cellar was in every way as ill-disciplined and wayward as the shop above was scrupulous and bland. Moving forward on a hotchpotch of mismatched and moth-eaten rugs, we were confronted at every turn with glass-fronted display cases filled with a bewildering array of artefacts, ranging from the downright hideous to the impossibly beautiful.

One case housed a myriad of specimen jars containing strange creatures suspended in preserving fluids. Vile-looking worms, their open mouths a circle of sharp little teeth, were placed next to a clutch of twisted embryos of indeterminate species which, in turn, were perched beside a collection of two-headed frogs and a large bell jar containing a human hand severed at the wrist. I opened the glass door and touched the latter...

Through the eyes of a condemned man I glimpsed an angry, baying crowd. A black hood was pulled roughly over his head. His heart thudded in panic at the tightening of the rope. The platform gave way... I pulled my fingers from the jar with a jolt.

Next to the hand there was a shrunken head, the lips and eyelids sewn shut, its leathery dark skin cracked and flaking.

I thought it wise not to touch this exhibit.

In the farthest corner stood another cabinet crammed to the gunnels with yet more bizarre curios; bundles of bound chicken feet, sprigs of white heather, crudely carved wooden goblets and a variety of animal skulls, including one apparently human specimen disfigured by the most alarming growths. All of these were interspersed with a great many bottles and jars containing, as evidenced by the handwritten labels, the most extraordinary ingredients; *Powdered Puffin Beaks, Essence of Nightjar Blood, Dried Starfish Hearts, Devil-bone, Salted Owl Eyes, Hangman's Rope Fibres, Witch Ash, Mermaid Scales, Consecrated Burying Soil...*

Overseeing these dubious treasure chests, a parade of bookcases lined the walls from skirting to coving, their shelves groaning under the weight of their blasphemous cargo. A library prodigiously stocked with all manner of occult texts and ancient grimoires, their spines stamped with an array of fascinating titles: *Witchcraftis Sorsarie and Necromancie, Quietus Est, Studio Incognitarum, The Rosicrucian Bible, Divination: Techniques and Applications, The Collected Witch Trials of Scotland – Vol VIII: 1600–1650.*

Hung with the dust of old deaths, the air tasted of slow decay. Each mote I inhaled came with a quiet cry of injustice. Ignoring this choir of misery, I concentrated on a collection of intricate talismans, amulets and rune stones, all decorated in a glittering profusion of elaborate, if profane, iconography. Molly lifted out one of the objects. A tiny coffin of larch wood nestled comfortably in her cupped hand. The lid was adorned with a metal plaque no larger than Molly's thumbnail. Though worn with age and rust, the suggestion of a shape remained upon its surface. A bird of some sort, its wings spread. Molly opened the lid and inside there lay a miniature wooden doll smartly attired in a cotton suit of blue and white plaid. The eyes of the diminutive corpse – white ovals with black dots at their centres – were wide open above a straight mouth.

'Ah! Beautiful are they not? Please, feel free to peruse the others,' smiled Finlayson, encouraging us to admire the little coffin's equally fascinating companions. 'They are remarkable. Such detail. I am so fortunate to have them in my possession at last. I cannot tell you the lengths it took to persuade Wishart to part with them. The cantankerous old fart! Four years he's had them squirrelled away in his paltry little museum. Four years! Do you know how much he paid those lads who found them on the Crags? Tuppence! The man is a swindler!' This last he emphasised with a raised fist. 'Suffice to say his pockets are weighed down with decidedly more than a tuppence now, I assure you. Come, let us sit.

'Did you know you are now in the very room where Major Thomas Weir and his wife once practised their demonic incantations? They were conjurers, meddlers in the darkest of magics. Many of these items once belonged to Major Weir. But he was a clumsy sort. And a drinker to boot. He ended his days swinging from the end of a gibbet. He haunts this cellar still, but I pay him no heed.'

Molly and I swapped a fearful glance. I looked into the shadowy recesses, half expecting to encounter some fiendish apparition.

'Now then, Joseph,' continued Finlayson, 'tell me precisely how you came to find yourself in this unfortunate predicament.'

I proceeded to tell my sorry tale mainly to the bookseller's back, for no sooner had I begun than Finlayson swept from his chair to harry back and forth across his extensive library, eyes rapidly scanning the shelves, hand poised to snatch his prey like a heron's beak preparing to skewer a fish.

He acknowledged the more pertinent points surrounding the parasitic chestnut, the craving to devour soil and the vicarious suffering I endured from every dead thing I touched, with the occasional murmur of understanding or sympathy. Happy he had all the books he needed tucked under his arm, Finlayson returned to the table and listened attentively as I concluded my story with the discovery of the documents hidden in Father's notebooks.

'I apologise for the discomfort the creation of this table, these chairs and all these books present to you, Joseph. I only hope you may find the strength to push those unpleasant

horrors aside for the duration of our meeting. You have certainly made a wise move in seeking me out. All may not yet be
lost,' he smiled.

My heart leapt at this small crumb of comfort.

'You believe there is hope?' I cried with unabashed relief.

'I do.'

Finlayson laid the McKay spell, its translation and the
receipt upon the table, then opened one of his books: *A History
of Arboreal Magic*.

'May I say before we continue, that I am a great admirer
of your parents, Mr Ware. I own every volume of *Botanica
Fantastica* and I am very much looking forward to the next.
They provide an invaluable resource to anyone with even
the remotest interest in the wonders of the plant world and
are rightly lauded for discovering and promoting its many
applications in the disciplines of science and medicine. That
being said, it is undoubtedly witchcraft that concerns us in this
instance.'

'How can you be so certain?' said Molly. 'Why not disease
or some kind of poison?'

Finlayson passed his magnifier to Molly and opened my
hand for inspection.

'Take a look for yourself. Pay particular attention to the
cuticles. This is very skilled work. Magic of the highest order.
I very much doubt there has ever been a finer application of
the *Ossa Lignum* curse. There were and are very few witches
capable of utilising the power of nature in such a delicate
manner. This is undoubtedly the work of Margaret McKay.'

'*Are*? You said there were and *are* witches capable of this.
You mean to say witches still exist?' said Molly, astonished.

'Why wouldn't they?' said Finlayson even more astounded
by the notion that there could be a world *without* witches.
'Centuries of persecution has, to our nation's great shame,
decimated their number, but happily there are a precious few

who live among us still, though none so great as Margaret McKay. How cruelly she was treated when all she deserved was our reverence and gratitude.'

'You will understand if I do not share your sentiment,' I said.

Finlayson reached for his pipe, filled the bowl with two pinches and borrowed the flame from the nearest candle.

'I do indeed,' he puffed. 'Though in time, when you are furnished with all the facts, I trust that may change.'

'How did Uncle Lachlan come to be in possession of the spell?' asked Molly.

'I believe he said it was bequeathed to him by his father. Part of a collection of similar documents, if I remember correctly. Sadly at my age there can be no guarantee of that! But not being a speaker of Gaelic, Mr Ware was unable to interpret the text.' Finlayson tapped the faded receipt. 'Hence my involvement. It is not every day one encounters something as extraordinary as this.'

'You say the Witch McKay was treated cruelly? What happened to her? What made her cast this horrible spell? How did she create the Witch Tree?'

'Never mind all that!' I snapped, annoyed by Molly's failure to ask the one question that truly mattered. 'Can the spell be reversed?'

Mr Finlayson smiled ruefully in the face of this inquisition. A slow cloud of grey blue smoke emerged from his lips as he gathered his thoughts. He turned the pages of *A History of Arboreal Magic* and drew our attention to a graphic illustration of a woman dangling by a rope from the bough of a tree while six men, one of whom appeared to be recording events with paper and quill, stood and watched. According to the woodcut's title, the men were witnessing:

The Hanging of the Witch McKay.

'The world is at a crossroads,' said Finlayson. 'A dangerous metamorphosis is underway which is set to encompass all the lands of the earth. Margaret McKay knew this and feared the path Man had chosen to pursue. In keeping with her beliefs, she advocated strongly that Science and Nature must work together, hand in hand, for the mutual benefit of all. But such is the way of Man, we have made it our mission to trample Nature under the wheels of our progress. Greed has no sympathy for reason.'

Molly glared in disgust at the disturbing image. 'Six men against one woman. They look so proud of themselves! Who are these cowards?'

In reply, Finlayson opened a drawer, collected a piece of charcoal and approached the one section of the cellar wall that remained unoccupied, where he proceeded to draw a strange symbol on the limewashed stone; a simple cruciform, scored through with a series of short horizontal lines.

'They call themselves Gladius Dei – the Sword of God. An elite society of witch-finders formed in the wake of the Scottish Witchcraft Act of June 1563. They were ruthlessly efficient. Hundreds died at their hand. Thousands more tortured. Not a single one deserving of their fate. The sole aim of Gladius Dei was to eradicate every last trace of Witchcraft in Scotland. And they very nearly succeeded. Some scholars believe the society to have disbanded in the early part of the eighteenth century. Others, and I include myself in their number, know only too well that Gladius Dei continue to pursue their nefarious objective to this very day. This is their mark – the sword and Jacob's Ladder combined.'

He returned to his seat to indicate the faint mark on the reverse of the original Gaelic copy of the spell. 'You see it again here. Much faded, I admit. But then this innocuous-looking note is of a very great age. Indeed, it was drafted the very day Margaret McKay was murdered.'

'How can you possibly tell?'

Unfazed by Molly's scepticism, Finlayson paused to indulge his pipe. 'It was a simple enough matter. When Lachlan Ware first presented the document to me, I made a thorough study of the handwriting. It was written by this fellow –' he pointed to the figure depicted in the woodcut holding the quill and paper – 'none other than Sir Malcolm Slater, secretary to King James VI. I have in my collection several writs and warrants relating to various witch trials written and signed by Slater. He, along with the other five men here present at McKay's burning, represent the original High Council of Gladius Dei. To have such a distinguished assembly bear witness to her death was a singular, if dubious honour. No one else was permitted to attend.'

'Why?' asked Molly.

'Because they believed her to be – and they were quite correct in their assumption – the most powerful witch in Scotland. In those days, it was common practice for witches to be executed at the Grassmarket gallows for the whole of Edinburgh to witness. But not McKay. These pages will shed further light on the matter.'

Finlayson selected another book from the pile...

The Royal Commission of Witchcraft & Daemonologie 1567.

'Let me turn to the index... Ah! Yes, here we are: The Braid Woods Execution.' He skiffed through the pages to find the corresponding chapter. 'December the tenth. Report of Malcolm Slater which states: Miss Margaret McKay, being seven and thirty years of age and without husband or child, who resides at Livingstoun's Close and who has been adjudged to be a practitioner of witchcraft through the legally established methods...'

Finlayson looked up from his book briefly.

'By which he means the preposterous methods of dunking and bodkin pricking.' Then, returning to Slater's report: '...

was taken into the custody of His Majesty's most obedient servants, the High Council, where she appeared before us in closed session. Sir William Ross examined the accused and discovered upon her scalp, the Devil's Mark. When asked for an explanation, the accused had none. When asked to explain the ungodly number of deaths her neighbours suffered at the hands of the pox whilst she herself remained unharmed, again, she could not. When confronted with the testimony of her gaolers, all men of good and trustworthy character, that Margaret McKay did bewitch them into the most bestial and foul forms of copulation in an attempt to facilitate her escape; again the accused offered no explanation. Despite the evidence gathered against her, the accused repeatedly denied all wrongdoing.

'The High Council in its infinite wisdom, afforded the accused every opportunity to confess and to repent. However, the accused remained silent and dismissed our benevolence with contempt and in so doing denied to us the merciful sentence we sought to pass. It is the firm belief of the High Council that the accused has made several attempts to place a hex on our lawful endeavours. We have each suffered instances of unnatural illness and fever, but by the strength of God we have overcome the evils of her witchcraft and fulfilled our lawful obligations. After four days of fair and rigorous examination of the facts, the court has ruled Margaret McKay to be the most profane instrument of the Devil we have yet encountered. Therefore, Margaret McKay shall not be executed in the usual manner and place lest she cast a final evil cantrip upon the crowd and fill their heads with violent hysteria. The witch shall be removed from the city and hanged and her corpse burned, then buried. And there shall be no stone nor any mark to dignify her grave. This sentence will cleanse the world of her evil for all eternity.'

Finlayson's impassioned eyes sparkled in the candlelight.

'Swines!' he cried. 'In summary, these cowardly monsters dragged this poor defenceless woman from her home, subjected her to the most sickening torture, performed what can only be described as a pathetic mockery of a trial and then, with the verdict predetermined, they threw a hood of sackcloth over her head and transported her to Braid Woods with no shoes and nary a stitch of clothing to protect her from the bite of the midwinter air!' Finlayson pushed his spectacles back up the bridge of his nose and turned the page. 'Ah! And here we arrive at the conclusion of Slater's infuriating report:

'As decreed by the High Council, the witch Margaret McKay was taken to a wood far from innocent eyes, where a tree was chosen for her gallows and the rope prepared. The witch was bound and her hood removed. Sir William Ross appealed to Margaret McKay to confess and so place herself at the mercy of the Almighty. The witch replied with a terrible scream. It was the scream of an animal! The scream of a demon! A scream to tremble the earth under our boots and shake the trees above our heads. She opened her mouth to the sky, and into it fell a chestnut which she swallowed whole. The witch wept tears of blood and from her mouth she spilled a yellow bile upon the earth. Using the Highland tongue, Margaret McKay did summon her master. And with the Devil's voice she did cast an incantation. At Sir William's command the rope was pulled and the heretic did rise off the ground and did hang in the air. And with eyes of blood, she smiled. Smiled at her executioners! And with her dying breath she did conclude her spell. The body we burned and buried in the hollow and with our Bibles held aloft, we thrice recited the Lord's Prayer and gave thanks to Him for choosing us to perform His duty.'

Finlayson's spectacles had slipped again. He nudged them back to meet his blazing eyes and closed the book with an angry thud.

'Scoundrels to a man! *High Council*? Never has such a

loathsome cabal of rogues been so misnamed. For High Council read *Lowest Order*, for that is what they are! Men of the lowest calibre with no respect for women, Nature or Magic. And Sir William Ross? Pah! He ranks as the lowest snake of them all. As Royal Physician to the House of Stuart, he had power and influence and was by no means reticent in using those qualities to satisfy his sadistic desires. My old heart aches for Margaret McKay and for all those murdered at the hands of these soulless tyrants. McKay marched at the side of the angels. She devoted her life and her magic to help those unable to help themselves. She believed the spirit of creation resides in every one of us. We are all Nature's children. We are all of us, hewn from the same clay. She believed it is our duty to treat everyone as our brothers and sisters for, in the eyes of Nature, that is precisely what they are. Margaret McKay believed it was incumbent upon us all to resist the temptation to divide ourselves into tribes or to spread baseless fears founded upon superficial differences. Sadly, there are many in this world who pocket a healthy profit from division. Division breeds hate. Hate breeds conflict. And with conflict comes opportunity. And so these men actively sow the seeds of division and grow fat on the harvest. Magic has no place in their world. This was why they murdered Margaret McKay. This was her reward for a lifetime of charity and love. This! Hanged, then desecrated for the sneering pleasure of men who cherish money and status above all else!'

The old bookseller ended his tirade red-faced and perspiring with righteous anger. He soothed himself with a long puff on his pipe. It was impossible not to be moved by the strength of his passion.

'Mr Finlayson, I too feel some sympathy for Margaret McKay but I fail to understand why I should be punished for the actions of others? Why am I to suffer for the crimes of these men?'

Finlayson lifted the rumpled scrawl of Gaelic from the table and read aloud:

Murderers of mine!
Heed this promise
From this dust I shall rise
And my dust become bone
And my bone become wood
From these branches will grow
The seed of my magic
And with Nature's justice
Thine actions I shall judge

For whomsoever will catch
My last autumn fruit
Before it enters the dirt
Shall taste my power
And with the blessing of the sun
The moon and earth
I curse to see as I see
A world of death
For you murderers of mine!

'Her motive is simple,' said Finlayson. 'She desires retribution. It matters not who caught the chestnut. I believe at the moment of her death she believed all mankind to be complicit in her demise. And who can blame her? For all her kindnesses to be rewarded with the noose, then ploughed into the dirt and forgotten? This spell is a cry of fury. And you are the unwitting recipient of that fury. You are the vessel through which she can share her pain. Share the injustice. And we must remember, it is not simply the words that create a spell. The witch's thoughts and feelings at the moment of inception are equally essential to the spell's potency.'

He tapped the cover of *The Royal Commission of Witch-craft & Daemonologie 1597*:

'*She opened her mouth to the sky, and into it fell a chestnut which she swallowed whole. The screaming stopped and the witch wept tears of blood and from her mouth she spilled a yellow bile upon the earth.* Here we have the precise moment of inception. The moment Margaret McKay summoned not the Devil, but Nature herself, and asked her to create new life from the dust of her mortal remains. What we now call the Witch Tree began to grow the moment her tormentors departed Braid Woods. A tree borne from a union of Nature and Magic waiting patiently to fulfil its purpose and curse one unlucky soul – *To see as I see, a world of death*.'

Finlayson returned the spell to my care.

'I have dedicated my entire life to the study of witchcraft and in all those years I have discovered not more than four written accounts of the Ossa Lignum curse. Never in my wildest imaginings did I foresee that one day I would bear witness to its effects first-hand. This is truly astonishing.'

'Ossa Lignum?' said Molly, staring in puzzlement at the spell.

'It is an extremely rare arboreal interpretation of the Maledicti Mutatio. A hex used to transform one creature into another. What is happening to Joseph is subtle, painstaking and, dare I say, quite beautiful in its way. He craves sunlight, fertile soil and water. In time his skin will become bark, his veins will run with sap, his arms and legs will spread roots and branches. And his bones will turn to wood. As a caterpillar becomes a butterfly, so you, Joseph, are becoming a tree.'

I laid my hands upon the table and spread the fingers. The sight of them sickened my heart.

'Mr Finlayson, there is nothing remotely beautiful about what is happening to me. I have listened to you with a great deal of patience. And I trust that you will understand I have not come here to astonish you, or to fascinate you, or to entertain you in any way. I have come here in the hope that you may be able to help. So, I will ask you one more time before I take my leave. Is there a counter spell?'

Mr Archibald Finlayson, leaned back in his chair and drew at length from his pipe.

'My dear Joseph,' he said. 'There is always a counter spell.'

CHAPTER TWELVE

The Lothian Witches

Thinking it important I familiarise myself with the woman whose magic continued to weave its diabolical threads through every facet of my being, Finlayson had presented me with a book bound in leather, its cover decorated in jade green marbling:

The Lothian Witches by Studley R. Knapp.

'A pseudonym for my humble and, I hope, informative biography of the most gifted practitioner of the art of witchcraft ever to have graced our country. Not many people purchased it, I'm afraid,' he sighed. Finlayson then bade us farewell with a promise to dedicate his every waking hour in the search for a counter spell. 'Do not despair, Joseph. The cure for the Maledicti Mutatio is at hand. Seek and ye shall find!'

And so I departed Finlayson's shop with an unexpected spark of hope in my heart, a spark Molly's scepticism seemed determined to douse.

'I don't trust him.'

'Why not?'

'Did you not see his collection of scrimshaws? They were in the cabinet next to the little coffins. Very much like those I sell for Pa, except Finlayson had them labelled as dragons' teeth!'

Molly and I were seated inside The White Hart, watching

the ebb and flow of the Grassmarket. The snow falling heavily from a sky of sour milk, failed to dampen the buoyant mood of the men unloading their carts outside the stables of Messrs Reid & Gleghorn. Faces flushed pink with the bitter cold, they exchanged a volley of foul-mouthed raillery with their counterparts at the neighbouring victual dealers of Young & Co.

'If he believes them to be dragon's teeth, then where's the harm?' I said with some dismay.

'If he believes them to be dragons' teeth, then he's a fool. Which makes us even bigger fools for believing anything the man says. And as for all this Maledicti Mutatio nonsense? I swear it's not tobacco he smokes in that pipe of his.'

My cousin, I noticed with some discomfort, had attracted the lascivious attention of one member of an impromptu choir of drunken cabbies singing raucously at the bar. The revellers were stoically ignored by a pair of elderly gentlemen, walking sticks hooked over the backs of their chairs, occupying a table close to the roaring fire. Their faces were pursed in such concentration on the chessboard under their noses, it would not have come as any great surprise to learn that the old adversaries had been sat in the very same spot, pondering the very same move for decades. A grizzled wolfhound yawned at the chess players' feet, rested its muzzle upon its paws and went back to the exhausting business of sleep.

The warm scent rising from the spiced liquor cupped between my gloves invoked fleeting visions of exotic hillsides bathed in glorious sunshine, where fingers plucked ripe grapes much to the irritation of their parent vines. A chatter of sorrow soon brushed aside this relative heaven. The ghosts of the table, chair and floor, blackened with age and smoothed with use, each giving voice to their own history of woe.

'I don't like the way some of these men are staring at you.'

Molly reminded me of the small but lethal blade concealed

inside her brooch.

'Let them stare.'

She sipped her mulled wine and opened *The Lothian Witches,* skipping to the final and lengthiest chapter: *Margaret McKay.*

'Finlayson must think us absurd. I imagine he is sitting in his shop laughing at what easy fools we are.'

'You seem intent on crushing my hopes,' I said, moodily addressing my drink. 'I realise you have plenty of your own problems to deal with, so I would perfectly understand if you'd rather not become further embroiled in mine.'

Molly took my hands and lowered her smile to meet my downcast eyes. 'Don't be upset with me, Jojo. If I seem harsh on Mr Finlayson, it's because I don't want you to place all your faith in him and Mr Studley R. Knapp when we have other options to explore.'

'Such as?'

'Father Slaven for one,' said Molly, brightly.

'A priest?'

'Why not? If this is witchcraft, who better to fight the forces of evil than a man of God?'

'But I am not Catholic.'

'That wouldn't matter to Father Slaven. Our old neighbour, Mrs Dumfries, often tells of how she and other folk have been cured at Father Slaven's hand. Folk who have been possessed by demons and the like. She told me of the time she herself would wake every night to find the Devil himself sitting on her chest with his mouth open, teeth dripping with blood. This went on for many weeks till she begged Father Slaven to come and bless her house. Now she sleeps in perfect peace.'

'Is that what you think this is? Demonic possession?' I asked, fearfully.

'If Margaret McKay's spirit has entered you, then you will need God's help to remove her. We can go now if you'd like?

St Mary's is not so far.'

I had little time to consider Molly's proposal when a shadow fell across our table.

'We meet again, young sir!'

It was Hugh Tulland, the cabinetmaker, beer gripped in one jaunty hand while the other thrust itself towards me. I greeted him with no great enthusiasm in the hope my disdain would dissuade him from further interaction, but it was not to be.

'And who is your charming companion,' he leered.

'My cousin.'

Hugh Tulland swayed on his feet as he digested this barrage of information. Balance restored, he lifted her hand and kissed it.

'It is an absolute pleasure to meet you, cousin of young Mr Ware. My name is Tulland, and I am entirely at your service.'

Molly withdrew her hand sharply before his ale-soaked lips treated themselves to a second helping. Undeterred, our unwelcome guest collected a spare stool from the adjacent table and planted himself between us, though markedly closer to Molly than myself.

'Rough weather, is it not? Will this snow ever end! But I see, Joseph, you are warmed by the wine and the excellent company, eh?' he said with a wink and a nudging elbow. He switched his rheumy gaze to Molly. 'So, you are cousins! Excellent. I have a son. Robert is his name. He and Joseph are the very best of pals. Did you know your aunt purchased an easel from my shop recently? Can you imagine? What an honour! Mrs Bility Ware no less, of the Botastic Fatantics! A true artist. Are you an artist, Joseph Ware's cousin?'

'Sir,' said Molly, a hand rising to her brooch, 'would you please leave us? We were in the middle of a private discussion.'

Tulland's mask of drunken bonhomie slipped. 'A private discussion!' he snorted. 'Concerning what?'

'That is none of your business, Mr Tulland,' I said.

Tulland wagged a slow finger at me. 'There is something not quite right about you, Ware. I cannot quite fathom what it is, but there is something twisted about you. And I'll wager it has something to do with this!' He snatched *The Lothian Witches* from the table and sneered at the cover. 'Reading about daft wee witches and their daft wee spells, are we? Burn them all, I say! Have you ever handled a wand, Miss Joseph Ware's cousin? I fancy those hands of yours are capable of all kinds of magic.'

Enraged by his insolence, I seized the book and pushed him from his stool. The raucous cabbies crowding the bar raised their glasses and cheered in amusement as Hugh Tulland tumbled to the floor, the remnants of his drink splashing his jacket and trousers. The old chess players broke from their hostilities and even the lazy old wolfhound raised an eye to watch the cabinetmaker wobble awkwardly to his feet and turn to address his audience.

'Look at them!' he cried. 'The Grassmarket Witches. Double, double, toil and trouble. I say let's burn the witches! Who's with me?'

The throaty jeers and mocking laughter pursued Molly and me to the door. Once outside, we hastened for Castle Wynd, where I chanced a backwards look and saw Hugh Tulland on the threshold of The White Hart, talking into the ear of a man whose dimensions threatened to engulf the doorway in which they stood. Tulland pointed in our direction. The huge man responded with a firm nod.

*

The cab driver pocketed his fare, wished us goodnight and with a single, sharp snap of his whip, wheeled away from Braid House and melted into the late evening fog. Rarely had I been so pleased to see the eccentrically angled gables and misshapen chimney stacks of home. These features, coupled with the ivy-smothered facades and blankly staring windows, usually engendered a slight sense of foreboding, particularly after dark, but my relief was such that had I been alone, I would gladly have wrapped my arms around its many grotesqueries and greeted the old house shamelessly like a long-lost friend.

After holding Molly to a sacred oath of silence on the subject of our day's adventures, we entered the drawing room to share a pleasant family evening of piano, backgammon and ghostly tales. By the time midnight arrived, everyone had retired for the night and I was left alone to enjoy the comfort of the armchair closest to the hearth. I applied the bellows to a fresh shovelful of coal and with the flames restored to the rudest of health, settled back to read Mr Finlayson's book. For the sake of my fragile sanity, I had by this point become somewhat adept at suppressing those harrowing testimonies contained within the memories of the objects I touched. Through the volume's cover I acknowledged the spectral whisperings of the tree felled, stripped, sliced and pulped to provide its paper before channelling them to the depths of my consciousness to join the baleful tales of a thousand others. I was now free to concentrate solely on the engrossing, if occasionally florid prose of Studley R. Knapp.

The pages of *The Lothian Witches* told the remarkable stories of five extraordinary women: Janet Black, Rhona McPherson, Mary Galbraith, Elizabeth Wilkie (known as Blind Lizzie) and Margaret McKay. These women were members of the same coven. However, as detailed at length by the author in his prologue, the popular notion of a coven – witches huddled tightly together adding pinches of dubious seasoning to a large pot of bubbling eye of newt and toe of frog – was far removed from the mundane reality. Covens were in fact more akin to church dioceses with the witches frequently spread across a large geographical area and coming together perhaps only once or twice a year to discuss matters concerning the principles of magic and to share knowledge and new ideas.

In the storm that followed the passing of the Witchcraft Act of 1563, the Lothian Witches were forced to practise in the utmost secret for fear of persecution. But the world is a cruel place where secrets are bought and sold with little regard for the consequences, and so it was for these prodigiously gifted women when inevitably, they fell into the murderous clutches of Gladius Dei. All that is, except for Blind Lizzie. When the witch-hunters broke down the door of her ramshackle croft overlooking Aberlady Bay, they found it empty save for a raggedy white fox that bolted upon their arrival.

Elizabeth Wilkie was never seen again.

Black, McPherson and Galbraith were hanged together in front of a baying mob of some ten thousand or more at the Grassmarket gallows on the morning of the ninth of December, 1567 in an act described as 'the most brazen example of cowardice ever committed by men against God's own daughters'. Margaret McKay, having been deemed too dangerous for a public execution, was taken to Braid Woods the following day.

The identity of the person responsible for betraying the Lothian Witches to the authorities was not documented in any of the contemporary records, but the book presented a compelling case against one individual in particular:

Charles Ralston-Wark.

Ralston-Wark owned a sprawling estate on the eastern fringe of Bo'ness, where he enjoyed all the customary trappings of a wealthy landowner including a castle with its attendant staff, one of whom was the maid Janet Black.

Finlayson, writing as Studley R. Knapp, described Black as 'a young woman of great beauty and immense charm who captivated the hearts of all who knew her'. To her great misfortune, Janet Black's beauty and charm had enraptured the wizened heart of Ralston-Wark. Janet repeatedly, though always with the greatest politeness and good grace, spurned his unsolicited advances, but the master of the house was a man well used to getting his own way and it did not take long before his frustration and impatience turned to tyranny.

In his blinkered mind Janet's gentle rebukes were an affront to both his manhood and his status. He simply could not fathom why this lowly orphan girl (who would doubtless have spent her life begging for scraps had the late Lady Ralston-Wark not taken pity upon the wretch and granted her a position within the household) did not seize upon his interest and embrace it for what it was: a truly remarkable honour. Charles Ralston-Wark reacted with extreme and petty-minded bitterness to Janet's supposed disrespect. He habitually berated poor Janet in full view of the other servants for the smallest misdemeanour. A poorly polished knife or an unsightly speck of dust upon the furniture were sufficiently criminal to trigger his wrath. He even blamed Janet for things for which she quite obviously had no responsibility. One morning, during his regular after breakfast walk around the grounds, he discovered a chaffinch lying dead under the eaves of the stable. He declared that Janet, as part of her duties, should have cleared the offensive bird from his path and buried it long before the little corpse insulted his poor eyes. An intolerable oversight for which Janet was severely reprimanded and docked half her already meagre wage.

Then, one rain-soaked October night, a terrible fever struck Ralston-Wark and it seemed he must surely die.

Much to her fellow servants' surprise, rather than rejoice at this news, Janet, whose heart was assembled in a manner that refused entry to all but love and affection, took it upon herself to nurse the old man in the hour of his most dire need. For days on end, she traipsed back and forth into the woods to gather wild herbs and mosses. What she did with this unusual harvest no one knew because Janet insisted on treating her patient alone and in secret. The nosy cooks and grooms eavesdropping at Ralston-Wark's bedchamber door were often rewarded with a peculiar grinding sound accompanied by the soft murmur of Janet's voice, though not one word did they ever manage to decipher. Then, after a mere five days under Janet's care the master, to everyone's utter amazement, was back on his feet, enthusiastically remarking to anyone who cared to listen that he had never felt better in all his life!

News of his miraculous recovery prompted further whispers of Janet Black's strange and uncanny abilities. Rumours abounded of her capacity to entice the shyest of woodland creatures to come and feed from the palm of her hand and her preternatural knack for predicting where the fish would run on any given day, a knack utilised for the benefit of the local fishermen, who filled their nets till they were fit to burst.

As a sign of his immense gratitude, Ralston-Wark presented Janet with the one thing he had vowed never to offer another woman in his life. A proposal of marriage. Janet humbly refused. She was, after all, already betrothed to a young blacksmith named Peter Fraser. This latest rejection sent Ralston-Wark into a fearsome rage. How dare she disrespect him so! She had no more right to dismiss his advances than a flea-bitten rat had to dismiss the roar of a noble lion!

Cowering in the corner of her tiny lodgings, Janet watched on helplessly as what few belongings she had were smashed, torn or broken apart. Amidst this shower of destruction, a small wooden box caught Ralston-Wark's attention. Inside he found a flat stone. Grey and sea-worn, it fitted snugly in the cup of his hand. A simple outline of a flower had been etched into the stone's surface. He turned the stone over and found five straight lines neatly scratched on the reverse. Janet begged for its return, but the flint-hearted old tyrant, upon seeing how much it meant to her, decided to keep it for himself.

The significance of the flower and of the lines scratched upon his little trophy eluded Ralston-Wark until it caught the eye of his friend Sir William Ross, who immediately recognised it as a coven-stone. The unfortunate Janet Black was removed to Edinburgh for trial but not before she received the most devastating news. There had been a terrible fire at the smithy. Peter was dead.

The coven-stone together with Janet's full confession (obtained, as one may imagine, under the greatest duress) proved invaluable in condemning Janet and her fellow witches (Blind Lizzie excepted) to their fates. In recognition of his role in what they regarded as a major victory against the forces of darkness, Gladius Dei invited Ralston-Wark to join their number, an invitation he accepted with unrestrained zeal. Janet Black's old master lived on for another three years, a short time perhaps, but time enough to help oversee the most ruthless purge of witchcraft in the history of Scotland.

Janet Black's story both appalled and fascinated in equal measure, but in my eagerness to turn to the most intriguing of all the five witches, I gave undeservingly scant attention to the lives of Rhona McPherson, Mary Galbraith and Elizabeth Wilkie and moved directly to the final chapter:

Margaret McKay.

Chapter Thirteen

Margaret McKay

Being an extract from *The Lothian Witches* by Studley R. Knapp.

*

On the 19th day of June in the Year of Our Lord 1566, the batteries of cannon lining the ramparts of Edinburgh Castle fired in unison to announce the news:

Mary Stuart had given birth to a son!

In olden times the arrival of a future King gave our nation cause to replace the wearied grimace of daily existence with a smile of unbridled joy and celebration. And seen in this light, the impartial observer, unversed in the ever-widening theological schisms tearing at the seams of the nation's loyalties at that time, may quite reasonably have expected every heart in Scotland to unite in jubilation at this most auspicious announcement. Caledonian hearts, however, rarely beat to the same rhythm and the birth of James, Duke of Rothesay, Prince and Great Steward of Scotland, stoked as much in the way of revulsion as exultation.

The infant heir had been born Catholic and when viewed through the expanding prism of Presbyterianism, this was a misfortune that could not be tolerated for long by the rebels plotting to align the Scottish throne with Protestant England.

The wellspring of their patience was approaching exhaustion as a result of the English monarch's infuriatingly arid womb. Inaction was a luxury they could no longer afford.

Mary, Queen of Scots was both an astute and a stubborn woman. A combination as likely to hinder as to benefit. She was acutely aware of the dark whispers bubbling up from the spiralling shadows of the castle's stairwells and the damp black alcoves of its deepest corridors. These feverish murmurings spoke of plots and conspiracies, of poison and 'unfortunate accidents'. For all its grand size and its constant bustle of attendants, soldiers and servants, Edinburgh Castle had become a lonely and oppressive cage for Mary Stuart. And now, when faced with the gloomy prognosis that her newborn son, as pronounced by every surgeon at her disposal, would not survive his first winter, the bars of her enclosure pressed Mary's wings ever more tightly to her sides.

As the nights lengthened and the prince's health steadily declined, Mary, fearing that someone was slowly poisoning the boy, removed herself to her estate in Jedburgh, where she decreed that she and she alone would attend to her son. Yet still the infant slipped inexorably towards oblivion and on Christmas Day, when all hope seemed lost, Mary at last consented to allow a priest to enter their chamber in order to deliver the Last Rites.

Mary, whose own health had suffered terribly as a result of months of debilitating despair, stood tearfully over the cot. Inside was the bairn, swaddled with extra blankets to counter the hard midwinter chill, and his tiny mouth twitched as if it were amused by the priest's prayer. At this bleakest of hours Annabell Murray, the Countess of Mar and Mary Stuart's most loyal ally and friend, of which the Queen had precious few, arrived at Jedburgh in a state of agitation. Apologising profusely, she begged Her Majesty's forgiveness for presuming to act on her behalf without prior instruction, for she had taken it upon herself to invite an old acquaintance to meet her Queen. Someone, Annabell firmly believed, who possessed the power to bring forth the dawn where others saw only the dusk. Mary listened intently as her dear friend espoused the virtues of a healer; a woman who had miraculously pulled Annabell's own sick daughter from the precipice of certain death a dozen years previously.

The priest turned on the Countess with unrestrained contempt:

'To consult with healers is to consult with the Devil himself! Such superstitious heresy has no place in any household, let alone a royal one!'

The Queen responded by ordering the sour-faced clergyman to leave and the healer, who had hitherto been waiting patiently outside, was called to enter.

History has no interest in recording the origins of the poor. The exact circumstances of Margaret McKay's birth and lineage have remained something of a mystery to this day. The daughter of hardworking fisherfolk, she is believed to have been born in Dunbar circa 1530. Beyond these basic scraps nothing is known of her childhood, but this screen of anonymity was to slip away as she entered adolescence, when word of young Margaret's precocious talent for harnessing the abundant remedies of Nature to cure the incurable spread throughout the burgh. Feted and adored by the people of her village, Margaret sought neither reward nor praise for her endeavours. Gaelic being her natural tongue, she also conversed in both English and Latin. In her journal, written at the time of the crisis, the Countess of Mar provides a more detailed account of Margaret McKay's qualities:

'She is erudite and strong-willed. Remarkably so for a woman of her situation. Her dress and shawl are fashioned from scraps of cloth stitched together by her own hand in a patchwork containing all the russet hues of autumn. She wears a simple deerskin hat adorned with the prettiest flowers and herbs. She possesses an intellect to rival any properly educated man I have ever met. She is both kind and courteous, pays no heed to a person's station be they nobleman or peasant – both are afforded the same degree of respect. For as she is wont to say – "You may keep your castles and your palaces. My roof is the stars and the mountains my walls."'

And thus Margaret McKay was introduced to the future King of Scotland. With Mary's cautious blessing, she collected the fragile bundle in her arms. Baby and witch looked at each other in silence. Then McKay rested a thumb on the tiny forehead and closed her eyes.

'There is poison in him.'

Mary recoiled at this devastating news. 'Mon Dieu! What kind of man would do this to a harmless baby?'

'Can you save him?' implored the Countess, her hands clasped to her bosom.

Margaret McKay replaced James in his cot. 'Aye. But be warned, the poison runs deep. I shall remove what I can, but he will likely carry its shadow for the rest of his days.'

'Do what you must!' cried the anguished Queen. 'I will provide anything you require. Save my child!'

The witch removed a small white stone the colour of a full moon from a fold in her sleeve and laid it carefully over the infant's heart. Then, collecting a dab of spittle on the tip of her forefinger, she applied the moisture to her patient's brow and whispered a spell. The baby succumbed to her soothing Gaelic tones and was soon fast asleep. The spell complete, McKay rose to Mary and instructed her thus:

'Leave the stone with the child. It will provide protection. I will return tomorrow after I have gathered all the things I need. Have patience. It may take another moon. It may take two. But your son will live.'

True to her word Margaret McKay returned the very next

day, carrying a basket containing, according to Annabell's journal, 'a peculiar cargo of tree bark, sycamore seeds, elm root, crushed urchin shell, a collection of the most hideous and foul-smelling mushrooms, dandelion milk, crow feathers and a sweet paste of sea water, rose hip, honey and willowherb.'

As the days progressed, wild rumours of the absent Queen's troubling association with a strange peasant woman reached the ears of the Privy Council in Edinburgh, provoking furious consternation. To a man, the Queen's closest advisors agreed that if the stories of the healer's use of spells and potions were true, then swift and decisive action was required to remove her humiliating presence. The men of Science and the men of God had found a common enemy in a woman of Magic. A woman who had further exposed the dangerous naivety of their Catholic Queen. The very idea that this lowly, uneducated heathen, with her dark medicines and cantrips, had been permitted unfettered access to a future King was intolerable. After much heated debate the Royal Physician, Sir William Ross, persuaded his unhappy friends to bide their time. What better way, he argued, to raise public ire against the feminine naivety of this papist Queen than to sit back and wait for McKay's intervention to fail, as it surely must, and therefore expose Mary's undeniable incompetence for turning to a witch rather than to God. An unforgivable lapse of judgement resulting in the most heinous of all crimes. The murder of the heir to the throne!

And so the great and the good kept their counsel, but within a few short days, to their utmost horror, came the news to scupper Sir William's clever plan. The baby had grown fat and pink and his robust lungs possessed a wail that shook all of Jedburgh to its very foundations! McKay's sacrilegious ministrations had succeeded where they, despite all their sophisticated education and unequalled intellect, had failed.

Sir William Ross composed a letter wherein he laid bare

in the most strident of terms, the myriad concerns of – *Her Majesty's most loyal servants* – and warned of dire consequences should the Queen – *Insist upon paying heed to those heretical influences which pose the greatest threat to the future and prosperity of our great and God-fearing nation.*

The letter ended with a demand that *Margaret McKay be immediately and permanently banished from all interaction with the Court.*

And here, with the benefit of hindsight, one may reasonably put forth the argument that this was the moment Mary made her greatest political misstep.

She failed to reply to Sir William's letter.

To a man burdened with so delicate an ego, there is no greater slight than to be wilfully ignored. Whether Mary deliberately chose to dismiss the letter or whether her failure to respond was merely an oversight, one of many tasks left unfulfilled in the midst of her all-consuming joy at her child's recovery, will never be known. There can be no doubt, however, that this perceived insult served to strengthen the resolve of Sir William and his allies to pluck this irritating thorn from the Protestant paw once and for all.

Her task complete, Margaret McKay handed her charge into the grateful arms of his mother, but not before impressing upon the Queen that although she had removed the poison from her child, she could not remove the poison from the minds of ambitious men.

As we have learned, Mary Stuart for all her fine qualities held at her core, a wilfulness capable of seriously impairing her judgement at the most inopportune moments. And so it was when, disregarding the entreaties issued by her dwindling band of trusted advisors, she returned to Edinburgh determined to bring her detractors to heel. Sir William Ross, fearing for his position, pledged with forked tongue his unswerving allegiance to Her Majesty, insisting her safety and well-being had always been his foremost priority. And for a brief while, the whispers of conspiracy retreated from the spiralling stairwells and long dark corridors and an uneasy hush descended upon the castle.

Then, as that long desperate winter gave way to the rejuvenating warmth of spring, a strange occurrence signalled an end to the fragile truce.

At the break of dawn on Good Friday, Mary awoke to something of a commotion. A cat, having somehow made its way into her chamber, had perched itself on the edge of her infant's cot, where it proceeded to mewl and hiss, its tail shivering in a state of extreme perturbation. Mary rose quickly from her bed, fearing the animal intended to do harm to the child inside, but when she approached, the cat dropped to the floor and proceeded to rub its russet coat against her legs, purring happily as it weaved between her ankles. The Queen peered into the cot to see James sound asleep and with not a scratch upon him.

The cat returned to its former vantage point, where it repeated its display of feline ire and clawed furiously at the baby's blankets. With the coverlet tangled in its paw, Mary lifted the cat aside and beneath the mass of fur and wool she saw the protective moonstone left by Margaret McKay lying at the bairn's shoulder. The stone began to glow, changing rapidly from a soft lunar white to a scorching coal of red. Mary quickly gathered up her son and emptied a jug of water into the flames rising from the cot. The stone hissed under the deluge and returned to its original hue, but as she continued to pour, it melted completely away, giving the extraordinary impression that it had been composed of ice all along.

The Queen recognised the sign for what it was: an omen. A portent of some imminent evil she simply had to acknowledge. Mary searched for the cat, but there was no sign of it anywhere. For once and for the sake of her child's safety, Mary managed to quell her characteristic stubbornness and set off that very morning for Stirling Castle, whereupon she placed James into the care of Annabell Murray.

On the eve of her return to Edinburgh, Mary Stuart cradled the infant James in her arms, kissed him gently on the brow and settled him to sleep. It is to be noted with a little irony that this tender exchange occurred on the Feast of St George 1567 and represented perhaps the last moment of happiness and peace Mary, Queen of Scots ever enjoyed. Alas, from this point forth, her life would know only pain and chaos. She was never to lay eyes upon her son again.

That fateful summer, in the aftermath of Mary's enforced abdication, the pack of scheming wolves who had so ruthlessly brought about her downfall, circled victoriously around their new cub. The very cub whom they had desired only a few short months earlier to rip apart with their bare teeth, they now sought to nurture, educate and mould in their own image. The cub who would be king represented a bottomless well of opportunity. However, these cunning wolves knew that the key to their continued power and influence depended upon the keeping of a secret. For nothing was as certain to poison the fount of all their future endeavours than the revelation that the King of Scotland and of England owed his life to a filthy witch.

Thus the dominant wolf, Sir William Ross, gathered his bloodthirsty dogs before God, in front of whom they swore a sacred oath to cleanse His world of Margaret McKay and of all who shared her wicked practices. A name was chosen for this select and clandestine band of witch-hunters.

Gladius Dei.

We can but speculate as to why Margaret McKay chose to remain in Edinburgh rather than flee into exile. A witch of her extraordinary talent must surely have been aware to some degree of the heinous forces rallying against her. After her success in Jedburgh, Margaret McKay returned to her home in Livingstoun's Close, where she lived in relative anonymity, generating a small but reliable income selling ointments and remedies renowned for their efficacy. Hers was a solitary existence without a husband or child, and she dedicated herself to the advancement of her art and to providing succour to those who had not the means to help themselves. The streets and wynds surrounding her own little Old Town hovel were collapsing under the weight of the most appalling destitution. Disease and hunger were her neighbours. And here we may cast all speculation aside in favour of certitude.

Margaret McKay's compassion for those abandoned both by God and their fellow men far exceeded her own instinct for self-preservation. Many of those who lived in the vicinity of Livingstoun's Close owed their lives to the kindly spinster and her potions, but none were aware of the toll the healing had taken upon the healer. For every time she employed her Magic towards the preservation of a life, so a little piece of her own vitality had to be sacrificed in order to preserve the equilibrium that Nature so demands. Perhaps it was the sum total of all these incremental sacrifices that led Margaret McKay to retire early to her bed unaware of the boots marching towards her door on that fateful December night.

The agents of Gladius Dei smashed down her door and, with swords raised, attempted to capture the witch. Margaret's wits, however, proved far sharper than their blades and, casting a spell into the embers still glowing in the hearth, she brought forth such a flash of light that the men were thoroughly blinded. Margaret fled into the darkness, but this was to be a temporary reprieve: within a few short days she was discovered exhausted and shivering inside a cave near the summit of Arthur's Seat.

It is impossible to comprehend the suffering Margaret McKay endured at the brutal hands of her gaolers. For a full week they inflicted the most horrible torture upon her body, but Margaret's spirit remained unbowed and unbroken. Finally, she was brought before the High Council of Gladius

Dei. The mockery of a trial lasted two days and nights, yet for all their ludicrous accusations and wanton violence the witch refused to grant them the confession and with it the vindication they so craved. Regrettably, however, Sir William Ross and his disciples would not be denied their lust for blood.

On December the tenth, 1567, a day after she had been forced to witness the execution of her friends Mary Galbraith, Rhona McPherson and Janet Black, Margaret McKay was taken from her cell and transported to a lonely corner of Braid Woods, where she was to be hanged by the neck. Feeling the noose at her throat, Margaret screamed to the heavens. In their ignorance, Sir William and his co-conspirators believed this scream to be one of anguish and terror, but when a chestnut dropped from the canopy above straight into the witch's gape, their sadistic delight swiftly evaporated. In the throes of a violent spasm Margaret retched a stream of hot bile upon the ground. Then, glaring into the affrighted eyes of her tormentors, she cast her final spell. A spell designed to preserve the influence of her magic in the physical world even as her soul was, at that moment, being cruelly ripped from Nature's earthly realm. The men, in a frenzy of panic, pulled hard on the noose and throttled the last gasp of life from the witch.

On Sir William's instruction, the corpse was laid upon the ground where, in front of the assembled High Council, the ghoul set about dissecting the body of the witch in the hope of discovering the *Viscus of Devilry* – the very source of a witch's magic.

Alas, the surgeon's efforts were to end in ill-tempered frustration and, with hands gloved in blood, he ordered the corpse to be burned, then buried and the tree from which Margaret McKay was hanged to be cut down. Wise precautions when dealing with so powerful a witch. Wise, yet futile. For the seed of Margaret McKay's magic had already been sown into the fertile soil of the woods, where it lies dormant to this day, like the seed in the desert awaiting the first drop of rain.

*

I feel it would be most remiss of me not to conclude my narrative with an account of the subsequent activities of the Gladius Dei murderer-in-chief, Sir William Ross.

During the course of my researches, I have been fortunate enough to come into the possession of certain documents, the authors of whom, I trust my readers will understand, must remain unnamed, as to reveal their identities even with the passing of centuries, may result in serious repercussions for their living descendants.

These records present a most telling portrait of a man consumed by a visceral hatred for witches and their art. Emboldened by the murders of those poor women collectively known as the Lothian Witches, Sir William pressed ahead with his ambitious plan to bring about: *the complete annihilation of all who kneel before the Devil.*

This became the central tenet for Gladius Dei, for whom he enthusiastically gathered support both political and fiscal by inviting the wealthy and influential to dine at his home in the Canongate. Once he had filled their bellies with wine and roasted grouse and their heads with outrageous tales of the Sutherland Witches' liking for stew cooked from the flesh of children, or of the notorious Witches of Arran who, under the light of the full moon climb Goat Fell to fornicate with Satan and upon their descent give birth to hideous demon-lambs, it was Sir William's custom to escort his esteemed visitors down into a large, musty basement. The home of his 'secret museum'.

How he smiled as he watched his awestruck guests survey the shelves and cabinets laden with a plethora of repugnant artefacts! These, he explained with great delight, were his 'prizes' drawn from the spoils of his never-ending battle against the evils of sorcery and witchcraft.

Candles trembled over the withered and desiccated carcasses of numerous small creatures pinned securely to boards. There were countless bowls and jars containing charred bones, strips of skin, broken teeth and other unsavoury ingredients Sir William claimed were used in the creation of potions and spells. But the most hideous thing of all, an object which caused many a refined and delicate constitution to swoon at the horror of it, was the skeleton of what appeared to be a human baby. However, this particular specimen boasted an extra element of hideousness by virtue of the fact that it possessed not one, but two skulls!

One would have expected this monstrosity to have been the 'jewel' of Sir William's collection, but not so. That honour he reserved for a small wooden box displayed by itself upon a stout little side table. Inside the box lay four small stones. Flattened, grey and sea-worn, each had a unique symbol crudely etched upon one side and five lines scratched upon the reverse. These, he explained with enormous satisfaction, were the coven-stones of Janet Black, Mary Galbraith, Rhona McPherson and Margaret McKay. The hard-won acquisition of these stones brought to an end the shameful era of the Lothian Witches and represented his finest achievement (though his failure to capture Blind Lizzie irked him to the end of his days).

Behind the coven-stones, in the darkest recess of the cellar, stood a door of solid oak. When inevitably, one of the guests inquired as to what lay beyond this firmly locked and bolted door, Sir William's mouth responded with a twist of displeasure before loudly announcing that the time had come for everyone to return upstairs where warmth and wine awaited.

Had the inquisitive guest thought to ask Sir William's wife, Lady Frances Ross, what lay behind the mysterious cellar door, they may well have received an altogether more satisfactory answer. Lady Frances had long since abandoned her affection for the man masquerading as her husband. He was not the man she had fallen in love with. This William Ross was an impostor. A stranger so consumed by hatred that all forms of joy and wonder were as salt to the open wound of his soul.

Lady Frances poured these miseries into the pages of a letter to her sister Isobel, in which she also spoke at length on the subject of her husband's monomaniacal quest to find what he himself had termed the *Viscus of Devilry*.

The theory of the *Viscus of Devilry* first struck Sir William as he stood in the Grassmarket to witness the executions of Janet Black, Rhona McPherson and Mary Galbraith. The sight of their limp bodies suspended from the gallows put him in mind of a trio of butterfly chrysalises suspended from a twig. This idle fancy provided the inspiration for an intriguing line of thought.

What strange and unnatural metamorphical force had transmuted these particular women into witches? What common trait separated these abominations from natural women such as Frances? There had to be something within. Something in their viscera. A gland perhaps, from which flowed the essence of Magic in the way that blood flowed from the heart. An organ absent from the physiology of ordinary men and women.

A *Viscus of Devilry*.

At Sir William's request, the bodies of the three witches were delivered directly to his basement, where they passed through the sturdy oak door and into a second, much larger chamber containing a solitary table at its centre.

In her letters to Isobel, Frances described one particularly unpleasant visit to the second room thus:

'The air was foul and filled with the smoke of a hundred candles. A dead witch lay upon the table. My husband stood over her. The blood upon his hands! Oh, my dear sister, I shall never forget the sight!'

Sir William begged his wife's understanding. His work, he insisted, was essential to the furtherance of science and knowledge and though unpalatable, dissection was nevertheless, an essential element of that work.

Night after night Frances retired to bed alone, leaving Sir William to his grisly research. Though separated from her husband by several floors, she could not escape the awful smell creeping up from the cellar. No matter how many flowers and scented oils she deployed to counter the effect, the noxious odour continued to permeate every part of the house.

Oftentimes, a loud knocking at the street door roused Frances from an uneasy slumber, whereupon she would rise to the window to witness a grimy outstretched palm on the pavement below accept a gold coin from her husband's purse in exchange for a large jute sack of a size and shape that made her shiver with dread.

Sir William's repeated failure to locate the *Viscus of Devilry* threw him into the blackest of moods, leading to frequent outbursts of violent temper, the like of which Frances had hitherto never thought him capable. Every attempt Frances made to lift her husband from the gloom was met with the most withering and heartless of ripostes. He cursed himself for marrying a woman who *though pleasing to the eye, held no attraction for the mind*. A woman whose ignorance rendered her incapable of understanding anything of his torment and of the dire consequences for all should he fail to discover the secret source of a witch's power.

He complained bitterly that his work was at every turn frustrated by a dearth of material. A fresh and reliable supply of corpses was the obvious solution. But from where? Sir William approached the Earl of Moray, regent to the infant king, and put forth an impassioned argument for a Royal Decree granting Gladius Dei the full legal authority to undertake the most extensive and thorough purge of witchcraft yet seen in Scotland.

The decree was granted.

Sir William's happy mood melted first to sorrow, then to rage when he returned home to find a letter from his wife awaiting him. Lady Frances, unable to withstand another day in that *unwholesome house of misery and horror*, had accepted an invitation to live with her sister. Sir William burned the deceitful pages and proceeded to the cellar.

A mere two weeks had elapsed when he received the sorry news from Perth. His wife was dead, her body discovered along with Isobel's amidst the charred wreckage of their home. The official verdict deemed the fire to be the result of a tragic accident. This, despite several sightings of a hooded figure seen riding out of town at full gallop moments before the first of the flames had set the night sky aglow.

The savage purge carried out by Gladius Dei introduced no fewer than two hundred victims to the gruesome attentions of Sir William Ross. Nevertheless, proof of the fabled *Viscus of Devilry* remained forever beyond his grasp. In later years he attributed this failure to the very thing he was trying to expose. Magic.

In a lecture presented to the guild of the Barber Surgeons of Edinburgh in September 1586, Sir William argued:

'The root of a witch's power is in itself enchanted and when any true and natural God-fearing Christian man attempts to set eyes upon it, the thing simply becomes invisible.'

Unconvinced by his own line of reasoning, Sir William continued his iniquitous quest. Many more innocent victims passed through his cellar door, which mercifully closed for the last time when old age forced him to lay down his scalpel. He spent his final days alone in his Canongate house contemplating his life's work and in a written correspondence to King James, concluded it to be:

'A humble life willingly dedicated to the service of God and to my King.'

The elderly Sir William was a lonely, embittered creature. His last act as chairman of Gladius Dei was to order the exhumation of Margaret McKay's remains from the Braid Woods. He wanted her bones to be mounted above the entrance to the society's meeting hall as a constant reminder to all members of their:

'Essential and holy pursuit.'

This last instruction was never fulfilled for, despite several extensive searches, no one could determine the exact spot where the witch had been buried many decades before. The repeated failure to locate the final resting place of Margaret McKay was not, as Sir William testily claimed, the result of mere incompetence and idleness. There are some things in this world that simply do not want to be found – a conclusion accepted by all but the irascible old surgeon who refused to countenance the strange experiences told by the men entrusted with carrying out his order. Each and every one of them reported that they had suffered a most inexplicable form of brain fever from the moment they entered Braid Woods. This peculiar affliction had a most disorientating effect on their memory, leaving them completely at a loss as to where they were, what they were doing and why they were doing it. In this horribly confused state, they patrolled the woods for hours at a time before eventually stumbling one by one into the open fields, where their faculties were returned to them. One of the party dimly recalled passing through a hollow where grew a young chestnut tree no higher than the hat on his head. At the top of the tree there hung a single chestnut as large as his fist. But when he made to pluck it free, he heard a terrible scream. A scream that set his blood to ice and had him fleeing like a frightened rabbit from the woods.

And so, on the fourth morning of February, 1607, with their grey scarves and austere robes of a uniform black, The High Council of Gladius Dei resembled nothing so much as a gathering of jackdaws at the deathbed of Sir William Ross. The men, eager to assume the task of appointing his successor, waited impatiently for their leader to die. Their fidgeting ended as the clock struck nine, when suddenly the witch-finder opened his eyes very wide and stared into a vacant corner of the room. Pointing a tremulous finger, he exclaimed in a voice rasped with terror:

'I see her! I see her!'

And then Sir William Ross was dead.

CHAPTER FOURTEEN

The Parasite

I could not move my head. The restraint had ploughed a tight, warm furrow into the flesh of my brow. But if I strained my eyes to the extreme limit of their orbits, then it was possible to see their expensive black plumage shining in the fringe of oil lamps lining the walls of a vast circular room. Giant crows with murderous beaks, they greeted each other with twitching, iridescent wings and a swirl of expectant cawing. Then all at once they settled down on their benches to stare in hungry silence towards the poor unfortunate laid upon the dissecting table below. I squirmed and strained, but the thick leather straps binding my arms and legs held fast.

A raven, much larger than all the others birds, hopped from the shadows and took to the stage where, to the delight of his enthralled audience, he spread his wings in triumph.

'Esteemed gentlemen and colleagues! I present to you, Mr Joseph Ware!'

The crows chattered excitely and made such a flap with their wings it seemed the whole building was in danger of breaking free from its foundations and taking flight.

'Silence!' commanded the raven. The crows obeyed instantly. 'Mr Joseph Ware has a secret to share! Is this not so, Mr Joseph Ware?' The raven cocked its head and thrust a soot black eye so close to my mouth I felt the cool breeze of its blink against my lips. A terrified whimper escaped my throat. The raven seized upon this and flew to the rafters. Circling the gallery, he repeated over and over in a dizzying blur:

'A confession! A confession! A confession!'

In paroxysms of fluttering ecstasy, the crows echoed his cry:

'A confession! A confession! A confession!'

Satisfied, the raven returned to his perch.

'Silence!'

The crows obeyed.

'Tell us your secret, Mr Joseph Ware,' said the raven, returning his inky glare to within an inch of my trembling mouth. 'Where shall we find the root of your devilrie?'

I tried to speak, to protest my innocence, but the raven did not want to listen. I watched in paralysed terror as it stepped upon my chest and used its colossal weight to crush the breath from my lungs.

The raven straightened itself to address the assembly once more.

'Esteemed colleagues I will now reveal to you the secret hidden inside Mr Joseph Ware.'

Shrill squawks of delirium erupted from the benches as the raven sank a claw into my skin and cleaved the flesh from sternum to abdomen. Spurred on by the crows' feverish bloodlust, the raven plunged its fearsome beak deep inside my belly. He pecked and pecked again, tearing at the innards and flinging them unceremoniously to the floor. The last of the entrails removed, he dipped his beak inside the hollow cave of my ribs and plucked out a familiar item.

'Behold!' cried the raven.

The spiky green shell of the chestnut split apart in the raven's beak and out fell the nut. The raven screeched in joy and invited all the crows to join the feast. I lay helpless as a hundred voracious beaks plucked strips of meat from my bones. And as the blustering, shrieking, frenzy of feathers, bills and claws rose to a calamitous maelstrom, the raven, who did not like to be watched whilst he supped, pecked out my eyes.

*

I woke with a fearful start and was much relieved to discover that I had not in fact been blinded by the malicious beak of a giant raven. The horrible dream of the crows faded into the nebulous mist of my imaginings, yet the echo of their piercing cries persisted. The drawing room had grown cold in the greyness of the early morning light filtering through the window. A lazy wisp of smoke rose from the white ashes in the grate. The reading lamp had burned itself dry, leaving Mr Finlayson's book, now closed upon my lap, in shadow.

The distressing shrieks of the crows stubbornly refused to die away. I vigorously shook my head, hoping to dislodge this last vestige of my nightmare, but stopped when I caught sight of someone staring at me with a look of pure horror. It was then I realised it was not the collective screaming of the crows I heard but the single scream of the little girl standing in the gloom.

'Grace? Whatever is the matter?'

My little cousin ran terror-stricken to the door and into the arms of my newly arrived parents.

'Look at Joseph! He's all wrong!' she wailed, clutching at Mother's dress. My parents turned to me, whereupon the blood immediately drained from their complexions.

'Why are you looking at me like that?' I demanded, deeply alarmed by the consternation I had unwittingly provoked.

'My God, Joseph,' said Mother, clasping a hand to each side of her astonished mouth. 'What has happened to you!'

My panic increased tenfold when I saw the source of all their distress. The cursed affliction had reappeared with a distressing vigour. From the fingertips of my left hand, fresh growths trailed across the floor, twisting towards the window where stood a large, ornately decorated vase housing a mature aspidistra. Thick and milky in colour, the spiralling shoots had ascended the lip of the vase and plunged inside to feed from the rich dark soil it contained. From the tips of my right hand had grown a tangle of slender, vinelike structures. These sickening appendages had fused themselves to the pages of the book on my lap so completely it was impossible to ascertain where the words ended and I began.

Father dashed to the window and threw the curtains to their widest extent, shedding as much light as possible upon the whole sordid scene.

'Please leave! All of you!' I begged. 'You mustn't see me like this! Go!'

I started to bite at the roots, gripping them firmly between my teeth, tearing and chewing them from my fingers. The intensity of the pain brought me to the verge of senselessness, but it was as nothing compared to the excruciating humiliation I so desperately sought to dispel. Drips of white sap splashed to the floor as I ripped the abominations from my body. Grace buried herself in Mother's waist and wept uncontrollably. At first my parents watched on in a state of appalled silence, but when I loosed a terrible wail of anguish as I severed the tip of my thumb, Father moved sharply to accost me in an attempt to prevent further self-mutilation. Determined to rid myself of every last unwholesome protrusion, I shouldered Father aside and stumbled for the door. Molly suddenly appeared to block my escape. Her tired eyes and the shawl thrown loosely around her nightdress spoke of a sleep rudely broken.

'Please,' I gasped, feeling my heart wither in despair. 'I beg you, do not look at me. Not like this.'

With an expression of unbearable pity, Molly watched as I slumped in giddy agony into a carpet of infinite blackness.

*

'Extraordinary! I have quite simply never seen the like. Have you?'

The question was posed by an unfamiliar voice.

'No, Fraser. I have not.'

The response I recognised as my father's.

'Is there a cure? A treatment? You must be able to rid him of this, yes?'

This from Mother, her words anxious and strained.

My palms itched terribly. And at the base of my neck I sensed a brief squirming sensation as my uninvited guest wormed around the vertebrae. I opened my eyes. Great blocks of hard frosty light filled Father's study, framing slow eddies of dust motes in a modest tribute to the snow falling lightly outside.

'He's awake!' Mother swept across to take my head in her hands. 'Oh, Joseph, how do you feel?'

'Come now, Mrs Ware, we must not crowd the boy'.

A portly man with abundant ash-grey whiskers propping up a bulbous nose made rubicund by the vagaries of winter, occupied the stool by the side of the couch where I lay. He fussed over my hands, busily scrutinising every finger in the minutest detail.

Wiping her tear-stained eyes, my mother reluctantly withdrew.

'Tell me you can cure him!'

The man had so absorbed himself in his task he appeared not to hear her appeal.

'We will do our utmost,' said Father, crouched at my feet, studying them with a curious excitement. A silver tray sporting a pair of scissors and ten neatly arranged cuttings rested on the cushion between my feet. He dabbed a damp cloth at the sap seeping from the freshly trimmed nails.

There was one more person in the study. Arms folded tightly across her chest, Molly stood beside Father's desk where a haphazard explosion of notes, diagrams, equations and lists smothered every available inch of its surface. Much of it had spilled to the floor, forming a patchwork paper rug at her feet. When our eyes met, Molly quickly lowered her gaze and shifted her weight from one foot to the other.

'Where is Grace? Is she still upset?' I said, addressing Mother.

'You mustn't fret, Joseph. Grace is in the drawing room with Bethany. Mr Maybury is watching over them. Try to rest. Dr Whittle will look after you.'

The doctor unclasped a bag of shiny black leather stamped with the initials FW. There was a bundle of roots and tendrils inside, the very ones I had bitten from my fingers. Half of them were still fused to Finlayson's book. The book itself was in a terrible state. The flaking pages had all but crumbled to dust and the cover had become so infested with thick black spots of mildew that the book's title and the name of its author were left indecipherable.

Dr Whittle removed a small, sharp pointed implement and proceeded to press and poke at the now very faint impressions left on my palm by the chestnut's spines. He pushed the tip of his probe deep into the entry scar at my wrist. When a trickle of brackish fluid escaped from the wound, Dr Whittle uncorked a small glass tube and collected a sample.

'Fascinating,' he mused, holding his prize to the light.

'A doctor is of no use to me,' I said, disdainfully.

Dr Whittle lowered his hooded lids and fixed me with a contemptuous glare. 'You still believe this to be the result of witchcraft? The work of an enchanted chestnut! Dearie, dearie me,' he tutted. I sat up ready to protest, but Dr Whittle raised a firm hand to indicate he had no intention of listening to a single syllable. 'With respect, Joseph, there is little to be gained in denying it. Miss Keane has told us all we need to know regarding how you arrived at this sorry state.'

'And it has nothing to do with witchcraft and everything to do with stupidity,' added Father, gathering the tray of cuttings and delivering them to his desk.

Unable to disguise my shock at so comprehensive a betrayal, I turned to Molly. Her face burning with shame, she hurried for the door and left.

Father carefully teased a sliver of root from the tray and placed it under his microscope.

'I must confess I have never been so disappointed in you, Joseph. What on God's earth possessed you to go wandering through those woods in the dead of night? And climbing trees in complete darkness! Molly could have died! Do you not think your Uncle Tam has experienced enough heartbreak in his life that you feel the need to supply more?'

'You are far from blameless, Lachlan,' said Mother with obvious irritation. 'You have been filling his head with your Witch McKay and her stupid tree nonsense from the moment he learned to walk.'

'I never expected the boy to take them as gospel,' muttered Father, somewhat distracted by the revelations unfolding in the microscope's eyepiece. 'This is truly astonishing!'

Dr Whittle, having gleaned all he could from my hands, now started to prod, pull and poke at my ears and hair.

'Do these growths only occur when your hands are buried in soil?' he asked.

'Not necessarily,' said Father when it became clear that I had no intention of answering. 'However, he told Molly that the rate of growth is far more vigorous when soil is in close proximity. Furthermore, when he comes into contact with the earth, he can sense the movement of every living thing it contains. And when he touches any material which once belonged to a living creature – be it wood or wool or ivory, for example – he experiences visions through which he relives that particular creature's dying moments.'

Dr Whittle expelled a snort of derision. 'Is that so?' Then with forefingers and thumbs, he lifted my eyelids and peered underneath. 'I am beginning to suspect the fever has reached your brain, Joseph.'

'There is more,' said Father. 'Molly informs me that he has, on more than one occasion, confessed to having consumed mouthfuls of dirt.'

The doctor took this revelation as a cue to press, squeeze and tap at my tongue and teeth. 'Most odd,' he mused.

I braced myself for further humiliation. What other secrets had Molly exposed? But Father was lost to his microscope once more.

'Astonishing!' he exclaimed after a period of silent study. 'Truly astonishing!'

Losing patience, Mother moved to her husband's shoulder. 'What can you see?'

'Look for yourself.'

She put her eye to the microscope and adjusted the focus.

'Note the position of the nucleus,' said Father. 'And is the shape of the cell itself not suggestive? More importantly, note the rigidity of the outer membrane.'

The fear in my mother's eyes chilled me to the marrow.

'How can this be?' she gasped.

'What is it? What is happening to me?' I demanded.

'That is precisely what we are seeking to determine,' said Dr Whittle. 'Now try not to overexcite yourself and allow me to complete my examinations.'

'Father? Please! What have you seen?'

My father rubbed slow small circles into his knitted brow, a habit he often employed when formulating an explanation for the benefit of someone less expert in his chosen field of study than he.

'It is difficult to say with any certainty. Further research is required. The evidence thus far suggests an unusually aggressive contamination of the blood. It is fungoid in nature. And it is creating what I can only describe as a form of biological alchemy inside you; subjugating your own healthy human cells and replacing them with structures remarkably similar to those we commonly associate with plant life. Truly astonishing.'

'Will you stop using that word?' cried Mother. To Dr Whittle's irritation, she returned to my side and gathered my hands in hers. The physician knew better than to chastise a distraught mother for a second time and so relocated his studies to my feet.

'There are parallels in the natural world,' Father continued. 'For example, there are certain parasitical fungi in the upper reaches of the Amazonian jungle, whose spores when ingested by an animal host, slowly germinate within the digestive system, where they draw nourishment and continue to grow. Eventually their stalks pierce the skin of the by now starved and desiccated body of the unfortunate victim...'

'Lachlan, please!' said Mother, scowling at her husband's insensitivity. Rather than the fatherly compassion she expected, he had the demeanour of a man on the threshold of some bright new discovery, bristling with nervous excitement. Father noted her disappointment and attempted to curb his scholarly enthusiasm. Placing both hands flat upon the desk, he straightened his back and faced me with all the calm assurance he could muster.

'I do not wish to alarm you, Joseph. I am merely considering every possibility.'

Anger and frustration boiling over, I snatched my hands from Mother's grip and held the resin-like substance crusting at what little remained of my deformed fingernails for all to see.

'Then why dismiss the most obvious one of all? The legend is true! The tree is cursed. I caught the chestnut! I watched it burrow through my skin and into my flesh. I can feel it now. Moving inside. And I have heard her voice! The witch communicates with me. She shows me things. Terrible things. What more proof do you need? It is witchcraft!'

Dr Whittle shook his head gravely.

'Delirium.'

'I will not tolerate any more talk of curses or witchcraft. Do I make myself clear, Joseph?' said Father. 'Chemistry is the key! Not magic! Chemistry will provide the answers we need. Once we understand the nature of the chemistry poisoning your blood, we will undoubtedly, hit upon a cure. You have my word!'

Mother gently encouraged my head back to the pillow. 'You must not excite yourself, Joseph. Look at you. You are shivering all over with fever.'

She applied a damp flannel to my burning forehead. The cotton fibres retained the warmth of the American sunshine that once sustained their growth. They shared the sudden trauma of their harvest by calloused hands which themselves spoke of unimaginable suffering.

'Witchcraft or not, that rotten old tree is behind this. I am certain of it,' said Mother.

'As am I,' said Father, thoughtfully. 'It is likely the tree carries a rare fungal blight, the spores of which must have entered Joseph's blood via the chestnut's spines. Though I confess, I have never heard of any previous instance whereby contact with a horse chestnut has resulted in a case as unique as this. There is, however, a precedent. The spines of the Abyssinian moonshadow elm contain a poisonous sap which, on piercing the skin of an unwary hand for example, result in the victim's fingers becoming permanently splayed and rigid. Over time, the skin hardens and cracks to the extent that it ultimately assumes a texture and appearance very much like the bark of the moonshadow elm itself.'

'And is there a remedy for this moonshadow poison?'

asked Mother with renewed hope.

'No. Not as yet. Do not look so disheartened, my love! Nature insists on balance. For every sting there is a salve. For every poison, an antidote. It is simply a matter of finding it.'

But this did not appease my mother. She left my side to stand, hands drumming impatiently on her hips, in front of Father's prodigious apothecary chest.

'Is there not something here which could help Joseph?' she asked, craning, stretching and bending to inspect the labels fixed to the countless number of drawers.

'Let me see,' said Father, joining the search. He rolled the ladder to the farthest corner of the cabinet and climbed till his head almost touched the ceiling. 'Now, where is it...? Ah!' He opened a drawer, removed a small tin box and held it proudly aloft. 'Glacier Moss! Highly effective at slowing down the advance of fungal growths, fevers and other diseases. This will grant us more time to find a permanent cure. It is also an extremely effective remedy for pain. But we must take great care with our measurements. Ingest more than a single pinch in the course of a day, and the results would be counterproductive to say the least.'

'Why?' asked Mother. 'What happens if more than a single pinch is taken?'

'The body falls into a state of prolonged inertia, much as the moss itself does in order to survive the extremes of an Arctic winter. The vital functions slow to the point of near death. The heart beats but once every minute, rendering the victim as little more than a living statue.' Father descended with his prize and responded to his wife's alarm with a cheery smile. 'But a single pinch taken once a day is perfectly safe.' He opened the tin box, dipped his forefinger and thumb inside and presented a pinch of pale green dust to my nostrils. 'Take a good deep sniff.'

The effect was immediate. A pleasant, rapid warmth

infused my lungs and flowed outwards in all directions. The soreness eased from every tendon and sinew as the parasite loosened its grip.

'Better?' asked Father.

'Much,' I said.

Dr Whittle raised a dubious eyebrow. 'I still say the young man requires something a little more radical than your powdered moss, Lachlan.'

'And what did you have in mind, Fraser?'

'You must permit me to transfer Joseph to my hospital, where I will perform a series of exploratory surgical procedures.'

The cold crawl of panic smothered the soothing warmth of the moss.

'No!'

'Absolutely not! I will not allow you to cut open my son,' Mother protested, as shocked as I at the proposal.

Dr Whittle's knees cracked under the strain as he stood upright to better present his argument.

'Mrs Ware. In all my thirty-two years in practice, I have never encountered a case so utterly confounding. So utterly unique. This is truly, truly exceptional. Look at his toes! Look at his fingers! Look at the discolouration and hardening of the skin at the knuckles.' He snatched my right hand and invited Mother to join him for a more detailed inspection. 'And see here? Where he chewed these extraordinary growths away with his bare teeth? Where is the blood? There should be blood here. The wounds should be sealed with dark red scabs, not this peculiar, translucent substance. I fear a rare and lethal strain of anaemia is at play. And that is why I beg you, Mrs Ware, to place all your motherly concerns, understandable though they are, to one side and allow me to take your son into my care. For the one thing he does not have, is time. It is my medical opinion that without proper and immediate treatment, Joseph will be dead by Christmas Day.'

'Do not listen to him! This man has no understanding of what is happening to me.'

'On that point, we are in total agreement, Joseph,' said Dr Whittle, calmly. 'I have absolutely no understanding of what is happening to you. Which is precisely why you must be admitted to my hospital, where you will receive the highest standard of care. I am not a man prone to idle boasts, so when I tell you that we have the most scientifically advanced facilities to be found anywhere in Scotland, you may rest assured I have told you an undeniable truth. We *will* discover the cause of your disease and we *will* defeat it.'

Recognising my mother's resilience was beginning to crumble in the face of his steadfast conviction, the doctor led her by the arm to join Father. A hushed conference ensued around the desk, during which each conspirator took their turn to glance in my direction.

'Agreed?' I heard the doctor say, finally. Father offered a nod of affirmation. Mother, after a moment of intense hand-wringing, reluctantly assented. 'Excellent!' said Dr Whittle, extremely pleased with the outcome. 'Then it is settled. At first light tomorrow morning, I shall send a carriage to collect our patient! In the meantime, it is imperative that he not be allowed to leave this house. Nor is he to be left unattended. The disease, I fear, has severely impaired his mental faculties, which may compel him to take flight before we have a chance to restore him to the young man we all knew and admired. Therefore, for the sake of his own well-being, we must bind his arms and legs.'

'Is that absolutely necessary?' said Mother.

'Regrettably so.'

'No!'

I tried to swing myself from the couch, but before my feet touched the floor, Dr Whittle pressed his substantial bulk to my chest and held me firmly in place.

'Help me restrain him!'

Father hurried to assist. The doctor delved a pudgy fist inside his bag to collect a pair of buckled straps and worked quickly to secure my arms.

'Please don't hurt him!' cried Mother.

'Mrs Ware, I assure you this will be but a temporary discomfort to your son,' puffed Dr Whittle, wrestling the second strap around my ankles. 'By this hour tomorrow, Joseph will be well on his way to a full recovery.'

'No! Please! He means to kill me!' The stories imparted by the leather straps served to increase my distress. Through the eyes of an old bull, tethered and helpless, I watched the slaughterman lift his blade... And, feeling the slice of steel at my throat, I shared the animal's final memory. The sight of its own reflection in the spread of hot blood on the abattoir floor.

'Save your strength, Joseph,' said Father, taking a small bottle of reddish liquid from his desk drawer. 'I understand you are frightened, but there really is no need to struggle. We are only trying to help you.' He poured the fluid into a spoon and raised it to my lips. 'Now, lay back and drink this. It will calm your nerves and allow you to rest.'

I swallowed the bitter medicine and as my head nestled once more to the pillow, the horrors of the slaughterhouse dissolved into a pond of blissful nothingness.

Through increasingly weighty eyes, I watched Dr Whittle gather his samples and instruments together. As he opened his bag to place them inside, I observed a small mark imprinted upon the interior. It was a mark I initially assumed to be the stamp of the bag's manufacturer, but then I realised I had encountered this symbol before and very recently. Fighting to hold back the leaden curtains of sleep, I tried to recall precisely where and when I had seen this long vertical line intersected with a series of diminishing horizontals.

'Do not worry, my good people!' said Dr Whittle cheerfully,

clasping his bag. 'We will rid Joseph of this awfulness, be in no doubt. After all, we have God on our side! Until tomorrow!'

And with a shiver I remembered Mr Finlayson drawing a symbol on the wall of his basement. The symbol of the Sword and Jacob's Ladder.

The symbol of Gladius Dei...

CHAPTER FIFTEEN

Lachlan's Encyclopaedia
of Horrors

The dreams played host to the strangest forms of torment. Acts of extreme violence slowed to the point of near imperceptibility. A scalpel, delicately poised in expert fingers, was brought to my forearm. Bound by the rules of this glacial timescale it took hours for the steel to pierce each layer of skin. The blade then spent several weeks cutting a leisurely tract from the wrist all the way to the elbow. Blood exuded painlessly from the incision and flowed with all the urgency of molten glass. The sluggish waves of brittle crimson hardened to a standstill long before they could drip to the table upon which I had been tethered.

The room was speckled with eyes and mouths, all of them melting into the candles held in their emaciated claws. And how those mouths laughed! Pendulum tongues striking rings of teeth with all the clarity of the Easter bells. Months elapsed as I turned my head away from the mocking assembly to watch a woman leap from the highest branch of the Witch Tree and fall slower than the lightest feather, the sun setting and rising twice over before she settled upon the deck of a whaling ship.

The *Majestic North* was cast adrift on a storm-tossed sea of autumn leaves. Tam was on board, growing old as he passed the decades slicing open the belly of a whale whose song was

destined to fill the mournful fog long after every living creature
on earth had answered the call of extinction.

The *Majestic North* herself was ablaze, her timbers black-
ening inside the slowest of flames, the cracking and splitting
of her death throes creating a thunder which rumbled into
infinity. The splendid ship began to sink into the turmoil of
leaves and, after three cycles of the moon had waxed and
waned, the tip of her mainmast disappeared forever. The
nightwatchman approached, eager to voice his displeasure. I
grew decrepit with age awaiting his arrival and saw through
failing eyes that he had acquired a new face.

'Wake up!'

The witch was extremely frightened.

'Wake up, Jojo!'

The branches of the Witch Tree buzzed and fluttered.

'Joseph…!'

With a dizzying quickness, the witch, the ship, the leaves,
the tree, the laughter, the scalpel… all plunged into the abyss,
leaving only Molly, her hands upon my shoulders, to shake the
last icicles of slowness from my mind.

'You gave me such a fright!' sighed Molly, slumping into a
chair. 'You stopped breathing for so long, I thought you were
dead.'

A solitary candle burned on Father's desk and in the
hearth, a modest fire glowed and crackled, casting palsied
shadows throughout the study. Behind the drawn curtains an
angry squall flung itself repeatedly against the windowpanes.

The mantel clock struck three times.

'Has everyone gone to bed?'

'Aye,' said Molly. 'Your mother was in tears most of the
night. Uncle Lachlan was sitting here with you, lost in his
books. He has not long gone. I volunteered to watch over you
in his place.'

'Why did you tell them?' I asked, more puzzled than angry.

'What else could I do? This disease is killing you, Jojo! I thought they would be able to help.' She glanced at the straps restraining my arms and legs. 'I didn't expect this. I'm so sorry.'

'Did you tell them of our meeting with Finlayson?'

'No.'

'Good. Then no real harm has been done,' I said. 'Did my father find anything in his books?'

Molly shook her head glumly. 'But he is confident Dr Whittle will put you right.'

'Dr Whittle means to kill me tomorrow.'

'Don't be silly. He is going to cure you.'

'He is going to kill me. Dr Whittle is one of them.'

'One of *them*?' frowned Molly.

'I saw it! As clearly as I see you now. Printed on the inside of his bag. The symbol Finlayson showed us. The symbol of Gladius Dei. Dr Whittle is a member of Gladius Dei!'

'That's the fever speaking, Jojo. Ignore it. Dr Whittle is not a witch-hunter!'

'I swear to you, I am completely lucid. If I am taken to Whittle's hospital, I will not come out alive.'

A hefty gust rattled at the windows. The draught parted the curtains a fraction. Enough to expose a sliver of night sky. The knot of fear pulled tight inside my chest.

'You must help me, Molly. Please, take these off,' I pleaded, wrestling with the restraints.

Molly eyed the straps. Her expression suggested an on-going struggle with restraints of her own. 'Uncle Lachlan warned me about this. He warned me your delirium would make you say anything to be freed. He told me I should not be fooled and to ignore everything. It's for your own good. That's what he said.'

'Look at me! This is not delirium. This is the truth. Whittle means to cut me open. In his eyes, I am an abomination. I am less than human. He *will* kill me!'

Molly weighed her options for a few agonising moments, then reached for the buckles. My relief proved short-lived when she hesitated, changed her mind and withdrew her hands.

'But where will you go? Where else *can* you go?'

'Yesterday, after we met with Finlayson, you mentioned a priest?' I said, trying to contain my mounting frustration.

'Father Slaven? I thought you hated the idea.'

'Please understand, Molly. Everything I thought I knew has been destroyed. I have not the slightest idea what is happening to me and if this is, as you yourself suspect, the work of the Devil, then what right have I to say otherwise? So let me talk to your priest. And if it comes to no avail, I promise I will gladly surrender myself into Dr Whittle's care.'

Molly undid the straps. 'I'll hold you to that promise, Jojo.'

I manoeuvred myself stiffly to the edge of the couch and sat awhile, stretching my limbs and arching my spine. The lack of new growth from my fingers and toes were testament to the efficacy of the Glacier Moss. Upon hearing a loud grumble from my empty stomach, I collected a handful of soil from a potted plant and swallowed it down with a gulp of water straight from the jug.

'Please don't do that in front of Father Slaven,' complained Molly.

'I shall try,' I said, wiping the residual dirt from my grin. 'Would you guard the door, please? Warn me if you hear any movement.'

Molly positioned herself by the door and teased it open just enough to afford a view of the staircase along the hall.

I dressed hurriedly, then quickly collected the little tin of Glacier Moss from Father's desk. As useful as this remedy had thus far proved itself to be, when I looked at the tin sitting in the palm of my hand, I could not help but feel it represented a woefully inadequate arsenal with which to confront the boundless resources of Gladius Dei.

I carried a candle to Father's vast depository of notebooks and cursed the author's lack of regard in his arrangement of what was arguably the country's (if not the world's) pre-eminent library on nature's rarest and most exotic fauna. Regardless of Father's slapdash methodology, it did not take long to locate the volume I sought. In marked contrast to all the red leather spines crushing in on every side, this particular book was uniquely bound in black and embellished with a silver skull and crossbones motif.

The candle balanced on the teetering jumble, I scanned page after page of my father's fastidious handwriting, the text frequently supplemented with sketches of seeds, pods, leaves, flowers and the occasional portrait of a tribesman suffering the effects of some horrendous affliction. Herein was a meticulous catalogue of the deadliest plants he had thus far encountered on his numerous expeditions, with their symptoms laid out in the most vivid and distressing detail.

'What are you looking for?' asked Molly.

'Weaponry.'

'What sort of weaponry?'

'Listen to this,' I said, arriving at an entry with a particularly gruesome illustration. 'The spines of the Trystle Cactus of Northern Australia impart a venom which causes the skin to slough free from the body of any creature unfortunate enough to have been punctured in a matter of minutes, leaving the poor flayed victim writhing in unimaginable agony upon a rug of its own discarded hide.'

'That is disgusting!' said Molly.

I turned to the next page. 'And this! "The fruit of the Malula, a rare flowering bush of the Cook Islands: These purple berries when reduced to a paste and heated over a flame, release a noxious vapour which when inhaled, causes the tissue of the lungs to liquefy, leaving the victim to drown in his own blood."'

'Even more disgusting!'

I skipped a few more pages. 'The hooked thorns of the Jacintha Rose, a native of the Agafay desert, are perfectly designed to puncture the thickest skin whereupon its poison will reduce the victim's mind to an empty, vacuous husk, rendering them devoid of self-determination and powerless to resist the instruction of others. However, if the thorn is permitted to remain in the skin for a period of several hours, it will then adopt a bright yellow hue and be safely plucked free, allowing the victim – with a few days' recuperation – to make a full recovery. But should the thorn be removed from the skin prior to the aforementioned change of appearance, then the damage to the victim's brain will be permanent.'

'Hurry, Jojo! Someone is moving upstairs,' whispered Molly anxiously.

I skimmed to the last entry in Father's encyclopaedia of horrors. Under the heading *Flos Veritas – The Flower of Truth,* there followed a succinct summary of this singular bloom's attributes and effects:

'An orchid unique to the eastern slopes of the Mountains of the Moon, the snowy peaks which fuel the very source of the River Nile. The powdered labellum of this flower when swallowed (preferably dissolved in a little sugared water to mask its prodigious bitterness) will induce a pronounced urge to confess to even the most trivial of wrongdoings. The Dinka tribe of Abyssinia have for generations used this tiny bloom as a truth serum, forcing confessions from the mouths of miscreants and enemies. If too large a dose is taken (a half-scruple being the prescribed norm), the victim will become so plagued with guilt, so overwhelmed with sorrow, that he rapidly descends into a sustained mania of self-loathing. This madness destroys their reason, and in extreme cases victims have been known to scoop out their own eyes or chew their own flesh from the bone in penance for their sins before at length, they resolve to kill themselves by whatever means is at hand; be it drowning, hurling themselves from a precipice or self-immolation.'

'Quick, Jojo!' urged Molly.

In keeping with all the other entries, Father had added a catalogue number to the top right-hand corner of the page. I dashed to the wall of apothecary drawers, scouring the labels until I alighted on FV1832. I swiftly transferred my prize – a small green bottle filled with a pale powder – to my pocket, returned the black book to its precise position among the slipshod bank of journals and hurried to join my cousin.

'Let's go!'

CHAPTER SIXTEEN

The Altar and the Alley

Wrapped tightly in the face of the gnawing chill, we set off along the driveway. Halfway to the gates, I stopped and looked back.

'Are you having second thoughts?' asked Molly.

I realised then, as I admired the slumbering eccentricity of its chimneys and gables thrown as black shapes against the moonlight silvered clouds, that I would never set foot inside Braid House again.

'No.'

The darkness was lifted somewhat by the abundant crust of frozen snow at our feet. The pavements and roads held an itemised account of yesterday's ebb and flow in the pits and ruts of footprints, hoof prints and carriage tracks. Gripping the crook of my arm for balance, Molly amused herself by skidding and skating along the treacherous surface.

Deep in my greatcoat pockets I sensed fresh growths splitting the cuticles of my gloved fingers. I resisted the temptation to slow the newborn shoots with a sniff of the Glacier Moss, as I did not wish to deny the priest the opportunity to experience them in all their twisted glory.

Passing through Marchmont we made for The Meadows, where our progress was hampered further by the haar rolling in from the Firth, carrying with it the distant peal of navigation bells. Between those doleful chimes I fancied I heard the sound of footsteps pressing heavily into the snow on the path behind us. I glanced over my shoulder and there, no more than a dozen yards from our heels, stood a figure cloaked in mist. The man abruptly turned and ran, his shadow melting away into black silence.

'Something wrong?' said Molly, oblivious to his presence.

'No. How far to the church?'

'Not far.'

We trekked on for the generous street lamps of the New Town where, on Broughton Street, St Mary's Chapel finally emerged from the ubiquitous fog. A peculiar sound accompanied us as we started up the steps. The vigorous and persistent scraping noise emanated from somewhere to the side of the building. We turned to investigate and came upon a figure crouched by the wall towards the rear. Sleeves rolled to his elbows, he rinsed a large brush in a pail of water, put it back to the bricks and scrubbed hard at the words someone had daubed in thick white paint:

NO POPERY.

'Wait here, Jojo. Let me have a word with Father Slaven first,' said Molly.

Upon hearing her friendly greeting, the priest abandoned his onerous task, picked up his lamp and reciprocated with a broad smile. He was a tall man and though advancing in years, he still retained an imposing air of strength and nobility. A brief exchange followed, during which his smile faded. Molly gestured in my direction and the priest, peering at me through narrowed eyes, dropped the brush in the bucket and strode towards me.

'Come inside,' he said.

The atmosphere within the church evoked a confusion of emotions. It had been some hours since the last congregation had departed, yet the air – heavy and still with the scent of

Scott O'Neill

incense – continued to hold fragments of the hope, despair, anxiety and grief that fuelled their prayers. But these were as motes of dust in comparison to the centuries of melancholy imbued in the wood of the pews, the grand oak doors and the ornate frames adorning the Stations of the Cross and, most of all, in the large crucifix suspended over the altar. I ached in sorrow for the Lime Tree slain and then chiselled into a rough-hewn representation of another's pain and sacrifice; its every grain pressed deep with the guilt and remorse of innumerable sinners. If anyone were seeking evidence of a miracle, they need look no further than the supporting pillars, for it was a wonder they had not collapsed under the sheer weight of all this accumulated suffering.

My palm began to itch so terribly as I followed Father Slaven and Molly towards the altar that I was forced to bite the irritation through the glove in order to find any relief.

'And how is Tam, Molly?' asked the priest, inviting us both to take a seat in the front pew.

'He's well, Father.'

'Glad to hear it. It was tragic what happened to the *Majestic North*. Tragic. And what a commotion! All those bells, the shouting, the firemen! I woke from my bed thinking the Apocalypse had descended on Leith. Now then, Joseph, are you a Catholic yourself?'

'No, Father.'

'Are you a man of faith?'

'What faith I may have had has been sorely tested by recent events, Father.'

The priest nodded thoughtfully. 'No matter. Here you sit in His church in your hour of need, which proves you have not ruled our Lord Jesus Christ out of your life completely.'

'I am in no position to rule anything out,' I said, scratching my palm.

'So, what vexes you enough to bring you here on such a

frigid morning?'

'Show him, Joseph,' said Molly.

I must have hesitated too long for Molly's liking because she lost her patience, snatched my hands, plucked away the gloves and thrust my fingers in front of the priest.

'Mother of God,' he muttered aghast, then crossed himself not once, but three times.

As expected, fresh growths had split from the tips of every digit. But a new and equally abhorrent development had occurred which sickened me to the core. There was a deep fissure cleaving the palm of my right hand. The split ran in a long curve from the base of the thumb to the first knuckle of the little finger. Beads of clear sap leaked from the wound and the skin on either side had curled apart, revealing a dark colour underneath. I gingerly parted the flesh further. Molly covered her mouth and gasped. The priest teetered backwards from the horrible sight. Beneath the broken skin a new layer had formed. Rough in texture and hard to the touch, it was a dark greyish green, like the bark of a young tree. I pressed a thumb around the wound and outwards across my hand. The extent of this new hard layer had spread as far as my wrist. With tears in my eyes, I lifted my head to the priest.

'Please, help me.'

'Wait there,' said Father Slaven before he dashed down the aisle to lock the church door. A sharp clang echoed to the rafters as he slid the sturdy iron bolt home, then hurried for the vestry, into which he disappeared for a brief while. He returned dressed in green and gold robes and carrying a copy of the *Rituale Romanum*. 'We must act quickly. There is not a moment to lose,' he said, hastily circling the altar to light the candles. 'But first, I need more details. When and how did these deformities first appear?'

I breathlessly recounted the legend of the Witch Tree and of Margaret McKay's curse and of my own sorry involvement in both.

'Does this affliction exhibit itself in other ways? For example, are you speaking in tongues? Are you hearing voices inside your head? Have you encountered any manifestations, apparitions, evil spirits of any form? Does being here in this church, in God's house, leave you feeling nauseous?' said the clergyman, firing the questions with bewildering rapidity.

I told him of the unsettling visions, of my ability to hear the laments of all the dead things that surrounded us, and of my disturbing craving for soil.

The priest shook his head gravely. 'Filling your mouth with dirt is the surest sign of Lucifer's influence. But be assured, we shall defeat him. Now Joseph, I must ask you to lay yourself here before the altar.'

I looked to Molly. Her attempt at a reassuring nod of encouragement did nothing to allay my anxiety.

'Have strength, Joseph. Trust in the Lord,' the priest continued, skipping through the pages of his book. 'No harm can befall you here in God's house. You must try to remain as still as you can. And Molly? You must resist the temptation to intervene, no matter what you may witness. Thank you. Good. Now...'

I settled upon the floor and fixed my gaze on the priest towering over my head, a silver aspergillum in one hand, the open book in the other.

'In the name of the Father and of the Son and of the Holy Spirit, amen,' began Father Slaven, sprinkling cold droplets of holy water as he spoke.

'Amen,' echoed Molly. Hands pressed in prayer, she raised her eyes to the crucifix.

'Oh! Glorious prince of the heavenly host. Saint Michael the Archangel, defend us in the battle and in the fearful warfare that we are waging against the principalities and against the powers of the rulers of this world of darkness...'

I flattened my itching palm against the cool smooth stone and permitted my gaze to drift with the blue spirals of candle smoke to the church's vaulted ceiling, where the rafters and joists whispered of cruelty and wilful violence.

'I exorcise thee, every unclean spirit, in the name of God, the Father Almighty...'

Constrained within my boots, the new shoots emerging from my toes began to throb in protest at their imprisonment. The priest spat into his hands, rubbed them together and knelt by my side.

'Devil, be gone!' he cried, touching first my ears, then my nostrils. 'For the judgment of God is at hand.'

His spittle reeked of smoked fish. My stomach spasmed and my bones quaked. And there was I, swimming amongst them in their teeming thousands. Fish caught in a net. A seething mass of panic fuelled by an invisible and ever tightening obstruction. The water churned to a glinting quicksilver storm of scales, fins, tails and frenzied eyes. Mouths gaped in silent screams where gills had become entangled in the fibres of the mesh. Others, driven frantic with distress and not understanding the futility of their actions, attempted to drive themselves through holes too small to accommodate their madly flexing bodies and suffered the same fate. The prisoners turned on one another, biting and thrashing at their immediate neighbour in a last frenetic bid for survival. Suddenly we found ourselves rising as one single entity from our Mother Sea into a bright airborne hell. I watched her waves fall away beneath our dripping ascension into the savage daylight whilst the suffocating weight of hundreds of slipping, writhing, wriggling and gasping bodies pressed down upon me...

'Do you believe in God, the Father Almighty, creator of Heaven and Earth?' asked Father Slaven, with a grim determination.

I gasped noiselessly...

'Do you believe in God, the Father Almighty, creator of Heaven and Earth?'

An invisible giant, determined to grind me to dust like a worthless insect, pressed his boot heel hard on my collapsing chest and crushed the answer from my throat.

'Joseph, you must respond, please,' implored the priest. 'Do you believe in God, the Father Almighty, creator of Heaven and Earth?'

The blade cleaved me open from abdomen to throat. Great fingers slipped around my innards, grasping at the guts and tearing them out.

'Do you believe in Jesus Christ, His only son, our Lord who was born and suffered for us?'

I tried to scream, to communicate the eviscerating pain, but nothing escaped my lips other than a useless, rasping exhalation.

'You must respond, Joseph!'

The priest dabbed a thumb in holy water and pressed it to my brow. His wet skin instantly burned a hole into my head and lit the fuse on a violent storm of convulsions. The acrid taste of brine flooded my tongue. I could stem the nauseous tide no longer. The sea spilled from my mouth, spreading a dark stain over the flagstones. Another purge lifted the suffocating pressure from my lungs and I was free to draw a precious breath and clamber to my feet.

'Joseph! You must finish this!' cried Father Slaven as I ran for the door.

'Wait, Jojo!'

My fingers, stiff and gnarled by the spasms, fumbled desperately at the bolt.

'If you leave now, he has won! Do not give him the satisfaction!' cried the priest, hurrying down the aisle with Molly.

At last the door parted and I dashed outside into the mist

now so thick it was impossible to determine one step from the next. I stumbled onwards into the street, relishing the cleansing sharpness of the open air, the oppressive sorrows of the church dissipating with each sweet intake. The tormenting itch at my palm abated almost immediately. Behind me, reduced to indistinct silhouettes framed within the dim yellow arch of the church doorway, stood Father Slaven and Molly.

'This is beyond my understanding. I have done what I can,' said the distressed priest. The door closed with a deep, baleful thud.

I pressed on with no direction in mind other than to increase the distance between myself and the horrors of St Mary's as quickly as possible but was forced to a halt when Molly hurried to my side and grasped me by the elbow.

'What happened to you back there? Talk to me,' she demanded.

'How can you tolerate being in such a miserable place?' I replied bitterly. 'So much sadness in one building. I was drowning in it!'

'Oh, Jojo, the Devil is making you say these things. We must go back. Please, let Father Slaven complete the ritual.'

'No. It was idiotic of me to have even tried.'

'Idiotic? Turning to God is not idiotic!' said Molly with some consternation. 'You mustn't say such things. God will help you if you will only ask. Please, come back to the church with me.'

Exasperated by her stubborn refusal to see sense, I pushed my hands close to her face, compelling her to view the roots spearing from my nails and the horrible wound slicing my palm.

'Have you not been paying attention? God has abandoned me! ... And so should you.'

Molly calmly took my wrists and lowered the monstrous appendages from her sight. 'No. He has not. And nor will I.'

The tears shining in her eyes filled me with shame. I had inexcusably piled all my resentment and rage upon the one person who had remained steadfast and loyal throughout my ordeal.

'Go home, Molly,' I implored, hiding the deformities back inside their gloves. 'You will only come to harm if you stay with me.'

'Not until we find a cure.'

A sudden pain blazed at my spine, forcing me to my hands and knees.

'Jojo!'

'The Glacier Moss,' I gasped. 'In my pocket. Quick!'

Molly delved into my coat, retrieved the medicine and held a pinch to my nose. The agony eased.

'The parasite?' said Molly, aiding me to my feet.

'It's growing stronger by the hour. I fear it will soon destroy me completely.'

'You mustn't think that way.'

'Why not,' I said, feeling an odd rush of warmth inside my chest. The sensation flowed to my head, leaving me momentarily dizzy.

'Because there is always hope,' insisted Molly.

The warmth settled at the back of my mind, producing a dull, nagging ache.

'Is there? I see none. The world used to be a place of endless wonder and discovery to me. Now all I can see, all I can *feel* is the endless cruelty we inflict upon its creatures every moment of every day. There is a rage burning within me, Molly. It is Margaret McKay's rage. A rage against the never-ending brutality. The destruction of all that is beautiful. And the perpetual slaughter of innocence. She has shown me the truth. And I thank her for it. For the truth is, what is happening to me is not a curse. It is an awakening! I *am* the curse! We all are! *We* are the parasite! In our arrogance and in our selfishness, we have become the architects of hell on earth. Margaret McKay knew this! Hope is for fools. Rage is the answer. Our rage is the only thing that will bring about their downfall!'

The ache intensified. Waves of colour ebbed and flowed behind my eyes. Each hue brought forth its own distinct emotion.

'I am so sorry, Molly,' I said, overcome by an intense, azure swell of remorse. 'But you must understand, it was this rage that drove me to burn the *Majestic*...'

A horrible realisation sparked in Molly's eyes and I knew I had failed to curtail my wayward tongue in time.

'You?' she said, the accusation no more than a strained whisper. 'It was you who burned Pa's ship? You burned the *Majestic North*?'

'Yes, but –'

'You might have killed him. You might have killed the whole crew. What were you *thinking*?' she said, retreating a step.

'I made sure there was no one on board. Molly, this is what I've been trying to explain. It wasn't me. It was this rage inside. I am so, so sorry.'

'You took away our home! You took away Pa's livelihood. No! Not another word. I can't bear to look at you.' Molly emphasised her dismay by obscuring my face behind her open palms before she turned heel and vanished into the smothering fog.

'Molly!'

The parasite jabbed repeatedly at my spine and again I collapsed in crippling agony on to all fours. I clutched frantically at my coat. Molly had returned the medicine to my left pocket. I reached inside and straightaway I knew, as I touched the glass phial, why the pain had refused to dissipate. In her haste she had mistakenly administered a pinch of Flos Veritas! I snatched the tin from the other pocket and managed, in spite of my quaking hands, to gather a measure of Glacier Moss.

The pain subsided at once.

Reeling with shame, I struggled to my feet and for an interminable moment, I stared into the silent grey confusion.

'Molly!'

The mist responded with a scuff of footsteps chasing off in the direction where last I saw her.

I blundered headlong into the morass and entered a close so oppressively narrow and gloomy I could hardly distinguish my own feet from the snow and ice stained with the spill of overflowing gutters. The stench rose up in murky wreathes to mingle with the hidden whisperings issued from an open window in the crumbling tenement somewhere over my head. I heard the footsteps chase into the distance; running, then slowing, then running again.

'Molly!'

A hefty splash exploded on the setts behind me, rapidly followed by the slam of a window. I quickened pace and within a few yards the alley dog-legged to the right where it assumed a pronounced upward gradient, which I took as an indication that perhaps I was soon to arrive on the Canongate or thereabouts.

The assumption proved entirely erroneous when I found my way blocked by a solid and unscalable wall. I aimed a kick at the infuriating bricks and leaned back against the dead end, cursing my own ineptitude. I thought I knew the city and all its geographic idiosyncrasies at least as well as any other man. How wrong I was!

The impenetrable fog folded in on itself, pressing and probing in slow waves. It too was seeking an escape route. I watched its curtains sway and weave, its fabric stretching and pulling at the seams. Then fleetingly, the threads of mist tore apart to reveal a dark mass sprawled upon the ground close to my feet.

'Molly!'

I dashed to her side and carefully lifted her from the puddles and the dirt. Her limbs splayed like a broken doll in my arms. Her eyes were closed and splashes of red speckled her face. The stains continued along the sleeve of her coat, culminating at the wet blade of the little dagger-brooch clutched in her hand.

I sensed the warm flowing urgency of the blood and nerves at work beneath her skin, and to my great relief I was able to discern that no serious damage had been sustained.

Molly's eyelids flickered hesitantly open. She started at the sight of someone looming so close, but her fear quickly turned to anger when she recognised the familiar face.

'Get away from me, Judas!' she hissed.

'What happened to you?'

'I said get away!' She pushed me aside and propped her aching body against the wall. 'How could you do that to us? How could you destroy your own family?'

'Molly, please. Let me explain. It's not me. It's the parasite!'

But Molly had no desire to hear my defence.

'You are the parasite! I will never –' The fright suddenly returned to her eyes.

'What's wrong?'

'Shhh! Listen!' Molly peered past me aiming her little dagger towards the alley. 'I think he's coming back,' she said, trembling.

I turned and stared anxiously into the fog.

The sound was short and sharp. Again it came. The strike of metal against a hard surface. And with it, the slow advance of boots. Closer they stepped, heavy and with purpose. Another strike. A spark briefly escaped the greyness. The coils of shifting mist separated to reveal a great brute of a man. Twice the bulk and a full head taller than myself, he had one hand clasped against a deep gash at his neck whilst in the other, the blade of a knife glinted menacingly. I recognised the murderous intent blazing in the man's eyes. It was the same man Hugh Tulland had conversed with outside the White Hart on the afternoon of our visit to Finlayson.

He stopped and once again sparked his blade against the side of the alley. A malignant twist of amusement played on his mouth as he watched me scramble to examine the wall at our backs, hoping for a ledge we could scale or a window to clamber through.

'Ah, the wee witches are feart!' the man growled. 'Well, fear not. My blade is sharp and quick.' He removed the hand nursing his neck and used the palm to smear a mask of crimson over his entire face. 'Sharp and quick!'

The man charged at Molly. I threw myself between them and wrestled desperately to divert the knife from its intended target, but it was a hopelessly one-sided contest. I was grappling with an arm forged from wrought iron. His blood-slicked fingers grasped my jaw and pushed my head hard against the coarse brickwork. Fearing my skull would soon crack under the intense pressure, I applied every remaining ounce of strength into halting the blade's progress.

My feeble efforts were brushed aside with contemptuous ease.

'Sharp and quick is good,' he hissed. 'Sharp and *sloooow* is bett –'

The Goliath's malicious smile suddenly quivered under a heavy, dull thud. Eyes bulging, he lumbered backwards, clutching the crown of his head.

Framed in a glow of swirling ochre another man stepped forward, brandishing a lamp and one broken half of an old plank of wood; the other half lay in splinters at his feet. A thick muffler and a wide-brimmed hat largely obscured the man's features, leaving only his eyes visible. The newcomer raised his bludgeon ready to land another blow, but the brute swatted it aside as if it were an irritating gnat and swung a fist to his attacker's jaw. Our would-be saviour toppled like a felled tree and as he collapsed in a dazed heap upon the ground, the hat and muffler slipped from his face.

'Wait!'

My cry produced the desired result. The knife travelling for Mr Maybury's chest hesitated. In one swift action I took the little tin box from my pocket and threw its entire contents directly into the thug's great cannonball of a head. The cloud of dust flowed freely into his gaping mouth and nostrils. Enraged, he redirected his blade towards my throat, but as the steel closed in, he lost all momentum and came to a sudden and complete standstill.

'Cover your faces! There's still some in the air.'

Heeding my advice to mask themselves from the few remaining particles of dust now dissipating into the mist, Molly and Mr Maybury lifted themselves from the ground.

I circled our cataleptic assailant. The exceptional slowness of his movement was fascinating to observe. The knife continued to travel towards the empty space previously occupied by my neck, albeit at an almost imperceptible speed, whilst his head began to turn at a similarly glacial rate towards my current location. But there was no slowing of the hatred which continued to flare within the furnace of his eyes.

'Glacier Moss?' asked Mr Maybury.

'Yes.'

'Ha! I suspect our friend has inhaled enough to paralyse him for a full month.' Mr Maybury searched the man's pockets, but they yielded nothing of interest. 'Are you hurt, Miss Keane?' he said, spying the patches of blood on her face and coat.

'That's not my blood,' said Molly. She sheathed her lethal little dagger back inside the brooch. 'What shall we do with him?'

Mr Maybury prised the blade from the man's grip. 'Leave him. The rats deserve to eat as much as we.'

'We can't do that!' said Molly, evidently shocked by the image she had conjured up in her mind's eye. 'Can we?'

'You have a merciful heart, Miss Keane. Merciful but misguided.' He raised the knife, inviting Molly to observe its every lethal facet. 'What mercy do you believe he would have afforded you, hmm?' Mr Maybury lifted his lamp for a close inspection of the stupefied man's head. It did not take him long to locate the object of his search.

'Ah! Here's our proof.' Mr Maybury folded back the left ear to reveal a small tattoo behind the lobe. Crudely executed though it was, its shape was all too familiar.

'Gladius Dei!' I gasped.

'This particular agent of theirs has been following you from the moment you left the grounds of Braid House.'

'How do you know?' asked Molly.

'Because he wasn't the only one. This fog has made it devilishly difficult at times, particularly when you had your wee disagreement back there at the church. Thankfully your footprints are fairly distinctive. Nevertheless, I can only apologise for not reaching you sooner.'

A deep croak began to rumble at the back of the assassin's throat and his eyes embarked on a journey towards Mr Maybury with all the haste of a flower turning for the sun. I had the impression he had only now realised he had been disarmed and was beginning the process of issuing a bloodthirsty threat which would take him some hours to impart.

'We must be on our way,' said Mr Maybury. 'I suspect our friend here will not be the only one out to seek mischief upon you, Joseph.'

'But where shall we go? Back to Braid House?' asked Molly.

'Out of the question, I'm afraid. Gladius Dei have at least

two men waiting for you there.'

'Doctor Whittle?' said I.

'For one. And he will not be best pleased to find you gone,' smiled Mr Maybury.

We turned in unison on hearing the furious barking of a dog deadened by distance and the enveloping grey gauze. Molly reached for her brooch.

'No,' continued Mr Maybury, 'we shall go to Archibald's.'

'You know Mr Finlayson? But how?' said Molly.

'I shall explain everything on the way. But we must make haste.'

Guided by Mr Maybury's lamp, we retreated from the alley and left the paralysed knifeman grumbling into the fog like the protracted creak of a door opening on rusty hinges.

A hazy dawn had draped itself over the Canongate when finally we escaped the labyrinth.

'You said Gladius Dei have at least two men waiting at Braid House,' I said to Mr Maybury as we made for the High Street. 'If Whittle is one, who is the other?'

Mr Maybury stopped and turned to me. His expression, normally so stoic, so resolute, was beset with turmoil. It was a look I shall never forget.

'The other is your father.'

CHAPTER SEVENTEEN

The Circle

'My dear, you must not be too hard on your cousin. He is at the mercy of Margaret McKay's spell and cannot be held responsible for whatever actions her magic compels him to perform. Be that the consumption of soil or the burning of a ship.'

Molly offered a small, tired sigh. 'I don't care.'

'And though I fully respect your beliefs, a priest is no more qualified in these matters than any of the hawkers on Princes Street. The issue at hand needs to be addressed with the cool dispassionate logic of the academic. I myself have studied these matters all my life and I can assure you that never in all my years of study have I come across a single instance where an exorcism has successfully negated the symptoms of a curse. Put simply, witchcraft is the cause, therefore witchcraft must provide the cure.'

'But surely we must put our trust in God!' protested Molly.

'Why? Why must we trust this God of yours? A God who doth smite far more than he doth smile. No. Far wiser to place your trust in Mother Nature. The one true Goddess of all the natural laws of the universe.' Mr Finlayson shook his head sadly. 'But no one is heeding her preachings. An oversight for which, I assure you, mankind will pay a very heavy toll.'

The long, excitable and at times heated conversation

between my cousin and the old occultist had flowed without interruption ever since Mr Maybury delivered us safely to Mr Finlayson's shop. I remained silent throughout, distracted by the single phrase echoing over and over inside my head:

'The other is your father…'

The revelation had bombarded my soul with all the force of a blast from Mons Meg, scattering the splinters of my wits and reason to the mercy of the Four Winds. And Mr Maybury had more to tell as he led us quickly through the city. Much more. For a man who had always affected a most taciturn and morose demeanour, he unleashed such a gush of words it was as though, after a lifetime of swallowing secrets, piling them up from the pit of his stomach to the tip of his gullet, the cork that was his tongue could no longer stem the intolerable pressure. Not that my fractured mind had the least capacity to concentrate on the ensuing verbal deluge. Nevertheless, a few salient headlines did force their way between the cracks.

Mr Maybury was a spy. Sixteen years ago, he had been assigned the task of gaining a position aboard *The Cygnet*, a ship chartered by one Lachlan Ware and owned by a company known to be connected to Gladius Dei. Securing a berth as a deckhand, he sailed to the South Seas on an expedition to gather rare flora from the Samoan archipelago. During this adventure and the others that followed, he patiently worked to gain Lachlan's complete confidence till at last, after almost a decade of loyal and diligent service, he was offered the opportunity to become his personal assistant. From this unique position of trust, he mined a treasure trove of information, all of which he forwarded to his companions-in-arms. For Mr Maybury belonged to 'The Circle' – a dedicated band of disciples sworn to protect the last of Scotland's witches from the scourge of Gladius Dei.

'Our purpose is a simple one,' he explained. 'To keep the flame of witchcraft alive. There are so few practitioners of

Scott O'Neill

the craft left that we must protect them as best we can. Ours is a doctrine enshrined in the laws of nature; one of peace, of positivity, of equilibrium. We must preserve its history, its teachings, its spells, its philosophy and the natural well from which it all springs. We must not allow it to die – or worse, fall into the hands of those who would use its many wonders to inflict harm.'

But lately the battle had become increasingly forlorn for The Circle. They had not the money, nor the power nor the influence that their enemy enjoyed in abundance. Gladius Dei utilised these three amoral bedfellows to extend the reach of their iniquitous grasp far across the globe, crushing all opposition, no matter how insignificant, under their brutish heel.

Over generations, The Circle had lost countless good men and women to their tyranny and now numbered fewer than a hundred souls scattered across all of Scotland. As for the number of true witches still in existence for them to protect? Mr Maybury unfurled four fingers before falling into a lengthy period of doleful silence.

We were gathered in the basement; Molly and I encouraged to sit by the hearth, where the sprightliest of fires allowed us to first dry and then brush the dirt from our clothes and boots. Mr Maybury had refused the very same comforts and decided instead to make straight for Braid House before the length of his absence raised suspicion.

Mr Finlayson watched me bite the buds from my fingertips with an unsettling mix of pity and fascination.

'Does that hurt?'

'A little. Mr Maybury has promised to collect a fresh supply of Glacier Moss.'

I dropped the trimmings into the flames. Her fingers tapping impatiently against the arms of her chair, Molly watched them boil and melt on the coals.

'Do you think us wise to leave that man there? Should we not go back and demand some answers from him?' she asked.

'By all means. Go and make your demands,' said Mr Finlayson, gesturing to the stairs. 'But I suspect the spring daffodils will be in bloom long before the Glacier Moss sufficiently loosens its grip to allow an answer to escape his lips. Oh! how I wish I could have been there to witness its effects! Ha! And serve him right! The Gladius Dei ruffian!'

Propelled by a sudden fury, I sprang from my chair and pounded a seeping fist upon the mantel.

'This is all wrong! My own father belongs to a society that routinely murders and tortures people? A society that would happily see me dead? Not possible! Mr Maybury has been having fun at my expense. When he returns, I shall not hesitate to impress upon him how little I appreciate his sense of humour!'

'Calm yourself,' said Mr Finlayson. 'You have had a terrible shock. Come and sit with me, both of you. Some hot tea will soothe our nerves.'

Molly and I joined our host at the walnut table where Mr Finlayson filled three cups from a silver pot.

'You are correct on one point, Joseph, Mr Maybury's sense of humour is indeed something of an enigma. However, and I truly wish it were not so, I'm afraid on this occasion Mr Maybury does not jest. Lachlan Ware has been a devoted follower of Gladius Dei since before you were born. It is Gladius Dei who finance his expeditions. Why? Because despite their avowed loathing of the magical and the supernatural, the one thing they have learned through centuries of persecution is that witchcraft is based on an undeniable truth. The truth that Nature holds all the keys. The keys to health, happiness and contentment. But Gladius Dei want to keep that precious set of keys for themselves and use them to unlock all of Nature's gifts. They want to plunder those gifts. To refine, bottle and sell the magical healing properties contained in the world's flowers, herbs and roots in order to fill their vaults with gold. For they understand that with gold comes power. The power to influence governments and lawmakers, who for twenty pieces of silver, will clear a path allowing unfettered access to Nature's bounty. A bounty they exploit with impunity wherever their agents may discover it afresh. Agents such as Lachlan Ware. No continent is beyond their reach. I fear they will not be sated until there are no fish left in the sea, no trees to reach for the sky and nothing to breathe but soot and ash. They *have* to be stopped.' Finlayson took a sip from his cup. 'Ah...' he sighed mournfully, 'but we are so few in number.'

'You burned the wrong ship. You should have burned Uncle Lachlan's,' said Molly, seething. She still could not bring herself to look at me.

The knot of fury in my stomach became a tangle of despair. I stared into the steam rising from my tea, its warmth imbued with a thousand little sharp shocks of plucked leaves and the last fear-struck memories of the cattle whose bones had been incinerated, then crushed, then combined with clay to make the china cup.

'I don't... I don't. Believe you,' I stammered. 'He is a good man. He wouldn't... He wouldn't...'

Taking care to avoid his motley collection of heretical exhibits, Mr Finlayson picked up his chair and carried it to his library. He stepped on to the seat and reached to explore the disorderly array of dusty boxes and papers perched on the lofty cliff tops of the towering bookcases.

'Your family's association with Gladius Dei stretches back many generations. As does its obsession with the legend of the Witch Tree. Your great-great-grandfather John purchased the Braid Estate not because he had any great love for the house, but because it provided exclusive access to the tree. However, interest in the Witch Tree waned over time and eventually it was relegated to the status of an insignificant old folk tale. Then, some years after the murder of your grandfather Malcolm, Lachlan discovered Margaret McKay's spell amongst his father's papers and the obsession was born anew.'

'Did you say, *murder*? You are mistaken. My grandfather's death was an accident,' I said, irritated by the old man's incessant rummaging.

'Ah yes, the Clyne's puffball incident. I take it you believe your father's version of events?'

'So now you accuse my father of being both a murderer *and* a witch-hunter?'

'Here we are!' said Mr Finlayson, lifting down a sandalwood box. He returned to the table and answered my scowl with a good-humoured smile. 'Not only is Lachlan Ware a murderer and a witch-hunter, he is also a liar,' he said, placing the box before him.

'This is absurd! If anyone is a liar, it is you!' I snapped. 'If, as you claim, my family has supported Gladius Dei for generations, why have I never heard mention of it?'

'Because you have not yet come of age. The men of the Ware family are traditionally initiated into the cause on the occasion of their twentieth birthday. In the normal course of events, you would have been presented before the High Council of Gladius Dei to be cross-examined regarding your suitability for inclusion into the fold on your very next birthday. A moment you have been prepared for all your life.'

'Prepared? How?'

'Think back to your childhood, Joseph. Think back to all those horrifying bedtime tales Lachlan told you. Stories of how the brave world of science is locked in a constant struggle to bring God's light to bear upon a world thrown into darkness by the Devil's magic. Think back to those long walks you shared, when Lachlan loaded your young mind with bloodthirsty tales of the heinous crimes perpetrated by witches. Tales of children killed in their sleep by the wicked spells of Margaret McKay. Every word designed to foster a loathing for witches and their craft in your heart.' Finlayson leaned back in his chair and gazed pensively at my damaged fingers. 'Year on year Lachlan has encouraged you to rise to the challenge of catching that chestnut. It is fair to suppose he never imagined for one moment you might succeed. But now that you have, he and Gladius Dei have new plans for you.'

'What plans?' I asked, warily.

Mr Finlayson suddenly spread his arms to encompass me in a gesture of astonishment. 'Look at you! You are the Holy Grail! An opportunity to study at first hand the intricate workings of the Ossa Lignum curse! They are of the belief that the key to all magic now resides within you. Placed there by Margaret McKay's spell. The very thing they have been butchering innocents for centuries in order to find. The *Viscus of Devilry*. And now they mean to cut you open and separate every last piece of you until they lay their hands upon it. To Lachlan, you are nothing more than a scientific curiosity. The means by which he and his rapacious brethren can better understand and exploit the secrets of witchcraft. You are but a sacrificial lamb on the altar of their greed.'

Molly folded her arms and eyed the old man sceptically.

'How do you know all this about my uncle?'

'Because I have read Lachlan's diaries.'

'That's not possible!' I exclaimed. 'His journals are kept under lock and key in his study.'

'And yet here, inside this box we have copies of some of your father's more pertinent entries. Take a look for yourself.'

Mr Finlayson pushed the box across the table. Aside from a few scratches and scuffs to the polished veneer, there were no markings of any kind.

I opened the lid.

'You have given me the wrong box,' I said flatly.

'I believe you'll find that is the correct box.'

'Then where are my father's diaries?'

'You are looking at them,' said Mr Finlayson, his eyes twinkling.

'What are you talking about? There's nothing but petals in here,' I protested, now fully convinced that the aged bookseller had lost command of his faculties.

Molly looked inside the box. It was filled with hundreds upon hundreds of flower petals. The petals buried at the bottom were browned and curled with age whereas those at the surface were markedly fresher and retained their vibrancy. With the waft of their heady scent came an inkling of the flowers' experience. A brief existence spent tracing the arc of the sun as it crossed the sky while the bees and the hoverflies drank their fill.

'Take one and read it,' came the infuriating reply.

I glared at him.

'Mr Finlayson, please. I am too tired, too angry and too confused for childish games.'

'And I am far too old to play them,' he said, holding my petulant gaze. 'Take one. Hold it against the light and look closely.'

I searched his kindly expression for signs of a seam or a join. A way to peel back his disguise and reveal the impostor beneath. I wanted to finally expose him as an elderly fool with nothing to offer other than an endless litany of nonsensical ramblings accompanied by a hatful of extraordinary eccentricities. For if I could dismiss this man as such, then I fancied I might comfortably dismiss all else I had experienced in much the same manner and still awake from this horrendous dream to find everything returned to its proper state. To my dismay, the eyes of the old man patiently awaiting my judgement, contained not a trace of deceit but rather an abundance of beneficence and a clarity of purpose, at once noble, honest and compelling.

I followed his instruction and held the petal of a corn-flower to the glow of a candle.

'Notice anything?' he asked.

'Only that I am being taken for a fool.'

Molly helped herself to a bright yellow buttercup petal.

'Are those holes?' she said, angling the petal this way and that. 'Aye, there! I can see lots of wee holes all over it.'

Mr Finlayson grinned and lit his pipe, his nostrils venting smoke as he watched us intently like some wise old dragon. Subjecting my own pale blue petal to a more thorough examination, I soon discovered that it too was perforated with scores of tiny little pinholes. Narrowing my eyes further, I began to realise that these assorted dots were not as random as they initially appeared but were in fact arranged in a series of deliberate shapes and patterns. Some were grouped in two and threes, whereas others formed geometric symbols, including a triangle and a square. Others still, were grouped into parallel lines, some vertical some horizontal, punctuated on occasion by a solitary dot.

'What do they mean?' I asked, now fully engrossed in the little mystery.

'They are coded transcripts. The petals carry some of the more pertinent entries taken from Lachlan's diaries and also letters he's received from his Gladius Dei associates,' explained Mr Finlayson. 'Your mother is a remarkably inventive and courageous woman. The bravest and cleverest soul I have ever met.'

'What has any of this to do with my mother?'

'Mr Maybury is not the only spy in your midst,' said Mr Finlayson.

'Aunt Bility is a spy! I think I love her more than ever!' proclaimed Molly, joyously.

'The Petal Code is entirely Bility's creation. Completely

unbreakable. Unless you have the key of course. Which I have.'
Mr Finlayson tapped his head. 'As you know, every second
Saturday she visits Greyfriars Kirkyard under the pretext
of sketching her lichens and mosses. Bility's real purpose,
however, is to furnish me with intelligence regarding Lachlan
and his Gladius Dei cohorts using the coded petals which she
leaves behind the loose stone at the base of old Mr Buchanan's
memorial for my collection. All this she does at great personal
peril, for should her allegiance to The Circle ever come to light
the consequences would be…' Mr Finlayson shook his troubled
head. 'Well, let us not pursue that unhappy thought,' he said,
removing his spectacles to polish them with a handkerchief.
'You should be immensely proud of your mother. Her work
has saved many a life.'

'I have had my fill of your lunatic ravings!' I cried, grasping
desperately as the walls of my past came tumbling down. The
memories piling up in ruins.

'Every word is the truth, Joseph. I believe you saw me
during Bility's most recent excursion to Greyfriars making a
very poor show of blending into the shadows as I waited to
collect her message. I fear I am not at all adept at subterfuge.'

'Even if I were to believe a single word of your ludicrous
fantasises, why now? Why would you risk exposing my
mother's secret now?'

'Because she asked me to,' said Mr Finlayson. He produced
a pair of dried rose petals from the pocket of his waistcoat,
one red, one white. 'She had Mr Maybury deliver these to me
yesterday.'

I snatched the petals from his fingers and held them to
the light.

'Your protection has been Bility's primary consideration
since the day you were born. She has spent her life shielding you
from the dangers that have always surrounded you. But now,
with all that has occurred, she accepts there is no longer any

value in keeping you in the dark. You must be made completely aware of the evil forces ranged against you. And none are more dedicated to their wicked cause than your father.'

'What do these petals say?' I said, growing ever more frustrated by my failure to decipher any semblance of meaning in the perforations.

'It's quite simple,' puffed Mr Finlayson. 'Red is the location. White is the hour.'

'You are to meet with her? Where? When?'

I had come to accept the reality of never setting eyes on my mother again, but this dark prospect now faded in the joyful pinpricks of light shining through the petals.

'Five o'clock tomorrow evening at Number Sixteen, Dalrymple Place. Your mother wishes to discuss plans on how best to secure your safety. I must confess I am more than a little troubled by the idea. Events have overtaken us. This arrangement was made before Lachlan apprised Gladius Dei of just what a wondrous prize you are. And now that prize has slipped from their grasp, we can be certain that at this very moment, they will be deploying every means at their disposal into finding you.'

Mr Finlayson drew thoughtfully on his pipe as he considered the implications.

'So, for the entire Edinburgh Division to congregate in one place at so dangerous a time? We would be taking a very grave risk indeed. Once again good judgement dies under the heel of desperation.'

'Who are the Edinburgh Division?' asked Molly, continuing to admire the box of coded petals.

'Myself, Mr Maybury, Bility and three others. All of whom you shall meet tomorrow. We six are all that remain of The Circle's network in Edinburgh. Three weeks ago there were seven of us. But then…' the bookseller sighed sadly, 'then they killed poor Francis Baxter.'

'The man murdered at Advocate's Close?' I said, recalling Mother's sorrowful mood when she learned of the young lawyer's death.

'Indeed. But let us put our troubles aside for the time being. You both have had a most vexatious day. You must rest. I shall prepare a room for you in my lodgings above the shop. It is not much, but it is comfortable and soon warms up once the fire is lit. Ah! Which reminds me. I have a gift for you, Joseph.' Mr Finlayson collected a pair of tongs from the hearthside and pushed them deep into the burning coals. 'Here we are,' he said, removing a dark and lustrous pebble from the fire. 'Baked to perfection!'

I leaned in for a closer look. Its surface gleamed like burnished copper. 'What is it?'

'It is a flame-stone. An ancient talisman. Celtic in origin.'

'It's beautiful,' said Molly. 'What does it do?'

Mr Finlayson's alarming response was to drop the stone from the tongs into the palm of his hand. 'Oh, it is not in the least bit hot,' he said, plainly amused by the consternation precipitated by this foolhardy act. 'All the heat is stored at its core. The exterior is quite cold to the touch. Here, try it for yourself.'

Molly took up the challenge without hesitation.

'How is it possible?' she gasped, closing her fist around the stone.

'That is a question I cannot answer,' admitted Mr Finlayson with a smile. He transferred the curious little object into my own hand.

The flame-stone was as cold as a snowball. Holding it to the light revealed a small hole at one end and some strange, intricate markings etched on the surface. Turning the stone on its head, I saw that they represented an owl, wings spread under enormous eyes.

'You wear it like so,' said Finlayson, revealing his own

flame-stone suspended from a thin leather cord around his neck. 'And when you are in the company of someone who means to do you harm, it will warn you by releasing some of the heat it has absorbed from the fire. The greater the threat, the hotter it will glow. But you will be perfectly safe here. Our immediate priority is to build up your strength with food and rest, for tomorrow promises to be another interesting day.'

*

The room above Mr Finlayson's shop was as comfortable and warm as promised, if a little cramped owing to the multitudinous books and papers leaning over our narrow cots. Its one small window afforded an excellent view of the West Bow's sweeping arc; a canvas of deep shadow and jaundiced frost picked out by the brush of the street lamp burning directly below. The steady fall of snow provided the scene's only movement. I tried to follow individual flakes as they materialised from the black sky and glittered downwards to the street, untroubled in their descent by even the merest wisp of a breeze. Most were lost to the darkness, but some I managed to trace all the way to the ground. One settled in the corner of the pane, bolstering the veins of ice crystals spreading inwards across the glass.

This rimy invasion of the window's terrain mirrored my own predicament. The parasite's wintry threads had advanced to within striking distance of my heart. I cut the growths unfurling from my fingers and toes, added them to the coals, then sat cross-legged on the floor to enjoy the performance playing out on the little theatre before me; a fiery drama filled with a cast of exuberant actors in costumes of gold and red velvet, all attacking their roles with gusto. The music of the blaze, the crackles and the hiss, added to the hypnotic quality of the production.

A face began to form inside the flames. The loathsome, blood-smeared face of the knifeman. I imagined his ossified presence still haunting that filthy alleyway.

The fire shuddered.

My blade is sharp and quick!

If, as Mr Finlayson suspected, the thug had been sent forth into those vile wynds under strict instruction from Gladius Dei to capture and return their precious specimen unscathed, then they owed Mr Maybury as great a debt as I for his timely intervention.

I looked at Molly sound asleep in her bed and I realised how selfish I had been. Her life had been thrown into turmoil as much as mine. And yet, in the face of all the dangers and all the risks, she had chosen to stick by my side. My one unwavering friend and ally in this endlessly spiralling nightmare. In her ceaseless efforts to help restore me to my former good health, she had asked for nothing in return and received, to my shame, not a word of gratitude. Cold-hearted betrayal had been her reward. It was little wonder she had rebuffed all my attempts to engage her in conversation and had retired to bed without a word. The world remained an immeasurably better place for her presence. But, in the face of so callous an enemy, for how much longer?

Why did God in His infinite wisdom deem it necessary to populate His world with people who, for the weight of a shilling, will happily inflict violence upon their fellow men? Why, in our supposedly enlightened age, does He continue to tolerate poisonous anachronisms like Gladius Dei? A relic from a time before science or logic. A time of superstition and ignorance. What they perceive as strength comes wrapped in a cloak of cowardice and false moralism. For would any individual amongst them have the courage to commit their atrocities without the protection of the hive to shield them from justice? Gladius Dei were a confederacy of leeches motivated not by reason but by base greed. A desire to accrue and control through the cultivation of fear and division. Shall we never be rid of these parasites whose appetite for misery and death can never be satisfied?

The fire slumped.

I added another scoop of coal and climbed into my bed. Lying back against the pillow, I felt the flame-stone settle at my throat; a foolish little token of security gifted by a well-meaning friend. The prospect of seeing my mother again gladdened my heart. There was so much I wanted to ask Mother. A whole heap of questions inspired as much by pride as by fear.

When did she first become a spy for The Circle? And how had she managed to inveigle her way into my father's life? Had there ever been a spark of genuine affection between them or had their long marriage always been an elaborate masquerade of deceit and duplicity? As for my own role in the charade, were her displays of motherly devotion simply a change of costume for the same fine actress who played the loyal wife with such consummate ease and carried no meaning beyond the confines of the stage upon which she performed?

The more I dwelled on Lachlan Ware's performance as a father, the more my heart soured with anger and betrayal.

Rat-tat-tat… rat-tat-tat…

My leaden eyes pulled back from the cusp of sleep.

Rat-tat-tat… rat-tat-tat…

I sat up and stared across the room, searching the shadows for the source of the persistent tapping sound. Molly's slumbering form rose and fell silently beneath the patchwork of her counterpane. The door remained closed, the handle motionless.

Rat-tat-tat… rat-tat-tat…

I raised a candle towards the window.

Rat-tat-tat… rat-tat-tat…

The unyielding, sulphurous glare of a sparrowhawk sparkled back at me from the snow-encrusted sill. Again it tapped its beak against the glass. I rose from the bed certain the bird would fly off at my approach, but the sparrowhawk showed not the slightest concern and resumed its drumming with increased urgency.

Rat-tat-tat, rat-tat-tat, rat-tat-tat…

I lifted the window. The bird immediately flew into the room and settled on the mantelshelf. Captivated by its lethal beauty, I carefully reached out and gently stroked its wings. The raptor blinked contentedly but at my second touch it ruffled its feathers, puffed out its chest and began to quiver and convulse alarmingly. The sparrowhawk's gaping beak choked and retched till finally it expelled a large pellet into my hand. Seemingly satisfied with its work, the bird launched itself back into the night.

Bemused by this most peculiar of encounters, I closed the window and returned to the warmth of the fire to study the raptor's strange parting gift.

I turned the still warm oblong over. The outer shell was comprised of the fur and broken skulls of several rodents. Each little mouse and shrew conveyed its last fleeting moment of panic as the talons gripped. I gave the pellet a shake. Something rattled within. The shell crumbled away as I cracked it open, and there inside were the unmistakeable remains of a human finger. The blackened and charred bones of the digit had been fused together by an intense heat. A heat that flowed under my skin.

The finger twitched.

At first I fancied an involuntarily spasm in my hand had caused the movement, but all doubt was removed when the finger revolved first clockwise, then anticlockwise, flitting of its own volition like a needle in the compass of my palm. I tried to drop the blasphemous article to the floor, but the paralysing warmth flowing from the charred bones rendered me powerless to do anything other than watch as it continued to seek its desired direction.

It arrowed briefly to Molly, then to the window, then it

hesitated at the flame-stone at my neck before revolving slowly towards the fire where it settled. The coals crackled and whined as if somehow wary of the bone-needle's attentions. The fire itself appeared intrigued by the stick of charcoal resting in my hand. The flames leaned forward, drawn by an unnatural magnetism. The same unseeable force dragged serpentine coils of smoke from the flue and guided them to my wrists, where they tied themselves together in tight bonds.

I tried to alert my sleeping cousin, but the smoke reacted quickly to fill my mouth with silence. The burnt bones were not to be interrupted in the telling of their story. A black oil seeped from the tip of the dead finger. I stared into the eldritch pool spilling across my palm and saw in its polished surface, a mouth. The mouth opened and loosed a terrible scream. From the howling chasm more oil sprayed forth in a great leaping eruption, extinguishing all the light from the room.

My own screams bubbled uselessly in the flood of hungry blackness. A deadly grip tightened at my throat and lifted me violently from the ground. And there I remained dangling in a void of nothingness till at length, the oil drained from my eyes to reveal, not the room nor the fireplace of before, but the wide hollow at the heart of Braid Woods. It was then I realised I was experiencing in the most excruciating detail, the demise of Margaret McKay.

The rope tugged harder. Margaret rose another few inches. Her bare feet reached vainly for a solid purchase of ground, or a rock or a fallen branch; anything to ease the strain on the vertebrae now separating at her neck. Through eyes shot red with burst blood vessels, she saw the satisfied faces of her Gladius Dei executioners, each man relishing her death throes the way a connoisseur of the fine arts relishes the most exquisite portrait in the gallery. And when she no longer had strength enough to prevent her head from dropping to her chest, Margaret heard the clap of a closing Bible and the slap of hands upon backs as the men commended themselves on a job well done.

Looking down to her swaying feet, the witch let her agony give way to rage. A rage that continued to thrive in the cold expanse of eternal darkness. For it carried with it the object of its creation, the cruel smile of the man who ordered the rope to be cut and the dead woman laid on the ground. The same man who then applied his blade to the remains and in his frustration at not finding what he so desired, had them burned and the ashes shovelled into the dirt.

Again and again I heard her voice whisper the man's name. A single syllable resonating outward to occupy the furthest reaches of the great endless nothing.

'Ross... Ross... Ross...'

The darkness lifted, banished behind the oak-panelled walls of a vast room. I stood under a high vaulted ceiling. Towering banks of display cabinets ran the entire length of the space to either side. Their shelves supported an army of bell jars, each playing host to a gruesome anatomical specimen suspended in preserving fluid. I made my way through this corridor of horrors, accompanied by a chorus of anguish. Every floating eye, lung, foetus and tumour all vying to impart their sorry tales. A closed door greeted me at the end of the aisle. There was a name printed in gold on the central panel, but before I was able to read it, the door abruptly vanished and I found myself returned, unharmed to the hearthside of the benevolent fire with Molly sleeping soundly in the darkest corner of the bedroom.

The last drop of black oil retreated back inside the tip of the witch's finger still balanced in my hand. The scorched bones now pointed directly to the window, where the snow continued to bury the pavements and setts of the West Bow under an unblemished layer of purifying white.

The flame-stone radiated a muted warmth at my chest, a

reminder that no amount of snow could ever hope to cleanse Edinburgh's sordid soul. For evil resided in its every street, lurked inside its every close, hid inside its every tenebrous vennel and stained the very foundation stones upon which the city was built.

CHAPTER EIGHTEEN

The Edinburgh Division

The boundary that separates sleep from wakefulness is, even when navigated by the most seasoned of dreamers, the least reliable structure in the architecture of the mind. Its frontiers are prone to last-minute changes of situation or of unexpected alterations to exits and entrances that had proved so reliable on a thousand previous crossings. Imagine then, how much more bewildering these eccentricities of construction are to the dreamer whose mind can no longer determine which side of the border his feet are planted.

And so it was when I awoke in the afternoon light to find the witch's finger still in my grasp like a grotesque memento from my travels into the Land of Sleep, which is where I had fully expected it to remain. I was alone in the room. Mr Finlayson had kindly left a glass of water and a plate of soil at my bedside. I ate my fill, dressed and made my way to the basement.

'Ah! Good morning. Or to be more accurate, good afternoon. I trust you slept well?' said Mr Finlayson, cheerfully pouring some tea.

'I did. Thank you.'

'I'll say. You snored like a pig the whole night through,' muttered Molly. It was abundantly clear that her antipathy towards me remained fully intact.

From somewhere above the tallest bookcases came the chink of a little bell.

'Please excuse me.'

Mr Finlayson ascended to the shop and soon returned with Mr Maybury, who wasted no time in sharing his news on the latest developments at Braid House.

'Your flight has caused quite a stir, Joseph,' said Mr Maybury, helping himself to a brandy. 'Dr Whittle is not a happy man. He spent the entire morning berating your father for his ineptitude. Angry as a cat in a bag he was! But we must be on our guard. They are determined to find you even if it means searching every room in every house in Scotland.'

'Did you see my mother?' I asked.

'I did. She was quite brilliant. There she was, acting the distraught mother, threatening to crash Lachlan and Whittle's heads together before she stormed out of the house.' Mr Maybury then turned to Mr Finlayson, 'Incidentally, she was most insistent that the meeting proceed as planned.' The old man nodded his assent, but it was apparent from his expression that he still doubted the wisdom of gathering the Edinburgh Division together. 'Ah! And Joseph, this is for you.'

Mr Maybury handed me a fresh supply of Glacier Moss. I helped myself to a pinch and spent the remainder of the afternoon in relative comfort, listening to our host cheerfully regaling us with tales of his exploits as a young lighthouse keeper. The stories were filled with great storms, perilous seas, shipwrecks and long periods of isolation with his fellow keepers, one of whom went raving mad with the loneliness of it all. Many of the details escaped my attention, distracted as I was not only by the ever-lengthening list of questions I wanted to ask Mother but also by the presence of the sparrowhawk's gift now tucked away in my pocket.

The moon and stars had taken full command of the sky when the hour of the meeting drew near. With the eyes and ears of so many Gladius Dei agents scouring the streets, Mr Finlayson advised we depart the shop via the rear. And so we set off across the courtyard, passed silently through a stable block and exited on to the Cowgate. Mr Finlayson's apprehension increased with every step we advanced. He cursed the clear sky and the snowy pavements for softening the shadows and again lamented the decision to hold a meeting at all.

Meanwhile, Mr Maybury surveyed every door, window and passage with hawkish precision and would not allow us to progress unless he was satisfied the path ahead was clear of danger. Travelling swiftly through a series of narrow closes and weed strewn yards, we entered an area of the city unfamiliar to me. At every turn of a corner, the bowed and canted facades of the tenement buildings became more and more decrepit. And of all the windows squinting down in suspicion, not one contained an unbroken pane of glass.

To claim that these slums were perfectly adequate for the needs of their inhabitants (as a vocal section of the New Town's more contemptible opinion-makers were wont to do) was an insult to common decency. But to those in possession of even a modest understanding of the plight of the city's poor, the greater insult lay in the inescapable truth that while these disintegrating hovels represented the worst form of degradation, there were innumerable families clinging hopelessly to the bottommost rung of Edinburgh society for whom these were palaces forever beyond the very limit of their aspirations.

Another squalid corner conveyed us into the dingiest street yet. At the far end, Salisbury Crags emerged from the night like a huge basalt mouth frozen in the act of taking a bite. Two emaciated little peg dolls crossed the road ahead of us. A boy and a girl. The pathetic entanglement of rags hanging from their shoulders offered scant protection from the rasping cold as they trudged barefoot through the grey-brown slurry. In each scrawny hand, they grasped the paw of a dead dog and were dragging the heavy carcass towards a tenement every bit as grubby and grimy as themselves. On spying us, the children, worried we might pounce to steal their booty, redoubled their efforts and hauled the mongrel's corpse into a doorway. Inside they met with a cheer of delight:

'We shall eat tonight!'

'We're here,' said Mr Finlayson, taking a key to the door of a slovenly old shop. The sign above the shuttered windows, cracked and weathered through years of neglect, read:

H. Fellowes & Sons, Butchers.

We entered. Mr Finlayson lifted a candle from a sconce beside the door and turned the key in the lock behind us. Once lit, the candle revealed a dank and gloomy space. The only meat on display came in the form of generations of dead flies and woodlice lying upturned on the counter and shelves. Covered in a damp and mouldy mat of ancient sawdust and crumbled plaster from the collapsing ceiling, the floorboards flexed and creaked under our weight. Decades had surely passed since the last parcel of mutton had been weighed on the rusting scales.

'This way.'

We filed in behind Mr Finlayson as he led us down a short corridor, its walls thick with blooms of mildew, and into a back room as dark and welcoming as a smuggler's cave. Our guide dripped a few splashes of wax on to a large oak table and set the candle upright in the rapidly solidifying pool. The flame's agitated glow exposed a multitude of scars criss-crossing the table's surface, delivered by countless blows of the butcher's sharpest blades. Many of those tools, dulled and tarnished with age, still dangled from hooks embedded in the table ends.

Eager to rest my aching bones, I reached for one of the eight rudimentary stools arranged around the table, seemingly in readiness to host our clandestine assembly, when, from the blackest corner of the room, there came a sudden rustle of movement. Holding our collective breath, the four of us stared hard towards the source of this unnerving interruption. A woman emerged from the darkness. She was dressed from her hat to her shoes in shades so dark she appeared to be wearing the shadows themselves, so it was not until she lifted her veil that I realised with any certainty that we were not, in fact, in the company of a phantom.

'Good to see you, Archie. It has been far too long,' said Mother.

'It is always a pleasure, Bility, but a necessarily rare one. I cannot say I am completely at ease with regard to holding this meeting. And I observe that you share my apprehension,' said Mr Finlayson with a nod to the pistol she held in her gloved hand.

'We have no choice. Things are moving apace.' Tucking the pistol into a fold in her skirt, she stepped across and wrapped me in her arms. 'Joseph, my love! How are you? I have been so worried. How are your symptoms? Have they worsened? Are you in pain?'

'Never mind me. What is happening, mother? I can hardly comprehend what Mr Finlayson and Mr Maybury have told me. Why have you never spoken to me about any of this. About The Circle? About Gladius Dei. About Father? Why are you putting yourself in so much danger? I can help. I want to help,' I said, the words tumbling forth in an anxious rush.

She placed a kiss on my forehead. 'I know. And I promise I will answer all your questions in time.'

'Aunt Bility, unless we find help soon, I don't think Joseph has much time left. What are we to do?'

Mother took her niece by the shoulders and smiled warmly. 'Dear Molly, I suspect you are the strongest and bravest of us all. The first thing we must do is not give up hope. We are not beaten yet.'

'Are Grace and Bethany safe?' asked Molly.

'They are.'

239

'Will I be able to see them again?'

'Soon,' replied Mother, with a shade less conviction.

Mr Maybury drummed his impatient fingers on the table. 'Where are the others?'

His reply came with the soft twisting of a key in the lock of the abandoned shop's front door. Listening to the creak of decaying floorboards straining under the weight of hesitant footsteps, Mother readied her pistol whilst Mr Maybury quietly took possession of the largest cleaver hanging from the table end. Mr Finlayson cupped his hands around the candle, throwing the room back into near pitch darkness. We all sat in rigid silence as the tentative footsteps advanced through the corridor.

'Are they here?' whispered a woman's voice.

'They better be. I have sacrificed an evening of cribbage and ale for this!'

With a chuckle Mr Finlayson immediately removed his hands from the candle.

'We are here, Campbell, you thirsty old sop!' Three new arrivals entered. Mr Finlayson leapt forward to greet them all but reserved his warmest embrace for the tallest. 'Campbell! You are becoming as wide as a Christmas goose! I fear Joan may be fattening you up for the slaughter.'

'It's her plum duff, Archibald. The crowning glory of the pudding world! How can any mortal man resist a second or even a third helping?' joked Campbell, patting his expansive belly. Then, peering over his brass-rimmed spectacles, he directed his genial gaze towards me. 'So, I take it this is the young man at the centre of all the fuss?'

'Indeed so,' confirmed Mr Finlayson. 'Joseph, I would like you to meet my brother Campbell.'

Though Campbell had twice his brother's girth and less than half his hair, the family resemblance was inescapable. The same mischievous eyes. The same easy, convivial manner.

'Pleasure to meet you, sir,' I said, shaking his hand.

'The pleasure is all mine,' he grinned. 'And this must be Molly. Delighted I must say. Absolutely delighted.' Molly blushed as he kissed the back of her hand in the manner of a true gentlemen. 'The likeness is uncanny!'

'What likeness, sir?' said Molly.

'Why, the likeness to your mother, of course.'

'You knew her?'

'I am very proud to say that I did know her… And still do.'

Campbell encouraged the only woman amongst the three newcomers to step forward into the light. Had it not been for the steadying hands of the brothers Finlayson, Molly would most certainly have collapsed to the floor.

'Ma!' she gasped.

Tears shining on her cheeks, Aunt Kathryn gathered her daughter in a tight hug and peppered her face with kisses.

'Oh, Molly. I have missed you so much!' she sobbed.

'I knew you were alive! I knew it!' wept Molly. But then a sudden cloud of anger and confusion rolled into to darken her joy. Pushing away from the embrace, she stared accusingly at her mother. 'How could you abandon us? How could you be so cruel?'

'Molly, you must understand, Kathryn's hand was forced,' said Mother, hurrying to her sister-in-law's defence. 'She left because her life was in immediate peril. If she had stayed, there is every chance she and quite possibly you, your sisters and Tam would all have been killed.'

'But why? What happened?'

Kathryn took Molly's hands in her own.

'Do you remember when we last saw each other?'

'How could I ever forget? It was the worst day of my life. You promised you'd be back soon!' said Molly with a curtness that stung Kathryn into a momentary silence.

'I am so sorry,' she said, her voice ragged with regret. 'I

pray that one day you will find it in your heart to forgive me. But I was in a desperate way. If I had not acted, Bethany would have died of her fever that very night. Do you remember the balm I gave you?' Molly, recalling the sweet-smelling muddy paste she had applied to her sister's chest and brow, responded with a small nod of acknowledgement. 'That remedy was her last hope. But to make it I needed to collect fresh flowers and roots from my mother's grave. I always collect my flowers from there. Her essence is still very strong. I chose not to tell you how close Bethany was to death because I wanted to protect you from the pain. So I left you sleeping in your chair and went to the kirkyard, where I sat at my mother's feet and gathered everything in my little bowl...' Overcome with emotion, Kathryn wiped her eyes, then paused a moment to compose herself. 'I should have used an ordinary stone. Any old bit of rock would have done. But I was foolish. I used my coven-stone to grind the elements together, hoping it would add further potency to the magic. Oh! but poor Bethany. I was in such a careless hurry. I did not think.'

Molly's eyes narrowed under the weight of her frown. 'Magic? Coven-stone? No,' she shook her head as if trying to dismiss an unwelcome notion before it was able to fully introduce itself. 'No. You can't be.'

Kathryn took an object from the pocket of her heavy winter coat and handed it to her daughter. Molly stared in amazement at the round, smoke-grey pebble resting in her palm. The size of a hen's egg, there was a symbol etched into its smooth surface; the symbol of a crescent moon.

'You can't be...'

Mother reacted sharply to steer Molly to a seat before she buckled under the giddying chaos of emotions unleashed by the startling, inescapable reality she held in her hand.

'It is time you learned the truth. Your mother has the Magic,' said Mother, placing a comforting arm around her niece's shoulder. 'She is one of the very few witches left in Scotland.'

'Do you have the Magic too, Aunt Bility?' asked Molly, her voice distilled to a stunned whisper.

'No. But Kathryn is not the only witch in this room.'

Molly's trembling fingers blanched around the stone.

'*Me?*'

'Like mother, like daughter,' said Kathryn, stroking a finger through Molly's hair.

A sudden bright smile dispersed the storm of anguish from Molly's face and she threw her arms around her mother's waist.

'Like mother, like daughter, you say? Let us hope not,' said the man who until now had been standing by the doorway silently watching the proceedings with a degree of impatience. A young man, crisp in both manner and attire, he had several rolled-up lengths of paper protruding from the crook of his arm, each a yard long and tied with a sliver of ribbon. He approached the table, whereupon he unfurled one of his papers. It quickly revealed itself to be a large map of Edinburgh, the curling ends of which he weighted down with his hat and gloves. Satisfied the map was in order, he positioned himself opposite Molly. 'You are still very young, but the Magic will soon present itself to you. With the proper training you will learn how best to harness its gifts, and perhaps in time, you will prove to be a more sensible witch than your dear mother.'

'Molly, allow me to introduce you to Mr David Olyphant,' said Mr Finlayson. 'Don't let his rudeness fool you. Like all lawyers he lacks social grace, but his dedication to our cause is exemplary.'

'You are confusing rudeness with candour, Archibald. Kathryn's actions that night were careless in the extreme.'

'What did she do that was so wrong?' I asked.

'She allowed herself to be seen,' snipped Mr Olyphant. 'Which is to be expected when you visit a graveyard in the dead of night to prepare a healing balm.'

Molly, slightly disappointed to find Mr Olyphant remaining impervious to what she had imagined to be one of her finest scowls, looked to her mother.

'Who saw you?'

'The church sexton,' admitted Kathryn. 'I thought I was alone, but I became so absorbed in making the balm that I did not see him till he was standing over me. I cannot say for certain if he saw my coven-stone, but he knew what I was doing. I gathered everything as quickly as I could and ran away, but he followed me. I must have turned every corner in Leith before I was sure he'd gone. Only then did I feel it safe to hurry home and pass the balm to you. But I could not stay, Molly. I had to tell someone what had happened. So I went to Mr Olyphant and sought his advice. It was he who opened my eyes to the full gravity of my carelessness and advised me, for the love and safety of my family, to flee without delay. Before the night was through, he had made all the necessary arrangements and I was smuggled out of the city.'

'And if I had not acted as swiftly and decisively as your mother describes,' said Mr Olyphant, 'then I say it is no exaggeration to suggest that not one of us would be alive to enjoy these salubrious surroundings in which we now find ourselves. It is a matter of fact that most, if not all, of Edinburgh's anatomists are members of Gladius Dei. It is a matter of fact that most, if not all, of Edinburgh's sextons are in the employ of Gladius Dei. The anatomists pay the sextons a handsome stipend in exchange for unfettered access to the graves of the recently deceased.'

I shuddered at this last. I had naively believed the gruesome trade of the resurrectionists to have ended with the demise of Messrs Burke and Hare a dozen years earlier.

'The sextons,' continued Mr Olyphant, 'are also expected to report, without delay, any suspicious activity they encounter within their churchyards. And for Gladius Dei, witchcraft is the very definition of suspicious activity, which is precisely what the sexton of St Nicholas witnessed when he encountered Kathryn.'

'Which is precisely why the sexton of St Nicholas now finds himself buried in his own churchyard!' Campbell Finlayson proudly exclaimed, slapping the map with one meaty fist while the other pulled a pewter flask from his pocket. 'I reached him before he had the opportunity to tell anyone what he saw. Of that I am certain.'

Campbell raised his flask to toast the unfortunate sexton and swallowed a mouthful of whisky. Mr Olyphant remained impassive.

'Nothing is certain. Need I remind you of what happened to poor Francis? We are swimming in very dark waters. As we speak Gladius Dei will be collating and examining every minute detail regarding everyone Joseph has ever met and every place he has ever frequented as they attempt to ascertain where and to whom he may have run to. Be under no illusion, they will peer under every last stone of his existence. Connections will be made. Not one of us is safe. If their investigations discover nothing of interest residing in the periphery of Joseph's life, they will inevitably turn their focus inwards. To you, Bility. And you, Mr Maybury. My advice to us all: trust no one beyond these walls and refrain from all unnecessary excursions.'

'What about my poor Pa? Surely he can be trusted? Please tell me he has no part in this?' pleaded Molly.

'No,' said Kathryn. 'Your father is precisely who he has always claimed to be: *The finest harpooner under the sun and over the moon!*'

Kathryn's impression of her husband's familiar boast raised a welcome laugh from all present. All, that is, except Mr Olyphant.

'It pleases me no end to see you all so happy and carefree,' he said, once the mirth faded. 'But may I suggest we return to the matter at hand and determine how best we can assist Joseph in avoiding the straps of a Gladius Dei dissecting table?'

Mother clapped her hands together. 'Quite right, Mr Olyphant. What other maps have you brought us?'

'I also have an atlas of the world, one of Europe and one of Great Britain should we require them,' he said.

'Then, dear Kathryn, I shall hand proceedings over to you.'

At Mother's invitation Kathryn drew herself closer to the map on the table. 'May I have it please, Joseph?' she said, holding out a hand towards me. Unsure as to what she was referring, I hesitated for a moment, then offered my own hand in return. 'No,' smiled Kathryn. 'I meant the gift. May I have the gift the sparrowhawk gave you last night?'

'How could you possibly know?' I said, astonished.

Her smile broadened. 'Who do you think sent it to you?'

Molly's incredulity outstripped even my own. 'You sent a sparrowhawk? With a gift? How did I miss this? What did it give you?'

I placed the charred bone on the map. Molly shuddered.

'That is the most disgusting gift I have ever seen. What is it?'

'It is our most treasured relic. Margaret McKay's left index finger,' Mr Finlayson explained.

'Did it offer you any insight? Any visions? Dreams?' asked Kathryn.

Molly and the assembled members of The Circle listened attentively as I detailed the magical relic's extraordinary effect. Of how the blackened bones invited me to share in the dying moments of the Witch McKay and her contempt for the sneering faces of her executioners. And how she reserved her greatest loathing for her chief tormentor, Sir William Ross. A rage she carried with her into the next realm. I then described how my dream shifted from Margaret McKay's ignominious burial in Braid Woods to the great room full of specimen jars and my journey to the door bearing a name I was unable to read.

'Did you enter the door?' asked Kathryn.

'No, the dream ended at that point,' I said.

'Not to worry, you've given me plenty to work with,' said Kathryn. 'Now, would you please place both your palms flat on the map.'

I did as asked and, like everyone else, watched in reverential silence as she lifted the candle and tipped several drops of hot liquid wax across the backs of my hands. One drip missed its target and landed on the map, prompting a twitch of chagrin from Mr Olyphant. Kathryn returned the candle to the table and then, sinking her fingers into the soft molten wax on my skin, she began to murmur softly in Gaelic.

The heat from the wax surged to my fingertips. Sap leaked from each cuticle as ten translucent wormlike roots split forth and slowly unfurled to feel their way blindly across the map. The sight of their twisting, curling progress sickened me; a disgust reflected in the shock and fascination displayed on all the surrounding faces. The shoots spiralled around one another, forming a single vine. The vine snaked over the streets and houses, weaved across Charlotte Square, looped around the castle and into the old town. It hesitated for a moment at Nicolson Street in order to allow one of the strands to separate itself from the bundle. The lone element rose an inch, advanced another, and stopped. A drop of pink fluid fell from the strand to stain the dark block of a large building indicated on the map.

'What is that place?' asked Campbell.

Mr Olyphant seemed far more perturbed at the appearance of another stain on his map than by the wholly unnatural means by which it occurred. 'The Royal Society of Pathology,' he remarked irritably, dabbing at the blot with the corner of a handkerchief. He reluctantly moved aside when Kathryn, continuing to murmur in Gaelic, placed a finger on the damp spot.

A brilliant burst of white light seared my eyes and with the next blink I was returned once more to the great room with its high vaulted ceiling and rows of tall cabinets with their grim assortment of pathological artefacts. Again I made my way towards the closed door at the far end of the aisle. The glare of an adjacent lamp rendered the gold lettering on the door illegible, but with each step I advanced, the light softened and eventually a name presented itself...

'Sir Edward Ross!' The force of my own voice hurled me from the museum and returned me to the equally unsettling shadows of the old butcher's shop. 'Stop staring at me!' I yelled, infuriated by the expressions of concern aimed in my direction. I snatched a blade from the end of the table, sliced off the growths and put an end to the indignity.

'Be careful, Joseph! You have cut a hole in Marchmont,' said Mr Olyphant, inspecting the minor damage my pruning had inflicted upon his precious map.

I angrily swept the cuttings to the floor and stepped away from the attentions of my startled audience. Molly rose, ready to offer some words of comfort, but Mother wisely persuaded her to leave me be.

'Edward Ross,' sighed Campbell. 'This does not bode well.'

'No, brother, it does not,' said Mr Finlayson, absently twisting the whiskers of his moustache as he considered the implications of my revelation.

'Why? Who is he?' asked Molly.

'Sir Edward Ross is the President of the Royal Society of Pathology and the current head of the Gladius Dei serpent. He is the direct descendant of Sir William Ross. The door Joseph described is the door to his office.'

'But what does all this mean? What are we supposed to do?'

Kathryn picked up the witch's digit and rested the tip on the map next to the black block representing the Royal Society of Pathology. She uttered another phrase in Gaelic. A question ending with the words *Edward Ross*. The response was immediate. Kathryn's hand twitched and spasmed violently. Her entire body stiffened and her eyes clamped shut. The candle flame guttered, swayed and briefly glowed a brilliant blue before returning to its natural yellow. The dead finger toppled from Kathryn's grip. She relaxed, opened her eyes and withdrew her hand.

Scrawled in a jittery dance of charcoal from the point of the witch's bone, a single word appeared on the map:

"*Marbh.*"

I returned to my seat for a closer look at the seemingly random jumble of letters.

'What does that say?'

Kathryn slipped the relic inside her coat and shared a troubled glance with Mother. 'It's an instruction.'

Campbell stared up at a sizeable hole in the ceiling where the sickly candlelight played amongst the decrepit timbers. 'As I said, this does not bode well.'

'I trust you have all finished vandalising my map?' said Mr Olyphant, briskly. An affirmative nod from Kathryn, and Edinburgh was smartly rolled up and tucked safely back in the crook of Mr Olyphant's arm.

The encroaching darkness had taken on a decidedly sinister edge. I picked anxiously at the now cooled and hardened scabs of wax on the back of my hands.

'You said it was an instruction? To do what?'

Kathryn paused to consider her reply. 'I asked what needed to be done to free you from her spell.'

'And what am I to do?'

'Kill. You must kill Sir Edward Ross. Then – and only then – will the charm be lifted.'

'Then what are we waiting for? Help me find him!'

Knife raised, I charged for the corridor, but Mr Maybury moved swiftly to block my way.

'Don't be a fool, Joseph!' he said, wresting the blade from my grip and forcing me back into my chair. 'Believe me, I share your impatience, but we cannot wander into the lion's den armed with naught but a few rusty chopping knives and a mean stare. We need to formulate a plan. We need to choose our moment. We need to catch Ross off guard.'

'And as Sir Edward is renowned for being a singularly paranoid individual, this is a most difficult ambition to achieve,' said Mr Olyphant. 'Ever since our dear departed Agnes took it upon herself to try and remove his head with a razor shell, he never sets foot in public unaccompanied.'

'I cannot be expected to sit here and do nothing!' I protested. 'With every moment that passes, this thing inside steals another little piece of who I am. I have to act now or soon there will nothing left worth fighting for!'

Mother turned to Kathryn. 'Are you certain there is no alternative? Something hidden in the Magic you may have missed?'

'I'm afraid the visions, both my own and Joseph's, were clear. To lift the spell, he must kill Sir Edward Ross.'

'Please mother, I beg you. This is not the time for hesitation. Look at us all cowering here in this filthy black hole like so many frightened rabbits waiting for the fox to strike. What kind of an existence is this? I propose we seize control and take the fight to them! Let them be the ones to cower in the dark!'

'I agree with Jojo.'

'You are not a member of The Circle, Miss Keane. Nor is your cousin. Therefore your proposals hold no sway,' said Mr Olyphant.

'Then how do we join The Circle?' I asked.

Mr Finlayson stood to address the assembly. 'I propose

that we invite young Joseph Ware and the fledgling witch Molly Keane to join our number. Any objections?' He glanced at each of his comrades in turn, all of whom responded with a shake of their heads. 'Good! Welcome to the fold!' He shook first Molly's hand and then mine. Soon we found ourselves vigorously shaking hands with everyone, including Mr Olyphant who, caught up in the enthusiasm of the moment, even managed the beginnings of a smile.

Molly embraced her mother tightly, eyes shining with tears. 'I am not leaving your side ever again.'

'Quiet, everyone!' snapped Mr Finlayson. The bookseller hurriedly undid the uppermost buttons of his coat and tugged the flame-stone from his neck. It was burning red hot. 'Joseph!' He pointed to the curl of smoke rising from under my own collar. Alarmed by the smell of burning fabric, I snatched the pendant from my throat and threw the smouldering talisman to the table. The flame-stone glowed a fierce white as it scorched a deep notch into the wood.

We all fell as silent as statues, our eyes hunting the walls, the ceiling and the doorways for any indication of the threat communicated by the stones.

A floorboard creaked under Campbell's shifting weight. Mother eased the pistol from her skirt. From the room above came the dull, steady drip, drip, drip of leaking water. Kathryn placed the witch's finger in her open palm and whispered to it. The burnt bones turned and pointed to the front room. Dismissing Mother's noiseless instructions to stay put, I followed Mr Maybury into the mildewed corridor.

Taking great care to keep ourselves hidden in the shadows we entered the dilapidated shop and crouched slowly towards the boarded windows. Peering between the gaps we saw a small crowd gathered in the street beyond. I counted a total of nine men standing in a line. Some were holding oil lamps. All were carrying weapons. I recognised the man at the centre, stooping

251

to place a coin into the outstretched hands of two raggedy children. Mr Maybury vented a small growl of frustration and signalled for me to return with him to the others.

'It's Hugh Tulland's men. Nine of them,' he reported.

'I didn't think Tulland's reach extended this far,' said Mother with a worried look.

'Evidently you were wrong. Oh, why did I ever agree to this reckless meeting? I should have trusted my instincts,' groaned Mr Finlayson, closing his flame-stone safely inside a snuffbox.

'What shall we do now?' asked Molly, fearfully.

'COME OUT, COME OUT, WHOEVER YOU ARE!'

The voice hollering from the street was Hugh Tulland's.

'SHOW YOURSELVES! I PROMISE YOU WILL COME TO NO HARM!'

My flame-stone buried its way a little deeper into the table.

'IT LOOKS A WEE BIT DARK IN THERE! WOULD YOU LIKE SOME MORE LIGHT?'

'Come, quickly!' Mother snatched the candle and motioned everyone towards the door leading to the rear of the building. Campbell Finlayson held his ground.

'I will not run from that rat-faced excuse of a man,' he growled.

'There are nine of them out there, Campbell,' warned Mr Finlayson.

'It is not my fault they are ill-prepared. If they desired a fair fight, they should have brought more men.'

'Patience. Ross is the one we want, not Tulland,' said Mr Maybury.

'My brother has no patience. Not when his stomach is full of whisky,' said Mr Finlayson.

Campbell opened his mouth, ready to challenge the affront, but his retort was stifled by the deafening crash of splintered wood and shattered glass. Then came the roar of an uncaged fire. The corridor flickered orange and red, a brightness soon smothered by thick black smoke.

'This way!' cried Mother. We hurried after her as the suffocating cloud flooded the meeting room. Before I passed through the door, I caught sight of the flame-stone burning its way through the table to drop against the stone floor, where it burst apart in an explosion of yellow and white sparks.

I tugged the rickety door to a close behind me and entered a tight hallway, my feet sinking into a deep carpet of collapsed plaster and pigeon mess.

'Hide your faces! And keep them hidden till you are far away from here. It is best we all head in separate directions. If and when it is safe to do so, send word to my office using a coded petal,' ordered Mr Olyphant as we gathered together at the rear door. Scarves and collars were duly raised. 'Godspeed to you all.'

With a sudden, mighty crack the door split from its hinges, sending the lawyer sprawling across the floor to land in a dazed heap at my feet. Two heavyset men wielding coshes barged inwards. The first man bludgeoned Mr Finlayson across the temple. Campbell seized the attacker's raised arm before it delivered a second blow and plunged a knife deep into the ribs beneath. The man howled and collapsed to his knees.

The second attacker was locked in a deadly tussle with Mr Maybury. Mother raised her pistol and fired. A crimson mist exploded from the assailant's head and he crumpled across the back of his stricken companion.

I stood senseless with shock in the midst of this whirlwind of violence. Mr Maybury brushed me aside to help Campbell tackle three more men who were trying to force their way inside.

'Get yourselves up those stairs! We'll take care of things down here!' he yelled, grasping the throat of the first of the newcomers. 'Go! Now!'

Mother and Kathryn dragged Mr Finlayson towards the adjacent staircase.

Molly and I snapped into action to aid Mr Olyphant, who was only now rising from the floor.

'Never mind me. I can manage,' Mr Olyphant said, pushing his precious maps deep inside his coat. 'Go and help your mothers.'

We hurried to assist Kathryn and Mother in hauling Mr Finlayson up the steps. The old bookseller rolled his bleeding head and moaned incoherently. Arriving on the first-floor landing, I happened to glance back down. Mr Olyphant had joined the fray with surprising zeal, punching and kicking at a shape writhing on the floor. Mr Maybury repulsed another assailant with a cosh snatched from the lifeless grip of the original aggressor. I saw Campbell's blade glisten wetly as it swept in range of the candle Mother had abandoned on the bannister's finial and bury itself inside the chest of the latest invader.

An oil lamp flew inside and smashed to the floor, spilling a mess of flames in every direction. I considered hurling my supply of Glacier Moss into the mêlée but the risk of incapacitating friend rather than foe was too great.

We stumbled upwards for the next landing, where we lost sight of our battling companions. Kathryn retrieved the flame-stone from Mr Finlayson's snuffbox and held it aloft, and as the pendant gently rotated in her grasp, she murmured a brief incantation. The stone instantly changed hue from fiery red to a lunar white as bright as any lantern. We followed the stone's light into the upper reaches of the abandoned tenement. On the fourth floor we paused to rest under the rotten sill of a broken window. Its shattered panes whistled an icy refrain as Mr Finlayson gingerly placed a hand to his injured head.

'This meeting was a bad idea. A very bad idea,' he muttered.

Kathryn dabbed gently at his wound with a handkerchief.

'Hush, Archie. Save your strength.'

The reek of rising smoke intensified, prompting the old man to cough and wheeze. I listened hard for further signs of the confrontation below but was met with a worrying silence. Mother recharged her pistol.

'We cannot stay here. We must keep moving.'

'But where?' asked Molly. She opened a despairing hand to the next flight of stairs. The middle section of the staircase had collapsed, leaving a gaping hole several steps wide. There was little time to contemplate this setback as a far more pressing concern arrived in the sound of boots bounding quickly upwards. Kathryn blew into the flame-stone. The light faded.

Mother placed a finger to her lips, requesting silence. Concealing her hands behind her back, she advanced cautiously to the top of the stairs and peered down into the dark. The stamp of the boots grew louder and there soon appeared on the crumbling walls the yellow cast of a lamp dancing ever higher. A man emerged from the lower floor. Seeing the woman standing above, he raised his light to her. His bloodied face twisted in delight at finding his prey with such apparent ease.

'Now you wait there, lady. Be a good lass and you'll come to no harm,' he said, tightening his grip around a length of lead pipe.

Mother waited till he was but four steps distant before revealing her pistol. The coward blanched, dropped his weapon and raised his hands in submission.

'Are you injured?' said Mother.

'Beg yer pardon, miss?' the man quivered.

'You have blood on your face? Are you injured?'

The man wiped a tremulous hand over his brow and studied the resulting stain on his fingers. 'I... I... I don't think so, mm, mm... Miss.'

'Is it not your blood?'

'No. I don't think so.'

Mother fired a shot into the man's chest. She watched impassively as the body tumbled downwards in a twisted mess of limbs to the landing below. The lamp rolled from the dead man's grasp. The light inside guttered briefly, then perished.

Mother turned to the broken window and tried to force it open. Even with my assistance the sash refused to budge.

'We had better move Archie aside,' she said.

Once Mr Finlayson had been shuffled out of harm's way, Mother took the handle of her pistol and smashed away the remaining glass and decaying frames. Her path cleared, she leaned out to assess the drop to the roof of the adjoining building.

'We will have to go through here. It's our only option,' she said. 'Do you think you can manage it, Archie? It's only a few feet down.'

From the depths of the stairwell came the steadily rising thud of more boots.

'Where you lead, I will follow,' said Mr Finlayson, attempting a smile.

Mother ushered first Kathryn, then Molly through the window, and no matter how hard I protested, she remained determined that I should be next. And so, with the wind whipping at the crust of snow covering the steeply sloping slates on either side, I reluctantly lowered myself on to the apex of the neighbouring roof.

A pall of orange-stained smoke climbed into the night sky, carrying with it the clamour of approaching fire engines and a volley of frantic shouting from the streets far below. The howling gusts had no impact on Molly's exceptional balance and she traversed the initial stretch to the next building with remarkable ease whereas myself and Kathryn, lacking such sure-footedness, opted to manoeuvre ourselves along the perilous crest on all fours.

We clambered to the relative security of a chimney stack,

where Molly awaited us. I peered backwards along the roof, expecting to see Mother and Mr Finlayson close on our tail, but saw only smoke rushing from the shattered window like steam from the spout of a boiling kettle. From the black rectangle I heard voices cry in alarm. Then came a flash of light quickly followed by the sharp crack of a pistol shot. The ensuing silence cut a chill far deeper than the wintry blast constantly harrying at my eyes and ears.

'Where are you going!' yelled Kathryn as I tentatively started back towards the billowing smoke.

'To help Mother!'

'It's too dangerous, Joseph! We must leave!'

'Don't wait for me. I will catch up with you, I promise!'

Kathryn and Molly begrudgingly pressed on for the next set of chimneys. Arms outstretched to counterbalance the buffeting wind, I stepped forward, placing one foot in front of the other. The distance to the gable end of the burning tenement closed inch by treacherous inch. I had advanced a mere yard or two when someone appeared at the window.

The smoke, agitated by the burgeoning gale, coiled around the coughing, gasping figure leaning out to a catch a clean breath. For one brief moment the squall changed direction and the smothering grey cloak was lifted from the choking man. Time enough to see him raise his head and wipe the soot from his streaming eyes before another gust obscured him completely. Time enough for Father to meet my horrified gaze.

I turned and fled as fast as I dared. Something smacked hard into the chimney stack, sending a little burst of stone whistling into the air. I dashed to the next roof. Kathryn and Molly were nowhere to be seen. Shielding myself behind the third chimney stack, I looked to the window. There was no one there and there was no one, friend nor enemy, pursuing me along the rooftops.

The tumult of alarm bells fading behind me, I arrived at

the point at which the roofs formed a sharp right angle as one street collided with another. I turned the corner and gingerly stepped on to a new row of tenement buildings in an even more perilous state than the first. In some places the roofs had bowed alarmingly whilst in others they had caved in entirely. I peered inside one such hole, hoping to find a way down, but encountered nothing but the blackness of an apparently endless abyss.

I noticed footsteps in the dusting of snow beyond the hole. Two sets of tracks descending across the sloping slates. I carefully retraced Molly and Kathryn's steps to the guttering, where they ended at the mouth of a drainpipe. Whether or not it extended all the way to the ground proved impossible to tell, as only the smallest section was visible. The rest was soon lost to the pitch darkness.

I knelt down and reached to take hold of the pipe. Something cracked and shifted under my weight. Another tile gave way.

I slipped over the edge and fell headlong into the void.

CHAPTER NINETEEN

FV1832

A pair of stubby beaks had taken a liking to the buds newly sprouting from my hands. The striking pink blush of their chests dipped and bobbed to plunder the sap oozing from the fingertips. The beautiful little bullfinches showed no sign of fear and happily continued to feed even when I managed to raise my sleepy head for a better view of my situation.

I had landed beneath a bright, uniform sky of flaxen cloud in the crown of an elderly beech tree some ten feet below the edge of the roof from which I had fallen. Looking to the base of the drainpipe I had hoped to descend before fate intervened to choose a somewhat quicker route, I saw a trail of footprints disappear into a courtyard choked with muddy snow, weeds and lumps of broken masonry.

The bullfinches took flight as the tree kindly released the twisting mesh of slender branches and twigs it had thrown around me to cushion my fall. The beech was in fine health and communicated a general contentment with its lot. It did not care much for the quality of the soil at its roots, tainted with an accumulation of filth deposited by the malnourished inhabitants of the surrounding buildings. And the tenements themselves cast the tree into shadow for more hours of the day than it would have preferred but these, the tree assured me, were minor quibbles.

I descended to the courtyard and hurried out through the nearest close into the street. Gathering my coat against the punishing cold, I waited as two fire engines rattled past, pulled by teams of horses all snorting great plumes of steam into the freezing morning air. The exhausted firemen, faces stained with soot and sweat, stared blankly at the road ahead. Head bowed to the ground, I set off in their wake and walked briskly away from the scene of the previous night's horrors with no clear plan as to where to go or what to do next.

The image of Father's face staring through the swirling smoke haunted my every step. I thought of Mother and my heart slumped. Had he captured her? Killed her? Left her to burn with Mr Finlayson in that godforsaken building? A thousand dire imaginings presented themselves before I chanced upon a tiny grain of hope. Perhaps she had somehow managed to flee with Mr Finlayson before Father's arrival. Quite how, I could not fathom. But I consoled myself with the certitude that my mother was a far more ingenious person than I.

And the others? When last I saw them, Campbell Finlayson, Mr Maybury and Mr Olyphant were valiantly holding their ground but they were hopelessly outnumbered. I took heart from Molly and Kathryn's apparently successful escape. But where had they run to? Where *could* they run to?

My own options, I quickly came to realise, were depressingly limited. I patted my pocket and was reassured to find the two little receptacles of Glacier Moss and Flos Veritas present and undamaged. My primary instinct was to seek out my father. His crimes deserved the most excruciating retribution ever devised by Man. Or better still, by Nature. I imagined no greater satisfaction than to sentence my father to experience for himself the effects of every poison contained within the pages of his own black notebook with the silver skull and crossbones emblazoned on its spine:

A venom which causes the skin to slough free from the
body...
Causes the tissue of the lungs to liquefy...
Victims have been known to scoop out their own eyes...
Writhing in unimaginable agony...

The parasite shifted, its filaments twining around the trellis
of my ribcage. A painful reminder that Father had nothing to
fear as long as I remained in this wretched state. If the path
to my salvation, presented so graphically upon Mr Olyphant's
map, was one fraught with difficulties even for a determined
band of eight souls, then – in the wake of The Circle's decisive
defeat – how much more impossible was it to achieve alone?

A snowflake melted into my eye.

The air had quietly filled with countless white dots softening the hunched shapes of the buildings and people along
Candlemaker Row. I rested inside the gates of Greyfriars Kirk
and helped myself to a measure of Glacier Moss. The pain
climbing to the summit of my backbone subsided. I was so
exhausted, I began to envy the eternal rest of the sleeping
denizens of the kirkyard. There was not a living soul to be
seen above the ground, but evidence of life lay all around.
Everywhere the snow carried a busy record of the comings
and goings of birds and cats and people. I closed my eyes and
pictured my mother painting and sketching the slow march of
the lichens over marble, sandstone and granite. The picture
shifted; a pistol replaced her paintbrush. The gun fired and all
became lost in a wall of smoke.

I stared across the cemetery to Mother's favoured spot and
prayed till I shivered with the effort. But my entreaties were
met by a cruel and indifferent God who steadfastly refused to
return my mother safe and unharmed to my side. Brushing
away the tears of frustration, I happened to gaze upon what
I now knew to be the true object of Mother's excursions to
Greyfriars:

Mr Buchanan's memorial.

A set of tracks approached the monument's base and then departed along the path towards the gates. Intrigued, I rose to look more closely. They were evidently the footprints of a man whose feet were a good deal larger than my own. Spaced at regular intervals, adjacent to the depression of the left foot, I noticed a series of dots pushed firmly into the ground. The visitor had walked directly to the memorial, paused, and then turned back for the kirkyard gates.

I was struck by the thrill of possibility. Were these Mr Finlayson's footprints come to collect one of Mother's coded petals? Perhaps he had left a message of his own? Perhaps they belonged to Mr Maybury or to Mr Olyphant or to Campbell Finlayson, one or all of them anxious to communicate with other survivors of the assault. I pulled the loose stone free and reached a quivering hand into the hole.

There were no petals... No notes... Nothing...

I retreated to the gates and sat glumly facing the street, chin cupped in my hands. The last lingering ember of hope turned to ash in my heart. There would be no vengeance. No breaking of the spell. No favourable outcome of any kind. All that remained was to acknowledge the crushing totality of the defeat and to negotiate the terms of my surrender. If I were to be assured that no further harm would befall anyone who had sought to help me, then Gladius Dei were welcome to do with me as they pleased.

The swell of a commotion roused me from this unhappy contemplation. Lured by a volley of horrific screams, people were hurrying towards the Grassmarket in their droves. Losing myself in their number, I hastened to investigate.

I joined a large and excitable crowd piling into the West Bow. A woman in a black bonnet was standing at the edge of the throng, craning her neck for a better view. I tugged her sleeve.

'What happened?'

'Murder!' she said, her round face flushed with excitement. 'It's murder!'

I pushed my way to the front, where I was greeted by a terrible sight. A constable battled manfully to keep the wall of curious faces at bay whilst his colleague examined a body lying in the doorway of a shop.

The body of Mr Archibald Finlayson.

The mischievous twinkle gone from his eyes, he gazed blankly at the sky. I noticed a symbol daubed in blood upon the dead man's brow. A cruciform intersected with several short horizontal lines. The Sword and Jacob's Ladder.

'Did anyone see anything?' demanded the policeman crouching by the bloom of red pooling from a great gash separating the bookseller's throat. His inquiry was greeted with a flurry of muttered denials and shaking heads.

The murmuring wall of onlookers dissolved into a single amorphous mass, their breaths rising as one to create a discordant cloud of noise. The buzz made my ears ache. Blindly, I pushed free from the suffocating crush and escaped to the foot of the Castlehill steps. I sat gasping for air and tried in vain to erase the nauseating sight of poor Mr Finlayson's savaged body from my mind. But then my thoughts turned to Mother and every atom of my being splintered with dread. I envisioned her murdered body lying as yet undiscovered in a lonely corner of the city painted exclusively in the colours of blood and snow.

'A terrible business, is it not?'

The voice, rich and forthright, came from behind and above. A man was sitting on the smooth stone of the landing separating the first flight of stairs from the second. He was dressed in a soldier's uniform, perhaps a shade too large for the ageing frame it clothed, but it remained in good repair with creases as sharp as the lines on his face and buttons as shiny as his sharp grey eyes.

'I said, it is a terrible business, is it not?' he said, gesturing with his walking cane in the direction of Mr Finlayson's shop.

'Yes,' I agreed, eventually.

'Come and join me,' he beckoned. 'I would come to you, but these old legs are to be used as sparingly as possible. Doctor's orders.'

I climbed to the second flight of steps and sat opposite the veteran soldier.

'I wonder if you could spare a penny for a retired officer of the Forty-Second Regiment of Foot fallen on hard times,' he said, poking a cap placed on the ground between his sizeable boots, in which lay a miserly collection of coins.

'I haven't any money,' I shrugged.

The man sat back and nodded sagely. 'Times are indeed hard for us all.' The hand that gripped his cane was missing the two fingers furthest from the thumb. His left hand was missing three, the skin around each stump reduced to a hardened mass of scar tissue. 'The French are to blame,' he announced proudly upon seeing my revulsion. 'Six and twenty years ago it may be, but I remember it like it happened this very morning. Captured I was at Quatre Bras en route to Waterloo. They tortured me. Cut off my fingers. Nice and slow. With a piece of flint. Thought I had important intelligence. Troop movements. Munitions. They were correct! But did I talk? No sir, I did not. But by God I sang! Such a rendition of God Save the King as you have never heard. Those Frenchies will go to their graves with my voice ringing in their ears!' He laughed and tapped the brass foot of his cane against the flagstone. '*La, la, laa, laaa-la-la!*' Then the old warrior leaned forward. 'You look like you've seen battle yourself, young sir.' He drew my attention to a lengthy tear in the sleeve of my greatcoat. Further investigation revealed the full extent of my unsightly appearance. My raiment was heavily stained with smoke and damp. There were gaping holes in both knees of my trousers and a split had appeared in the toe of my left boot.

'It has been a difficult few days,' I said.

'Not as difficult, I suspect, as for the poor fellow lying just around the corner.'

'No,' I conceded. 'I suspect not.'

'Did you know him?'

'No. Did you?'

'I hear he was a bookseller. But I can't recall the man's name. My memory is in a shocking state these days. Did you see his body? Was it gruesome?'

'I did not stop to look,' I said.

'No matter,' the soldier grinned. 'If only he sold books on the subject of how to avoid being murdered, eh?'

'If only.'

The man thrust forward his right hand. 'Captain Malcolm Hay at your service. And you are?'

Leaning forward to accept his greeting, I saw a few spots of dried blood on the collar of his shirt. The pattern of stains extended to the breast of his red tunic. Evidently, he did not take as much pride in his appearance as the polished buttons and starched creases had led me to assume. The reek of sweat, tobacco and whisky suggested it had been some considerable time since the man had last acquainted himself with a sponge.

'John Black,' I replied, his acrid odour stifling my quest for a more imaginative pseudonym.

'Pleased to meet you, Mr Black. And what is your profession?'

'Harpooner.'

'Ah! A killer of leviathans! The noblest profession of all.' He shook my hand with renewed vigour. 'You will forgive an old warrior for his uncouth ramblings. I should not speak ill of the dead. After all, Christmas is soon upon us and the good Lord demands we impart goodwill to all men. Living or dead.

Even to our cantankerous neighbours across the Channel. Treacherous scoundrels though they are. What plans have you for Christmas, John?'

'I have none.'

'No plans!' cried Captain Hay, aghast. 'For the love of God man, you must spend Christmas with your family.'

He slumped against the wall and sat awhile silently contemplating the top of his cane – an eagle's head carved from ivory, which he twisted absently back and forth around the shaft – lost in some painful reminiscence. His eyes, now devoid of their earlier glee, began to glisten.

'I have come to a conclusion, John,' he said, a small melancholy smile playing on his lips. 'I will no longer do their bidding. It is over. I have seen far too many good men fall. On both sides. Women too. Most lived scarcely long enough to have witnessed a score of Christmases. Their lives sacrificed to service the vanity of our great leaders who fill their cellars with wine, whilst we fill the battlefields with our blood. Tell me, John, do you see it? I admit my sight is not as sharp as it was when I fired a shot through that French infantryman's eye socket from a thousand yards distant, but I sincerely hoped, after searching for all these years, I would have seen it by now. But you, John, with your young eyes? Do you see the glorious spoils of victory? Do you see God's shining light bathing us all in untold riches as reward for our sacrifice? They promised us joy and prosperity but they gave us squalor and decay. I did not go to war for this. I did not kill for this. I fought for King and Country!' Captain Hay stamped his cane furiously against the ground with such force he sent a spark arcing into the air. Venting a hefty sigh, he motioned to the hubbub still rising from the West Bow. 'Listen to them! Half-witted dullards crowing over the sight of a dead body like they had discovered a rare jewel. Turn a corner or two anywhere in this city, and the same filthy scene awaits. Ha! If they knew how commonplace a severed throat truly was, they wouldn't offer Finlayson's corpse a second's thought.' His doleful smile returned when he realised his mistake.

I closed my fingers around the small bottle in my pocket. 'Your memory has improved, I see.'

'Aye. It comes and it goes. Have you ever considered a military career, Mr Ware?'

The name fell so casually from his lips I thought I must have misheard. 'I beg your pardon?'

'Come now, Joseph! I know who you are. It's not so surprising, is it? You are a very poor liar. *John Black?* Those French mongrels took my hands, not my brains. And I'll wager you wouldn't know one end of a harpoon from the other. I ask you again. Have you ever considered a military career?' His mutilated grip tightened around the cane.

'No, I have not.'

'Pity,' he said. 'You have the makings of a fine soldier. It's in your eyes. A determination to pursue victory whatever the cost.'

'Who are you? Truthfully.'

'Captain Malcolm Hay at your service. That much is the truth.'

'How do you know my name?'

'Oh, I know everything about you, *Tree Man*,' he sneered. 'I have orders to seek you out. To capture you alive. Unlike your friend.'

I stared horror-struck as Hay pointed his stick towards the scene of the murder. 'It was you?'

'It was,' he admitted, with not a hint of remorse.

'You are an agent of Gladius Dei?'

The captain looked suddenly very weary. 'For ten years I have been doing their filthy bidding. But no more. Finlayson will be my last. I want no further part of their wretched business. I am tired of wearing this colour,' he sighed, rubbing at the stains on his tunic.

Watching the pitiable manner in which he preened himself, I struggled to fathom how so broken an individual possessed the wherewithal to murder an ant let alone another human being.

Another human being...

My heart stuttered.

'Have you killed anyone else?'

The old soldier snorted derisively. 'Every kirkyard within a hundred miles of where we sit has benefitted from the fruit of my labours.'

'I meant since last night. Aside from Mr Finlayson, have you killed anyone else since last night?'

'Ah! I see. You want to know what happened after the attack on your little gathering? Specifically, you want to know what happened to Mrs Bility Ware?'

'Yes!' I said, with mounting fury. 'Is she still alive?'

'I hope so. She is a fine woman, in every respect. The world would be much the poorer for her loss.'

I snatched him by the collar and pulled his thin, sanctimonious smile close enough to catch a waft of rank breath. 'Is she alive?'

'You are a very fortunate young man,' said Captain Hay with quiet malice. 'Under normal circumstances these steps would be running with your blood for daring to lay a hand on me. Howbeit, these are not normal circumstances. I say again, I want no further part of this filth. But there are others. Many, many others. So, I strongly advise you to stop wasting your time with me, Tree Man, and start running before they come to chop you down.'

I lifted the little green bottle from my pocket and removed the stopper. 'Not before you tell me everything I need to know.'

Captain Hay peered at the label. 'FV1832. Flos Veritas. I have used this on many a Circle sympathiser in the past. Very effective. Your father is a genius.'

'Then you know what will happen if you refuse to answer me willingly.'

'I do. The question is, do you?'

With the deftness and precision of a cat's paw, the assassin's three surviving digits dropped the cane, plucked the bottle from my grasp and tipped the contents directly into his mouth. Face contorting as the intense bitterness assaulted his tongue, he tossed the bottle back to me.

'I fear you may be disappointed,' said Captain Hay forcing the powder down and reclaiming his cane. 'What knowledge do you believe I possess? Look at me! I am a lowly foot soldier! The generals do not share their grand plans with the likes of me. But please, help yourself. Ask away. But be quick before the mania takes hold.' His fiery eyes fixed on the near empty bottle in my hand with a perverse delight.

Astounded by his recklessness, I watched him intently, waiting for the first harrowing symptoms of an overdose, as detailed in Father's journal, to appear.

'Is my mother alive?'

'I cannot say. I heard Hugh Tulland say she had been taken prisoner. That's all I know. Ask me another. Quickly now!'

'Who else was captured?'

'The traitor Maybury and your friend Finlayson.'

'And Campbell Finlayson?'

Killed and left to burn in the fire.'

'What will happen to the prisoners?'

'They will be questioned. Tortured if need be. And there is always a need,' grinned Hay. 'The bookseller was proof of that.'

'What did you do to him?'

'I gave him the Flos Veritas of course!' Captain Hay chuckled ironically, 'But the conniving old cheat must have used some type of magic because it had no effect. So I tied him to a chair and put a candle to his fingers. Even then, the stubborn fool refused to tell me anything useful. Although, he did tell me where to find these.' He produced two petals from his tunic. One yellow, one blue. I took them and held them to the sky. There were no perforations. No indication of a message.

'Did he explain their significance?'

The soldier suddenly burst into a fit of uproarious laughter and began to sway his head from shoulder to shoulder. 'The buttercup and the cornflower are free! The buttercup and the cornflower are free! The buttercup and the cornflower are free! That's all he said. Stupid cretin! So I cut his foolish throat and dumped him in the street outside his shop. Ask me another! I am starting to enjoy this!'

'Do you know Sir Edward Ross?'

He paid no attention. A sudden cloud of despair snuffed the manic glee from the captain's face. Chin slumped to his chest, the decrepit soldier muttered into his topmost button. 'I feel it. It is coming. My reckoning. I am not worthy of the Lord's forgiveness. I know this. I am an instrument of the Devil. I shall burn a thousand times over in Hell. This is my fate.'

'Do you know Sir Edward Ross?'

Again the question went unheeded. A tear trickled to the tip of Captain Hay's nose.

'But the Devil pays well,' he said. 'And I never want for whisky. Whisky helps me forget the faces. So many faces! How can they see with long dead eyes? But they can! They watch me. Stare at me. I enjoyed killing them. Every one. But no more. So help me God! No more! No more dead eyes!'

'Do you know Sir Edward Ross?' I persisted, shaking him by the shoulders.

Captain Hay raised his waterlogged stare. 'He is a fine man. I am but a slug in comparison.'

'If I offer myself in return, will he leave my friends be?'

'Edward Ross needs a new chair. Edward Ross needs a

new chair. Edward Ross needs a new chair...' Rocking his head from side to side, Captain Hay repeated this juvenile mantra over and over and over.

I clasped him firmly by the jaw and forced him to meet my gaze. 'Can he be reasoned with?'

Hay's entire body tremored with supreme effort as he battled to share one last shred of lucidity before the madness claimed him for good. 'NO!' he roared. 'Ross means to cut you open and steal your guts. For science, he says. It is all for science! He will show you no mercy. You must run! You must –' Captain Hay gesticulated to the stairs, urging me to flee, but the sight of the squirming stumps of his missing fingers silenced him. He peered at them with a shuddering disgust as though he had never before set eyes upon them. 'I am unwholesome,' he wept. 'Dear God, forgive my many, many sins. Many, many sins. Many, many sins...' He beat his head against the wall in time with his sobs, producing an awful, dull, rhythmic thud. 'Many, many sins. Many, many sins...'

I tried to haul him away from the wall, but the captain beat me back with a vicious swish of his cane and continued to bash his skull all the harder.

'Many, many sins. Many, many sins. Many, many sins...' He stopped abruptly and leaned forward. A bloodied smear of hair and scalp clung to the wall. 'Can you hear their screams? Merciful Lord, make them stop!' His face a study in abject sorrow, Captain Hay pulled the handle from his cane. The eagle's head doubled as the pommel of a long thin blade which, when freed from its walking-stick scabbard, measured a good eight inches in length. Captain Hay inserted the tip of the dagger into his right ear and with a scraping motion that turned my stomach, worked it deeper inside. 'Many, many sins. Many, many sins...'

A little lump of flesh plunged into the blood pooling at his shoulder. Another glistening morsel dangled from the lobe...

Unable to tear my eyes from the captain's grisly magic trick, I stumbled backwards against the steps watching the steel disappear further into his head.

'Many, many sins…' his eyes fluttered and rolled. 'Many, many sins…' Blood dripped from his nostrils. 'Many… maneeeee… ssssiinnnnnssss. Mayyyyynnn… ssss.' The words gurgled wetly. Spluttered and rasped, then ceased altogether. Now only the hilt was visible. The eagle's beak pressed to the side of his head. Captain Hay's lifeless body folded over itself and flopped to the flagstones.

A woman, as wide as she was short, arrived at the foot of the steps from the West Bow. She took one look at the hideous display sprawled above and screamed at the top of her lungs.

'Murder! Murder!'

Down the High Street and into Blair Street I ran. Weaving between drays and barrows, I reached Cowgate and paused under the South Bridge to gather my strength and catch my breath. The space beneath the great arch echoed with a burgeoning hiss as curtains of rain spilled down on either side. Coats and shawls tugged over their heads, people scurried for shelter. Too many people. I had to hide myself from their suspicious glances, real or imagined.

On the opposite side of the road, occupying the narrow gap between the massive supporting column of the bridge and the shabby tenement building leaning to its shoulder, stood a tall barrier hastily constructed from a patchwork of mismatched planks designed to prevent access to the adjoining arches of the viaduct. A makeshift and lopsided door occupied the centre of the barrier. When the rain abated and the people returned to their business, I crossed to the door. It was locked and bolted, but as I tested it, the cause of its crooked appearance became apparent. The hinges had all but parted from the rotten timbers of the frame, leaving only two or three screws valiantly holding on. I wrenched the door from the frame till I created a gap wide enough to enter.

Once through, I pulled the broken door to and set off between the bridge and the tilting slums along a path made slick with a dubious, foul-smelling black mud. The majority of the archways which shouldered the great thoroughfare above, were inaccessible. Some entrances barricaded by walls of thick stone, others by insurmountable piles of rubble. After a short trek I came upon a substantial hole in one such arch and crawled inside.

The hole led to a dank and airless vault. I waited, staring into the pitch black, listening for any sign of movement. I had heard the rumours. The chambers beneath the South Bridge were supposedly home to the city's vilest inhabitants, both living and dead. Thieves and murderers living cheek by jowl with the ghosts and demons from whom they received their evil inspiration. To find your way down here was to enter the depths of Hell itself.

The feeble shaft of daylight accompanying me through the hole revealed nothing beyond a midden of oyster shells and the skin and bones of a long dead foal. I soon began to feel quite safe inside my own little corner of hell. I blocked the hole with a few hefty stones, sealing myself away from the very real horrors in progress above, and settled down to wait for nightfall.

Huddled in the blackness, I listened to the muted rumble of hooves and wheels passing overhead. The rhythm steady and unbroken. The ebb and flow of the city's lifeblood. The blood which pooled in its doorways and trickled down its steps.

Many, many sins... Many, many sins... Many, many sins...

I thought of Mr Finlayson, his throat cut. Of his brother Campbell, slain as he sought to protect his friends. Of Mr Maybury, captured, tortured and most probably murdered. Of the others, Mr Olyphant, Molly and Kathryn, fleeing for their lives.

I thought of my mother...
And the arrow of my fury settled upon its target.
Edward Ross had many, many sins to atone for.

CHAPTER TWENTY

Sir Edward Ross

The night-time pavements of Nicolson Street were an enter-taining riot of silvery sparks. Each cone of light cast by the street lamps, gradually diminishing into the distance, played host to its own glittery display as the unremitting downpour melted the last traces of snow. This fusion of water and light provided a welcome counterpoint to the singular lack of activity arising from the building opposite.

The steps of the Dunedin Playhouse afforded a fine and sheltered view of the grand, classical façade of the Royal Society of Pathology, and in the hours since departing my dark cave, I had grown intimately acquainted with every minor detail of its construction. From the small chip in the scrolled capital adorning the leftmost column to the missing stud adjacent to the keyhole. This last came to my attention on the sole occasion the doors parted during my long watch, when a group of elegantly dressed gentlemen stepped forth and climbed into a waiting carriage. I had no inkling as to what Sir Edward Ross looked like, yet some deep-seated instinct assured me that he was not amongst them.

The playhouse released a boisterous flow of theatregoers into the night. I joined the exodus as far as Drummond Street, then turned for Roxburgh Place. The meagre radiance leaching from the lane's solitary lamp showed me to a tall, locked gate.

I scaled the iron railings, dropped to the other side and swiftly crossed the garden to obscure myself behind the trunk of a fine sycamore. The tree conveyed a mild frustration at the propinquity of the boundary walls and of a large outbuilding all combining to restrict the expansion of its root system.

I stared through the harsh, unbroken sibilance of the rain. The Royal Society of Pathology's rear door and windows offered no indication that my intrusion had been detected. The parasite shifted with renewed intensity. Spooling and burrowing. He was very close.

Very close indeed.

I had arrived at my destination with no discernible plan in mind other than the crude intention to somehow force my way into close proximity with Sir Edward Ross and (I tapped my pocket, reassured by the presence of the tin and the phial) pour my entire supply of Glacier Moss and what remained of the Flos Veritas down his wretched throat.

The door clanked open.

Two men sporting thick leather aprons mottled all over with dark stains appeared. Each had a grip of one end of a heavy canvas sack, its bulging middle scraping over the path as they struggled to manoeuvre their awkward cargo. Arriving at the outbuilding, they dumped the sack unceremoniously to the ground. The taller man proceeded to launch a volley of profanity into the darkness and rain, cursing them both for his frustrations as he made several unsuccessful attempts to marry his key to the lock. His wheezing partner used the lull in proceedings to wipe a grimy rag across his brow.

Finally, the lock was released. The men took up their load and entered.

Smoke began to rise from the outbuilding's chimney and a murky orange glow filled the small square of its window. The men reappeared with the now empty sack and returned to the main building. A slit of light revealed they had left the door tantalisingly ajar.

I dashed across but as I reached for the handle, I was met with a clamour of scuffling steps and a barrage of breathless cursing. Crouching behind a spread of cotoneaster, I watched the two men huff their way across the garden with an even heavier sackful than the first. The taller man stubbed a toe on the outbuilding steps and hurled a fresh barrage of expletives into the rain. When at last they ventured inside with their cumbersome load, I seized my opportunity.

The door opened on to a long passageway of white tiled walls gleaming in the light thrown by a line of regularly spaced sconces. Treading as softly as I could, I advanced towards the first of a series of doors lining both sides of the corridor and peered cautiously inside.

The room was adorned with the same white tiles, their polished surfaces reflecting the flame of a single candle placed between the feet of a grim centrepiece. The naked cadaver lay on a bed of white marble. An old man, his torso split from throat to abdomen. Sheets of skin hung from his sides to touch the floor where blood choked the mouth of an inadequate drain. His vitals had been arranged around his butchered frame like so many discarded toys whilst his frosted eyes stared dully at the ceiling. I sensed the man's dying moments; filled with fear and hopelessness. And questions. So many questions...

Revulsed by the intense odour of his decay, I fled from the room to the end of the corridor and passed into another hallway transecting the building left and right. A sign affixed to the wall indicated the route to various rooms. Straight ahead lay the *Library* and the *Anatomy Theatre*. To my left, the *Dining Room* and the *Laboratories*. I instinctively turned right and made for the *Committee Rooms*. With not a soul around to question my presence, I progressed without hindrance to the third floor, where I came upon a door labelled *The Ralston-Wark Museum*. I eased the door ajar and peeked inside at the oak-panelled walls surrounding row upon regimented row of tall display cabinets reaching halfway to the beams of the vaulted ceiling. Satisfied the room was deserted, I stepped inside.

My head swirled as I moved between the massed ranks of bell jars, all intricately catalogued and labelled to form an exhaustive index of human suffering. I had seen their gruesome treasures before; the consumptive lung, the sclerotic brain, the atrophied liver, the tattered heart. Every diseased eyeball, malformed foetus, misshapen skull, ulcerated tongue and parasitical worm; all floating in the same pale yellow fluid. The whole morbid display corresponded exactly to the visions implanted into my fevered dreams by the witch's finger during the night I spent in the room above Mr Finlayson's shop.

The tumult of despair howled forth by those unfortunates from whom these relics had been plundered, clashed with the omnipresent distress of the trees destroyed in order to house these artefacts and provide the floor upon which the entirety now stood.

Yet, in the midst of this constant, mournful thrum of death, I became increasingly aware of the presence of life. Not merely the mice or the insects or the spiders hiding in the cracks and the dark corners, their presence relayed to me through the fabric of the building we shared, but substantial life. People.

Him!

I closed my mind to the cries of the ghosts and continued for the door at the end of the aisle till the smear of gold lettering printed upon its midsection fell into sharp relief and a name presented itself:

Sir Edward Ross PRSE FRCPE.

Heart thudding madly, I put my eye to the keyhole and saw a man seated behind a desk of solid mahogany. His white shirt sleeves extended from a black waistcoat, where a gold fob chain drooped from the pocket. Perched at the tip of a thin nose protruding from a long, clean-shaven face, a pair of spectacles gazed keenly downwards to a pen tapping impatiently upon a sheet of foolscap. As evidenced by the deep furrows scoring his brow and the continuous stroking of his chin between the forefinger and thumb of his free hand, the document was posing some difficulty. An inspired smile cleared the impasse and, with a quick dip of the nib, the words set off across the paper with an enthusiastic flourish.

I stood upright, gripped the door handle and barged inside.

'Ah! Joseph! Come in, come in. You arrive at a most opportune moment. I am attempting to resolve a few trifling difficulties with my forthcoming lecture,' Sir Edward Ross boomed, entirely unfazed by my sudden intrusion. Resting the pen upon the desk, he returned his spectacles to the bridge of his nose and reclined with hands clasped, to study me with the patience of a teacher long since used to dealing with the ill-mannered and unruly. 'There are some details I would be extremely grateful if you would be so kind as to clarify. Firstly, how tall are you, Joseph?'

The door clicked to a close behind me. The room was spacious and bright. A gallery of sombre-looking men, most of them old and heavily whiskered, stared dispassionately from ornately framed canvases. The largest portrait of all hung above the mantelshelf of a generous fireplace. A full-length depiction of an austere, gaunt man of advancing years dressed in a surcoat, doublet and hose of a uniform black with gold trim. In his left hand he held a scroll secured with a wax seal. The seal bore a familiar symbol. The symbol of Gladius Dei. A brass plaque set in the lowermost edge of the frame bore the name of the subject:

Sir William Ross: 1536–1607.

The man behind the desk possessed the same hollowed cheeks, the same weakly tapering jaw and the same stone-grey eyes.

'You appear to be under some misconception,' I said,

determined not to betray the slightest hint of the apprehension and doubt building within. 'I am not here to engage in any form of discussion. I am here to put an end to you, Mr Ross.'

He drummed the ends of his fingers together, eyes glinting in amusement as he scrutinised me.

'The misconception is entirely on your side, Joseph. You are making the wholly erroneous assumption that your cooperation is in any way negotiable. Willingly or otherwise, you will furnish me with all the answers I need. *That* is why you are here. Incidentally, you will address me as *Sir.* My title is well earned and is to be shown the proper respect.' The surgeon leaned forward to peruse the document on his desk. 'Now, I have no issues regarding the practical element of the lecture. However, it is the subject's history – *your* history, Joseph – that will add the necessary seasoning to the proceedings. Lachlan has kindly furnished me with all of the salient facts, but I need more than the dry bones of mere biography. I need the colour and spice of first-hand experience. Your case is truly exceptional. No incident of this kind has been recorded in over two centuries. For the furtherance of science and to help us protect the vulnerable from the filth of witchcraft, it is your duty to provide a full account of the progress of your mutation. From the first moment of your infection right through –' Ross smiled, a bloodless, flinty smile – 'to the first moment of your dissection.' He calmly reached for a little bell sitting on the corner of his desk and rang it vigorously as I sprang for him. The door to an adjoining room flew open and two men raced inside to prevent my enraged fingers reaching his neck. 'Gentlemen, would you kindly accompany Mr Ware to his seat?' said Ross, indicating the vacant chair facing him across the desk.

I struggled vainly as the men forced me down, then bound me by the wrists and ankles to the chair.

'Search his pockets.'

The men complied and handed the contents to their master.

'Glacier Moss...' he mused, inspecting the tin box. 'And what have we here...?' He held the little green bottle to the light. 'Flos Veritas,' he confirmed. 'Hardly a grain of truth left inside, I fear. You have met Messrs Tulland and MacGregor previously, have you not?'

My pockets picked clean, both men stepped back from the chair and for the first time since their arrival, I had a clear view of their faces.

'Oh, we have met on several occasions,' said Hugh Tulland with a supercilious leer. 'We have become close friends. Is that not right, Joseph?'

The second man, MacGregor, I instantly recognised as the thug whose knife had so nearly dispatched Molly and me in that grimy, fogbound alley.

Ross pulled his seat to the front of the desk and placed it uncomfortably close to my own. The chair's legs splayed a little loosely and the whole frame creaked in complaint when he sat.

'We are all friends here,' he said. 'And in the spirit of friendship I am sure Mr MacGregor has forgiven you for the rather ungracious way you treated him. It is fortunate that your father has a ready supply of counteragents for all his wondrous concoctions. The Glacier Moss included. You do forgive Mr Ware, do you not, Stuart?'

'I should have killed him,' I said, glaring at the hulking brute.

'Yes. That was a serious error of judgement on your part,' agreed Ross.

MacGregor's mouth twitched.

'One I will not repeat.'

My defiance was met with a thin reedy, laugh.

'Lord bless you! This boundless optimism does you great

credit! And I thank you for your kind, if entirely unnecessary assurance. I admire you, Joseph. Truly I do. Lachlan has often boasted of your many fine qualities; your sharp scientific mind, your insatiable thirst for knowledge, your good manners and keen sense of duty. We had high hopes for you. But hope is a fragile thing and so easily lost.' Ross looked sadly at the pair of items pilfered from my pockets. 'I dare say you had hoped to force these potions down my throat and watch me die a thousand agonising deaths. Ah! but then – *The best laid schemes o' mice an' men, gang aft agley.*'

'I will see you die yet! I promise you,' I hissed, tugging at the restraints.

Ross smiled and leaned closer still. 'You may keep your promises. I have no need of them. Your bones, however,' he shifted his weight from side to side testing the rickety chair to its limit, 'will prove most useful. What say you, Mr Tulland?' he said, turning to the cabinetmaker. 'Will these bones meet my needs?'

'A moment, sir.'

Hugh Tulland produced a measuring stick, which he presented firstly to my legs, then to my arms, shoulders, spine and ribs, carefully calculating the length and width of each. Whilst Tulland's stubby pencil busily jotted the results inside a tired old notebook, Ross treated himself to a detailed examination of the growths coiling at my fingertips. I felt his own hands trembling with excitement as they pressed and prodded at the sticky buds. He wore a ring on the middle finger of his left hand; a gold band embossed with the mark of Gladius Dei.

'Tell me? What is it like to have the roots of evil growing inside you?' he asked, the question soft and awestruck. 'Can you feel them moving?' Impatient to discover more, Ross removed my shoes. His eyes widened in wonder at the mesh of shoots and tendrils tightly furled at the ends of my toes.

MacGregor applied his considerable mass to my shoulders, pinning me helplessly to the chair as I tried to twist away from the scalpel Ross collected from his desk.

'Get your hands off of me!' I howled.

Ross drew the blade across the bridge of my foot. A clear, viscid resin oozed from the wound. 'No blood!' cried the surgeon, extremely satisfied with the result of his experiment.

A timid knock at the office door brought an end to his moment of triumph.

'Enter!'

A young servant stepped inside, his head bowed meekly to the floor. 'The guests are starting to arrive, Sir Edward.'

Ross found the news irksome. 'Very well. Tell Dr Whittle I shall be down presently.'

'Yes, sir.'

'What are your findings, Mr Tulland?' asked Ross, once the departing servant had closed the door. 'Is there sufficient material here to furnish me with an excellent new chair?'

Since concluding his calculations, Hugh Tulland had been quietly sketching a diagram in his notebook. He handed the results to Ross.

'The measurements are satisfactory. We have everything we need.' Tulland turned to me with a sardonic grin. 'And I do so enjoy working with new and exotic materials.'

'Oh! this is splendid! You have excelled yourself, Hugh! What say you, Joseph? Is this not a most fitting tribute to your sacrifice?'

Ross showed me the grisly diagram of an elaborate chair constructed from bones. My bones. The femurs and tibias arranged to create a very different set of legs. The ribs, spread wide, provided a cage for the sitter whilst the spinal column offered rigid support for the living back. The arms of the chair were to be formed from my own reconstituted humeri, ulnae and radii. The seat itself was to be created from the pelvic bones laid horizontally within the structure.

Eager to share the finer points of his creation, Hugh Tulland crouched by my side.

'Please excuse its crudeness. This is only a preliminary sketch. You must imagine it upholstered in the finest leather, fixed with brass studs and castors. And all your bones will, of course, be thoroughly polished and varnished.'

I averted my eyes from the stark, crushing inevitability of my fate. A fate from which, I now conceded, there was to be no hope of escape.

'Why Joseph, it vexes me to see you look so downhearted. Be of good cheer. This is a great honour!' crowed Sir Edward, rising from his seat to collect a decanter. 'Every part of you is to be preserved for all eternity. Nothing shall be wasted. Least of all your secrets.'

He filled the bottle containing the last few specks of the Flos Veritas with whisky and swirled the mixture, round and round. The green glass sparkled as he returned to me.

'I trust you allowed yourself some time to enjoy our museum and its many fine exhibits before you honoured us with your presence? It is the finest collection of its kind to be found anywhere in the Christian world.'

Ross held the bottle in front of my eyes.

The contents spinning inside.

Round and round… Round and round…

'The rarity of the samples is unequalled. This is due to the singular nature of the subject matter. Every last specimen sourced exclusively from witches or their sympathisers. It is by no means an exhaustive collection. There is always room for more artefacts. Why, only this afternoon we set aside an entire shelf for your friend Mr Henry Maybury.'

Round and round…

'And this will be your final humiliation, Joseph. Your every organ placed in a jar of preserving fluid and displayed in our cabinets for generations of young children and delicate women to point at in both disgust and amusement. I shall set aside a special cabinet for your head and place a suitable label on the jar. Perhaps *Hominis arbor* or, *Lignum hominis*. I cannot quite decide which. Hold him.'

MacGregor's arm swept around my throat, locking my head firmly in place while Ross gripped my nose and waited till I was forced to draw breath whereupon he swiftly poured the liquid down my throat.

The mixture infused my core with an oddly soporific warmth, its radiance spreading outwards to envelop my skin like the breath of a late afternoon breeze on a cloudless summer's day. All the tension, all the fears and anxieties melted away and, in their stead, came a state of complete relaxation and ease. The room rippled and shimmered as though I were looking at it through the clearest and slowest of waterfalls, the languorous cascade washing it clean of all its previous malice. Even Sir Edward, his face bending to mine, assumed an air of sweet benevolence.

'Now, Joseph,' he smiled amiably. 'I know there are others who escaped your little gathering at Dalrymple Place. I had hoped to ask Mr Maybury who else was in attendance, but the coward poisoned himself before I had the opportunity. As for the bookseller, I understand you met his executioner, Captain Hay? The Captain, rest his soul, possessed many admirable traits, but sadly, subtlety and patience were strangers to him. If there is one thing I have learned from all my years as a surgeon, it is that you cannot expect a man to tell you very much when you have cut his throat.' He laid a friendly hand upon my shoulder. 'Therefore, in the regrettable absence of Mr Maybury and Mr Finlayson, I turn to you, Joseph. Who else was with you in the old butcher's shop?'

A dim warning pealed from a rapidly darkening recess of my mind. A warning to resist. To remain silent. But then I saw them. Smiling warmly. Molly and Kathryn encouraging me to confess. All would be well. No need for secrets or deceit. The truth must be told.

Ross angled his ear to meet my confession.

'That's right. Tell me their names.'

I ground my teeth and breathed hard. Molly and Kathryn scampered from the rooftop.

'Tell me.'

'Robin Hood and Joan of Arc.'

Sir Edward's mouth twisted in irritation. The surgeon collected a white clay bottle from his desk, removed the stopper and used the contents to dampen a handkerchief.

'We have dallied long enough. Our guests have been most patient. It would be very bad form indeed to keep them waiting a moment longer.'

He pressed the cloth firmly over my nose and mouth and as I inhaled the sweet cold vapour, the shadows crept forth from all four corners of the ceiling to smother me in their darkness.

CHAPTER TWENTY-ONE

The Dissecting Table

The darkness whispered and shuffled with slight sounds of movement. The flavour of wool crammed hard inside my mouth made every breath a challenge. The air was cold. I had been laid supine on a hard, unyielding surface, every limb thoroughly restrained. Suddenly struck with a terrible fear that I had been made blind by the smothering vapour, I rolled my eyes to their widest extremes, seeking the merest trace of light in the disorientating blackness, and found some reassurance when the lashes twitched against a thick layer of fabric.

Footsteps approached. The creaking and rustling in the background intensified.

'Esteemed gentlemen, colleagues and guests. Before we begin, I must respectfully request that you put aside any preconceived notions as to what you expect to witness here, this night. For I am not here to fulfil your expectations. I am here to defy, confound and surpass *all* expectations!'

The voice, delivered with a forthright assuredness and authority, was unmistakable.

'I have invited you here on this Christmas Eve,' Sir Edward Ross continued, 'to share with you at this time of miracles, the single most astonishing discovery of our age. This is a defining moment in our history. It is also a delicate moment. And so, I must insist on your discretion. Tonight's events are not to be discussed with anyone outwith our noble order. Anyone who does so will be sanctioned accordingly. The reason for this precaution should be obvious to all. The layman has not the mental capacity to fully grasp the magnitude of what lies upon this table. If he understood the true extent of the evil in his midst, the evil that walks with him every day in the streets and in the parks; that stands by his side in the factories and in the churches, in his own *home*; then inevitably, we would be swept aside by the ensuing hysteria. Fear and destruction, the very qualities upon which our enemies thrive, would reign in our absence. Your patience, however, will soon find its reward, for it is no exaggeration to say that at this very hour we find ourselves standing together on the threshold of ultimate victory. The tide has turned for the last time, dear friends. The filth we and our predecessors have fought so long to eradicate now faces its final annihilation. The war is almost at an end!'

This declaration was met with a thunderous outburst of cheers and rapturous applause. It was a terrible, paralysing noise. I now knew the stage upon which I had been placed and the role I was expected to play.

'Gentlemen!' said Ross, forcibly. 'We are men of science! A little decorum and dignity if you please. These are the virtues that separate us from the vermin we have sought so long to defeat.'

The excitement dimmed to a murmur.

'Thank you. Now, if you will permit me, let me present our subject for today... Mr Joseph Ware!'

The blindfold was snatched from my eyes.

Sir Edward's introduction was met with a flurry of polite appreciation from an audience now dimly coming into focus as my sight adjusted to the scorchingly abrupt brightness.

Slowly, through narrowed eyes, a few details began to emerge.

Save for a piece of cloth covering my feet, I lay naked and

utterly exposed, strapped to a table directly beneath a simple chandelier formed of six glowing glass bowls. My hands were buried under piles of dirt. The balled rag stuffed inside my mouth stifled a small cry of alarm when I spotted an array of fearsomely sharp blades, saws, pliers and other implements whose function I dared not imagine; their highly polished surfaces glinting expectantly from a tray placed on a table near my head.

Seeking a better view of my situation, I managed to extend my neck the fraction allowed by the restraints and saw a hundred and more stares watching hungrily from the benches arrayed beneath the blaze of oil lamps encircling the walls. So many faces! Some portly and ruddy-faced, others thin and drawn, but all hunched forward in eager anticipation. The entire assembly dressed in black. It was the nightmare of the crow-infested dissecting theatre made real!

Every last seat had been taken, the occupants mostly men with a few women scattered sparingly throughout, including one I recognised as the woman who screamed "*Murder!*" from the foot of the Castlehill steps. The table at my back told the sorry tale of the tree felled to supply the carpenter with his material. The blow of the axe and the pull and push of the saw echoed also from the benches and the floorboards, all butchered to provide a comfortable setting for learned men to indulge their ignorance.

Tiny vibrations of distress troubled the air, signalling the presence of another endangered life. A moth, entranced by one particular lamp, fluttered repeatedly towards the flame, scolding its fragile wings till they could fly no longer.

I noticed other familiar faces... Dr Whittle whispering excitedly into his neighbour's ear... The surly MacGregor, his imposing bulk dominating the uppermost row... The nightwatchman from Leith docks taking off his hat to wipe the perspiration from his brow... Robert Tulland, affecting an air of studied indifference. Beside him, Professor Gilchrist, arms folded, waiting to be impressed...

And there, sitting in the front row, scribbling furiously into a notebook, was my father. He appeared entirely unsympathetic to my plight. The same could not be said of the little girl perched at his side. Grace, sucking her thumb, her cheeks wet with tears, had her head bowed to the bairn cradled in her lap.

Bethany was fast asleep.

'Let us see his heart!' came a yell from the shadows.

The outburst was countered from several quarters with a terse, '*Shhh!*'

Sir Edward Ross circled the table, blocking my father and cousins from view. His bloodless lips curled in malign amusement as his eyes bore down upon mine.

'His heart, you say? But why, when his heart is of little interest? Mr Ware has a selection of far more intriguing delights to share. He has acquired a most remarkable and deadly affliction. A malady three hundred years in the making. One from which he will not survive. But do not pity him. He is a willing disciple of witchery and deserves his fate. This creature is no longer human.'

With a dramatic flourish, Ross pulled my hands from their blankets of soil and held them aloft for all to see.

'Know thine enemy!'

The crows gasped in unified astonishment at the dirt dripping from the long pallescent tendrils dangling loosely from my fingertips. He then lifted the cloth at my feet to reveal the shoots trailing from the toes prompting a second wave of cawing incredulity.

'Here lies before you an insult to the very laws of nature. A spit into the face of God Himself. And it is our holy responsibility to rid the world of this filth. The filth of witchcraft, magic and devilry. There is no place in this modern world for such abominations. But to defeat them, and defeat them we shall, we must first understand their innermost secrets and use them to our advantage. Science is our sword, gentlemen, and we shall use it to pierce the heart of evil. Let us proceed therefore, with a closer examination of these remarkable appendages.'

The benches creaked under the craning necks of the multitude as they leaned forward to watch Ross collect a pair of scissors from the instrument tray.

'Note how they germinate from the cuticles,' he said, taking a firm grip of my right wrist and raising the tendrils to the light of the chandelier. 'Some of you may regard my choice of the word *germinate* to be an odd one, implying as it does, the roots of a plant emerging from a seed. But the description is apposite, for that is precisely what they are. I have studied with great interest the excellent report made by the good Dr Whittle, whose microscopic studies have shown that the cellular structure of these deformities share more in common with the biology of plants than of animals. They absorb both moisture and nutrients from the soil via tiny hairs extending from the epidermal tissue. There are no bones within their length and nor is there any blood. Yet observe what happens when I cut one off.'

I screamed mutely into my wool-filled mouth as Sir Edward snipped the obscenity from my thumb.

'As stated, there is not a drop of blood to be found. Yet did we not witness the subject react with a good deal of pain when I amputated this strange little limb? This suggests that the nervous tissue does not end at the natural flesh of the fingertips but extends throughout the entire length of the protuberance. Now, observe this strange viscous liquid seeping from the wound. As it comes into contact with the air, it hardens in much the same manner as the resin of certain trees will harden around an injury.' Ross tapped the scissors against my damaged thumb. 'See? The cut is now completely sealed. Dr Whittle proffers the theory that this resin is the result of an extreme form of white blood disease. However, this does not explain what we find here at the palm. A deep laceration approximately four inches in length. If I stretch the wound to see what lies inside, I should expect to encounter soft red muscle and flesh but –'

I writhed helplessly as Sir Edward tore the split wide open.

'Instead, we find a second layer of skin of a dark green hue and a rough, hard texture. It is not, in my opinion, too fanciful to suggest that it bears a remarkable resemblance to the bark of a young tree.'

A derisory chuckle emanated from somewhere amongst the farthest benches. One dark glower from Sir Edward, and the mirth promptly evaporated.

'Nor does white blood disease account for the green hue of chlorophyll present in many strands of his hair. And so, as we proceed with our investigation, we may well ask: Is this peculiar secretion restricted solely to the tips of the fingers and toes?'

Sir Edward leaned over to adjust the gag which, in the throes of my agony, had partially escaped my mouth.

'To answer this question,' he continued, pushing the wad behind my teeth, 'we must dig a little deeper.'

The crows ruffled their feathers and murmured excitedly.

'But before we proceed, I am sure you will agree that this momentous day must be recorded for future generations of scholars to study and admire. And who better to document our findings than the subject's father, Mr Lachlan Ware!'

Sir Edward thrust his arms towards the front row, where Father proudly rose to accept the noisy acclaim of the audience. Whilst all eyes were on my father, the surgeon aimed a surreptitious nod to a man hovering by the nearest door.

Hugh Tulland acknowledged the command and stepped out.

'And our good fortune does not end with the presence of

one of our nation's foremost scientific minds,' said Sir Edward, once the fuss had settled. 'No, ladies and gentlemen! For we are doubly blessed to have with us, one of its finest artists.'

The cabinetmaker returned to the room, carrying an easel and a stool, both of which he set down at my feet.

'I speak, of course, of Lachlan's radiant wife, Bility Ware!' pronounced Ross, throwing a theatrical sweep of his arm to the door.

Her face obscured behind a veil of black lace, my mother entered to a confusion of hesitant applause, spiteful hisses and full-throated booing. Sir Edward raised his hands, requesting silence. Order was immediately restored and everyone resumed their seats.

'Bility, if you would be so kind,' he said, inviting her to take the vacant stool. Once seated, Mother lifted her veil. Her expression remained as blank as the canvas Tulland had placed on the easel alongside a box of pastels and charcoals. She looked at me through the vacant, dispassionate eyes of a doll. All trace of their customary verve and spark had gone. It was as though someone had reached inside and stolen her very soul.

I wrestled despairingly at the restraints... *What have they done to you?*

Mother selected a piece of charcoal.

'If I may say so,' said Sir Edward, peering over her shoulder, 'the next volume of *Botanica Fantastica* is set to become the most informative and ambitious yet!'

The surgeon's prediction was met with a great outpouring of laughter and the rumble of stamping feet. I turned to Father, daring him to see the hatred in my eyes, but his attentions were once more buried in his notebook. Grace, however, did raise her disconsolate gaze from the sleeping tot, but her eyes quickly diverted when Sir Edward, after some careful deliberation, picked a blade from the tray. Points of light gleamed from the knife's pristine surface to flitter in a mad dance across his face. He held the scalpel high for all to see, and a perfect hush descended till all that remained were the rapid strokes of charcoal on canvas.

'I will now make an incision immediately above the styloid and proceed as far as the olecranon.'

The pain hit me with the force of a steam hammer. I clenched and chewed at the saliva-soaked rag, squirming and writhing, the torture shaping my spine into an arch so rigid I feared I would surely hear it snap. With excruciating precision, the surgeon's scalpel cleaved my forearm, releasing a flowing warmth as it journeyed through the flesh.

Sir Edward rested the honey-stained blade upon the table and then, working his fingers deep inside the incision, he pulled the opening apart.

'We have now exposed the ulna and radius. Note how his veins run not with the pure red blood that sustains good Christian men and women, but flow instead with the same singularly unwholesome fluid we first encountered at the fingertips. Note too the extensors, the flexors; indeed all the muscles have surrendered their usual healthy scarlet hue in favour of an insipid, diluted shade of amber. The fasciculi have lost their characteristic flexibility and do not stretch when pulled. This, as Dr Whittle ascertained with the digital growths, is a result of the fibres becoming progressively vegetal in nature. We now move to examine the skeleton, where we uncover yet more irrefutable evidence of the unnatural forces at work. The bones have lost their typical whiteness and are now a shade of pale ochre. The surface has a distinct grain, reminiscent in structure and texture to that of a piece of untreated timber. Admittedly I am no carpenter, so perhaps if I remove the ulna our own Mr Tulland would care to furnish us with his expert opinion.'

Sir Edward selected a small saw and brought it to my arm.

I felt the draw of its teeth work steadily through the exposed bone at the wrist. I squirmed and pulled, testing the limits of the shackles to their absolute extreme. The saw moved to the elbow and as it set to work once more, I unleashed another frantic, muzzled scream. The lamps began to dim. As the blissful embrace of unconsciousness beckoned, the surgeon snatched a bottle of salts from the tray and held it to my nose. He wanted me to remain alert. Like the ringmaster of a circus, Sir Edward appreciated his audience's desire for spectacle. He knew they wanted an experience beyond the scope of the anatomical lecture they were ostensibly here to observe. They wanted an exhibition of suffering. My torture was for them, entertainment of the highest form. A sadistic smile of triumph stretched his mouth when the waft of concentrated vinegar and peppermint snapped me back to the full, agonising glare of wakefulness.

I looked at Mother through streaming eyes, imploring her to intervene, but she was not to be disturbed from her mission to faithfully recreate the grim tableau arranged a mere arm's length from her easel.

One final bite of the saw and Sir Edward tugged the bone free.

'The marrow is virtually non-existent,' he stated, taking a close look at the most recently severed end of the ulna. 'In its stead we have a waxy, lignin-like substance. Mr Tulland? Your thoughts?'

In the cabinetmaker's hands the bone became a precious, glistening treasure. Cradling it with the utmost care, he marvelled with unconstrained relish at the prize he never dared imagine would one day fall into his possession. Tulland produced a clasp knife from his pocket and carefully teased the tip into the bone.

'It responds well to the blade. Close-grained and smooth.' He put the sample to his nostrils and sniffed. 'No odour to speak of. If I didn't know otherwise, I'd swear this was horse chestnut wood.'

Sir Edward Ross seized the bone from Tulland's grasp and, with the priceless trophy raised high over his head, he turned to address his increasingly agitated audience.

'There you have it, my friends. Proof! Comprehensive, undeniable proof! His transformation is almost complete! This is not the result of some hitherto undiscovered disease. This is not, as has been suggested by one or two of my learned fellows, the result of some exotic fungal infection passed through the skin via the burr of a diseased chestnut. This is witchcraft! A spell cast from the darkest magic and lain dormant for over three hundred years. The Witch McKay is mocking us from beyond the grave. For this, gentlemen, is none other than the Ossa Lignum curse itself!'

Sir Edward's conclusion stirred up a storm of consternation from the benches.

'Its rarity is matched only by its potency,' he added, once the commotion had dimmed sufficiently, 'and to find it here, made manifest in the body of this naive young man, is testament to Margaret McKay's mastery of the evil arts. The curse changes the zoological into the botanical. Turns man into tree. She intended this vessel to be the agent of our downfall. His sole purpose now is to quite literally take root and sow the poisonous seeds of McKay's magic to the winds, where they will foul the earth at our feet and the very air we breathe with her unholy pestilence. Everything we hold sacred would be lost to an eternal night of famine and plague.

'*This* is why Sir William Ross, my revered ancestor and the founder of our great and noble institution, left no stone unturned in his sacred mission to reduce her filthy existence to dust! *This* is why we cannot rest till we complete the work he began all those centuries ago. *This* is why we must guard against complacency! For not till the very last member of their vile tribe has been hurled into the flames and their ashes consigned to the dirt so that never again will they insult the sun with their foul presence, can we raise our swords in victory!' Flecks of spittle escaping from his enraged mouth, Sir Edward pounded a fist against the dissecting table. The congregation rose as one and unleashed a torrent of unrestrained rapture.

Sir Edward turned to me, a maniacal gleam darting from his eyes as he gestured for silence which duly arrived.

'Sir William Ross bequeathed another legacy. Gifted to us in the form of a theory. A theory to which I wholeheartedly subscribe. Many of you may have heard of it. The theory pertaining to the existence of what he described as the *Viscus of Devilry*. My forefather believed this organ, the *pythonissam organ* if you will, to be a unique anatomical aberration found only in witches. The function of the pythonissam organ is to secrete a preternatural fluid into the bloodstream, and it is from this fluid that the witch derives their powers of magic. Remove it, and you effectively render the witch impotent. Sir William's lifelong quest to find the pythonissam organ ended in failure. And I believe I know why. He was, quite simply, searching in the wrong place.

'At first he believed the *Viscus of Devilry* occupied a fifth chamber of the witch's heart; a hypothesis soon discarded after the dissection of the Perth Coven – a group of six witches, four women and two men – revealed no deviation in the structure of their hearts to those of Christian hearts. He then expanded his research, focusing in turn on the lungs, the liver, the kidneys, intestines, genitalia, spinal cords, tongues and even the humours of their eyes; but no obvious anomalies were found. Sir William also conducted numerous studies of the brains of witches, but the results were understandably limited by the crudeness of the methods and tools he had at his disposal. Tools totally unsuited for the study of so complex and delicate a structure. But we are blessed to live in an age where the light

Scott O'Neill

of science has never burned so brightly. Our understanding of human anatomy is as day compared to night when we consider the limitations of Sir William's era. He was a man out of time and out of place. A visionary working in the darkness of the sixteenth century. His lack of success in no way detracts from his undoubted genius. Think what he might have achieved if he too had access to the guiding light of phrenology! Through phrenology we have learned how to map the functions of the brain into specific regions relating to personality and emotion.'

Smiling a thin, sympathetic smile, Sir Edward stroked a trembling hand over my head.

'Therefore it is upon the brain that I have decided to concentrate my own humble attentions. After all, does not every spell and curse begin with a thought? It is my belief that the pythonissam organ resides somewhere in this area here,' Sir Edward gave the spot above my left ear a sharp tap. 'The region responsible for secretiveness and destructiveness. The two most potent character traits inherent in all witches. My efforts to date have been blighted by the same hindrance that affects all our work. A distinct shortage of specimens.'

The crows murmured in agreement.

'But I must not grumble. As here, upon this table, lies the key to our ultimate triumph over the forces of darkness. Look at him! His every cell is loaded with witchcraft. Is it not, therefore, reasonable to assume that Joseph Ware has within him the pythonissam organ? Could not the chestnut that wormed inside his body be the seed of McKay's own *Viscus of Devilry* regrown? Through her use of the Ossa Lignum curse, the witch sought our ruination but she has instead, supplied us with endless opportunity! Imagine, gentlemen, what its discovery may lead to! Think of all we might achieve should we learn how to harness the power contained within its mystical fluid! We would have within our grasp the means to enchant entire populations. To control their every need and desire. For control allows exploitation and exploitation allows profit!'

The Gladius Dei faithful erupted.

'Control! Exploit! Profit!' they chanted.

'Control! Exploit! Profit!'

'Control! Exploit! Profit!'

Sir Edward hushed them with a wave of his hand.

'Before I open the skull, let us join together in the Lord's Prayer so that God may take mercy upon this wretched soul.'

'*Our Father, Who art in heaven...*'

The words rolled around the benches in a joyless, monotonous drone. Father prayed with eyes closed and head bowed to the notebook on his lap, offering no comfort to the sobbing Grace nor to the sleeping infant she gently rocked.

'*Give us this day, our daily bread...*'

Mother continued her work, a pastel of burnt umber adding depth to the canvas. But a subtle change had overtaken her blank, impassive demeanour. Her fingers had lost their usual fluency and confidence and trembled visibly. The beginnings of a tear betrayed further evidence of the tremendous struggle taking place behind her eyes. Then, quaking with extreme effort, she dropped the pastel and reached behind her neck. Before I could determine what it was she grasped for, Sir Edward fastened a strap across my brow so tightly I was left with no other option than to focus all my pain into the six bright stars burning directly over my head.

'*... The power and the glory, For ever and ever. Amen...*'

I heard Ross choose another instrument...

'Joseph, we thank you for your sacrifice. May the Lord forgive you for your sins.'

I closed my eyes...

'To access the brain we must first remove the calvaria...'

The sound of a hard, rasping thud struck very close to where I lay. Then came a sharp, wheezing gasp followed by a crash of clattering of metal and exploding glass.

A spray of warmth rained against my chest and the strap slipped from my brow.

I dared to open my eyes. The room had descended into a fiery, chaotic hell of smoke, screams and stampeding feet. The flames spilling from two smashed oil lamps were spreading in a widening curve across the floor towards the frontmost benches. The smoke writhed and flowed in a most unnatural fashion, rising both upwards and sideways to form a perfect curtain around the theatre, blocking everyone from view... Everyone except a terrified Grace still cradling the sleeping Bethany in her arms.

Molly scooped up her sisters and took them to the doorway, where Kathryn, deep in concentration, stood busily reciting an incantation, the words inaudible under the swelling panic thundering behind the thick grey screen. She moved her hands in broad circling gestures, the smoke responding to her every instruction like the sections of an orchestra following the commands of a conductor, and with a flick of her right hand, the gap where Grace had been seated was closed.

His face blanched with shock, Sir Edward Ross staggered against the dissecting table. Hugh Tulland reached a tentative hand towards the harpoon protruding from his master's shoulder.

'Leave it!'

The menace in Uncle Tam's glare sent the cabinetmaker fleeing for the comparative safety of the smoke but not before he had managed to steal the precious bone away.

Tam gripped the barbed end of the harpoon and pulled the shaft from Sir Edward's howling body inch by agonising inch. With the fearsome spike removed, Tam stripped Ross of his frock coat and trousers, then set to work on my restraints.

'Can you move?' he asked, pulling the rag from my mouth.

'I think so.'

'Good. Put these on.' Tam helped me from the table and

into the surgeon's clothes. A thick crust of resin had sealed the horrendous scar left by his scalpel, but there was to be no salve for the relentless, withering pain.

'I will see you both flayed alive for this!' hissed Sir Edward.

Tam swung the tip of the harpoon to within a hair's breadth of the surgeon's nose.

'Not if I pluck yer eyes out, ye won't,' he growled, raising the spike in readiness to deliver a mortal blow. Sir Edward cowered under the dissecting table, one hand shielding his waxen, perspiring face, the other pressed against the blood flowing from his punctured shoulder.

'No! It has to be me! I have to be the one who kills him!'

Uncle Tam handed the weapon to me, 'Be my guest.'

I held the harpoon to Sir Edward's chest. I let the tip breach the skin and paused it there, keen to savour the last panic-stricken thuds of his heart as they travelled the length of the iron lance to warm my grip.

'May the Lord have no mercy upon your soul.'

A violent crash from the other side of the table brought the whimpering surgeon a stay of execution. I turned to see Tam hurrying to his sister's aid. She had collapsed to the floor, pulling the easel with her. Trembling in distress, she grasped weakly at the nape of her neck. Sir Edward seized the distraction and scuttled into the cloud of smoke.

'Joseph, no!' urged Kathryn, as I made to chase him down. 'We must leave! Now!'

The strain of the magic had taken its toll on my aunt and she was losing control of the surging smoke and flames. Tam hoisted Mother into his arms and together we fled from the dissecting theatre before they engulfed us completely.

Molly bolted the door behind us. Onwards we travelled through a long corridor of white tiled walls, following the direction indicated by the burnt bones of the witch's finger balanced in Kathryn's palm.

'We must hurry,' she said, leading us to a stairwell at the end of the passage. A sign pointed to the *Repository* below and the *Accounts Office* above. The enchanted compass stubbornly refused to choose either option and continued to aim itself towards a cracked tile upon the wall. Kathryn placed a hand to the tile and pushed. To my amazement a large section of the wall swept backwards to reveal a secret door.

Tam gently lowered Mother to her feet.

'What've they done to you, sister o' mine?' he said, placing a hand to her feverish brow.

She tried to speak, but the words failed her. Again she raised a feeble hand to the back of her neck but lacked the strength to complete the movement. And then, protruding from the delicate mass of curls gathered at the top of her spine, I saw the root of her torment.

A bright purple thorn as big as a thumbnail.

I vividly recalled Father's account of the rare desert rose in his infamous black book.

'A Jacintha thorn.'

'A what?' said Tam, spying the object of my concern.

'A Jacintha thorn. Its poison renders the victim a mindless slave, powerless to resist the instruction of others. No! Leave it in,' I said, grabbing Tam's wrist before he could pull it out. 'Remove it now and the damage will be permanent. She will be lost to us forever. It must remain in place till it turns yellow. Then – and only then – can it be safely removed.'

'Is there one in me?' cried Grace.

Molly parted Grace's tangle of hair.

'No. Nothing,' she confirmed. Happily, a search of the sleeping bairn returned the same result.

'Is it really you, Ma? Are you really here?' Grace whimpered. The poor, befuddled and terrified soul's little fists had been clinging to Kathryn's skirt at every step, refusing to let go for fear of losing her mother again.

'I am, Sweet Pea.'

'Are you going away again?'

'Never.'

Kathryn squeezed her tightly.

'Is this Lachlan's doing?' asked Tam.

'Yes,' I said.

Tam pressed a thumb to the tip of the harpoon I had adapted as a staff to support my weight. 'He will find this particular thorn a perfect fit for the back of his own cowardly skull.' His anger folded into a confusion of sympathy and unease when his gaze fell upon the repulsive growths dangling from my fingers. 'What have they done to you? What have they done to us all?' He spread his mighty arms and enveloped us all in a heartfelt embrace. 'I do not pretend to understand one stingy tot of the powers at work here. My family is in danger. That's all I need to know. The rest I will ponder later.'

The pounding of fists at the dissecting theatre door reverberated throughout the corridor.

'Hurry!' Kathryn ushered us inside the secret opening, closed it firmly at our backs and led us down a flight of steps into a long, narrow tunnel hewn from bare rock. We advanced in single file, Tam and myself forced to stoop our heads to avoid the jagged ceiling. The damp passage appeared endless, all sense of distance lost in the blackness beyond the jittering light of Kathryn's lamp.

'What is this place? Where does it lead?' I asked, still somewhat overwhelmed by the giddying speed and turn of events.

'It's a secret tunnel used by Gladius Dei to smuggle bodies into their dissecting rooms,' said Molly, taking care to shield Bethany's head from the jutting walls. 'It goes on for miles. All the way to the Crags.'

'How did you find me?'

'I performed a location spell. Me! Can you believe that?

Ma taught me how to do it. And she's promised to teach me everything...' Molly's pride and excitement suddenly faltered. She stopped and turned to me with penitent eyes. 'I am so sorry we didn't find you sooner, Jojo. After we climbed from the roof, we waited for you and Aunt Bility, but it became too dangerous. We had to run. Mum used her magic to find Mr Olyphant. He managed to escape to his office. He told us there was nothing to be done for the others, though we might yet hope to rescue you and Bility, but we needed help. Mum summoned a sparrowhawk. It was so beautiful! We dispatched it with an urgent message.' Molly looked fondly towards Tam gently guiding his sister through the tunnel, both figures silhouetted in the light of the lantern ahead. 'Our prayers were answered at first light this morning.'

It took me several moments to summon the courage to seek an answer to my own little prayer.

'Molly? Can you ever forgive me what I've done?'

Molly looked at me. There was no trace of the bitterness of recent days. 'I can,' she said, simply.

'Have you told your father about what I did to the *Majestic North*?' I asked with some trepidation.

'No,' she said. 'The poor man is bewildered enough. Besides, I think we all have far more important things to worry about right now. So, best we keep that as our own wee secret. Agreed?'

'Agreed.'

Our ragged little procession continued for a further two hundred yards or more when the air about us grew decidedly colder. The tunnel ended at a gate, its ironwork latticed against the slow parade of moonlit clouds beyond. The lock bore the scars and dents of an earlier forced entry and scraped uselessly against the wall as Tam pushed the gate open.

Between frosty mounds of whin and gorse sparkling in the light of a gibbous moon, we stepped into a crisp, still night. The unmistakeable profile of Salisbury Crags towered before us. On the road under the cliffs, two carriages awaited, clouds of impatience billowing from the horses' nostrils. Their heads bobbed and jerked at the distant stir of raised voices and clattering boots rising from the depths of the tunnel.

Tam blocked the gate with several hefty rocks and urged us forward to the man standing at the open door of the larger carriage.

Mr Olyphant greeted us all in turn, nodding appreciatively as he patted his gloved hands against the cold.

'Good, good. Well done. Now, we must hurry. The followers of Gladius Dei are especially tenacious when aggrieved.'

He aided first Kathryn and Grace aboard, then Mother, who sat mutely at her sister-in-law's side, head bowed, eyes staring blankly at the floor. Kathryn took Bethany from Molly and kissed the dozing bairn tenderly on her head.

Before I could say goodbye, Mr Olyphant closed the door.

'Thank you, Mr Keane,' he said, shaking Tam warmly by the hand. 'You remember my instructions? I do not wish to labour the point, but it is imperative you follow them to the letter.'

'Understood,' said Tam. He turned to Molly and embraced her so tightly I saw the gasp escape her mouth. 'Take care, sweetness. I shall see you again in three days' time. And you, Joseph. Farewell.'

'Gently Pa, mind his arm,' warned Molly as I too fell victim to one of Tam's rib cracking hugs.

'Forgive me,' he said, stepping back with a horrified glance at the limb hanging uselessly by my side.

'No apology necessary, Uncle. I didn't feel a thing.'

I was as surprised as he at this revelation. The embrace should have provoked a paroxysm of agony, but I endured not a hint of discomfort. And pain was not the only sensation to have deserted me. Standing there, in Sir Edward's ill-fitting clothes, I should have been shivering half to death, but somehow I remained perfectly unaffected by the freezing air. I felt nothing. No cold. No warmth. No aches or pains of any description.

'You see? A man with your fortitude should not be wasting his time picking flowers. You should be out at sea with me, hunting whales!' said Tam, forcing a smile.

'Thank you, Uncle. Thank you for everything.'

I offered to return the harpoon to its rightful owner.

'Ach, keep it. It suits you.'

Spying a faint light rolling inside the tunnel, Mr Olyphant clapped Tam on the back. 'We must away, Mr Keane.'

Tam hoisted himself up to the driver's seat. 'Godspeed to you, Mr Olyphant.'

'Godspeed to us all,' replied Mr Olyphant.

And with a sharp flick of the reins, off they went with hooves and wheels leaving a trail of frozen puddles splintering in their wake.

'Come,' said Mr Olyphant taking the reins of the second carriage, a hansom pulled by a fine piebald mare. 'Make yourselves comfortable. We have a long journey ahead.'

We wheeled off in the opposite direction to the other carriage; Molly and I sitting in silence as the streets of Edinburgh gave way to the thoroughfares of Leith. Soon the street lamps and buildings disappeared altogether and the moon became our travelling companion, illuminating a landscape of slumbering hills to our left and the wide ink-black ribbon of the Forth to our right. The steady rhythm of the horse's progress and the sway and roll of the carriage left me feeling quite drowsy.

'Where are we going?' I yawned.

'Somewhere safe,' said Molly.

I raised my sleeve and scratched idly at the damage done by Sir Edward's scalpel. The process of repair was underway. Encased within the protective varnish of resin, long fibrous strands were reaching out from the elbow and wrist, seeking to fill the space vacated by the pillaged bone.

'There is no salvation for me now.'

'You are wrong, Jojo,' said Molly. 'There is hope yet. Ma knows someone who can help. Mr Olyphant is taking us to see her.'

'Who?'

'Her name is Elizabeth Wilkie. She lives on the Isle of Bute. That's all I know.'

Elizabeth Wilkie... The name was familiar but its origin remained hopelessly lost in the fog of my exhausted mind.

The parasite pressed home its advantage. Its network of filaments and fibres made their final connections and the system was complete. And for the first time I welcomed their advance as the benign, comforting embrace of a friend. No longer to be feared or mistrusted but rather to be accepted and celebrated as a new and exciting reality. I was being delivered into another form of existence, an existence far removed from the insidious interplay of everyday human society with its currency of deceit and falsehood. I recalled the primal hunger in the eyes of all those finely dressed savages who bayed for my blood as I lay on Sir Edward's dissecting table. How fragile the thread that clothes both kindness and cruelty!

I remembered the moment I first held the chestnut in my palm and the shock of its invasion into my flesh, and thanked Margaret McKay for her extraordinary blessing.

I closed my eyes and listened to the thrumming lullaby of wheels and hooves. My only desire was to remain perfectly, beautifully still. To banish all motion from my being. To never have to suffer the indignity of movement ever again.

'What day is it?' I asked on hearing the distant toll of a church bell.

'It's Christmas Day.'

'A merry Christmas to you, Molly.'

'Merry Christmas to you, Jojo.'

CHAPTER TWENTY-TWO

Home

'We must leave him here for the time being.'

'But I don't understand. Why can't we take him with us?'

'Because the locals in these parts cherish only two things: bad whisky and good gossip. And who can blame them? What else is there to do in this godforsaken wilderness? Even the unremarkable traveller does not pass by unnoticed here. Therefore, imagine how quickly rumours will spread of the stranger with the twig-fingered hands. And never forget, the eyes of Gladius Dei are everywhere. We are safe only if we avoid attention. No. We hide Joseph here, then sail onwards to Bute as planned. He will be perfectly safe here... Ah! Good morning, Joseph.'

I stepped from the carriage, yawning and stretching. It had been the most blissfully untroubled night's sleep. The grey morning sky scraped its sagging belly across the white capped hills. We had stopped by the shore of a loch, its waters a great black blot amidst the frost and snow. Mr Olyphant and Molly watched me intently.

'What is the horse's name?' I asked, stroking the mare's flank.

'Sally,' said Mr Olyphant.

'She is a fine animal.'

'She is indeed.'

Sally kept her nose buried in the bag of grain at her feet. She was content. The long journey had tired her but not excessively so. A good meal and a drink, and she would be set fair to continue.

'She likes you, Mr Olyphant.'

'I am pleased to hear it.'

'You are a considerate driver. You have no need of the whip, unlike others she has experienced.'

'Aside from wanton cruelty, I believe it serves no purpose.'

'Incidentally, Molly, I wholeheartedly concur with Mr Olyphant's plan. It is merely good sense to hide the *twig-fingered stranger* from prying eyes.'

'I meant no offence,' said Mr Olyphant ashamedly. 'I was merely emphasising a point of concern. I trust you will forgive me.'

I held up my hands and smiled. 'How can I forgive the truth?'

'We will return as soon as we possibly can,' said Mr Olyphant. 'First we must seek Elizabeth Wilkie's counsel. She will have the answer to your predicament, I am sure of it.'

'Yes! Elizabeth Wilkie! I remember the name now. So Blind Lizzie is still alive! She must be three hundred years old.'

'Three hundred and sixteen years to be precise,' Mr Olyphant confirmed.

I left Sally to her breakfast and with the harpoon as my walking stick, I walked stiffly to the water's edge. Not much more than a stone's throw from where I stood, an islet rose from the depths of the loch, home to a small community of oaks and poplars. The dormant trees were enjoying their winter slumber. Their branches completely bare save for a crop of old nests.

It was a beautiful place. A place of stillness and serenity.

'Where are we?'

'Near the Bridge of Orchy.'

'A long way from home,' added Molly, ruefully.

'I'm not sure I agree. I cannot recall a time when I've felt more at home than I do here,' I said.

Mr Olyphant gestured to a rowing boat beached nearby: 'Shall we?'

We launched the little vessel into the water and stepped aboard. I watched the oars dipping in and out of the loch as Mr Olyphant steered us towards the islet of trees, the blades trailing little rainstorms in their wake. Each drop a tiny explosion of silver upon the placid surface. A short-lived pockmark on an otherwise perfectly smooth complexion.

'I shall wait here while the two of you bid your farewells,' said Mr Olyphant as we made landfall once again. 'Remember, this is but a temporary inconvenience, Joseph. We will meet again presently.'

'Thank you for all you have done for me, Mr Olyphant.'

The solicitor responded with a curt nod.

Molly and I headed into the trees. Together we forged a path through an undergrowth of bracken and holly till we entered a clearing at the very heart of the little island. The treetops bending in the breeze whispered and watched as I speared the harpoon into the ground. We threw our arms around each other and I clung on, absorbing her warmth, knowing in all likelihood it represented the last human contact I would ever share. Molly finally pulled away.

'You're safe now.'

She stood before me, her face a fresh spring blossom against the slow fade of winter hues.

'All thanks to you,' I said.

'Promise me you won't give up hope. Think of all the magic I will learn from Elizabeth Wilkie and Ma. I'll be back soon with the counter spell, you wait and see.'

'You will be the finest witch of them all, I have no doubt. I will miss you more than you will ever know.'

'I'll be back soon. You wait and see,' repeated Molly, her voice faltering at the last.

'Goodbye, Molly.'

'Bye, Jojo.'

And then, wiping her damp eyes, she turned and left. The light now melting from my failing sight, I watched her dissolve into the bushes and listened till the final trace of her progress was swept away by a cold, scouring wind.

I was alone.

Albeit briefly.

For I was welcomed at every turn by the gregarious trees. Each individual oak, poplar and alder keen to share their stories and to learn of mine. The considerate gorses greeted me in a hushed, respectful tone so as not to disturb the slumbering roots, seeds and rodents patiently waiting under the ground for the dormancy of winter to make way for the vibrancy of the spring sun. And as they reposed, the insects and fungi were busily feasting on dead wood and leaves whilst in the canopy, crows kept a wary eye on the buzzard swooping high above the loch in whose waters the pike and the perch played their deadly game of hide and seek.

Impatient to introduce myself to this new world of infinite wonder, I removed my clothes and planted my bare feet into the soil. The growths splitting from my toes immediately pushed their way deep into the ground. The parasite forced the last breath from my redundant lungs as I entered the final stage of my transmutation. I stretched my arms skywards where they set as solid boughs never to bend again. New branches burst from my hands to reach higher still. My legs fused together to form a single, immoveable trunk. Skin, muscles and organs dissolved to make way for bark, cambium and sapwood. I sensed the roots strike ever further into the earth, infusing me with its vitality. The soil tasted as pure as the air and I felt stronger than I ever thought possible.

My eyes hardened into sightless knots, but nothing was hidden from me. Nature welcomed me as one of her own and permitted me to see all things as she Herself saw them. A trillion lives in progress. Each individual with a role to perform in the great tangled skein of existence where every thread was connected and every connection was essential in maintaining the balance of all creation. Cut a single thread, and the whole delicate tapestry would surely unravel. Everything mattered.

Everything and nothing.

About the Author

Scott O'Neill spends much of his free time exploring the hills and shores of his homeland the Isle of Bute, an island in the Firth of Clyde in Scotland. The landscape of Bute is full of history and mystery which inspires much of his writing including two published novels: *The Buzz Building* (2014) and *The Hectic Headspace of Abigail Squall* (2018). He has written several screenplays including *Underground*, a crime thriller which was sold to Celtic Films, *The Circle*, an indie horror film starring Ross Noble (2017) and *Sketches of Bute* (2024). The sequel to *The Circle* called *The Circle: Awakening* will be released in 2025.

Scott is writing the sequel to this book focusing on the witches of Bute published in 2026.